THE

NEARLY

DEPARTED

BOOK TWO

THE HALSTON SERIES

THE

NEARLY

DEPARTED

C. T. WENTE

Text copyright © 2017 Christopher Todd Wente
All rights reserved.

ISBN-13: 978-1548493813
ISBN-10: 1548493813

For James Joseph,
who escaped beforehand.

PROLOGUE

The projectile entered her with the force of a hammer.

She spun and faced her assailant. He stood in the distance, the pistol poised in his hand, a thin smile parting his lips. With casual calm he fished a pack of cigarettes from his pocket and lit one. His smile grew as he took a drag, his eyes never leaving hers.

Her instincts told her to run, but it was useless. The damage was already done. She removed the tiny projectile and tossed it on the ground. Soon enough a familiar warmth would spider up her spine, leaving a void of paralysis in its wake. She told herself not to fear it. Fear would only hasten the effect, and she needed all the time she could get. There were too many unanswered questions. Too many unsaid goodbyes.

She turned and continued on.

The old downtown stood frozen and lifeless, like a faded photograph from the past. Even under a fresh blanket of snow it was nearly as she remembered–the wide streets, the tree-lined sidewalks, the timeworn facades neatly stacked in a row. But she wasn't here for what remained. She was after what was lost.

The gap in the row of buildings was as obvious as it was

1

unremarkable. To the casual observer it would have appeared to be little more than a vacant lot. But this was far from the truth.

A pang of sadness seized her as she drew closer, elevating her pulse. The warmth in her began to stir, draining the strength from her legs. *No,* she commanded silently. *You can't have me yet. Not until I've seen it. Not until I know.*

Upon reaching the gap, she paused and forced herself to look.

The remnants told her everything—a narrative of destruction told in shattered brick and black, heat-twisted steel. Nestled in the snow-dampened ash, small, grotesquely shaped stones reflected the light. She puzzled over them for a moment before concluding there was only one thing they could be—the molten remains of bottles and glasses. Her eyes traced a path to the area where the bar once stood. Only charred fingers of wood remained, rising up in a withering line that terminated at a deep spherical depression in the earth.

Ground zero.

She stared at it solemnly and shuddered at the cold. A torrent of memories began to fill her mind, but she quickly shut off the flow. Perhaps this was an outcome of her training. She couldn't be sure. All that was certain was the devastation. All she could feel was a void.

Something rustled behind her.

She turned unsteadily, her hair tossed by a sudden wind. Around her, tall grasses danced in the breeze. The first golden rays of dawn shimmered on the eastern horizon. She noticed the narrow path edging the high alpine meadow in which she was now standing and frowned.

This was where she'd found it.

She marched into the meadow, ignoring the warmth now creeping into her chest. It had to be close. The boulder. *Their* boulder. Large and flat and perfect for basking in the sun. A heart with her initials carefully carved into its surface, its arrow pointing precisely where to look. She remembered the moment she'd first noticed it—how the meaning had suddenly clicked, how she'd scraped at the hard earth until finally exposing its secret, how everything she thought was real was destroyed upon finding—

She looked up and froze. The boulder stood before her, an island in a sea of swaying grasses, just as she remembered. At that same moment the warmth seized her chest, reducing her breath to short, shallow gasps. Soon enough it would be over.

But that wasn't why she'd stopped.

The woman sitting on the boulder was sobbing, her slender body rocking gently beneath a heavy winter jacket. A mournful cry rose from her hidden face with every plume of frost-smoked breath.

She watched quietly, feeling the woman's sorrow infect her like the poison now coursing through her body. What was she doing here? Why was she crying?

As if hearing her thoughts, the woman looked up. Her large green eyes warily scanned the meadow while strands of short blonde hair whipped at her face.

She stepped back and gasped—

Allie!

She raised her hand and waved, but Allie kept her gaze focused on the edges of the meadow. A moment later, her best friend scrambled to the far side of the boulder and dropped from view.

No, don't go—I'm not ready!

She stepped forward to follow after, expecting her legs to obey. Instead she found herself teetering on two lifeless columns of flesh. A single thought filled her mind as she toppled toward the ground.

Goodbye Allison.

She opened her eyes to find herself lying on an oak floor yellowed with age. In it's creases, tiny shards of crayon shined like lost gems. She raised her head. Around her, carefully drawn stick figures waved from sheets of discarded typing paper. A half-dressed Barbie doll lay twisted by her hand. The tiny bedroom stirred distant, faded memories. The memories began to arrange themselves into something almost recognizable when a sudden noise sent them scattering.

The clack of the typewriter rang out sharply from the next room as unseen fingers raced to keep up with their owner's thoughts. At regular intervals the clamor was interrupted by the raspy groan of the carriage before the mechanical melody erupted once again. She closed her eyes and smiled, listening to the familiar sound fall around her like quenching drops of rain.

The warmth crept further upward.

Time was running out.

She propped her failing body onto her elbows and dragged herself into the hallway. Thankfully, the distance to her destination was short. Each agonizing inch across the floor brought the sound of slapping type bars closer until finally she reached an open doorway. Upon peering into the room, the typewriter fell silent.

"Wake up, Jer-bear," a baritone voice exclaimed. "It's time to go."

She looked up at the desk in the center of the small study. The thin, angular face of a young man hovered over a Smith Corona typewriter, his dark eyes studying her reproachfully. She felt her face blush as if she were a child. "Go where?" she asked, her voice barely a whisper.

"You know where," her father replied, gesturing toward the window behind him. "What, aren't you ready?"

"Ready? I . . . I don't know. I just wanted to—"

"Whatever you think you're looking for, you can't go back to find it, sweetheart. You have to keep going forward."

"But . . . but *you're* the one that started this!" she exclaimed, unable to summon the breath to shout. "And now I'm in it too!"

"Is that why you're here? To blame me for everything that's happened?"

She dragged herself into the room and collapsed against the wall, the last of her strength now gone. "No. I . . . I just wanted more answers. The ones only you could know."

Her father frowned. "I've already given you all my answers. The rest must come from you."

The warmth completed its task, reducing her to a paralyzed body crumpled against the wall. A knot of panic began to tighten in her throat. She closed her eyes and willed the words to come. "But I . . . I want to know the truth."

"The truth?" he scoffed. "You have the truth. You've *always* had the truth. The only question is what to do with it."

She opened her eyes. The room was darkening, the air turning colder. She gasped for breath, the knot in her throat growing tighter. "But you . . . you haven't told me if—"

"Enough," her father commanded, his voice growing distant. "It's time for you to wake up."

"No! Not until I . . . know . . . "
"Wake up, Jer-bear."
"Dad . . . *please* . . . "
"I said wake *UP!*"

Jeri Stone bolted up in bed and took a gasp of breath. The heavy wool blanket fell back, exposing her sweat-drenched skin to the frigid air. Her eyes swept the murky darkness of the small cabin. Then, as the dream faded and reality crept back, she shook her head and sighed.

I'm still dead to the world.

She climbed from the bed and shuffled to the cabin's lone window. In the thin strip of sky visible over the mountains, the stars of Cassiopeia twinkled in the predawn light. Beneath them, the world stood lifeless—the snow-dusted cliffs forming the border of their remote valley compound, the skeletal maples snaking along the dry creek bed, the dark windows of the training cabin. All of it as barren and unchanged as the day before. As *all* the days before.

Or maybe the world is just dead to me.

Jeri rubbed her toned arms against the cold. The training had hardened more than just her physique. Endless hours under the demanding eye of Whip, her masochistic instructor, had made her stronger—in every way possible—than ever before. And with this newfound strength had come an even greater confidence. A few months ago, Jeri *Halston* might have believed she could handle anything. This morning, Jeri *Stone* had no doubts. Despite all she'd been through—or rather, because of it—she now felt ready for anything. Even Whip's silent nods during these last days of training seemed to confirm it. She turned from the window with a pensive frown.

So why was she still having the dream?

A loud knock shattered the silence. "Rise and shine, freshman," a low, female voice commanded. "Special delivery."

Jeri turned and looked at the door. The shadow of Whip's stout frame hovered beyond the thin gap of the threshold. An envelope appeared in the gap and slid across the floor.

"You know what to do." The shadow turned to go. "Breakfast in twenty!"

Jeri marched over and picked up the blue and red bordered airmail envelope. *Ten weeks*, she thought, examining the postmarks and large PRIORITY label plastered across the front. Ten weeks since joining the agency. Ten weeks since the death of Jeri Halston and the birth of Jeri Stone. Ten weeks of brutal training and maddening isolation—

And it all came down to this.

She tore open the envelope and removed the folded sheet of stationary inside. As expected, a Polaroid photo slipped from the fold into her waiting hand. Jeri held it up and gazed at the face of an unfamiliar man carefully centered in the composition. Large brown eyes gazed calmly from a gaunt face framed by a short, neatly cropped beard. She committed the face to memory before turning her attention to the letter.

The letter's handwriting was all too familiar, the rambling message of the writer the same as every letter that had come before. But now everything was different. Now she knew how to read the *true* message.

She moved to the small desk in the corner of the cabin and sat down under the light. Her stomach growled with hunger. Her body shivered with cold. Jeri disregarded both as she picked up a pencil and quickly set to work—scratching out certain words, underscoring others. Within minutes she was finished. She dropped the pencil and carefully read the letter again in its translated form, ignoring the nervous excitement beginning to stir in her chest. After reading the message once more to be certain of its meaning, she stood and began collecting her things.

She'd have to move quickly.

Her first assignment was waiting.

PART I

Welcome to the agency.

Our first requirement of you is trust.
Not only in us, your colleagues, but also in yourself.
You see, in order to accept everything we're about to tell you
—why we recruit, whom we recruit, how we recruit them—
you must first trust in what you already suspect to be true—
The corporate state is destroying the global ecology,
and the hands controlling the mechanisms of global power,
are too few, too self-serving, and too myopic to be left unchecked.
If you truly believe this,
then you have no choice but to trust us.
Because our very existence underscores this truth.

Of course, this doesn't mean your trust won't be tested,
along with everything else.
But that's okay.
After all, trust is never recognized
until it's tested.

Audio Recording #03.173 // 0846
Reference Index: >NewAgentOrientation<
Narrator: Shafer, R. >Shepherd<

1.

J-

I woke again this morning to the smell of stale hookah and discarded hookers and knew I'd found rapture. How do I even describe it? The fact that every slack-jawed American miscreant from Bourbon Street to the Vegas strip hasn't hopped the big pond and resettled here is beyond my comprehension. Where else can your average loathsome alcoholic with a fetish for cheap thrills and cheaper tequila find his pleasures and poisons on a single street? I barely had time to slip out of my mescaline-induced beauty rest before the morning street urchins were massaging my nether regions and serving up plates of freshly fried patongo.

Of course, none of this can fill the void of your absence, my sweet.

I know you're ready to kill me for running off so suddenly,

but of course I can explain. Sometimes a man stands at the precipice of greatness, at the crossroads of brilliance and fate, and has to make a choice. That's the deal with this career choice, baby. Fight or flight — it's as simple as that. I think it was Paul (the Beatle, not the Apostle) that summed up my affliction best with that song "It's all in the genes, fucknuts." Not that a guy with the voice of an angel and the face of my great aunt should be taken seriously, but maybe he's right.

And now for the reason I'm writing.

Don't read too much into this, but I'll be stateside by the time you're holding this letter in those lissome little mitts. Yes, that's right waan jai, you'll be cursing my name before the evening fog erases bodies from the San Francisco streets. Remember the spot where we first met? The south end of the embarcadero where the mendicants like to piss? You were taking photos and I was watching you like Adam gazing at the forbidden fruit. Is your hair still as brown as a Ghirardelli gift bag? It better be, or I swear I'll snatch your keys and steal your car as surely as you've stolen this terminally enlarged heart. Our kids will be gorgeous, J. Even if we have to send one back.

Right. Well, you've got dinner plans to break and I've got five minutes to fist-pump the monks at Wat Chana Song-kram before my bargain-basement flight hobbles into the skies. Don't bother picking me up at the airport, I've still got enough American faloose in my wallet for a cab ride all

my own. Besides, the last thing you need to see is my pretty
mug stepping off the plane in a piss-stained snuggie. Have
a shot of Fortaleza waiting for me, and remember—this is
only the beginning.

Ta!
-C

p.s. The enclosed photo is an example of what I might look
like if I dropped the tan and splurged for facial hair plugs.
And don't tell me you don't go for the lumberjack look. You
love flannel like a second hand loves smoke.

p.p.s. Have you listened to that Paul Simon retrospective
I sent you? And don't say "over my dead body." Man that
guy's got chops. Just be sure to finish the first three
collections before you graduate to the bigger stuff.

2.

Nice evening for a walk, freshman.

Jeri Stone was strolling north along the embarcadero when the familiar baritone voice punctured the silence. She paused and glanced around. Only a scattering of pedestrians was visible on the wide path that edged the water, none close enough to overhear. She adjusted the earpiece concealed under her dark, wavy brown hair. "Freshman? Is that really the best name you can do?"

Every neophyte is called freshman, the voice in her ear replied. *You should be seeing the time by now.*

Jeri looked ahead. A long building graced with arched windows stood regally along the waterfront. Rising like a replica of the Venetian Campanile from its center was a large clock tower. "Correct," she said, judging the distance to her destination with her current pace. "Two minutes until arrival. So I'm a neophyte until I've finished three collections?"

That's right. And make it five minutes—your date is still parking his car.

"Got it." She paused and pulled a small digital camera from her jacket pocket. Looming over the water, the massive steel-girdled deck of the Bay Bridge stretched toward the mist-shrouded shores of Yerba Buena Island before vanishing in the distance. She snapped photos with mock interest for several minutes before the voice spoke again.

I'd like to see those photos.

"Yeah?" Jeri replied. "Well, I would have liked an occasional word from you during these last few months of hell—but that didn't happen. So I guess we'll both just have to deal with disappointment." She turned to the sprawling San Francisco skyline and continued taking photos.

What about my letter?

Jeri laughed reflexively and glanced around. The only person within earshot was a young woman jogging with a stroller. She tucked the camera back into her pocket and continued heading north. "What about it?"

Didn't you read it?

"Of course I did. But in case you've forgotten, I know *how* to read them now. Code words and instructions don't count. A little pep talk from my mentor would have been nice—especially after Whip started the psych drills. My personal favorite was the morning I woke up with a cadaver sitting next to my bed. Tell me—was that one part of your standard new-hire training, or something special just for me?"

Hard to say. Whip keeps her training plans pretty close to the vest. But you know she was just trying to rattle your cage. The good news is you passed all of her tests. And now here you are . . . part of the team.

Jeri marked her position from the clock tower and resumed her previous pace. "Yeah, lucky me. I suppose if I'd failed, I would've never heard from you at all." She glanced at her watch and quickened slightly. "Anyway, it's nice to be working with you, Chilly. Your freshman has successfully killed two minutes and is now proceeding as directed."

Good, Chilly replied. *He's waiting for you inside.*

$$\sim$$

Adam Cowell anxiously spun his car keys around his index finger and gazed up at the Ferry Building's high ceilings. On any other occasion, the intricate latticework of iron that formed the historic building's long transom would have interested him. But an inkling of doubt was now gnawing at his stomach. *Maybe the sweater had been a bad choice* he thought again. Was aquamarine even his color? It had looked so good on the mannequin at the store, but the twenty-seven-year-old research assistant was beginning to think it wasn't the best complement for his fair skin and thin, reddish-blond hair. He scratched again at his neck. The latest issue of GQ magazine said wool was the "in" fabric, but fuck it was itchy. And hot. He pulled at the sweater's tight collar and imagined a cloud of steam rising from his chest. As he did, the keys spun from his finger and soared across the restaurant's waiting area. A rush of blood colored his already red cheeks as the hostess looked over and gave him a smug grin.

God, he hated first dates.

Adam marched his short, pudgy frame across the room and picked up his keys. To his surprise, a young woman was standing in his spot when he turned around. He adjusted his glasses and looked closer. The woman was a mirror image of the picture he'd memorized from the dating site—amber eyes, fair skin, an attractive oval-shaped face framed in long curls of dark brown hair. It had to be her. Adam pocketed his keys and straightened his itchy blue sweater. A look of suspicion clouded the woman's expression as he stepped forward and reached out his hand. "Hi. You must be Carrie."

"I am," the woman replied, taking his hand. She smiled and her looks abruptly elevated from beautiful to stunning. "And you must be Adam. It's nice to meet you."

"Likewise," Adam replied, forgetting the discomfort of his sweater. He turned and nodded at the hostess. "I think we'll be seated now."

"Of course, sir." The hostess smiled and grabbed two menus. "Right this way."

Jeri followed her date into the dark interior of the restaurant. The hostess was steering them towards a table by the window when Chilly's voice echoed into her ear.

Max reserved a romantic table in the corner. Make sure you take it.

She glanced around the room. As expected, a table for two sat empty in the far corner. At the next table, two men in business suits were talking over their plates. The eyes of the gentleman facing her flashed in her direction. They exchanged a brief nod.

"Here we are." The hostess dropped their menus on a window side table and gestured at the view. "Best seats in the house."

Jeri turned to Adam. "I'm so sorry, but would you mind terribly if we sat somewhere else?" She caught his look of confusion and shifted her gaze toward the water. "I know this sounds ridiculous, but a good friend of mine drowned near here a few years ago and it's . . . well, it's just . . . "

"Oh my god, I'm—wow, I'm so sorry," her date exclaimed. "Of course. Whatever you want. We can even go somewhere else if you'd like. There's a nice restaurant near my apartment just over the—"

"Could we have that one?" Jeri interrupted, pointing at the table nearly hidden in the far corner.

The young woman looked at both of them with disbelief before picking up the menus. "Sure. Follow me."

Jeri gave Adam an apologetic smile as they followed the hostess to the table. Her earpiece crackled again as they sat down.

Nicely done. But don't get too elaborate with your stories. And in case I didn't mention it before, no drinking.

"I think I'm ready for a drink," she said, sinking into her chair. "How about you?"

Her date adjusted the collar of his horrid blue sweater and nodded with enthusiasm. "Absolutely. Shall I order us a few glasses of wine?"

She leaned forward and flashed him a mischievous grin "Make it a bottle."

Twenty minutes into their evening, Adam was pouring another round of wine and wondering what had caused such a monumental change in his luck. It had been months since he'd gone on a date that qualified as average, let alone good. But this? This one had the potential of being exceptional.

He took another sip of the Mendoza Malbec while his date finished her story about a recent ski trip to Austria. His eyes studied her face as she spoke. Carrie S—no full names yet—wasn't just intelligent, engaging and interesting. She was also drop dead gorgeous. The thought of her sweeping down a perfectly powdered slope in a tight ski outfit made Adam blush with arousal. He tossed back the wine and inwardly scolded himself for never learning how to ski.

His date paused and shook her head. "I'm sorry, I haven't stopped talking since we sat down. Enough about me. Let's talk about you."

"Well I'm sure my life isn't nearly as interesting as yours," he replied. "Let's see . . . grew up in a Portland suburb—boring. Went to Penn State for my undergrad—also boring. And now I'm here in the bay area doing post-doctorate research in, you know, genetics." He let the last word linger for a moment and took another sip of wine.

"Oh . . . wow. So you're one of those brilliant genetic researchers, huh?" Carrie asked, pointing her wine glass at him.

"Well, research *assistant.*" Adam shrugged. "But they've pretty much guaranteed me a full-time position once I wrap up my PhD this year."

"And who are they?"

"Velgyn Pharmaceuticals."

"Velgyn? Aren't they like the largest bio-pharmaceutical company in the world?"

"Yeah, something like that." Adam caught a flash of approval in his date's eyes.

"Very impressive. Oh—speaking of pharmaceuticals, that reminds me!" Carrie reached over and fished a small bottle from her purse. "It's time for my little miracle workers."

Adam watched curiously as his date poured two pills into her palm before popping them into her mouth. "Miracle workers?"

"Supplements," she replied. "I found this obscure little shop in Chinatown that sells them. They're just herbal, but I swear they do everything. Ever since I started taking them I've been *so* much sharper. And, I never get sick—I mean never." She held the out bottle. "Care to try some? I'm serious—they'll change your life."

Adam grabbed the bottle, brushing his fingers against hers in the process. The temperature inside his sweater immediately spiked. *Oh Christ, don't blush—don't blush!* he commanded himself. He adjusted his glasses and squinted at the bottle. Columns of bright red characters ran down the label. "How do you know what's in them? Everything's in Chinese."

"I just asked the woman at the counter. She said they were the best supplement you can get. All organic, all natural."

"And you just believed her?"

His date regarded him with a hint of irritation. "Well, yeah . . . I did after trying them." She held her hand out. "It's fine if you don't want to. Not everyone can be a risk taker."

Adam's eyes widened with surprise. Despite just meeting him, the woman sitting across the table had managed to strike a particularly sensitive chord. How many times had he heard it before? *Adam? Oh no, Adam's not a risk taker. Adam's the 'safe' guy.* And it was true. The biggest risk he'd taken in recent history was buying this itchy fucking sweater. No wonder he rarely got a second glance—or date—from women like Carrie. Did girls like her ever choose the safe guy?

Of course not.

"Who says I'm not a risk taker?" Without thinking twice Adam dropped three pills into his palm and tossed them back with a sip of his wine. "How's that?" he asked, handing back the bottle.

Carrie gave him a sly grin back. "That's perfect." She reached up and gently scratched at her ear before raising her wine glass. "To taking risks."

Adam raised his glass and toasted the beautiful woman across from him. This was it. After years of boring dates and banal women, he'd finally found what he was looking for—someone who made him feel alive. And with some more wine and fearless gestures, who knew where the night would take them? *Hopefully to my apartment* he thought with a smile.

"Hers do daking wisks."

His date raised an eyebrow. "Excuse me?"

"I said, hers do—" Adam paused and furrowed his brow in confusion. What the hell was going on? He reached up and touched his cheek. Something was wrong. A strange numbness was spreading over his lower face. His tongue felt swollen and clumsy in his mouth.

"Are you okay?"

Adam studied the glass of wine in his hand and slowly set it on the table. "I don . . . somedings happ'ning do me."

His date glanced around the restaurant before grabbing her purse and slipping around the table until she was behind him. To Adam's surprise, she then leaned down and wrapped her arms around his neck in a loving embrace.

"I can tell that you're nervous," she whispered, her mouth pressed to his ear. "And I get it. First dates are awkward for everyone. But if you play your cards right—and just re-lax—this could be your lucky night."

Adam felt a sudden pressure against his neck, followed by the sharp prick of a needle. "Waa . . . wad are you doin do me?" he mumbled softly.

"What did we just say about taking risks?"

Adam felt the awareness of his own body begin to fade. He tried to stand, but his date gently pressed against his shoulders until he resigned himself to staying put. "I don unnersan," he said, his thoughts growing cloudy. "Wire you—"

"You're telling me so many interesting things tonight," Carrie continued, her voice calm and precise. "Politics and religion, movies and art. You're telling me about your last visit to Portland, and how your mom drives you crazy. And we're both drinking far more wine than we should."

"My mum does dive me cazy," Adam chuckled. He rolled his head back and smiled up at her with vacant, unfocused eyes. "Did…did I aweddy tell you dat?"

"You did," Carrie replied, patting him on the shoulder. "Now, let me see your hands."

∾

All right, freshman—the clock's ticking.

"I know," Jeri said under her breath, fishing a silver compact from her purse and unclasping the top. She grabbed Adam's left hand and pressed his fingers firmly against the mirrored surface inside.

Two minutes.

"I know," Jeri hissed. She pressed a small button on the edge of the device and a flash of white light briefly illuminated Adam's hand. After returning the compact to her purse, she fished out another one and repeated the process with his right hand. "Prints are done," she whispered, moving her hands down his torso.

Now the wallet.

Jeri pried Adam's wallet from his pant pocket and

quickly thumbed through a thick collection of cards before finding the item she was looking for. "It's here."

Good. Get going. Max will handle dinner.

Jeri pocketed the wallet and wrapped a hand around her date's neck. "Okay, now listen to me," she whispered, squeezing gently. "You just spilled wine all over my dress and now I have to go to the bathroom get the stain out. I want you to stay right here until I get back and think about how you're going to make this up to me." She glanced at the two men seated at the next table next and nodded. Both men rose in unison. The closest man—a tall, hulking frame of muscle concealed within a tailored Italian suit—shifted his chair over and swung a friendly arm around Adam.

Jeri smiled. "Happy babysitting, Max."

"Thanks, freshman," Max replied.

Jeri made her way out of the restaurant with the second man following after her. Halfway down the Ferry Building's skylight concourse, her short, pudgy colleague fell into stride next to her. "Evening, Dublin."

"Freshman," the man replied with a heavy Irish accent. He slipped off his jacket to reveal a tightly-fitting aquamarine sweater underneath.

That's quite a popular look this season."

"The fook it is," Dublin grumbled, pulling at the collar. "Itchy shite." A few steps further he tossed his jacket onto an empty sitting bench.

"Happy as always, eh Dublin?"

"Happy? I had half my fookin' hair chopped off 'tis morning, and the other half dyed red. What do I have to be fookin' happy about?"

They stepped outside and headed west across the embarcadero toward the street. A black SUV materialized from traffic and stopped along the curb. Jeri followed her colleague into the backseat. They'd barely taken their seats before the vehicle sped forward.

"Welcome aboard, Jer—sorry—*freshman*," a voice said cheerfully. Jeri looked up to find a strikingly handsome face grinning at her from the driver's seat. "I was just listening to your performance," he continued, tapping his earpiece with his finger. "Sounded like you've been doing this for years."

"I doubt that," Jeri shrugged. "But thanks. It's nice to see you again too, Tall Tommy." She looked over at the man sitting next to him. "I don't believe we've met."

"We haven't." The man nodded. "I'm Sly."

"Is that your name or your best quality?"

"Both."

"Jaysus Christ," Dublin grumbled next to her.

"Hold on!" Tall Tommy pulled the SUV into a sharp U-turn and steered them south toward the Oakland Bay Bridge.

"Have you met Art?" Sly asked, pointing over her shoulder.

Jeri turned to find a slight, spectacled man with a ponytail of gray-streaked hair sitting in the far back row of seats. "Nice to meet you, Art."

Art nodded and slipped a hand over the seat. "May I have the goods?"

"Yeah, of course." Jeri pulled the two silver compacts from her purse and handed them over. Her colleague quickly removed a memory card from each and slipped them into a small device resting on the seat next to him. He then turned his attention to his laptop.

"Art's our forger," Sly continued with a look of amusement. "He can make practically anything—with the exception of small talk."

"And you?" Jeri asked, studying her colleague's dark, angular face and large brown eyes that revealed his Indian heritage.

"Me? Oh, I love small talk."

"No I mean . . . what do you do for the agency?"

"Ah, that. I'm just your run-of-the-mill G.A."

Jeri knew from her training that every assignment team had at least one G.A.—short for guardian angel. As the name implied, the G.A. watched over everything and helped modify or terminate a mission if something deviated from the plan. She looked him over and nodded. "Nice. I hope I never need you."

Her colleague smiled. "Oh, don't worry—you will."

What's your ETA? Chilly asked.

Jeri realized he was now broadcasting to everyone as Tall Tommy answered from the front seat.

"Eleven minutes."

Fine. Let's walk through it again.

"Take the southeast entrance, park in the lower garage, then prep Dublin," Tall Tommy replied.

"I'll intercept any physical security," Sly added.

"I'll snatch the fookin' keys," Dublin snapped.

Tall Tommy glanced up at the rearview mirror and leveled his blue eyes on Jeri. "And then our freshman here will take a nice scenic drive."

Art, how much time?

Art peered at the box on the seat next to him "First set of prints are almost done. Ten minutes, tops."

Good.

Okay freshman, time for act two. What's your name?

"Rachel Barnes," Jeri replied.

And you're . . .

"The executive assistant for Doug Taylor, Vice President of Genomic Research."

And why hasn't our recruit noticed you before?

"Gosh, I'm not sure," she answered with a mock tone of surprise. "I mean, I've been working for Velgyn for more than two years now. Of course, I spend most of my time at the corporate campus, not at the annex labs. And I did just change my hairstyle."

Right. And what's our recruit's name?

Jeri stared out the window as the SUV sped eastward over the bridge. Ahead, the low, undulating back of the Berkeley hills began to appear through the fog. "Paul," she said quietly, the face from a memorized photograph flickering to mind. "His name is Dr. Paul Obermeyer."

3.

Dr. Paul Obermeyer stared at the cascade of numbers compiling on the screens in front of him with a weary sense of relief.

The data was conclusive. His summary was complete.

The thirty-four-year-old genetic engineer glanced out his laboratory window inside the Lawrence Berkeley National Laboratory and felt a jolt of panic. The heavy coastal fog was already beginning its evening migration inland towards the state-of-the-art research facility nestled against the hills. Paul cursed under his breath. Had he scheduled the last Micro-PAT test earlier, he could have taken a run at lunch. But such was the life of a researcher.

Especially a researcher on a deadline.

He studied the approaching fog cloud and roughly calculated its arrival at twenty or thirty minutes—more than enough time to change clothes and get in a few miles. By the time it caught up to him he'd be warm enough to manage the twenty-degree temperature drop that came with it. Of course, visibility was a different matter. Motorists were notorious for ignoring the speed limit on the scenic road that connected the lab to the rest of the university. But Paul needed the run. And who knew when he'd get another chance? Once his research was in the hands of his executive sponsors, things were going to get very interesting. He glanced again at the compilation of data on his screen and nodded.

Very interesting indeed.

Paul saved the finished report to his research folder before marching off to the bathroom to change into his running clothes. In the server cabinet in the corner of his laboratory, the mirrored hard drives whirled to life and began re-encrypting the data that summarized the last two years of his life.

～

Traffic along Centennial Drive was thankfully light as Paul made his way upward along its narrow, winding route into the hills just west of campus. A light wind stirred the leaves of the eucalyptus trees that grew in thick groves on both sides. He focused on the sound of his breathing and quickly fell into a comfortable pace.

A short distance into his run, the road widened and gave way to a large parking lot. Beyond the lot, the squat, bunker-like profile of the Lawrence Hall of Science stood overlooking campus. During the day the Hall normally bustled with tourists and schoolchildren clamoring to see its planetarium and hands-on science exhibits. But now, nearly an hour after closing time, only a single vehicle remained. Paul glanced at the parked sedan and absently noted the badge-shaped logo of a private security company stenciled on its doors as he passed.

Just beyond the planetarium, the road turned and steepened sharply. Paul leaned into the grade and quickened his pace. Beads of perspiration soon appeared on his temples and ran down the back of his neck. He was just starting to find his rhythm again when he felt it—a cold breath of air tickling at his neck and shoulders. He turned and looked back.

What should have been a sweeping view of Berkeley and the bay beyond was now gone—replaced by a formless wall of white. Paul increased his speed once again. He was almost convinced he could outrun it when the first ghostly tendrils slipped past, weaving silently through the boughs of the surrounding foliage before rolling toward the ground. Within seconds the veil of mist had consumed him.

Despite the sudden lack of visibility, Paul held his pace. Slowing now would only expose him to the sudden drop in the air temperature. And after weeks spent cooped up in the lab, it felt great to be outside running again. The stress of his work slipped further from his mind with each stride up the winding road. As the light of the setting sun filtered through the fog with an ethereal glow, a smile appeared in the genetic researcher's face.

He was once again at peace.

The gentle hum of an engine was so foreign at that moment that Paul barely registered it. Only after it deepened to a growl did he glance down and realize his mistake—he'd drifted from the road's shoulder to the center of the lane. The sound of the approaching vehicle abruptly rose to a threating level. A moment later, two focused beams of light pierced the fog around him.

"Oh shhh—"

Paul spun in alarm as a blur of silver materialized behind him. Without thinking he hurled himself sideways toward the protection of the nearby trees. The scream of brakes filled the air. The blur swerved violently. Then time slowed to a dreamlike crawl. Paul watched with adrenalin-induced clarity as the silver sedan slid past his airborne body, barely missing his legs. His stare shifted to the window and locked onto the face of the driver. Wide eyes stared back in terror. Then time flashed to normal and the car vanished into the haze. Paul slammed into the ground with a dull thud. A short distance away, the red glow of brake lights shuddered to a stop.

"—iittt!"

Paul lay motionless by the edge of the road while his mind and body caught up with what had just happened. He vaguely recognized the sound of a car door opening, followed by the *click-click-click* of high-heels running on pavement. A moment later, a figure dashed from the fog and stood over him.

"Oh my god! Oh my *god*! I'm so sorry!" the woman gasped, placing a shaking hand on his chest. "Are you hurt?"

Paul lifted his head and gazed at legs. To his amazement, nothing was missing or looked broken. "No," he replied, sitting up slowly. "No, I think I'm fine."

"I'm *so* sorry," the woman repeated, helping him to his feet. "I shouldn't have been driving that fast in the fog. I was . . . god . . . I was in a hurry, you know, and I just didn't think anyone would be—"

"Stupid enough to go for a run in heavy fog at dusk?" Paul interrupted, nodding. "I can see why you might think that." After brushing himself off and confirming he was okay, he studied the woman more closely. Behind her worried frown was an exceptionally attractive face. "In case you're wondering, I don't consider this your fault."

"But it *was* my fault. I'm just glad you're—"

The woman paused and narrow her eyes on him.

"Wait . . . *Paul*?"

Paul narrowed his eyes on her. "Yes?"

"Oh my god—I can't believe this! Of all the ways to run into you again!" She grimaced at the unintended joke and caught his confused stare. "I'm sorry, you don't remember me, do you? I'm Rachel Barnes—Doug Taylor's assistant."

Paul blinked with surprise. "Oh," he mumbled, racking his brain. Why on earth couldn't he remember meeting this woman before? "Oh, of course—Rachel."

"Don't feel bad, I had really short hair the last time we met. I wouldn't have recognized myself either."

"Well, it's good to see you again, Rachel . . . even under the circumstances."

"You too. I'm just glad you're okay. I would've had a lot of explaining to do if I'd killed our company's most talented researcher."

Paul shrugged. "I'm hardly the best researcher at Velgyn. But yeah, you still would've had some explaining."

Both of them turned at the sound of an approaching vehicle. "We should probably get off the road," Rachel said, glancing at the fog. "How about I give you a ride?"

Paul considered the offer for a moment before shaking his head. "Nah, thanks . . . you go on ahead. I'll be fine."

Rachel shot him a look. "You *do* realize it's going to be dark in about twenty minutes, right?" She started walking toward her car. "C'mon, I think we've both had enough excitement for one evening. Let's get you back to the lab before someone else tries to kill you."

Paul studied the short stretch of road still visible through the fog. The light had faded noticeably in the few minutes they'd been talking. His body was beginning to chill and a dull ache was announcing itself in his right knee. Regardless of what he did next, his run was over. He turned and regarded his coworker, dropping his gaze to her left hand.

No ring.

"Sure it's not an inconvenience?" he asked.

"Positive." Rachel flashed him a smile over her shoulder. "Besides, it'll give us a chance to talk."

Paul nodded. She did have an excellent point. He smiled and followed her to the car.

~

Jeri slipped the BMW into gear and turned back toward the lab. Next to her, her recruit glanced around at the immaculate, leather-trimmed interior.

"Wow. You're as much of a neat freak as I am," Paul said admiringly.

"To be honest, I just haven't had it long enough to get it dirty."

"It's funny, I have this same model," Paul muttered. "Even the same color." He shook his head at the coincidence.

"So does half of San Francisco," Jeri replied. "And the other half drive Porsches. If nothing else, at least we're both perpetuating another California cliché. But enough about that—let's talk about something interesting." She gave him a prying stare. "Are you done?"

"Done?"

"With the project. The buzz around corporate is that you've finished. Even Doug mentioned it, and Doug never says anything about early phase research—unless he thinks it's going to be huge. That's why it was kicked it up to E-1 in the first place, right?"

Her recruit's eyebrows rose with surprise. "Everyone at corporate knew it was E-1?"

"So you *are* done."

"I am," Paul admitted. "But, you know, I can't really talk about it."

"Right, of course. I shouldn't ask. But I'm betting it'll cause quite a stir once you hand it over."

Paul stared out at the fog-shrouded view. "I think that's a safe bet."

They rounded the next corner and the entrance to the Lawrence Hall of Science materialized in front of them. Jeri downshifted and turned into the parking lot. Her recruit looked over curiously as she parked and shut off the engine.

"My lab's another half-mile down the hill."

She turned and smiled at him. "So—what now?"

Paul shook his head. "What do you mean?"

Jeri studied her recruit's face. Although he was a top researcher in human genomics, Dr. Paul Obermeyer's appearance more closely resembled that of a Brooklyn hipster. A crop of disheveled, jet-black hair capped his gaunt face. Framing a square jaw and surprisingly full lips was a short, neatly groomed beard. And his dark, deep-set eyes stared back with nervous interest. "I mean, what are you going to do now that the project is done?" she asked. She reached over and touched his hand.

"Oh, *that*," Paul replied, sounding both relieved and disappointed. "Well, I'm not sure. I generally don't think that far ahead. When one project is finished, there's always plenty more waiting for me."

"So how do you decide which one to take next?"

"I don't. That decision's made by your friends at corporate. They're the ones that determine priority in the research pipeline. And, of course, which ones get elevated to E-1." He paused and looked at her. "I would've assumed anyone working for Doug Taylor would already know that."

"I've only been under Doug for a few months," Jeri shrugged. "Anyway, I'm just surprised they don't allow *you* to have any input." Her earpiece crackled to life.

Freshman, what are you doing?

"Wouldn't it be nice if you could select the projects you're given?" Jeri continued. "After all, you're the one doing the work."

Paul scratched at his beard. "Well, if new drug development was left up to the people doing the actual research, it sure as hell wouldn't be focused on erectile dysfunction, or age—" he paused and shook his head. "But it's not up to us. Velgyn's like everyone else—we follow the money, not the need."

"But what if it were up to you? What if you were given the opportunity to work on something that really mattered?"

You're going off-script.

"Like what?" her recruit asked.

"Like curing cancer, or—I don't know—helping to develop a new alternative energy? You know, something that mattered to everyone. That mattered to the entire world." She leaned toward him. "Would you do it?"

Freshman, are you hearing me?

"Of course I would," Paul said, giving her a cynical grin. "But how? Researchers like me can't do much without sophisticated lab facilities and the big budgets needed to maintain them—which means you're right back to big corporations or corporate-sponsored universities who put economic opportu-

34

nities over moral obligation." He shook his head. "Sorry, Rachel, but what you're talking about doesn't exist."

"What if I told you it did?"

Paul's grin faded. "You know, if you and I weren't co-workers, I might get the impression you were a recruiter."

Take him—now.

"You don't work for Doug Taylor, do you? You don't even work for Velgyn."

"Of course I do," Jeri replied. "Look, I'm sorry for bothering you. I was just curious to know if you—"

"Wait a minute." Her recruit's stare was frozen on the keys hanging from the ignition. He opened the glove box and grabbed the registration. "This . . . this *is* my car!" His eyes flashed to Jeri. "Okay, Rachel, here's the deal—you have about ten seconds to explain what's going on before I call the police. Do you understand?"

Now! Chilly shouted in her ear.

Jeri held her recruit's stare. "What do think I've been trying to do, Paul?" She sighed and gestured at the back seat. "Okay, fine. Would you mind handing me my purse?"

"Why?"

"There's something in it you need to see. Something that will explain why I'm here."

Paul grabbed her purse and laid it on his lap. "What am I looking for?" he asked, opening it.

"My compact," Jeri replied. "In the second pocket."

Her recruit pulled it out and held the gleaming object between them. "This?"

"Yes."

"And what—I'm supposed to believe there's something in your compact that will explain what this is all about?"

"There's only one way to find out," Jeri answered, holding his stare. She then turned and gazed out the driver side window.

~

Paul examined the compact in his hand.

Nothing on the outside of the small, silver object aroused his suspicious. But then, nothing about the woman sitting next to him had seemed particularly suspicious either. After a moment of hesitation he held it away from his face and pressed the clasp. The two sides separated in his palm with a sharp metallic *click*. He gently opened it and studied the contents inside. Like any normal compact, one side contained a glass mirror. The other side held an unmarked panel of black plastic. On one edge of the panel was a small, button-like depression. Curious, Paul rubbed his finger over the depression. Nothing happened. He glanced at Rachel, who was still staring out the window. After another brief pause he pressed the button.

The flash of light was blinding.

Stunned, Paul dropped the compact. He could hear Rachel moving next to him and instinctively reached for her. His left hand latched onto something in her hand. "What is that?" he demanded, tightening his grip on the cold metal object. "Is that—is that a *gun*?" A wave of fear and anger washed over him as she tried to pull it from his grasp. Paul seized her wrist with his other hand and an awkward game of tug-of war ensued.

"Paul, listen to me! I'm not trying to hurt you!"

A high-pitched laugh escaped the researcher's mouth.

"Then why do you have a gun?"

"It's not a gun!"

Paul blinked his eyes until the blindness subsided and looked at the object locked in both of their hands. "Yes it is!"

"It's not a gun—it's a *tranquilizer*." Rachel corrected. "Now listen to me. I can explain."

Paul's eyes flashed to her face. Was this really happening? Was he really sitting in his car playing pistol tug-of-war with a woman that minutes before had nearly run him over? He took a deep breath and stopped pulling.

"Thank you," Rachel replied. "Now, I understand that this seems absolutely crazy, so let me just clarify a few things. First of all, you're right—I don't work for Velgyn. And yes, I am here to recruit you—"

Paul only half-listened as she spoke, his senses on full alert. Outside, the dense fog continued to roll and twist around them.

"—just not in the normal manner. The truth is, I work for an agency that specializes in the selective recruitment of scientist and innovators that have the capacity to change the world with their ideas. The reason I'm talking to you—"

Beyond his assailant's side door window, the fog suddenly thinned to reveal another car parked under a light at the far end of the lot. A large badge shimmered like a beacon across its doors.

"—and while I can't tell you the specifics of where you're going, I can assure you that the work you'll be doing will play a key part in restoring the global economic—"

Paul glanced briefly at Rachel and nodded before again studying the security vehicle he'd jogged by earlier. Was that the silhouette of a head leaning against the driver's headrest? He was beginning to doubt his eyes when the silhouette moved. His pulse quickened as he calculated the distance—thirty yards at most.

The fog thickened and the vehicle vanished from view.

Next to him, Rachel smiled. "You may not believe this, but I'm really on your—"

"Wait," Paul interrupted. "Can I ask you a question?"

"Of course."

He gestured behind her. "Who's that?"

Paul waited for Rachel to look over her shoulder before lunging forward and slamming her head against the driver side door. The sound of the impact echoed in the small interior. He ripped the tranquilizer gun from her hand and tossed it in the back seat. Charged with adrenalin, he shoved her again. "Who are you? Why would you do this?"

His assailant moaned and reached for her head.

Paul grabbed the keys from the ignition and scrambled from the passenger seat. He ran into the fog toward the private security guard. "Hey! I need help!" he screamed as the vehicle came into view. Inside, the head of the slumbering guard snapped upright. Paul reached the car as the man stepped from his vehicle.

"Okay . . . okay, easy," the security guard said, raising his hands. "What's going on?"

Paul stopped and caught his breath. "What's going on?" he scoffed, angered by the man's obliviousness. "How about an attempted kidnapping thirty yards from where you're napping!"

"Say again?" the guard asked, raising an eyebrow.

Paul glared at him. For a private security guard, the man looked surprisingly fit and polished. A neat crop of dark hair curled out from below his cap and rested against his tanned face. His badge and nameplate sparkled like new in the murky light. Even the man's uniform was pressed and spotless, as if worn for the first time. He turned and pointed in the direction of his BMW, now shrouded in fog. "There's a woman in a car over there . . . in *my* car . . . who just tried to kidnap me."

"A woman . . . in *your* car?"

"Yes!" Paul shot back. "She must've stolen it from my office while I was out running."

The security guard stepped closer, a thin smile on his lips. "Help me understand this, sir. You're saying a woman stole your car while you were out running?"

"Yes!"

"Then just how'd you end up in it?"

"She almost ran me off the road!" Paul exclaimed, throwing his arms in the air. "Then she stopped and helped me and told me she was my colleague and . . . and so I got in the fucking car!"

"Okay, alright," the security guard said, gesturing for Paul to calm down. "Just take it easy a minute. How about we start with your name?"

"My name's Paul—Paul Obermeyer. I'm a researcher with Velgyn Pharmaceuticals. I work at the lab just down the hill." He turned and again pointed into the fog. "Now, will you please call the *real* authorities and have them arrest the woman in my car?"

The security guard's smile vanished. "Tell you what, Mr. Obermeyer. Before I call the *real* authorities, how about I just walk over there and see what I find?" He took a few unhurried steps and paused. "By the way, how'd you get away?"

"I . . . I shoved her against the door and took her gun."

"Gun?" the guard repeated, raising both eyebrows.

"Yes, she had a gun!" Paul exclaimed, exasperated.

"And where is it now?"

"I tossed it in the backseat."

The guard's face went slack with a *you fucking idiot* look. "What kind of gun?"

"I don't know! She said it was a tranquilizer gun, but I have no idea. All I know is she was planning to shoot me with it."

The guard nodded. "Yeah, well, it'd be hard to tell the difference anyway. Especially for someone under, you know, *duress*." He reached down and pulled something from his belt. "Did it look anything like this?"

The researcher instinctively stepped back at the sight of another pistol. "Yeah . . . yeah, I suppose it looked like that." He met the guard's eyes. "So what—you guys carry tranquilizer guns too?"

"We do, Paul," the guard replied. "And I'm sorry."

Before Paul could react the guard raised the gun and pulled the trigger. A low *thump* echoed against the fog. At the same instant something punched him in the leg. "Jesus Christ!" he screamed, looking down. A thin metal cylinder protruded grotesquely from the center of his right thigh. Without thinking he pulled it free and stared dumbfounded at a blood-covered needle. "What are you *doing*?" he demanded, shifting his gaze to the impassive expression of the guard.

The guard holstered his gun. "Sit down please."

"Sit down?" Paul held up the tranquilizer dart. "This is evidence," he hissed, glaring at the guard. "Do you realize you're going to jail for this?" He started to step forward when he realized his right leg was numb. "Oh shit."

The guard rushed forward and grabbed his arm. "Please," he replied, gesturing for Paul to sit. "While you still can."

Paul shrugged off the man's hand and carefully lowered himself to the ground. Seconds later, the lower half of his body was numb. "You and that woman," he said, glancing in the direction of his car. "You're working together?"

The guard slipped a small radio from his belt and spoke into it. "We're ready." He smiled and gestured at the fog. "I have to say, Paul, you couldn't have picked a better night for us. Thank you."

"My research," Paul muttered, shaking his head. "That's what this is about, isn't it?"

The guard glanced at his watch. "Do me a favor and lie down while you still can. Otherwise you're going to flop over and concuss yourself, and I don't want anything happening to that precious brain of yours."

Paul lay back as commanded. Halfway down, his lower back gave out and his head slapped painfully against the concrete. "God*dammit*—what's the point of all this? Are you going to kidnap me, or just kill me?"

The guard knelt beside him. "Both." He pulled something from his breast pocket and leaned forward. "Now hold still."

Paul winced at the sting of a needle entering his neck. Almost immediately an unsettling warmth filled his chest and began moving toward his head. "What was that?"

The guard tucked the empty syringe into his pocket before checking the researcher's pulse.

"What was that?" Paul asked again, the anger slipping from his voice. Seconds passed. "Please," Paul whispered. His pupils were now dilated, his breath coming in slow gasps. "Will you at least tell me what you're giving me?"

The guard leaned in closer.

"A brand new life, Dr. Obermeyer," he said, a wide grin stretching his tan face. He gently brushed the hair from Paul's forehead. "Can you hear me? I said a brand new life."

4.

Jeri opened her eyes and glanced at the passenger seat. Paul Obermeyer was gone.

She sat up and immediately cringed as a bolt of pain shot down her neck. The attack by her recruit had been a complete surprise—and an unforgiveable mistake. She grabbed the gun from the backseat and stepped out of the car.

"My recruit has escaped," she whispered, raising her pistol at the surrounding wall of mist. "Repeat, my recruit has escaped."

Okay, alright. Just take it easy for a minute. How about we start with your name?

Jeri furrowed her brow in confusion. "Why would you ask—" she froze at the sound of another voice answering a short distance away.

"My name's Paul—Paul Obermeyer. I'm a researcher with Velgyn Pharmaceuticals. I work at the lab just down the hill. Now, will you please call the real authorities and have them arrest the woman in my car?"

Jeri slowly lowered her gun and listened to Chilly's calm, baritone voice respond. A wave of dread struck her at the realization of what was happening beyond the veil of fog in front of her. Moments later, the muted report of her colleague's pistol rang out.

"Jesus Christ! What are you *doing*?"

Jeri crept forward until both men were visible. She studied Chilly's strange outfit before noticing the private security car. *Of course,* she thought irritably. *Of course he knew just where to be.* She waited for her colleague to deliver the second injection, then marched over to him.

"Is he okay?" she asked, peering down at Paul Obermeyer's body.

Chilly said nothing as he stood and faced her. It was the first time they'd exchanged a look in nearly two months. He glanced at his watch. "You've got thirty-seven minutes."

Both of them looked up as a pair of headlights turned off the main road and cut their way forward through the fog. A moment later the team's black SUV rolled to a stop.

"Well, *that* was interestin'," Dublin said, stepping from the vehicle. He opened the rear hatch and, with Sly's help, removed a long black bag from the back.

Tall Tommy walked over to Jeri. "Keys?" he asked, holding out his hand.

"In the ignition," Jeri answered, pointing toward Obermeyer's car. "It's parked over there."

Her colleague nodded and disappeared into the fog.

Dublin and Sly carefully laid the bag on the ground next to their recruit. "How's our boy doing?" the Irishman asked.

"Fine," Chilly replied. "But we're behind schedule. Start prepping the package."

Dublin unzipped the bag in a single swift motion and pulled back the sides. A cloud of frost-white air escaped to reveal a glistening male corpse inside. Jeri looked on while Dublin and Sly donned latex gloves and began slowly moving the corpse's limbs back and forth. A memory from her training came rushing back, Whip's voice echoing in her head—

Upon death, the average human body begins muscular contraction within two to six hours and achieves maximum stiffness—or rigor mortis—within twelve hours. However, as enzymatic decomposition continues, rigor mortis begins to subside approximately twenty-four hours after death and decreases rapidly as endogenous and bacterial activities accelerate. The process works faster in warmer temperatures and slower in colder ones. Now—why is this important? It is important for one simple reason: forensic investigators often measure the amount of rigor mortis in a corpse to determine the victim's approximate time-of-death. This is why we always acquire our corpses—or, as we like to call them, "packages"— within two hours of death. This is also why we immediately chill them to thirty-three degrees Fahrenheit. Doing so delays the process of rigor mortis and effectively prevents investigators from determining the true time of death should any portion of the package remain int—

"Hey," Tall Tommy said, suddenly next to her. "The keys aren't in the ignition. Are you sure you don't have them?"

"I'm sure," Jeri responded. She glanced over to find Chilly eyeing her.

"Then where are they?" he asked.

Jeri glanced at their recruit. "He must've taken them."

Chilly knelt down and searched their recruit's pockets. Within seconds he found the keys.

"Why'd he take them?" Tall Tommy asked.

"To make sure I couldn't get away," Jeri replied.

"No, I don't think so," Chilly countered, studying the ring of keys in his hand. Hanging from one end was a small, heavily weighted metal cylinder. He noticed a button on one side and pressed it.

A shaft of brilliant blue crystal slid from the cylinder and gleamed in the light of the SUV's headlights.

"I think there's something here he didn't want you to have." Chilly removed the cylinder from the key ring and tossed it to Art. "What do you make of that?"

The agency forger held it up to the light. "Oh wow— sapphire! Laser etched. Dude, I've never seen one this intricate before. Must've cost a fortune just to make it." He carefully closed it before handing it back to Chilly. "It's an encryption key. The etchings in the crystal work like a long string passcode for decrypting sensitive files when you plug it into a particular computer. That's some sophisticated shit."

"Why sapphire?" Jeri asked.

"Because sapphire is virtually indestructible. And once it's made, it's almost impossible to duplicate." Art shook his head. "Pretty stupid to keep it on your key ring if you ask me."

"Well, we can't expect geniuses to be smart about everything." Chilly pocketed the security key and raised his hands. "Alright, listen up. Due to the unexpected alteration in tonight's script,"—his eyes flashed to Jeri—"we're now several minutes behind schedule. So, change of plans. Dublin and Tommy will stay here and help me with staging. Sly, you and Art will take the rent-a-cop car and drive our freshman back to the restaurant to wrap up dinner. We'll see everyone back at the airport in ninety minutes." He turned and marched toward the SUV while the rest of the team hurried into action.

Jeri followed after him until they were out of earshot. "Chilly, wait. Can I talk to you a second?"

Her colleague spun and regarded her coldly.

"Look, I'm sorry about what happened. You have to understand, I wasn't—"

"Thirty-*four* minutes," he interjected, pointing at his watch.

Jeri shrugged. "What? I don't understand."

"Of course you do. That's how much time you have before Mr. Cowell wakes up and realizes his wallet is gone and he's on a date with a large bald man. Had you stuck to the script like you were supposed to, you would've had more time."

"But I—"

"Stop. I don't want hear it. You made a bad decision tonight. And now you're making another one by wasting time with excuses." He paused as Sly and Art walked past them. "We'll talk about this later," he said, gesturing toward the car. "Now go."

≈

Adam Cowell stared at the plate of food in front of him. The glazed salmon nestled on a bed of rice pilaf looked delicious, but he made no attempt to try it. Something told him to wait. Or had it been some *one*? He glanced at the man sitting next to him. *How long has he been sitting here?* he wondered. *Do I know him?* He studied the man more closely. *Jesus, he's huge!*

As if reading his mind, the man draped his huge arm around Adam's shoulders.

Adam smiled. *What was it the man told me? Oh yeah—*

the fish. His gaze slowly returned to the plate of salmon in front of him. Wisps of steam curled upwards from the pink flesh. *Too hot. Gotta let it cool down.*

The arm around him shifted. Something tugged against his back pocket. Adam again looked over at his large friend. The man's gaze was drawn to something else. Then suddenly he rose and was gone. *Where you going?* Adam wondered, gazing at the rest of the room. *Such a nice guy to keep me company while Carrie is . . . where? Oh yeah—the restroom.* The thought of his date brought a grin to his blushed face. *What a fun woman. We have so much to talk about.*

"What are you grinning about?" a petulant voice demanded.

Adam looked over to find his date once again sitting across from him. He sat up and straightened his aquamarine sweater. *My lucky sweater* he thought, blinking his eyes into focus. "Shou're . . . shou're back!" he slurred, smiling at her. "Whatook you s'long?"

Carrie gazed back with unmasked irritation. "I was trying to get the stain out of my dress."

"Tha stain?"

His date pointed to a dark splotch on her sleeve. "Your Malbec, remember?"

"Oh no, oh noooo. I'm . . . I'm so sorry." Adam rubbed a palm into his forehead. "That is unacc . . . unaccelpable."

"Yeah, well, maybe you shouldn't have ordered a third bottle of wine." Carrie crossed her arms and gave him a derisive grin. "Especially since you stopped sharing after the first one."

"I'm so glad you're nod mad," Adam sighed, misreading her expression. He reached for his wine glass. "Led's have a toast!"

"No Adam, wait . . . don't—"

Adam misjudged the distance and clumsily toppled the half-full glass. A crimson stream of Malbec arched through the air and splashed into his date's chest. Both sat frozen for a moment before Adam leaned forward with a blank look of shock. "I'm . . . I'm soooo sorr—"

"God*dammit*!" His date grabbed her napkin and frantically wiped at her chest. A moment later she resignedly tossed it on the table. "That's it—I'm done," she said, bolting up from the table. "Thanks for a great night, Adam—and good luck with your drinking problem." She stormed past him, then abruptly turned and marched back. "In case you're too drunk to interpret my sarcasm, let me be clear. Never contact me again—got it?"

Adam gazed up at her and nodded. The shock of the moment left him suddenly clearer, as if awakening from a strange dream. "Yeah . . . yeah," he mumbled, his mouth hanging loosely. "I wouldn't. I mean . . . I . . . I won't."

Carrie flashed him a final venomous smile. "Good. Be safe getting home."

"Yeah . . . uh, you too. It was nice meet—" Adam's voice trailed off as his date turned and stormed out of the restaurant. He sat quietly for several minutes, staring at the untouched plate of salmon in front of him. He gazed down at his sweater and sighed.

God, he hated first dates.

5.

"May I suggest the Sauveterre piece, L'âme Perdue?" the art dealer asked.

Michael Manning tore his eyes from the stock market report flashing across his computer screen and glanced at the open catalog in front of him "The what?" he asked gruffly at the speakerphone.

"The Sauveterre, Mr. Manning." The young woman's British accent echoed against the coffered ceiling of his private library. "You'll find it on page thirteen."

Manning flipped through the thick pages of the gallery catalog as the art dealer briefed him on the work of Renee Sauveterre, the master of late twentieth-century neo-whateverism. He paused on the page showcasing the L'âme Perdue and grimaced. The large square canvas was nearly untouched with the exception of several small blue spheres of equal size that appeared randomly painted on its surface. In one corner, one of the spheres was encircled by a haphazard stroke of mustard-yellow. *Hardly my taste* he thought, glancing at the price. An elegant font listed the painting's appraised value at $310,000. His gaze dropped to the photo of the young art dealer at the bottom of the page.

Definitely my taste.

"What's the pre-auction price?" he asked, interrupting her monologue.

"Excellent question, Mr. Manning," the dealer replied, deftly shifting to the negotiation portion of the call. "While I have no doubts this piece will go for well over the appraised price, as a distinguished patron of our gallery we're prepared to offer you this seminal work of Renee Sauveterre for only two hundred and fifty thousand dollars."

"Two-fifty, huh?" Mannng closed the catalog and let his eyes absently drift across the books that lined the walls around him.

"That's correct. And let me just say, Mr. Manning, for a Sauveterre of this caliber, this price is absolutely extraordinary."

"I agree. Selling a painting of blue balls and yellow circles for a quarter mil definitely qualifies as extraordinary."

The dealer laughed softly. "Yes, I'm afraid art is a very unique world, Mr. Manning. It's sometimes quite difficult to appreciate the true value of—"

The buzz of another call interrupted her response. Manning glanced at the screen and furrowed his brow at the name of the caller.

"—but I can assure you that the piece we're discussing is well worth—"

"I've got another call," Manning said bluntly. "Why don't you call me tomorrow when you come up with a less extraordinary price?" He glanced again at her photo. "Or better yet, stop by my office and we'll handle this face-to-face."

"Oh—well yes, of course," the dealer replied, the surprise evident in her voice. "I'm sure we can come to a mutually acceptable arrangement, Mr. Manning."

"I'll look forward to seeing what you can offer," he said, ending the call. *Oh well*, he thought dismissively. His wife's birthday present would just have to wait. He picked up his cellphone. "Manning."

"There's been an incident," a man's voice answered.

"What kind of incident?" Manning rose from his chair and paced to the library's western wall of glass overlooking Richardson Bay. His new yacht bobbed gently in its moorings in the black waters below.

"I've just gotten a call from the Berkeley Police Department," the man replied. "There's been an accident near the genomics lab. Bad fire. One fatality. Not much left of the car—or the driver for that matter. But they did recover a wallet." He paused. "One of our employee ID cards was inside."

Manning rapped his knuckles against the glass. "Who?"

"Paul Obermeyer."

His hand froze.

"Michael?"

"I'm at the Belvedere house," Manning replied. "Send a car—and make sure you're in it. I want to see this for myself."

The half-dozen officers and investigators looked on curiously as the white Bentley Mulsanne limousine slowed to a stop near the line of police tape and two men in tailored suits stepped from the back seat. The closest officer swaggered over with an air of authority and began to raise his hand when the tall, dark-haired man leading the way reached out and shook it.

"Evening, officer." The man flashed an appreciative grin before glancing around grimly. "I hope we're not interrupting, but I needed to see what happened here."

"Are you related to the victim?" the officer asked, studying the man's thin face and sharp, angular features.

"It feels like it, but no. My name is Michael Manning. I'm the CEO of Velgyn Pharmaceuticals." He produced a card and held it out to the officer. "Dr. Obermeyer—Paul—was one of our top researchers. He was also a close friend of mine. Can you tell me what happened?"

The officer palmed the card and shrugged. "I'm sorry, but there's not much I can tell you until our investigation's been concluded."

"I see." Manning turned to his companion. The man was broad and muscular, with Scandinavian blond hair nearly shaved to the scalp. His pale gray eyes settled on the officer with piercing intensity.

"Are you the investigator in charge?" he asked.

"No," the officer replied. "That'd be detective Madsen."

"Then would you mind getting detective Madsen for us, please?"

The officer's stare lingered on the man for a moment. He turned and marched over to a stocky middle-aged woman in a police jacket hunched over the wreckage. The two briefly exchanged words before the woman shot a sidelong glance at Manning and his companion. She nodded and trudged toward them.

"Can I help you?" the detective asked, pausing at the line of police tape.

Manning's companion handed her a card. "Detective, I'm Lars Nielsen, Director of Security for Velgyn Pharmaceuticals. Your team contacted me earlier tonight after finding Dr. Obermeyer's identification."

The detective's expression softened. "Yes, we did."

"What can you tell us?"

"Well, we're still analyzing the scene, but so far the evidence looks pretty cut and dried." She raised a hand toward a crumpled light post across the street. "It appears Dr. Obermeyer was driving at a high rate of speed when he struck that post. Based on the impact location and subsequent tire marks, the car spun clockwise for two revolutions before rolling to a stop in this clearing." She paused and turned toward the charred remains of the vehicle behind her. "Hard to say if he survived the initial impact, but at some point the fuel tank ruptured and the heat of the engine ignited the fumes. As you can see, there was enough in the tank to burn things up pretty good."

Nielsen started to ask a question when his cellphone buzzed. He glanced at it and immediately excused himself.

Manning gestured at the wreckage. "Is his body still in there?"

The detective shook her head. "No, sir, the victim's remains have already been removed and sent to the coroner."

"And just how bad was it?"

"Well, let's just say it's a good thing his wallet was found mostly intact, because there wasn't much else left to identify."

The Velgyn security director ended his call and marched over to the detective. "Would it be possible to look at the vehicle or any other personal belongings you may have found?"

"Why would you want to do that?" she asked bluntly.

"I thought I just overheard you say you haven't confirmed his identity yet. If that's the case, perhaps there's something else you've found that we could take a look at."

The detective glanced over at the scene and shrugged. "Appreciate the offer, but I've got protocols to follow. Any evidence we collect here tonight will be sealed and sent to the crime lab before it's released to the victim's family. That's assuming there's no criminal investigation." She regarded Nielsen with sudden interest. "Something in particular you're looking for?"

Nielsen shook his head slowly. "Just trying to understand what's happened here."

"I'm sorry gentlemen, but this is as close as I can allow you to the scene tonight. Someone will give you a call as soon as we know more about the situation. For now, I suggest you go on home."

Both men took a final look at the blackened wreckage before returning to the waiting limousine. The moment they were inside, Manning pointed a finger at his security director.

"I want some fucking answers, Lars—and you're going to get them."

"Of course. But I need more information, Michael. Starting with what you're not telling me."

The CEO shook his head. "Excuse me?"

"The call I just took." Nielsen held up his phone. "Vick Blass, head of our network security team. I'd asked him to review Obermeyer's personnel files for anything out of the ordinary. He said the file itself didn't raise any red flags, but for some reason it doesn't include Paul's current research work." His gray eyes narrowed on Manning. "So, let me guess—is it E-1?"

"That's right."

"Okay, so we have a dead researcher who's current

work is an Executive-One priority. What else should I know?"

"The timing."

"The timing?" Nielsen repeated.

"He was *finished!*" Manning snapped. "Obermeyer wrapped up his discovery phase research last week. We were scheduled to have a review of his findings the day after tomorrow. How's that for timing?"

"What was the nature of the research?"

Manning turned to the window. "Get to the bottom of this," he grumbled. "Immediately."

Nielsen studied the CEO for a moment before nodding. "My team's sweeping Obermeyer's lab as we speak. By morning we should have all surveillance video of the facility in our hands for analysis. If there's anything more to this than an accident, we'll know shortly."

Manning shrugged indifferently. "You're first priority is to secure his research. I want every project file pulled from Obermeyer's lab and in my hands by tomorrow morning."

"Understood."

"What time is it?" The CEO glanced at his Gruebel Forsey watch and pressed a button on his armrest. In front of him, the privacy glass slipped from view. "Just take me to my condo downtown," he ordered the driver.

"Wait," Nielsen said, opening the door.

"What are you doing?"

"Obermeyer's lab is just down the road." The security director stepped out into the cool night air. "I think I'll take a walk."

"Fine. I want a full briefing first thing tomorrow—along with those files."

Nielsen nodded. The limousine pulled away and vanished around the first bend in the road. He glanced over at the officers and investigators still hovering around the accident scene. The officer who had stopped them earlier pretended not to be watching him, but Nielsen noticed the man's furtive glances.

He was trained to notice everything.

The growl of an engine caught his attention. A large flatbed truck labored up the hill and was quickly waved into position by the officers. The investigation was already wrapping up. Soon, what remained of Obermeyer's car would be shuttled off to the police impound lot. The security director smiled at the thought. He was certain that whatever security existed at the lot, it could easily be breached.

As with anything, you just had to find the weak spot.

But that would come later if necessary. For now, his focus was here. Nielsen stared again at the tire marks on the road and committed their pattern to memory. He then slowly made his way down the hill.

6.

"Stop kidding around, Jer-bear."

Jeri looked up at the desk in the center of the small study. The face of her father hovered over his typewriter, his dark eyes studying her reproachfully. She felt herself blush like a child. "What do you mean?" she asked, her voice a breathless whisper.

"You know exactly what I mean." Her father gestured toward the door. "No go back to your friends and apologize."

"But it's not my fault! They're not playing fairly!"

His handsome face frowned. "That's true. But you can't always play fairly when the world itself isn't fair."

The warmth completed its task, reducing her to a paralyzed body crumpled against the wall. She closed her eyes and willed the words to come. "What if I don't . . . don't want to play this way?"

"You don't have a choice."

Jeri opened her eyes. The room was darkening, the air turning colder. She gasped for breath, the knot in her throat growing tighter. "I could start a new game."

Her father shook his head. "There are no other games."

Jeri snapped awake as the private jet turned and banked north. She sat up and peered out the window. On the wingtip, the plane's navigation light flashed red against an ink-black night.

"We're somewhere over the Midwest."

She looked over to find Chilly studying her from his seat across the aisle. Behind him, Paul Obermeyer's body was spread across the couch. An IV line ran from his arm to a half-empty saline bag hanging from the ceiling. "Can't sleep?"

Chilly shook his head. "Don't want to." He swiveled his chair toward her. "Ready to debrief on tonight's collection?"

"Sure. What do you want to analyze first—how I nearly ran over our recruit while searching for him in the fog, or my carelessness with the gun?"

"Neither. I want to know why you decided to change the script."

Jeri narrowed her eyes on him. "What do you mean?"

"You know exactly what I mean. Tonight's script was very simple—acquire your recruit and tranquilize him at the first appropriate chance. And yet, you didn't follow it."

"That's ridiculous."

"Then why didn't you dose him when he was lying on the side of the road?"

"Because I thought he was hurt!" Jeri retorted. "If I recall my training correctly, the safety of our recruits supersedes all other considerations—including the opportunity for collection. Or am I wrong?"

"No, you're right. But even after you knew he was fine, you didn't take the shot." Chilly leaned toward her, a thin smile on his lips. "So tell me—at what point did you decide that talking our recruit into joining was a better idea than administering fifty cc's of chemical persuasion?"

Jeri leaned toward her colleague. "Per *your* script, upon determining that our recruit wasn't injured, I decided the best plan of action was to persuade him into the car and drive him to a private location for dosing and collection. Along the way, I chose to discuss matters relevant to his work in order to gain his trust. Everything was going absolutely fine until he noticed I was driving his car. And why was I driving his car? That's right—because *your* script called for it." She smiled back smugly. "If you want to question something, maybe you start with your choice of script."

Chilly glanced over his shoulder at their recruit. "If you were having second thoughts about our collection methods, you should have discussed them with me first."

"Oh, and just when should I have done that?" Jeri demanded. "Before you dropped me in the middle of nowhere with a psychopathic trainer for ten weeks? Or should I have reached out this morning in those few minutes between decoding your letter and flying to San Francisco to do this assignment?" She fell back into her seat. "You haven't exactly made yourself available, *Sam*."

Her colleague shot her a look. "We don't use real names in the presence of recruits, *freshman*."

"Oh for god's sake—he's unconscious."

Chilly sighed. "Okay, let's try this again. I apologize for the lack of communication during your training. I apologize for throwing you into all of this so quickly. But the simple fact is that we don't have the luxury of time, and if there's anything you should've learned after ten weeks with Whip, it's how things operate in this agency. Everything follows a protocol, or a plan, or a script. *Everything*. Regardless of what comes up, regardless of how you feel or whatever doubts you're having, you stick to the script."

"But I—"

"Yeah, you *almost* ran over your recruit. So what? So you improvise a little. That's your job. Your job is to do whatever's necessary to finish the collection. Your job is not—repeat, *not*—to toss out the script and change your method of collection because you have a sudden crisis of conscience."

"But I had him!" Jeri exclaimed, rising from her chair. "Did you not hear him when I asked if he'd rather be doing something of real value? He said 'of course I would.' But no—we can't just let these people make their *own* choices, can we? We can't let them *want* to come in. We have to dart them like some endangered animal and cart them off to the zoo."

"That's right, we do," Chilly affirmed. "Look, of course your recruit said yes to your question—who wouldn't? That's not the problem. The problem—the *risk*—doesn't come from the recruits. It comes from the people surrounding them." He stood and stepped closer. "Like it or not, our method of collection is the best way we know to minimize the risk for everyone. Going off-script like you did tonight only reintroduces that risk." He paused and studied her temple. "Of course, you already learned that the hard way. How's your head?"

Jeri leaned back as her colleague gently grabbed her head. "It's fine. Don't worry—"

"Turn to the right."

Jeri sighed and did as she was told. Chilly's hands slipped down to the base of her neck.

"Tell me if I hurt you."

"Why—is that the goal?" She closed her eyes as his fingers slowly moved upward, his breath tickling her neck.

"Where does it hurt?"

Jeri opened her eyes to find Chilly's face just inches from hers. "A little higher," she mumbled, watching him. An odd feeling began to overtake her, as if gravity had suddenly shifted. She felt her body being drawn forward. Then, without warning, his fingers found their mark and a sharp pain ripped her back to reality. "There," she gasped, recoiling from his touch. "Mission accomplished."

She fell back into her seat.

A strange look briefly clouded her colleague's eyes. He shrugged dismissively. "Probably just a contusion. But it could've been much worse. From the sound of your head hitting the window in my earpiece, I was convinced you'd been knocked out cold. Good thing I was there." He gestured toward the back of the plane. "I'm going to make myself a nightcap. Should I grab you some ibuprofen?"

Jeri nodded, then looked up at him sharply. "Wait a minute—you *knew*."

"Knew what?"

"That I was going to fail. *That's* why you were in the parking lot posing as a rent-a-cop. You knew I was going to make a mistake and that he'd run—run straight to someone he thought he could trust. And . . . Jesus . . . you were right." Her eyes swept over him with disbelief. "How did you know that?"

"I didn't *know* anything. But I was prepared for the possibility of something going wrong. That's how this agency works, freshman. Not just on protocols, plans, and scripts, but on redundancies. You didn't think Whip turned you lose without giving me a full breakdown of your training, did you? You tested off the charts on nearly everything. Unfortunately that included compassion and a distrust for authority. So I planned accordingly."

Jeri's stare turned suspicious. "Tell me the truth—was this a real assignment, or just another test?"

Chilly nodded toward their recruit. "Why don't you ask him? But then, who says it can't be both? Everything's a test, freshman."

"And you—have *you* ever failed this test? Ever looked in the eyes of a recruit and had second thoughts, or questioned your scripts and protocols?"

"No. Never."

Jeri shook her head. "Wow, Chilly. I think I'm finally starting to see how you got your nickname." Her stare shifted to their sleeping recruit. "Tonight I helped kidnap a man whose only crime is being brilliant. And tomorrow he'll wake up from a nice long rest and realize his life has been ruined."

"No, not ruined—*redirected*," Chilly countered. "You want to know why I've never had doubts about what we're doing? Because it's necessary. Because brilliant people like him are the key to solving everything. They're the single most valuable commodity that exists in the world today, and neither their fates nor their life's work can be left solely to the whim of some goddamn corporate shareholders."

He walked over and checked Obermeyer's pulse before adjusting his blanket. When he spoke again his voice was softer.

"I've never once dismissed what we're doing to these people. But it's nothing compared to the consequences of not doing it. This agency exists because the world can no longer afford to *ask* brilliant people for their help—so do us all a favor and stop trying." Chilly turned and looked at her. "Three collections and you're officially an agent. One down, two to go.

And it does get easier—I promise. You just have to get comfortable with the process."

Jeri turned to the window. A thin line of lights now shimmered on the horizon. "I'm not sure I *want* to get comfortable with the process."

"All the more reason to keep trying." Her colleague glanced at his watch. "We'll be landing in Newark soon to refuel. From there, I'll escort sleeping beauty here to his new employer. You'll take a flight south and meet up with the rest of the team. Our next collection is in two days." He turned and headed toward the back of the plane. "Two ibuprofen coming up."

Jeri watched him walk away. "So when will I get instructions on the next collection?"

"Check your bag," he replied without looking back. "You already have them."

Jeri reached into the pocket of her travel bag and found an airline ticket and a sealed envelope. She checked the destination on the ticket before turning her attention to the envelope. As before, the heavy paper envelope was bordered with the blue and red stripes of an international parcel. But instead of a recipients name or address, a simple instruction was scrawled across the front—

Open upon arrival.

She stuffed the ticket and envelope back into her bag and sighed. *Was this a joke?* she wondered. Were Chilly's letters really part of some 'standard' new-agent protocol—or just some demented form of fraternity-style hazing? And if so, was everyone in on it but her? Were they all quietly laughing at what the freshman was being made to do?

The sound of her colleague exiting the galley stirred Jeri from her thoughts. She curled up on the seat and pretended to be asleep. Whatever the truth was, she'd find out soon enough. For now, all she could do was continue. Continue south to the next collection, continue deciphering Chilly's letters, continue following protocols, plans, and goddamn scripts.

And, most importantly, continue telling herself that what they were doing was right.

The plane nosed downward into its descent into Newark. Jeri heard the rustle of Chilly returning to his seat. She listened to him sigh over the gentle whine of the engines, and felt the certainty of his stare on her face. She took a deep breath and forced her eyes to remain shut.

7.

Michael Manning read the first few lines of the article in the morning paper once again—

Car crash near university leaves one dead

A single car accident claimed the life of an Oakland man last night near the Berkeley campus. Thirty-four year old Paul Obermeyer was driving on Centennial Drive at approximately 6:30 pm when his car apparently struck a light post and caught fire. Fire fighters arrived on the scene to find the victim's vehicle engulfed in flames.

The CEO spun his chair toward the window and took in the twenty-six acre corporate campus spread out before him.

Everything was in jeopardy now.

After months of planning, the special shareholder meeting was just three weeks away. Every facet had been painstakingly planned and executed in absolute secrecy. No phone calls. No emails. Not even the normal attendees list. The carefully worded invitations to Velgyn's top executives and majority shareholders had been hand-delivered by couriers and re-collected upon confirmation of attendance. No details had been provided, except the importance of the meeting itself. Such were the necessary precautions of doing business in the brutally competitive world of pharmaceutical development—especially when you had something that was nothing short of a miracle.

Or almost had it.

Manning turned to the draft of his opening speech on his laptop. A lone sentence caught his eye—

Gene recombination therapy delivered into living cells by viral vectors not only represents the newest and brightest opportunity in both cellular regeneration and gene resubmission, it promises to be the key to a miraculous new era of youth-restoring pharmaceuticals.

Of course, the final draft would read more like a Hollywood script—telling the story of a brilliant genomics scientist who investigates an under-explored area of cellular research. Of initial findings so striking that the project is quickly elevated to E-1—the highly secretive Executive One research classification reserved solely for the most promising of projects. Of two years of groundbreaking work by Dr. Paul Obermeyer and his team. Of how Velgyn Pharmaceuticals now stood on the precipice of having what every major drug company sought most—drugs that could counteract an entire spectrum of age-related issues from gray hair and baldness to liver spots and wrinkles.

The mere thought of it made the CEO once again shudder with excitement.

For decades, the search for such so-called "Holy Grail"

cures—a name that referred as much to their revenue potential as their rejuvenating effects—had been the stuff of folklore and legend among the major drug companies. Billions had been spent in the pursuit of finding them. But now, thanks in no small part to Manning's clear guidance and unwavering demands, it was Velgyn alone that nearly held them in its grasp.

Manning knew it was the perfect story for enrapturing his high-power audience—with the exception of the part where the brilliant researcher drives himself into a fucking streetlight and dies in the flames. He was still pondering this when the speakerphone on his desk chirped to life.

"Mr. Nielsen's here, sir," his secretary announced.

"Send him in."

A moment later, Lars Nielsen marched through the door of the lavishly furnished corner office. Manning regarded his director of security expectantly. "So?"

"I spoke with the police again this morning," Nielsen answered. "The coroner isn't scheduled to examine Obermeyer's body until tomorrow. Unfortunately, we're not going to have access to their findings for several days."

"I don't need a goddamn coroner's report to confirm that he's dead. Just tell me you secured his research files."

"Yes, Michael. Obermeyer's lab computers were moved from his Berkeley lab to a secure room onsite this morning. His research files are perfectly safe."

"Good. When can I get my hands on them?"

Nielsen stepped to the window and admired the view. "We need to discuss something else first."

"Such as—?"

"A few circumstances surrounding the accident." The director of security watched as two men in lab coats emerged from the oncology research building and headed across the central courtyard toward the cafeteria. One of the men walked with a short, stilted gate, his hands gesturing wildly at his colleague. *He's angry about something,* Nielsen concluded. He turned to the CEO. "Have you read Obermeyer's personnel file?"

Manning shook his head.

"Then I'll give you the highlights. In the four years he worked for Velgyn, Paul Obermeyer took no sick days and only three of his sixty accrued vacation days. His health records indicate he was enrolled in our best medical and dental plans, and from what I've gathered so far he visited his primary care physician and dentist like clockwork every six months for routine examines and check-ups. He has no wife or significant other, no children, and no family to speak of—which explains why he never purchased any life insurance through the company. However, he did take full advantage of our retirement packages. When I checked a statement from his 401k that my team found at his house last night, I noticed his portfolio was almost entirely invested in bonds and treasury bills."

"And your point?"

"My point is that, on paper at least, Paul Obermeyer is one of the most *risk-averse* workaholics I've ever profiled. So I'm curious to know why a career-focused man with absolutely no desire for danger decided to drive his BMW at twice the posted speed limit on a winding road at dusk during heavy fog."

Manning considered the security director's point for a moment before waving his hand impatiently. "Okay—what else?"

"He was driving north towards Berkeley Hills at the

time of the accident, which is strange considering Obermeyer lived in Oakland—directly south from his lab. And as far as I can tell, he had no known friends that live in Berkeley Hills, nor any known activities or interests that would have compelled him to go north. In fact, I haven't found a single reason for him to be in that area at all—except for maybe one."

Manning's eyes narrowed. "What?"

"The area itself," Nielsen said, glancing around the room. He'd been in the CEO's office on several occasions since the multi-million dollar renovation of the executive floor the previous fall, but the sheer opulence still overwhelmed him. His gaze paused on a large, intricately detailed model of Manning's yacht *Comfortably Numb* mounted on the far wall between two Chagall paintings. Crowding the top of an eighteenth century English cabinet were professional photos of the executive's wife and three teenage children.

"I don't understand."

"Did you notice how quiet it was there? No buildings. No homes. Minimal traffic at night. Not a soul around to see or hear what's happening. It's a horrible place for an accident to occur—unless you wanted it to go unnoticed."

The CEO scoffed. "What are you suggesting—that Paul committed suicide?"

"No," Nielsen replied. "All I'm saying is that nothing about Dr. Obermeyer's behavior last night fits with his normal routine or personality profile. Given the circumstances, anything out of the ordinary should be examined very carefully." His gray eyes flashed to Manning. "And there's something else."

"You mean something *other* than the fact that my top researcher died last night under suspicious circumstances?" Manning rubbed his temples. "Christ, Lars, just tell me."

"His encryption key is missing."

"His *what*?"

"His encryption key," Nielsen repeated. "It's a security measure—an algorithm stored on a laser-etched crystal that encrypts the researcher's files to prevent unauthorized access. Every senior researcher in the company is required to use one. Normal protocol is for each researcher to encrypt all data and materials on two mirrored computers in their laboratory until that particular research phase is completed. The files are then moved to the central server and the encryption key is handed over to us. Unfortunately, Dr. Obermeyer hadn't turned it over yet."

"But you just told me his files are perfectly safe."

"They are. We just can't access them."

Manning shrugged. "The hell you can't—just hack into the fucking hard drives!"

His security director shook his head. "That's exactly what the encryption key has been designed to prevent. The algorithm's far too complex. No one can reasonably hack it—not even us."

"That's ridiculous. What if Obermeyer himself had lost it?"

"Then he would have used a series of passcodes to temporarily access the files until we produced a new encryption key. But only he would have had those passcodes." Nielsen noticed the scowl growing on the CEO's face. "You have to understand, these are industry-standard security protocols for managing highly classified information. The system was designed to always require either the researcher or his encryption key to gain access. We never planned for a situation where we lost both."

Manning slammed his fist against his desk. "You've got to be fucking kidding me!" He stood and started pacing the room. "None of this makes any goddamn sense," he hissed, his Italian leather shoes clicking hollowly against the black granite floor. "Could it have been destroyed in the fire?"

"These encryption keys are designed to be practically indestructible," Nielsen replied, standing stoically by the window. "If he'd had it with him, it would've most likely survived and been found by the investigators. Unfortunately, when I spoke with them this morning and described the *corporate property* Obermeyer may have had on him, nothing like it was on their list." The security director shrugged. "Perhaps, for some reason we have yet to understand, he destroyed it."

"Bullshit," Manning retorted. "Destroy two years of his own research? You said it yourself—it doesn't fit at all with Paul's personality or work ethic. So why—" the Velgyn CEO abruptly paused. "Son of a bitch. Someone else did this, didn't they? One of our competitors—maybe Symphexia, or G&F?" He turned and glared at Nielsen. "That's it, isn't it? Someone killed Paul and made look like an accident."

"Perhaps," Nielsen answered. In truth he was pleased Manning had arrived at the same conclusion he had. Experience had taught him that the best way to get anyone to support an idea was to make them believe it was their own. Now he just had to get the CEO on-board with the rest of his theory. "But if so, it was highly professional," he continued. "And it certainly would have required several people to pull off."

"They killed him and took his encryption key." Manning nodded, now certain of the idea. "But how did they get to his files?"

"They didn't. Obermeyer's computers don't have any

external access ports, except a unique one for the encryption key. Nor were they on any network. Everything was completely locked down. Anyone who knew enough about our security protocols to recognize an encryption key would have known it wasn't even worth trying."

"But that doesn't make any sense!" Manning snapped, pacing again. "Why would someone go to the trouble of killing Obermeyer and taking his encryption key if they knew they couldn't get to his research files?"

Nielsen raised his eyebrows. "To level the playing field."

"What do you mean?"

"I mean maybe this wasn't about *gaining* access to Paul's research. Maybe this was about *preventing* it."

"From who?"

"From us."

Manning froze. "You're saying someone killed Paul and took his encryption key specifically to keep us from accessing his research?"

"It's just a theory," the director of security conceded. "But given the importance of Dr. Obermeyer's research, it's not inconceivable. And you can't deny the timing—a researcher who's just finished two years of highly classified research dies the day before his work is to be submitted to corporate?" He gave Manning a thin smile. "You tell me—if one of our competitors was on the brink of developing a major new drug that you couldn't get your hands on directly, but had the chance to keep from them, what would you do?"

Manning walked back to his desk and dropped heavily into his chair. "Jesus Christ. It's . . . it's fucking brilliant."

"As I said, it's just a theory."

"Presume that it's not. Presume, for a moment, that

your theory is exactly right." The CEO studied his director of security carefully. "What are you prepared to do about it?"

"Everything necessary."

"To—?"

"To correct the situation. Or prove my theory wrong."

"*Every*thing?"

Nielsen read his tone and nodded. "Yes, Michael."

Manning spun his chair and again studied the view. The morning sun had slipped through the clouds and was now bathing the campus in golden light. "Paul Obermeyer's dead," he said flatly. "I have to accept that. But there's no goddamn way I'll accept losing his research. It belongs to this corporation. It belongs to *me*."

"I understand."

"Good. Then let me know what you find on those surveillance tapes."

Nielsen turned to go. He was nearly at the door when Manning spoke once again.

"And remember, Lars—everything necessary."

Nielsen paused and allowed a brief silence to acknowledge the weight of Manning's words. "Everything necessary," he repeated before slipping past the door.

8.

Paul Obermeyer opened his eyes.

A florescent light flickered overhead. He blinked up at it, waiting for a memory of where he was to materialize, but none did. He turned his head to find the steel railing of the hospital bed pressed against his left shoulder. Above it hung a half-empty IV bag. He glanced at the needle buried in his vein before noticing the heart rate monitor clamped to his finger. An obvious question flashed to mind—

What happened?

Paul sat up carefully. His body was stiff, his mouth dry and metallic tasting. A dull pain gripped his right leg. He tossed back the bed sheet and gazed dumfounded at a large bruise on his thigh. Centered in the purple-black skin was a small blood-crusted puncture wound. He brushed a finger against it, trying again to recall what had happened. Again nothing. *What the hell?* he wondered, noticing he was wearing his running clothes. A disjointed stream of images drifted through his mind—rolling banks of fog, wet pavement, blinding headlights—but Paul couldn't tell if it was real or imagined. He sighed with a growing feeling of frustration and looked around.

Even in the dim light it was obvious he wasn't in a hospital. The large industrial room was little more than four ash-colored walls of concrete rising from a white tile floor. Other than his bed, heart rate monitor, and a folding chair sitting a few feet away, the room was empty. Above the fluorescent lights, a labyrinth of massive air ducts and electrical conduits filled the high ceiling.

Paul's gaze settled on the steel door in the corner. A sign written in a strange, sweeping script was stenciled in bright red paint across its center. He narrowed his eyes on it and shook his head.

I must be dreaming.

Next to him, the heart rate monitor began to beep with alarm. Paul glanced around anxiously before ripping the monitor from his finger. The beeping grew louder. "Come on!" he hissed, punching buttons on the display until it stopped. He carefully removed the IV needle from his arm and slipped off the bed. The concrete floor was surprisingly warm beneath his bare feet. He shuffled to the door and studied the sign up close. The only thing he was sure of was the language in which it was written.

Please tell me I'm dreaming.

Paul slowly worked the door handle. It was unlocked. He pressed the heavy door open and found himself staring directly into the eyes of a thin, olive-skinned man sitting behind a laptop.

"Ah, you're awake!" the man said cheerfully through a thick Italian accent. "I wasn't expecting you for several more hours."

"What the hell's going on?" Paul demanded, eyeing the man warily. "Who are you?"

"Just getting the last few things in order." The man stood and gestured toward an observation window in the thick wall of concrete next to them. Through the heavy glass, an array of new sequencers, thermocyclers, spectrophotometers and other equipment gleamed under rows of futuristic-looking lights. "Your new laboratory, Dr. Obermeyer. I think you will not be disappointed." He raised a finger. "Scusami for one moment."

Paul watched as the Italian man fished a two-way radio from his pocket and pressed it to his mouth.

"Father, the sleeper has awakened. Repeat, the sleeper has awakened."

A moment later a sleepy male voice responded.

"Already? Shit, okay . . . I'm on my way."

The Italian gave Paul a sheepish grin. "I've always wanted to say that," he said, tucking the radio back into his pocket. "It's from the movie *Dune*. Are you a science fiction fan?"

"Am I—what?"

"You see, we can't use our real names on the radios or phones here. You never know who's listening. So I like to use lines from some of my favorite movies. It's funny, yes?"

Paul shook his head. "Look, I have no idea what you're talking about. Where the hell am I?"

"Yes, of course you have many questions."

"*Questions?*" Paul released an incredulous laughed. "Yeah, I have questions. And I want some fucking answers. Like this—" He pulled up his shorts to reveal the wound on his leg. "Can you explain this? Can you explain why I don't remember how it happened or how I got here?" He pointed behind him. "Or why the sign on that door is written in Arabic?"

"Yes, of course," the man answered. "But first, may I show you to the restroom?"

Paul blinked, dumbfounded. "What?"

"The restroom. May I show you where it is?"

"Christ, maybe I *am* dreaming. Why on earth would you ask me that?"

"Because it's what everyone asks for first when they wake up," a commanding baritone voice answered from the doorway.

Paul turned to find a stocky man with thin brown hair and a cleft chin marching into the room. He looked strangely familiar, but at the moment the researcher had little faith in his memory.

The man stopped next to the Italian and smiled. "Marcello, did you need to pee when you first woke up?"

The Italian nodded. "Very much so."

"Me too." The stocky man slapped his colleague on the shoulder. "I must've pissed for five minutes. It was nearly a religious experience." He smiled at Paul. "So, what would you like first—a toilet, or some answers?"

Paul sighed impatiently. "Answers."

"Fine. Ask away."

"Where am I?"

"Saudi Arabia. Roughly sixty miles southeast of the city of Al Hofuf, in the beautiful Al Khali desert."

"I'm serious."

"So am I." The man kept a steady gaze on Paul.

"Okay, then how did I get here?"

"The agency hired to recruit you brought you in."

"Recruit me?"

The man shrugged. "Well, the term *recruitment* is used kind of liberally around here. Perhaps a better way to say it would be a *non-volitional scientific appointment*. That's what I tell myself anyway." He glanced at Paul's leg. "Nice contusion. That's from the tranquilizer dart. Seems a little barbaric, but it does the trick. Marcello had the same wound."

Paul gazed at his wound. "Why don't I remember any of this?"

"The drug," Marcello answered. "It seems to wipe out several minutes of memory around the time you're injected. At least that's how it was for me. One minute I was sitting on a rickshaw in Assam, the next minute,"—he snapped his fingers and smiled—"*Che palle!* I was here."

"Wait a minute," Paul said, catching the Italian man's meaning. "You ended up here the same way I did?"

Both men nodded. "About three months ago," the stocky man said. "Marcello was recruited first. The rest of us followed shortly after."

"The rest? How many of you are there?"

"Five," Marcello replied. "Well, six, now that you have joined us."

Paul turned and gazed at the laboratory through the window. "Recruited? For what?"

"A project," the stocky man replied.

"What kind of project?"

"There's a gentleman that'll explain that in the morning. I hate to make you wait, but it's two a.m. here and we're all a bit overworked these days. I'll collect you around eight. In the meantime, Marcello will make sure you've got everything you need. It sounds ridiculous, but I suggest you try to get some more rest." The man yawned and shook his head. "Sorry, I should've introduced myself earlier. I'm Derrick Birch."

Paul raised his hand and paused. "Wait—did you say Derrick Birch?"

"That's right."

"But that's impossible. Derrick Birch is dead."

"Exactly." The man seized Paul's hand and shook it firmly. "We're *all* dead here, Paul. And you just joined the club."

Paul felt the color drain from his face. His eyes searched the grinning faces of both men before dropping to his shorts. An intense pressure suddenly demanded his attention. He cupped his genitals and leaned forward, a weak moan escaping his lips.

"Oops, there it is." Derrick Birch smiled at his colleague. "Marcello, would you mind escorting Dr. Obermeyer to the restroom before he pisses himself?"

"Yes, of course."

Paul fell in step behind the Italian man as his colleague stifled a laugh. He was almost out the door when Derrick Birch called out behind him.

"Welcome to the *nearly departed crew*, Paul!"

9.

"Christopher Adam Cowell—is that correct?"

Adam Cowell fidgeted in his chair inside the director of security's office and nodded. "That's correct."

"But you go by Adam?"

"I do. My parents always called me Adam, so, yeah, I go by Adam."

Across from him, Lars Nielsen studied the research assistant with a neutral expression. "How long have you been working in Dr. Obermeyer's lab?"

"Almost two years."

The Velgyn security director nodded as he opened a manila folder and silently read something. A second folder with Adam's name written on the tab sat on his desk. "Sad he's dead?"

Adam blinked at the question. "What? Well, yeah, of course. Paul is—*was*—an incredible mentor and teacher. I still can't believe he's gone." He glanced around at the director's tidy, sparsely furnished office. "What's this about, anyway?"

Nielsen continued reading the document in his hand. "What was happening in that lab between you and Paul, Adam?"

"What do you mean?"

"You tell me."

"Well, nothing," the research assistant said defensively. "I mean, Dr. Obermeyer may have been a little more irritable lately, but that was no surprise. He was under a lot of pressure to finish the project."

The security director's gray eyes flashed up at him. "What project?"

Adam shook his head. "Oh, I'm sorry, I don't know if— am I even allowed to talk about that? I mean, are you—"

"I have executive-level clearance to everything pertaining to this investigation, Mr. Cowell," Nielsen said flatly. "What project?"

"Oh, okay. Well then you probably know more about it than I do." Adam fidgeted again and began rubbing his hands on his thighs. "The official project name is IO-22, but Dr. Obermeyer always referred to it as *Project No-Time*, which is kind of ironic considering the number of hours we've spent on it. I could tell he was stressed—everybody could—especially last week when he was compiling all the final research data. But he and I never actually spoke about it."

"What was the purpose of this project?"

Adam shrugged. "No idea. They never share that stuff with the lab assistants. I mean, no offense, but the knockout rats get more attention in the lab than we do. I just worked on a very specific area of research within the broader project, and most of my samples were given coded names so even *I* didn't always know what I was looking at."

"And exactly what is *your* specific area of research?" Nielsen asked.

"Apoptosis."

"Which is—?"

"Well, it's kind of complicated, but basically you could say it's the science of programming cells to know when to die."

"To die?" the security director repeated.

"Yeah." The research assistant caught the meaning of Nielsen's tone and shook his head. "But don't get any crazy ideas. Almost all cells in a complex multicellular organism are naturally programmed to know when to die. My research just focuses on ways to activate biochemical agents that trigger things like chromosomal DNA fragmentation and chromatin—"

Nielsen raised his hand. "So you're telling me you've spent two years working in Dr. Obermeyer's lab teaching cells how to die for a research project, but you have no clue what that research is for?"

"That's correct."

Nielsen's eyes lingered on him for a moment. He dropped the folder he was holding onto his desk. "You're a smart guy, aren't you, Adam?"

"What do you mean?"

"I mean do you agree that you're smart?"

"Yeah . . . I suppose."

"Do you think *I'm* a smart guy?"

"I . . . " Adam shifted in his chair. "I don't think my opinion of you probably matters."

Nielsen's face eased into a grin. "You *are* smart."

Adam visibly relaxed as the security director's grin expanded into a friendly smile.

"I once spent six month interrogating detainees at Gitmo—that's Guantanamo Bay Naval Base for you non-military folks. I'm telling you, if you're ever looking for a tough job—" Nielsen shook his head. "By the time I was brought in, those poor guys had already been through it all—waterboarding, electroshock, emotion-warping—you name it. And yet, believe it or not, some of them *still* weren't talking. So it was up to us *echoes*—that's what they called us second wave interrogators—to get really creative. So one day, one of my fellow echoes traps a bunch of sewer rats, throws them in a cage, and starts feeding them cheese whip. You know the stuff I'm talking about—comes in a can? There probably isn't a drop of real cheese in it, but anyway, this guy does it. Feeds them that junk and nothing else. Next thing I know, he's tying naked detainees spread-eagle on the floor and telling them all about his new pets. *Cutest little things*, he'd say to them. *But goddamn were they hungry. Boy did they love that cheese whip—do anything for it. And those teeth? Even sharper than their claws.* Somewhere along the line he'd ask the detainee if they knew that a rat could fit its entire body anywhere their heads could go. Then he'd pull out a big can of that cheese whip and spray a little up their rectal cavity. If *that* didn't get them talking, he'd come back carrying a little cage with a towel draped over it." The security director paused. "Ever heard the sound a pack of hungry sewer rats make when they smell their favorite food?"

Adam's mouth fell open limply. "Uh uh."

"Be glad you haven't, because it's awful . . . like women screaming for their lives." Nielsen shuddered. "And believe me, it works. Those poor bastards would practically break their wrists trying to get free when they heard that cage hit the floor."

He paused and gave the research assistant a mischievous look.

"But you know what the best part was? There weren't

any rats. Not one. It was just a tape recorder in a cage playing the sound. Sometimes our own minds are our worst enemies, Mr. Cowell."

"I guess so."

Nielsen's smile vanished. "You're eyes are awfully red," he observed. "Out late last night?"

"No, not really."

"Hard to sleep after doing something awful, isn't it?"

"I'm sorry?"

Nielsen opened the folder again and slid the document he'd been reading across the desk. "That's last night's activity log for the annex lab. It shows me every person in and out of the facility between 2:30pm and midnight."

The research assistant gave him a quizzical look.

"Take a look."

Adam rubbed his eyes before picking up the one-page document and scanning the list of time-stamped entries and their corresponding badge IDs—

> Depart/14:43:31 Genom04076BYamanaka
> Depart/15:25:59 Genom04123ACowell
> Depart/15:56:02 Genom04092PRichards
> Depart/16:07:13 Genom04162VSarabhai
> Depart/16:20:40 Genom04027CRaman
> Depart/16:35:04 Genom04088LCheng
> Depart/16:36:32 Genom04102LBennett
> Depart/16:42:26 Genom04018JWalsh
> Depart/17:21:12 Genom04056PObermeyer
> *Entry/17:23:34 Genom04123ACowell
> Depart/17:27:08 Genom04123ACowell
> *Entry/20:02:13 CorpSec01060RFoster

*Entry/20:02:17   CorpSec01075SWilson
*Entry/21:13:20   CorpSec01006LNielsen

As he neared the bottom, he paused and shook his head. "Wait—this . . . this isn't right. This can't be right."

"What isn't right?"

"This says I was in the lab last night." Adam looked at the security director, confused. "Why would it say that?"

"You tell me. According to that report, you left the lab at 3:25pm, but then returned at 5:23 and spent about four minutes inside before leaving again." Nielsen's eyes narrowed on the research assistant. "So why did you come back?"

"I didn't, I mean—" Adam shook his head vehemently. "I wasn't even there!"

The security director smiled.

"I'm serious!" Adam exclaimed, seeing the skepticism on the director's face. "I left the lab yesterday at 3:25, just like this says." He shoved the report back across the desk. "But that second entry is wrong. I never went back."

Nielsen held his stare on Adam. "You know as well as I do that it takes a security badge and a corresponding thumb print to enter that lab—both of which are recorded by the system."

"Yeah, I do," Adam nodded. "But I'm telling you, it's wrong."

"Is it possible that you went back and simply misjudged the time?"

"No, it's not."

Nielsen settled back into his chair. "Let's presume for a moment that you were *not* at the lab last night at 5:23pm. Then where exactly were you?"

"On a date."

"A date? How nice. Where'd you go?"

"A place called The Wheelhouse on the embarcadero."

Nielsen nodded. "Food nice?"

"Sure."

"And your date? Does she—or he—have a phone number we can call to confirm this?"

The research assistant's face went slack. "She," he muttered, his eyes falling to the floor. "And no, I don't think she would."

"Wouldn't what—have a phone?"

"No, I mean I . . . I don't think my date would have any interest in seeing me again."

"Why's that?"

"Because I might've had a little too much to drink last night."

The security director raised his eyebrows. "Are you telling me you have an issue with alcohol, Mr. Cowell?"

"What? No! I . . . I just was having a good time last night and, um, from what I recall, I may have spilled wine on my date's dress."

"From what you *remember*?" Although he was already recording their conversation on his cell phone, Nielsen pulled a notepad from his desk drawer and began taking notes. "Interesting."

"No, wait!" Adam sat up with alarm and ran a shaking hand through his hair. "Look, I'm just saying there might be a few moments from last night that aren't, you know, perfectly clear. But that's all there is to it. I went on a date, I had a little too much wine, I did, um, whatever it is that I did, and my date got mad and left. End of story."

"But you see, Adam, that's the problem. It's not the end of the story. In fact, it's not even half of it."

"What do you mean?"

The security director dropped the notepad and once again opened the file. "Let review the circumstances as *I* see them—from an *investigator's* perspective."

The research assistant regarded the file as if it were a cage of hungry rats.

"So—" Nielsen thumbed past a few pages and pulled out a document. "I went ahead and checked the log files from the past few months, and I couldn't find a single occasion—with the exception of last night—where you left the lab before four o'clock. In fact, most nights you normally work until six. But on the same night that Dr. Obermeyer died, you left early." His eyes flashed up at Adam. "That's the kind of anomaly that catches my attention."

Adam sat frozen.

"Then of course there's that four-minute return visit recorded by the system—the one you deny happened—which, curiously, occurred just two minutes after Paul Obermeyer's last departure. Once again, I checked the log files from the past few months, and there wasn't a single record of you having done this before. Let's call that anomaly number *two*."

"I'm telling you," Adam said, his voice taking on a hollow, pleading tone. "I did *not* go *back*!"

Nielsen watched as the research assistant took a deep breath and again ran a hand through his thin, reddish-brown hair. "You may not believe it, Adam, but I'm trying to be on *your* side in this matter. I'd like to believe the only thing you were up to last night was a bad date. But I've got your badge and fingerprint both recorded entering the lab last night at

5:23 pm—and all you're offering in your defense is an alibi who doesn't want to speak to you and a memory that is admittedly incomplete. And if that isn't enough—" He pulled another document from the file and slid it across the desk. "How do you explain this?"

Adam leaned forward and gazed at a series of grainy, still-frame images composed on the page. "What's this?"

"That's *you*. Captured by entrance surveillance camera number three last night at 5:23pm. Those are just a sample of the images taken from the recording."

The research assistant looked closer at the images. In them, a male figure could be seen scanning his ID card and fingerprint before heading toward the genomics lab. Despite the high angle of the camera, Adam could easily make out the figure's bright, aquamarine sweater and reddish-brown hair. "No way, it's not . . . it's not fucking possible," he stammered, shaking his head.

"Look familiar?" the security director asked.

Adam sat back and nodded.

"Then I'll ask again. What were you doing at the lab last night?"

"I wasn't there."

"Try again."

"I wasn't . . . Jesus—look, if I *was* there, I have no idea why. I don't remember any of this."

Nielsen collected the documents and placed them back in the folder. "Well that's unfortunate, because I can tell you right now that anyone pushing for a criminal investigation into Dr. Obermeyer's death would look at this evidence and suggest you get a good defense lawyer. And your *I-don't-remember-anything* story isn't going to help you."

"What are you *talking* about?" Adam exclaimed. Beads of perspiration were now visible on the assistant researcher's forehead. "Even if I did go back to the lab, what does that have to do with Dr. Obermeyer's accident?"

"I don't know. But I guarantee you that if there *is* a link, I'll find out. And since you've been lying to me from the moment you sat in that goddamn chair, I have no choice but to believe there is one."

"You can't be serious."

"You'll see how serious I am in a moment. But first, you need to understand something." Nielsen rose from his chair and marched around his desk until he was standing in front of the now pale-faced young man. "I've been given one primary directive in the matter of Paul Obermeyer's death. But don't get the wrong idea. I'm not here to determine if his death was an accident, or go after the people responsible if it wasn't. That'll be for the police to decide. My directive, my *sole responsibility*, Mr. Cowell, is to locate any information belonging to this corporation that may have been stolen or otherwise jeopardized by this incident, and see that it's returned."

"Okay," Adam said weakly. "And what does that have to do with me?"

The security director grinned. "I'm glad you asked. You see, I have a theory. My theory is that you went back to the lab last night for Dr. Obermeyer's encryption key. After all, you're one of the few people that knew his patterns and where he kept it. You also knew the research was completed but not yet in the hands of the corporation. And—given the secrecy—you obviously must have known that this project was particularly important." He raised a finger as Adam started to speak. "Now, before you deny everything again, let me tell you what's about to happen."

Nielsen reached over and pressed a button on his desk phone. Seconds later, his office door opened and a tall man with short, precisely parted brown hair and a muscular physique walked in and stood behind Adam's chair.

"I'm going to give you two options, Mr. Cowell," the security director continued, "and you get to decide which is best for you. Option number one involves the immediate termination of your employment with Velgyn Pharmaceuticals under suspicion of criminal misconduct—including theft and corporate espionage. This option would also necessitate handing over all of the evidence I've just shown you to the Berkeley PD. As a bonus, I might even throw in a few interesting notes from your personnel file—like our concerns of alcohol abuse. Personally, I think there's enough circumstantial evidence here to warrant a homicide investigation. But even if I'm wrong, this option will almost certainly destroy what might have been a very bright career." He waved a dismissive hand in the air. "Anyway, that's option number one. Would you like to hear option number two?"

The assistant researcher nodded sullenly.

"Option number two allows you to keep your job for the time being and avoid any outside investigation—on the condition that you do *exactly* as I ask and tell me everything you know about the whereabouts of that encryption key."

"And what if I don't know anything?"

"You know *something*. And between me and Mr. Foster here, I'm sure we can help you remember. So, what will it be?"

"As if there was a choice." Adam dropped his head to his chest and sighed. "Option two."

"See, you are smart." The security director nodded to

his colleague. "Mr. Foster's going to escort you to his office to sign a few forms. He'll also be collecting your cell phone and keys. Later today, while his men are searching your car and your apartment, you're going to be drug tested, psychologically evaluated and given a polygraph test. I expect your full cooperation until we find what we're after. And who knows—maybe you'll even recall something useful from your date last night."

Adam looked up at the security director with tired, lifeless eyes. A torrent of emotions ranging from hatred to fear briefly clouded his face. Then, to Nielsen's surprise, the research assistant's smiled with a sudden look of defiance.

"What's so funny?" Nielsen asked.

"Carrie," Adam said, his voice low and steady. "Her name was Carrie."

10.

"You're kidding me, right?"

Jeri tore her eyes from the dress in Tall Tommy's hand and glared at him with disbelief. The Australian man stood in the doorway and shook his head.

"But I already have a dress."

"Chilly thought you'd say that." Her colleague gave her a crooked grin. "He said to tell you this is the *right* dress."

Jeri studied the kaleidoscopic collection of sequins, jewels and fabric dangling from the hanger and grimaced. "But this . . . this is *horrible*."

"He said you'd say that too. But he insists that this is what the script calls for."

Jeri waved him into her hotel room. "So let me get this straight—not only does Chilly get to script everything I do and say, he also gets to decide my wardrobe?"

Tall Tommy nodded and shut the door behind him. "When it comes to the script, Chilly has the final say on everything."

"And what—he makes you his little messenger?"

A look of irritation briefly clouded Tall Tommy's face. "I volunteered. Chilly won't be arriving until tomorrow."

"Fine, I'll take it up with him then."

"Don't count on it. He's only got about three hours to prep the package before the collection. Chilly never talks to anyone when he's working."

Jeri snatched the dress from his hand and marched over to the window. "Well, since he's so good at predicting what I'd think of this bejeweled nightmare, let's see if he's got a plan for its demise." She pushed aside the curtains in search of a latch. Twenty stories below, the bustling streets of São Paulo stretched toward the smog-clouded horizon.

"I don't think the windows on this floor open." Her colleague shrugged apologetically.

Jeri slapped hand against the window frame. "Did he plan that too?"

"Nah . . . that's just bad luck."

"Of course it is." She flung the dress onto the bed and released a resigned sigh. "What about shoes? Don't tell me he went to the trouble of ordering a dress and forgot the shoes."

"On the contrary." Tall Tommy reached into the satchel slung over his shoulder and pulled out a pair of sparkling, gold-plated stiletto heels. "Size seven, right?"

Jeri gazed dumfounded at them and nodded.

Her colleague handed them over. "Hey, if it's any consolation, I think you'll look fantastic. And don't worry about standing out—not in this crowd."

"Thanks." Jeri tossed the shoes onto the bed with the dress. The ensemble looked like something out of a pirate's treasure chest. "Anything else? Jewelry? Makeup? Perhaps a hair style recommendation from the all-knowing Chilly?"

"Nope, that's it." Tall Tommy glanced at the desk next to him. A Polaroid of a tall, corpulent man with a scraggly beard and thin, deep-set eyes stared back. "Are you ready?"

Jeri ran her hands through her freshly dyed, strawberry-blonde hair. "I was until you showed me that dress." She noticed the concern in her colleague's eyes and shook her head. "Don't worry, I'm fine. I just don't particularly care for the script Chilly's written for tomorrow night's collection."

"You mean your part in it?"

"I mean everything—the setting, the plot, the climax, and yes,"—her eyes drifted back to the outfit lying on the bed—"definitely my part in it."

"Does that mean you've got a better idea?"

Jeri caught the wry grin on the Australian man's face. "Yeah, okay—I get it. I'm the new girl on the block. What the hell could I know, right? But just look at this guy." She snatched the Polaroid from the desk and held it up. "What is he—two-eighty, maybe three-hundred pounds? He's a goddamn heart attack waiting to happen."

"So?"

"So why not follow *that* script? Why not give him something that causes a few chest pains and pick him up in an ambulance?"

Her colleague shook his head. "Too clean. You've got to have an end that's messy. Well, you know, at least messy enough to destroy any recognizable evidence. If we picked up this bloke in an ambulance, anyone looking for him would eventually find out. And the next obvious question would be *where'd he go from there?*"

"So we leave a paper trail," Jeri countered. "A paper trail that says he died in the emergency room and his body was sent to the morgue. And when his body isn't found in the morgue, there'll be a paper trail showing it went to a mortuary for cremation."

"Yeah, maybe," Tall Tommy conceded. "But paper trails are just that—trails. You have to remember that we're not dealing with an average person here. This guy's important . . . *very* important. He works for the kind of people that will come looking for answers when he turns up dead. And they won't be stupid. Paper trails will be followed. Questions will be asked. *Where's the doctor that signed the death warrant? Where's the mortician that cremated him?* Any holes in the evidence would only raise more suspicion."

Jeri shrugged. "Maybe."

"Look, I get why you don't like this script. I don't like it much either, and I'm not even the one being asked to—" Her colleague paused and shook his head. "It's not an easy job for any of us. But believe me, it's absolutely impossible if you don't trust your team. And vice versa. We've managed a perfect collection record with Chilly's scripts so far. And no offense, but considering how your improvisation on the Berkeley job worked out, you should be the last person questioning his judgment."

Jeri shot him a petulant look before turning to the window. "I suppose I deserve that." She studied the blocky skyline of dilapidated, gray-stained high rises around them. "You trust him completely, don't you?"

"I do. Chilly's better at this that anyone. That's why he's in charge."

"Ever seen him have any . . . doubts?"

"About what—the recruits? Or how we collect them?"

"Both."

"Absolutely not. In case you haven't noticed, he's a bit of a machine."

Jeri looked at her colleague. "What about you?"

"No," he replied firmly. "Flashes of occasional panic perhaps. But no doubts. I trust my team—including you—to do the job right. I also believe in what we're doing." His stare softened. "Hell, if any of us should believe in what we're doing, it's you."

Jeri watched as Tall Tommy reached into his satchel and produced a thick hardback book. She immediately recognized its age-faded cover.

"He knew what he was talking about when he wrote this," he said, handing it over. "And we all know this is why we're here."

Jeri silently examined his copy of *Predictions in the New Business Ecology*, the weight of it offering a sense of comfort. She turned it over and stared at the handsome young face of its author, James H. Stone. As it always did, the black-and-white photo of her father stirred a well of emotions for the man she'd once loved more than anything in the world. *What the hell would you think of all of this, Dad?* Jeri wondered, stroking the weathered image with her finger. *What the hell would you think of me?* She felt her colleague watching and abruptly handed the book back. "You carry that everywhere you go?" she asked, blinking the wetness from her eyes.

The Australian man nodded. "Keeps me inspired."

"Well, you're just full of surprises, aren't you?" Jeri gestured at his satchel, anxious to change the subject. "What else have you got in there?"

Her colleague peered inside his bag. "Not much. Just some vitamin supplements and a new hair gel I'm trying out. Oh, and a few Playboy magazines from home. The ones here are in Portuguese."

"Does it matter?"

"Well, yeah, if you want to read the articles."

Jeri studied her colleague's handsome face. She suddenly realized he was probably her own age, if not even younger. "How long have you been in the agency?"

"About a year."

"Do you remember how you were brought in?"

"Yeah, I was working on my engineering degree in Melbourne when Sly showed up at my flat one night. Ballsy wanker just walked in like he knew me and asked if he could bum a cigarette." Tall Tommy shook his head and laughed. "Had me so confused I didn't even see him pull out the tranq gun. Next thing I knew I was waking up in a fucking river shack on Victoria River with our pal Whip. Of course, we both know the story from there, eh?"

Jeri nodded. "Do you know who brought Chilly in?"

A slight grin twisted his mouth. "I suppose it was Chip, but who knows. Maybe you should ask Chilly."

"I get the feeling he wouldn't tell me."

"Yeah, probably not. Chilly's one of the few around here that takes this nondisclosure shit seriously. Ask most of us where we came from and we'll tell you—but not him. Nobody's gotten a word out of him about his past as far as I know. I assume he was probably a doctor of some kind before someone stuck a dart in his ass. He has that doctor look."

"Which is what?"

"You know, that smug asshole look."

Jeri laughed. "Yeah, I suppose he does. Well, anyway, thanks for the talk—and the laugh. I needed both."

"No worries." Tall Tommy glanced at his watch. "This time tomorrow you'll already be wrapping up the collection.

Don't worry . . . it'll go fine."

"That's easy for you to say. You don't have to wear that goddamn dress."

"That's true. But then no one could look better in it than you."

An awkward silence hung in the air as Jeri and her colleague exchanged looks. Tall Tommy abruptly turned to the window.

"Look at them," he said, gazing down at the growing throng of revelers on the streets below. "Regardless of how shitty their lives may be, however poor or overworked or unimportant to the rest of the world, they find a way to keep going. How's that even possible?"

"It's called alcohol," Jeri asserted. "I used to serve it, remember?"

"You miss it?"

"Bartending? Not in the least. But my blissfully ignorant life before the agency? Absolutely."

Tall Tommy pressed his head to the glass and sighed. "Don't we all." He turned and marched toward the door. "Right. Well, I'll see you tomorrow. Get some rest. And if you can't sleep, just read Chilly's letter again. That shit'll knock you out faster than Ambien."

Jeri sighed. "I think I'd prefer one of your Playboys."

"I'm not sure you'd want them after I'm done."

"I thought you said you *read* them."

Her colleague paused at the entry and smiled over his shoulder. "I do . . . first."

"That's disgusting, Tommy." Jeri said to the closing door. Her smile faded with the unwelcomed return of silence. She glanced around the room, her gaze falling briefly on the outfit on the bed before settling on the desk. The dark eyes of her target seemed to follow her as she marched over and brushed the Polaroid aside. She picked up the letter Chilly had slipped into her bag the night before.

Her colleague's precise handwriting stood crisply against the white page of stationary. Jeri scanned the sentences and shook her head. *He has time to write me encrypted letters, but couldn't manage to find a better dress?* She pushed the thought aside and sat down at the desk. It was important that she concentrate. Any mistakes in decryption might cause her to misinterpret a portion of the script, and that was the last thing the team needed from their freshman.

She tucked a lock of curly, strawberry-blonde hair behind her ear and picked up a pen. Her mouth silently formed the words as her eyes moved across the page.

Twenty stories below, the cacophony of the celebrating crowd began to rise.

11.

J-

I don't know if I was looking for trouble, but I've found it. Oh man, have I found it. That big, surly type that presses up against you and keeps mobbing your pockets for loose change. Not that I haven't had my share of experience with such things before. But this time it's different.

This time the trouble's with you.

This quick jaunt to the sands of nowhere reminds me of that first sultry night we spent gazing into each other's peepers. Or was it the last night? Christ, my mind's slipping like the tongue of a trombadinha with Tourette's. All I know is that once again someone's got their eye on me like one of those fat cats in the back alleys of the Vila Madalena. And they're prowling for a meal, baby. Big time.

Don't think the growing rift between us isn't weighing

heavy on my mind, meu amor. But if you'd just trust in what I'm saying, everything would be right as rain. It's like we're taking samba lessons from that passista in the carnival (remember the tall one I was convinced was a man but you said was just "big-boned"?) and you keep trying to lead. Sometimes you just have to let your partner put their hand on your back and tell you where to go. Even if that partner has had too much to drink and smells like cigarettes and stale cachaça.

Our kids will be gorgeous.

I've booked us a cozy one-star hotel for our upcoming rendezvous. If all goes well, you'll be dragging me to the bed for a performance that will make Cirque du Soleil look like a clumsy band of rogue sea monkeys by comparison. Just make sure you bring the right personal lubricant, love-bug.

We don't want to make the same mistake again.

Right! Well, it's wheels up soon and I'll be back before you can say 'don't come back'. You know I'm not one to take the road more traveled, unless that road leads to tequila or a magic mushroom milkshake on Gili Trawangan. But for you I'd happily go mainstream, J-girl. Just as long as it doesn't include any reality TV. I get enough reality right here.

Ta!
-C

p.s. The enclosed photo is not of me, but my cousin Jay. Jay's an Aries who loves cooking, salsa dancing, and hallucinogens by a warm fire. Oh wait, no—that's me. Anyway, Jay's been looking for love in all the dark places, and I thought you just might know someone that could look this bloated mug in the face and say "¡Ay, caramba! This hombre's the one!" Mind circulating his photo amongst your less virtuous and legally blind friends?

12.

"How'd you sleep?"

Paul Obermeyer spun to find Derrick Birch smiling in the doorway and rose from the bed. "How did I *sleep*? Your friend Marcello locked me back in here after you left!"

"Sorry. Safety precaution." Birch held up a steaming mug. "Want some coffee? We got this Kenyan medium roast in yesterday. Fucking out of this world."

"No! I don't want coffee," Paul exclaimed, his voice echoing against the walls of his concrete holding cell. "I want to go *home*! And I want to speak to a lawyer! Do you have any idea the size of the lawsuit I'm going to file against whoever's responsible for this? I can think of about five different felony charges alone that—what? What the hell's so funny?"

"I'm sorry, I don't mean to laugh," Birch replied, fighting the smirk on his face. "It's just that you sound just like me after my first night. I actually punched Marcello in the face when he opened the door that morning. Poor guy didn't even see it coming. Anyway, I promise by this time tomorrow you'll feel quite differently. For now, my advice is to pretend that you've landed in Oz and I'm one of those singing dwarves trying to help you out." He gestured at the door. "Speaking of

Oz—are you ready to meet the wizard?"

Paul glanced at the Arabic words written in bright red across the heavy steel door. "The wizard?"

"Yeah, you know . . . the big man."

Paul regarded him skeptically "What . . . are you going to lead me down a grand hall to some giant green head and balls of fire?

"Oh, I think we can do better than that," Birch replied. He took a sip of his coffee and shook his head. "Goddamn that's good. Sure you don't want some?"

Paul nodded and gestured at the door. "Lead the way."

The two men marched through a series of windowless corridors before eventually entering a large room containing a long, polished steel table. An older, immaculately groomed Middle Eastern man with hair that matched his silver-gray suit looked up from his newspaper and smiled.

"Dr. Obermeyer, it's a pleasure to finally meet you," the man said, rising from his chair. From behind tortoise-shell glasses, his large dark eyes sparkled with vitality. "My name is Faheem Razam. I am—"

Paul gestured for the man to stay seated. "Are you in charge here?"

"Indeed I am. And I'm sure you would like an explanation for why you are here."

"Yes, I would."

"Please," Razam gestured for both men to take a chair.

Paul reluctantly sat down and surveyed his surroundings. Like the rest of the strange facility, the room was a model of industrial scale and minimalism, this one with massive steel louvers spanning most of the wall behind his smiling host. "I want to know what the hell's going on." He pointed to the man next to him. "But first—who is this man?"

His host furrowed his brow. "I was under the impression that Mr. Birch had already made his introduction."

"Oh, he did. I just don't believe him."

"Why is that?"

"Because Derrick Birch is dead. He died last year in some kind of boating accident, if I remember correctly. It was all over the news—which means this man can't be him." Paul shifted his finger to Razam. "Or are you going to give me the same story about everyone here being dead?"

His host exchanged a brief look with Birch before nodding. "Yes, I'm afraid I am. But I assure you that none of us around here are what your Hollywood movies would call zombies, Dr. Obermeyer. We are only dead to the outside world." He slid the newspaper across the table. "Have a look for yourself."

Paul glanced at the paper. To his surprise, it was the morning edition of the San Francisco Chronicle. He was about to ask the purpose of its presence when a headline at the bottom of the page caught his attention—

Car crash near university leaves one dead

"Wait—*what*?" His eyes widened with each line of the short article detailing his death. "No, this can't be happening. This can't—" Paul looked at the man across from him and shook his head. "This can't be real."

"Real seems such an inadequate term for situations such as this," Razam responded, his tone soft and paternal. "Of course it isn't real. You're obviously alive and well despite what that paper says, just as surely as Mr. Birch is alive and well next to you. But I understand that you are upset by the circumstances as they currently appear."

"Upset?" Paul scoffed. "Everyone thinks I'm dead! If that's true, it doesn't really matter if I'm *alive*—you've just destroyed my entire fucking *life*!"

"And for that I offer my sincerest apologies. Now please, allow me to explain why such measures were necessary."

Paul silently glared at his host.

"I believe Mr. Birch has already informed you that you are now in Saudi Arabia," Razam continued, taking on a formal, lecturing tone. "To be more specific, you are now sitting inside the *Ras Jazan* refinery—the largest oil refinery in the country until regular operations ceased in 2011. Of course, a fact of this nature would normally be trivial to you. But the reason this facility is no longer refining oil—and the nature of what has occurred here since—are both directly linked to your presence here now."

He stood and began to slowly pace the room.

"It may be hard to believe, Dr. Obermeyer, but there was a time when oil was of no interest or value to the people of Saudi Arabia. Less than a century ago, the ruling king, Abdulaziz, was content to fill his coffers on nothing more than the taxes collected from the poor souls on pilgrimage to the holy cities of Mecca and Madina. But then the great depression hit, and even the most devout of our Muslim brothers stopped coming. It didn't take long for Abdulaziz to realize another form of income was needed—and quickly. So our great king raised his hands to the sky and prayed for a solution." Razam paused and mimicked the gesture with dramatic flair. "And what did God provide him in return?"

"The richest goddamn oil fields the world's ever seen," Derrick Birch answered.

"Precisely!" Razam exclaimed, his eyes alive with excitement. "From 1980 until 2010, Saudi Arabia extracted eleven million barrels of crude oil from its oil fields every single day—far more than any other country. But perhaps even more incredible is the fact that more than half of that oil came from a *single* oil field. It's called the Ghawar oil field," he paused and pointed at the floor. "And we're standing over it now."

Paul nodded with impatience. "Great. Are you getting to the part where you explain why you've ruined my life?"

"Yes." His silver-haired host resumed pacing. "As I said, this facility was the largest of its kind in the country. At the peak of production, it was capable of refining over six hundred thousand barrels of crude oil per day—nearly twice that of any other facility. But *Ras Jazan* was more than just an example of cutting-edge technology applied on an immense scale. It was an icon of this country's indomitable oil wealth."

"So?" Paul asked.

"So," Derrick Birch responded, his mouth curling into a crooked grin as he raised his eyebrows at Paul. "Why did it stop refining oil?"

Paul shrugged. "I don't know—cost?"

Razam nodded. "Indirectly, you are correct. This facility covers eighteen square kilometers of desert and once employed over nineteen hundred workers. Its annual operating budget was equivalent to a small country's GDP. Of course, such costs are negligible compared to the profits generated when the oil is flowing." His dark eyes narrowed on Paul. "But one day that stopped happening."

"What do you mean?"

"I mean the great Ghawar—the world's largest and richest oil deposit ever to exist—is virtually empty."

"Well, I'm very sorry to hear that," Paul replied. "But again, what's that have to do with me?"

His host cupped his hands together in a slow, deliberate manner as he formulated his answer. "Imagine if the economy of the United States was almost solely dependent on one sole resource, Dr. Obermeyer. Then imagine that resource suddenly vanishing." Razam separated his hands and flashed his empty palms at Paul like a magician. "It doesn't take a brilliant mind like yours to understand what would happen. Every pillar of stability—economic, financial, political, social—would vanish along with it. That's what Saudi Arabia was facing when we lost Ghawar and realized our oil reserves were indeed finite. Just as it had been a century before, our future was suddenly uncertain. But we were certain of one thing—if no solution was in place before the oil stopped flowing, blood would flow in its place." His somber expression slowly eased into a smile. "So . . . we created a solution. Well, perhaps I should say we've *almost* created a solution. And that is why you're here. You see, our solution requires some, shall we say, assistance."

"Assistance?" Paul leaned forward. "To sum up what's happened in the last twenty-four hours just so we're clear— you've drugged me, kidnapped me, falsified my death, destroyed my career, ruined my life, brought me to the middle of nowhere—and now you want my assistance?" He pushed his chair back and stood. "How about this? How about we all agree that this was a huge misunderstanding and you give me my life back? And in return, I won't press charges." He turned and gestured at Derrick. "Or say anything about the other scientists you've stolen from the world."

Razam smiled. "We prefer the term *recruited*."

"Call it what you like. I want no part of it."

"But you don't even know what it is." Paul's impeccably dressed host raised his hands. "Surely your curiosity is aroused, is it not?"

Paul shook his head. "No, it's not. Maybe under different circumstances. Maybe if you'd *invited* me here and *asked* for my help. But you didn't. And I have no intention of working as a slave. So good luck with whatever it is you're doing here, gentlemen. Good luck with your empty oil field. Now—who's going to take me home?"

Razam's smile vanished. "Dr. Obermeyer, if I had simply invited you here, you really would be dead."

Paul regarded him with annoyance. "What's that supposed to mean?"

"It means you have no idea how the *real* world operates," Birch replied. He stood and faced him. "Sorry to tell you that, Paul, but you don't. I didn't either until after I arrived here. And once I got past being pissed off, I started to grasp the bigger picture. Ghawar isn't just an empty oil field, it's a *barometer* of what's to come. And what it's saying is that the end of oil is coming sooner than anyone expected. Do you have any idea what this means? The substance *every* industrialized nation relies upon is running out. Unfortunately, we can't just go out there and announce that to the rest of the world."

"Why not?" Paul retorted. "If it's the truth, then people should know."

His host nodded. "That's a wonderful sentiment, Dr. Obermeyer. But you're looking at this from a scientist's point of view. Unfortunately, it's corporations and their puppet governments that run the world. To them, this is precisely the kind of information that destroys stock markets and starts wars. Regardless of what the truth is, most of them are still betting trillions of dollars on oil for the long run—and I've seen firsthand what those in power will do to avoid jeopardizing that bet. Knowing what we know about the remaining reserves of crude oil in this country would be threatening enough. If they also knew what we were doing in this facility?" He shook his head gravely. "They'd have no choice but destroy us."

Paul studied the grim expressions on both men before addressing Razam. "Why should I believe you? I mean, how do you *know* it's empty?"

Razam's eyes shined with intelligence. "Because I was the man who discovered it. You see, Dr. Obermeyer, among other things, I'm also a scientist like you."

"What do you mean, among other things?"

"I'm afraid you didn't allow me to finish my earlier introduction." His host offered his hand. "I'm Faheem Razam, Saudi Arabia's Minister of Petroleum and Mineral Resources."

Paul shook his host's hand with a dumbfounded stare. "You're the—?"

Birch grinned and slapped him on the back. "And you thought I was a big deal."

The minister released Paul's hand and laced his fingers together thoughtfully. "I hope you are at least willing to accept that what I've told you is the truth."

Paul nodded slowly.

"Good. Then I have a proposition for you. I propose that you allow us to show you what we're doing here. If you are impressed, I ask that you stay and help us."

"And if I'm not impressed?"

"Then I will grant you your wish. I will return you to

your *previous* life as you've requested. Are we agreed?"

"Fine," Paul answered, the skepticism in his voice obvious. He crossed his arms. "So—where's this solution of yours?"

The minister nodded to Birch, who quickly walked to the wall and tapped a glass panel. "Please keep in mind that what you're about to see is just a small portion of what we're doing here," his host said as the overhead lights dimmed and the din of something large and mechanical began to reverberate through the room. "But it should give you a good idea of the scale of our operation."

The massive louvers that formed the far wall began to rise upward into the ceiling. Paul winced and raised a hand against the intense light that immediately streamed in beneath the retreating blades of steel. A burst of hot, dry air rushed into the room, stirring the men's clothes. Moments later, everything stopped with a sharp, metallic shriek.

"It'll take a few seconds for your vision to adjust," Birch advised. "Then you'll see."

Paul stepped closer, his eyes starting to make out vague shapes and colors in the chamber beyond. Then, as his vision took focus, he dropped his hand and stood motionless. "I don't . . . I don't believe it."

Behind him, Birch and Razam exchanged a smile. The minister walked over and gently rested a hand on Paul's shoulder. "Welcome to Ceres, Dr. Obermeyer. Are you impressed?"

Paul continued to stare transfixed.

Moments later, he slowly shook his head.

13.

"What in god's name is it?"

The question escaped Paul's lips with a tone of awe as he gazed up at the engineering marvel above him.

Next to him, the minister laughed softly. "A rather appropriate way to phrase your question." He stepped through the opening onto a catwalk and raised his arms dramatically. "This, my friend, is one of our photoreactors—though I prefer to think of it as Ceres' heart. The design you see here has proven the most efficient we've come up with so far, but of course we're always trying new configurations in the test lab." He looked over with a wide, boyish grin. "It's quite beautiful, isn't it?"

Paul nodded and followed his host onto the catwalk, his eyes following the intricate network of suspended tubes that filled the enormous, atrium-like chamber. The tubes, which appeared to be made of glass, were approximately four inches in diameter and slightly elliptical in cross-section. Upon closer study, Paul noticed that they were arranged into precise, helically shaped groups of twelve or more, with two groups intertwining to form a symmetrical bundle. Smaller tubes of gleaming steel followed the countless bundles as they ran in concentric circles from high above to an enormous cylinder mounted beneath the catwalk on which they were now standing. The sheer size and complexity of the structure was astonishing. But what Paul found even more intriguing was what it contained. Inside each spiraling bundle was a shimmering, fluorescent green fluid pulsing through its glass veins like blood through a living body.

He reached up and gently brushed his fingers against one of the tubes. It was warm to the touch. "What is that?"

"Botryococcus braunii," Birch replied. "Nearly four hundred million liters of it between the phototube matrix and the pump station beneath us."

Paul looked at him with shock. "You're growing *algae*?"

"Yep."

"But why?"

"Ceres was the mythological goddess of agriculture and fertility, Dr. Obermeyer," the minister interjected. "It seemed only fitting to name the world's largest biofuel production facility after her."

Paul's eyes widened. "So *that's* what all this is about—making biofuel?"

"No," Birch countered. "This is about creating an economically viable alternative to oil. And we've done it." He shot a quick look at Razam. "Well, we've *almost* done it."

"Please," the minister said, gesturing them forward. "There's a great deal more to show you."

Paul continued to gaze around in wonder as they moved along the catwalk. While his two guides explained various details of the operation, he noticed several white-uniformed workers shuffle by on the network of catwalks overhead. "I don't understand. How could you possibly keep something of this scale a secret?"

"By hiding it in plain sight," the minister replied. "It may seem ironic, but a petroleum refinery is the perfect facility for retrofitting into a biofuel production plant. Most of the key modifications are what you see here—modifying the largest fractional distillers to function as closed-loop bioreactors. This particular facility has six of them."

"Wait," Paul interrupted. "You're saying you have *six* of these reactors here?"

Razam nodded. "When petroleum operations ceased, we simply told the media we were upgrading the facility and conducting some much-needed maintenance. Not a single question was asked."

"And the workers?" Paul gestured at two men examining a piece of equipment on a nearby platform. "Did you recruit them as well?"

"I handpicked the engineers and operation managers myself. They are all fully aware of what is happening here, and they understand its necessity. More importantly, they are loyal to me. As far as the rest of the workers—" The minister's mouth curled into a mischievous grin. "We've had to get a bit creative."

"What do you mean?"

"It was far too risky to hire our own Saudi countrymen for the normal operational jobs Ceres required. They might tell others about the strange things they were seeing here. So we hire our crews from Oman—and tell them they're working at a facility in Kuwait."

"And they believe you?"

"They don't have much choice. Everyone's flown in on cargo planes—no windows, of course—and once they're here, they never leave the compound. Even if they had doubts—" The minister shrugged. "One lifeless desert looks like any other, does it not?"

The three men continued across the catwalk.

"That's the conditioning station," Birch said, pointing to another massive steel tank beneath them. "It pumps carbon dioxide and water into the system and regulates the system temperature. Botryococcus prefers a constant temperature of thirty-four degrees Celsius—but of course you already knew that."

Paul looked at him with surprise. "How did you know that?"

"What—that you studied this particular class of algae as part of your doctorate thesis? Of course I know that, Paul. That's why you're here."

Paul stopped and threw up his hands. "Alright, let's get to the point. What exactly are expecting of me? Because I don't know the first damn thing about biofuel production."

"Of course you don't," Birch replied. "But you *do* know the genetics of the microalgae we're using. And you also happen to be one of the best genetic engineers on the planet. So what we expect from you, Dr. Obermeyer, is to find a way to make it better."

"Better?" Paul scoffed, shaking his head. "What do you mean, *better*?"

"More efficient, Dr. Obermeyer," Razam interjected. "You see, we've already made the operational aspects of Ceres as efficient as possible. Yet we're still coming up short on our production levels. Not by much, granted, but enough to warrant some . . . concerns. That's why you're here. We'd like you to genetically refine our algae stock."

Paul looked up at the intricate network of tubing suspended like a colossal chandelier over him. "Oh, that's all? Just take apart one of nature's most efficient microorganisms and make it better? Sure, no problem." He smiled sarcastically. "When do you need it—next week?"

"We know what we're asking for isn't simple, Paul," Birch replied. "That's why we recruited *you*."

Paul flashed both men a look of contempt. "I'd really appreciate it if you'd stop using that word."

"Of course!" the minister exclaimed, his eyes glistening with eagerness. He gestured toward a door at the end of the catwalk. "Shall we continue?"

The corridor leading from the sunlit reactor chamber was cave-like and claustrophobic by comparison. Paul fell in step behind his two hosts, who led him through a disorienting labyrinth of narrow passageways before emerging into a wide, high ceilinged hallway. There, a procession of enormous concrete columns framed glass walls on both sides, each punctured by a human-scale glass door. Rays of natural light filtered through thin skylights overhead and shimmered like gold on the burnished concrete floor. To Paul, the effect was like rising from a dark catacomb into the nave of a modern cathedral.

"These are the main research laboratories," Derrick Birch remarked with a tone of pride. "We wanted to have your lab here as well, but there wasn't enough space."

Paul looked through the nearest wall of glass at a large room gleaming with expensive, state-of-the-art equipment. To his surprise, a woman with short, dark brown hair was typing away at a laptop in the far corner. As if realizing she was being watched, the woman glanced over her shoulder. The two exchanged looks for a moment before the woman nodded tersely and returned to her work.

Razam turned and faced him. "So, Dr. Obermeyer, are you impressed?"

Paul noticed the smug grin on the minister's face and recalled their agreement in the conference room. "For the most part, yes. But there's something you haven't mentioned."

"What else would you like to know?"

"What's in this for me?"

The minister's grin faltered. "You mean other than helping to change the world?"

"Yes, other than that."

"I'll take this one," Birch said, stepping forward. "Look, Paul, no one's going to deny that you were brought here under less than ideal circumstances. But if you can just accept that, and the reasons for it, I think you'll see that everything from this point forward—including compensation—will be more than fair."

"And exactly what does fair compensation for destroying a person's life amount to?"

"Thirty million dollars," Derrick replied matter-of-factly. "That is, *if* you solve the challenges we brought you here to solve."

Paul studied the faces of both men, waiting for the smile that would tell him they were joking. Both men watched him solemnly. "Thirty million dollars," he repeated, trying not to reveal his shock. "Okay. And if I don't solve the problem?"

"We'll still give you ten million for your time. Regardless, this contract ends after thirty-six months or when it's mutually agreed that you've done what we've asked for—whichever comes first. At that time, you'll be given a new identity and all the legal paperwork to back it up, as well as access to an account with your money. All the details are spelled out in a contract you'll receive later, but that's essentially our offer." Birch raised his eyebrows. "Sound fair?"

Paul stared back at him. "Ten million dollars—even if I fail?"

"You won't fail. But yes."

"Alright. And how does the new identity thing work?"

"Those details are handled by our recruiting firm," the minister replied. His dark, handsome face softened into a grin. "But I assure you, when the time comes, no more tranquilizers will be necessary."

For the first time since his arrival, Paul smiled. "Good. But I still need more information—starting with some kind of quantifiable measurement of what you consider success. I don't want to ruin your parade, but it's very likely that what you're asking for is impossible."

"Maybe," Birch replied. "But that's our risk, not yours."

The minister shuffled his feet impatiently. "So, will you help us?"

Paul eyed both men silently.

"Dr. Obermeyer?"

"Just a moment." Paul turned and paced back down the corridor where they'd entered. He gazed up at the narrow shafts of sunlight filtering through skylights, trying to ignore the pounding in his chest. *What the hell am I doing?* he asked himself. Was he really negotiating terms with his captors? Yes, he was. But then, it was hardly the most outlandish thing he'd been confronted with this morning. Was he really somewhere in the Saudi Arabian desert? Could Derrick Birch really be alive? Was Ceres really what these men were insinuating—an answer to the world's fuel energy crisis? Were they really going to pay him millions of dollars, even if he failed?

It all simply defied credibility.

And yet, accepting just one of these things as real seemed to validate the others—as if the whole of the story was more believable than any sum of its parts. And what was the alternative? If not Saudi Arabia, then where? If not Derrick Birch, then who? If not some top-secret alternative energy facility, then what? As crazy as it all sounded, was a more viable story even possible? More importantly—did it even matter? After all, if the men standing behind him *were* lying, a refusal of their offer was probably a death sentence. But if they were telling the truth, how could he possibly say no?

He glanced into the laboratory next to him. To his surprise, the woman he'd noticed earlier was now staring directly at him. Upon meeting her gaze, the woman's stare hardened and her mouth twisted into something resembling disdain. She turned away before Paul could be certain.

"Perhaps you need more time?" the minister asked.

Paul turned and regarded both men. "If anything—and I mean anything—you've said turns out to be a lie, do I have your word you'll let me leave?"

The minister's smile returned. "You have my word."

"Mine too," Birch added.

Paul nodded. "Okay, fine." He marched past his hosts toward the next set of labs, his running shoes squeaking on the concrete. A moment later he paused and shrugged.

"What—is the tour over?"

14.

"He did it, didn't he? The pale-faced little sonofabitch took it."

Michael Manning tossed the surveillance images of Adam Cowell back into the folder on his desk and slapped it closed. A brief silence passed before he turned and glared at his security director. "Well—are you going to say something?"

In the chair across from him, Lars Nielsen shifted his gaze from the window and nodded. "It appears so."

"*Appears*?" Manning tapped the folder with his finger. "You've got everything but a signed confession in here."

The security director studied Manning's face and noted the dark circles under his eyes. These, along with the deepening creases on the sides of his mouth now made the CEO look older than his forty-six years.

"I wish that were true. But apart from Mr. Cowell's reappearance at the lab, we have very little to act on. He passed the psychological evaluation, his polygraph test was inconclusive, and a search of his home and vehicle turned up nothing. The only thing noteworthy was his drug test results. There was alcohol and traces of what appears to be benzodiazepine—a depressant—in his system. But even this seems to check out.

We found a prescription for Xanax in his medicine cabinet, and the presence of alcohol was in line with his admitted drinking that night."

"Then what was his reason for returning to the lab?"

"He didn't have one," Nielsen replied. "Mr. Cowell has no recollection of going back to the lab."

Manning grunted. "Obviously he's a better thief than he is a liar."

"If he's guilty. But that's the problem—we still don't have anything definitive. We don't even know if Obermeyer's encryption key was in the lab when Cowell went back that evening." Nielsen shrugged. "Lots of circumstantial evidence, but no proof."

Manning glared at him with disappointment before picking up his cellphone and tapping out a brief text. The security director started to think their meeting was over when his boss cursed and shook his head. "I asked the sisters if they've picked up any chatter about sabotaged projects. None of them have heard a goddamn thing."

Nielsen nodded. The *sisters* Manning was referring to were three executive assistants operating as moles within Velgyn's largest competitors. All three were young, attractive women, each one personally vetted by the CEO in private, "closed-door" meetings. For this reason alone the security director placed little value in the occasional information they provided. He knew from experience that loyalty gained by money—or other favors—was always on the lookout for a better offer.

Manning tossed his phone onto the desk. "What now?"

Nielsen stood and moved to the window. "My team and I are continuing to investigate under the presumption that

Cowell's involved. But if any of this was planned beforehand, I'm quite certain it wasn't by him." An image of the research assistant's pale, terrified face as he was dragged off to his drug test flashed through the security director's mind. "I'm keeping him at the retreat house in Sonoma until I'm sure."

Manning raised his palms to the sky. "That's it? Two days since Obermeyer's key vanished, and our only suspect is lounging around the goddamn retreat house?"

Nielsen turned from the window. "There is another lead we're pursuing. But it's a long shot at best."

"Elaborate."

The security director started to speak when a heavy-set man with small, hawkish eyes stormed through the CEO's door and marched toward his desk. "We need to talk," the man commanded, glaring at Manning from across the desk.

"Good morning, Mark," Manning replied warmly. "I didn't realize we had a meeting scheduled."

"Don't do it, Michael," the man threatened in a low, quivering voice. "Don't kill Avolaquine. Nearly a year of successful phase-one trials completed, and you want to just—"

"Shut it down?" Manning interjected, raising his hand. "Yes, I do. That's why I called accounting last night and asked them to immediately suspend funding on any further trials."

The large man stepped back as if he'd taken a blow to the gut. "Do you . . . do you realize what you're *doing*?" he hissed. "Avolaquine represents the most promising malaria vaccine ever tested. It has the potential to save tens if not hundreds of thousands of lives per *year*. My god, to kill it now would be simply—*immoral*!"

"You might be right," Manning conceded. "Unfortunately, as CEO, I have to make decisions based on economic *reality*, not moral justification. The cost analysis for Avola-quine shows that moving forward simply isn't feasible."

"Bullshit! Development costs have been well within normal cost parameters at *every* stage—I've checked the numbers personally."

Manning held the man's stare. "Cost is only half the story here, Mark. The other half is revenue projections. Avola-quine's primary market is developing countries. And in case you haven't heard, those governments and their favorite NGOs no longer have the funds for humanitarian campaigns like malaria prevention. I hate to say it, but the profit opportunity on this drug disappeared the moment that Ebola pandemic hit West Africa."

"*There's* the truth!" the man exclaimed, stabbing a finger at Manning. He turned and gazed at Nielsen. "Did you hear that? Our CEO just admitted his interest in saving lives is measured solely by the profits he can gain from it."

Manning smiled. "Lars, this gentleman is Dr. Mark Fiennes, Director of Research for our infectious disease programs. Mark, this is Lars Nielsen, my Security Director."

The research director stiffened noticeably upon hearing Nielsen's title. He turned back to the CEO. "This isn't what I signed on for, Michael. And it won't stand. I'll take this matter directly to the executive board if I have to."

"You can take it to the executive board or Jesus himself if you want," Manning replied. "I've already cleared my decision with the board. Avolaquine's dead, Mark—may it rest in peace. I even went ahead and got the board's blessing to terminate your employment if I deemed necessary. And given your remarks, I'm afraid it is."

Fiennes froze, a stunned look on his face. "You're not

serious."

"Of course I'm serious. There's obviously a large delta in our philosophical and moral perspectives, Mark. And these types of differences aren't easily resolved. So I think it's best for everyone that you move on." Manning gently rapped his knuckles on the desk. "I'll expect your letter of resignation by this afternoon."

The research director's brow creased into a menacing scowl. "You're really going to fire me for putting lives before profits?" he asked, leaning his large frame over the CEO's desk.

"No. I'm firing you for not accepting that my decisions are in the best interest of this company. This is a *for-profit* corporation, Mark. We don't have the luxury of spending millions of dollars developing drugs just to dispense them for free under a banner of goodwill. I thought you understood that. You've certainly never complained about your salary or your research budgets. Where do you think *that* money comes from—charitable donations?"

"You self-righteous bastard, you can't—"

"Hand in your resignation by two o'clock, or I'm firing you." Manning interjected, rising from his chair. "And if you utter one slanderous word regarding this mutually agreed upon decision to anyone, I'll make sure our lawyers destroy your reputation so thoroughly you'll be lucky to get a job with the goddamn Peace Corps—understood?"

Fiennes slowly looked over at Nielsen. "I can see why he keeps you close."

The security director gave him an impassive stare.

The researcher director twisted his large frame around and lumbered toward the door. "Fuck all of you."

"Mark, I appreciate all the great work you've done for

Velgyn," Manning said to his departing figure. "I know I speak for everyone when I say I'm very disappointed to see it come to an end."

Fiennes vanished through the doorway without a word.

The CEO returned his attention to Nielsen. "What lead?" he demanded.

Nielsen gave him a brief look of confusion before picking up their previous conversation. His gaze shifted to the window. "Cowell insists he was on a date at the time of the incident. We're trying to track down the girl he says he was with to see if she can corroborate any part of his story."

"And?"

"Nothing yet. We've checked the online dating site where he says they met, but no matching profile seems to exist. All we have for now is a first name. I have some men scouting the area around the restaurant to see if any surveillance footage of either of them might exist."

"Did Cowell describe her?"

"Caucasian, about five-six, thin athletic build with hazel eyes and long, dark-brown hair. He said she was—" the security director hesitated before quoting Cowell directly. "Not easily forgettable."

"Right, of course," Manning quipped, flashing a sarcastic grin. "He wasn't at the lab stealing his mentor's research, he was out having dinner with a beautiful brunette. For Christ sake, Lars *you're* the investigator here—can't you see this guy's playing us? Stop wasting time on things that don't exist and start hurting that pudgy fuck until he tells you where he put the key."

Nielsen's stare shifted to the CEO.

"I'm not kidding," Manning said as if reading his security director's thoughts. He nodded toward the door. "I just destroyed that man's career and killed a drug that would've probably saved countless lives. And he was right—I did it because it didn't make financial sense to continue. Now, just to put that into context, the research locked away on Paul Obermeyer's computers has more revenue potential than every other drug in our pipeline *combined*. So just imagine what I'm prepared to do—and ask you to do—to make sure nothing jeopardizes that opportunity."

Manning sighed and dropped back into his chair.

"Maybe I didn't make myself clear in our previous conversation about doing *everything* necessary to get that key back," he continued. "I don't want to hear about psych tests and home searches. I don't even want to know how many nails you have to pry off Cowell's fingers to get him to talk. I just want to know you're doing whatever it takes to get answers. Because until I've got access to the research on Paul's computers, this is your *only* fucking mission. Are we clear?"

The security director nodded.

"Good. Then I'll let you get back to it."

Nielsen turned to leave when Manning raised a hand. "Oh, by the way—I didn't just tell accounting to kill the Avolaquine funding, I had them roll it to *your* operating budget. You've got enough to hire a goddamn army if necessary, so don't waste time coming to me if you need something."

"Thank you, Michael."

The CEO's mouth twisted into a grin. "Don't thank me yet, Lars. I've just removed every limitation to resolving this matter possible. The rest is up to you. I'm betting the future of this company on your ability to resolve this matter quickly—and we both know what's at stake if you fail, don't we?"

"We do."

"Good." Manning nodded dismissively. "I'll be giving a TED talk tomorrow on corporate ethics. Brief me by phone."

"Understood."

Nielsen marched past the desks of the CEO's young entourage of executive assistants and stepped into a waiting elevator. The doors closed and the forty-three year old security director checked his watch before releasing a deep breath.

Everything necessary.

As the doors opened to the lobby, his cell phone buzzed to life. He glanced at the caller ID and snapped the phone to his ear. "What have you got?"

"Video," his Security Manager, Ray Foster, replied.

"Of—?"

"The Ferry Building. Exterior views of northwest and southwest entrances. Their security company gave us digital recordings from four different surveillance cameras covering the time Cowell says he was there."

Nielsen paced through the executive lobby toward his office in the adjacent administration building. "What story did you give them?"

"I told them a Velgyn employee was assaulted after leaving one of the restaurants and their assailant may have been caught on tape," Foster replied. "They were more than happy to help."

The security director nodded, unsurprised. Between Ray Foster's imposing six-foot-three physique and authoritative demeanor, he could have probably walked out with anything he asked for. "Have you watched it?"

"Some. Enough."

"And—?"

"He was there, boss."

Nielsen quickened his pace. "Who's covering our research assistant right now?"

"Harris and Reyes."

The security director stepped out into the cool morning air. Around him, the striking glass and white steel buildings of the Velgyn corporate campus gleamed in the sun. He paused next to a large reflection pond at the edge of the courtyard and scanned the surface. "Alright, listen," he said, eyeing a large Kohaku koi rising to inspect him. "We're escalating everything. I want you at the archive warehouse on Brannan Street within the hour. If anyone's there, escort them out and tell them no one's allowed access until further notice. Use whatever excuse you want—just get them out. Then change the locks and make sure you and I are the only ones that have a key."

"Okay."

"Have Cowell brought to the warehouse when you're done, and have those videos queued up and ready to watch. Once everything's in place, call me."

"Got it, boss," Foster replied. "Shouldn't take more than a few hours."

Nielsen watched the fish's gold and white-flecked form swim closer. He leaned forward and placed his hand over the water. "Tell Harris and Reyes to keep quiet. I don't want Cowell to know what we're about to do."

"What *are* we about to do?"

"Get some answers." The security director shoved his phone in his pocket and watched the koi now circling beneath his outstretched hand in anticipation of a meal. *So predictable* he thought, lowering his hand to the water's surface. The koi rose in response. Nielsen waited for its wide head to break the surface before poking it on the forehead. The large fish instantly slapped its tail and vanished, leaving a whirlpool of black water in its wake.

Especially when frightened.

Nielsen turned and headed toward a four-story building that stood opposite the executive offices. He entered the sunlit lobby and slipped through a doorway marked 'Authorized Personnel Only'. A tall, frail-looking woman behind a counter studied him curiously as he approached.

"Can I help you?" the woman asked.

The security director flashed his credentials and explained what he was looking for.

The woman's expression mutated from acrimonious to outright suspicious. "If you're in security, why on earth would you need something like that?"

"I'm not at liberty to say."

The woman shook her head. "And what—you think we just keep that sort of thing inventoried here?"

"We have four research labs on campus," Nielsen replied. "So, yes, I do."

The woman's eyes widened to reveal powder-white crow's feet on the sides of her face. "Well, I suppose I can check. But you'll have to fill out a requisition form just like everyone else." She disappeared down a narrow corridor lined with sealed storage bins and returned with a shoebox-size package. "I'll need to make a copy of your driver's license and employee card while you fill out the paperwork," she continued, dropping the box on the counter and looking around for a pen.

Nielsen read the label. "Perfect. Thank you." He slipped the box under his arm and marched toward the door.

"Hey, *wait* a minute!" the woman called after him. "You

can't just walk out like th—" Her words were severed by the shutting door.

The security director sighed with impatience at the sound of the woman rushing into the lobby behind him. A moment later her thin frame stood between him and the door.

"Take one more step and I'll call—"

"Who—*security*?" Nielsen shook his head. "Listen, Miss—"

"Ross. Laina Ross. And don't even try to walk out of here without following protocol."

"I don't have time for protocol, Ms. Ross. So you can either get out of my way, or I can call one of my men and have you detained. Which would you prefer?"

The woman drew her mouth into a scowl. "You wouldn't dare."

The security director pulled out his phone and dialed a number. "This is Director Nielsen. Send someone over to laboratory supply immediately to—"

"Okay, fine . . . fine!" The woman raised her arms and stepped aside.

"Never mind." He hung up and smiled. "Thank you, Laina," he said, stepping past her. "I'll be sure to have this back to you by tomorrow."

The woman's gaze followed after him as he reached the door "You can't return *used* supplies!" she exclaimed angrily.

The security director nodded without looking back. "I know," he muttered before slipping out the door.

15.

Javier Salas was hungry.

The HACKCON conference had proven even worse than expected—three days huddled in a large, dimly lit hall with the world's best programmers and software developers while a procession of presenters droned on about their latest apps, IOs and APIs.

Even the breakout discussions had been almost unbearable—especially when the thirty-nine year old programming genius realized how far *behind* everyone else was. Earlier that afternoon he'd barely managed to contain himself as a database architect from Google stood onstage lamenting over an issue his team was currently plagued with. *Could they not see how easy the answer was?* he mused, shaking his head at same problem he'd solved nearly two years before. Were it not for the identity of his own employer, Javier probably would have stood and smugly offered the twitchy, twenty-something Googlean the solution. But that would have gotten attention. Too much attention. Everyone in the audience would have turned and looked at the tall, corpulent figure dressed in a black tracksuit at the back of the room and started asking questions. And his employer definitely would not have liked that. After all, Javier wasn't there to show everyone he was the smartest guy at the conference. He was there to make sure no one else was even close to his advances in decryption modeling.

And besides, fuck Google.

So, as he'd done the previous days, Javier kept his mouth shut. But now, with the conference over, he was finally free to focus on what he really came to here to do—satisfy his cravings. And what better place to do it than São Paulo during carnival? The entire city was transformed into a miasma of exotic delicacies that tantalized the senses and stirred the blood. The food, the drink, the dancing, the women—each a unique flavor just waiting for the right appetite. It was the perfect playground for the genius programmer whose own bosses affectionately referred to as *el hombre voraz*—

The voracious man.

Javier stepped from the second restaurant of the night and steered his broad, six-foot four-inch frame slowly onto the street, the taste of feijoada still lingering on his tongue. The pungent, musky-sweet smell of jasmine hung heavily in the warm evening air, spiced with earthy hints of tobacco smoke and human sweat. Javier rubbed his sizable abdomen with satisfaction and studied his surroundings.

The Vila Madalena was a riot of sights and sounds. Revelers fresh from the festivities of the Sambadrome were now pouring into the quaint, tree-lined neighborhood's bars and cafes to continue the party. *A caipirinha would be nice,* Javier thought, recalling the delicious cocktail made from cachaça and lime. He lit a cigarette and drew the smoke deep into his lungs. Then something he craved even more caught his eye—a group of young women in tight, radiantly colored dresses and sparkling high heels. He licked his lips as they sauntered past, his wide nostrils inhaling their sweetness, his gaze devouring every sumptuous curve and crease of young flesh. As they disappeared into the growing mob, Javier took another deep drag and smiled.

With his belly now full, it was time to turn his attention to more pressing appetites.

He released the half-used cigarette from his fleshy fingers and plodded forward. Within moments *el hombre voraz* was absorbed by the throng, his massive figure bulldozing aside those smaller and weaker around him. He moved slowly, his dark eyes flickering with a predatory light. Like his earlier meals, Javier knew exactly what he was craving.

Now he just had to find it.

He's coming toward you from the east. Thirty yards.

Jeri nodded at Chilly's voice in her earpiece and continued dancing. Overhead, the samba music poured from large speakers like water onto the crowded street, stirring the revelers into a rhythmic frenzy. A hand abruptly slipped around Jeri's waist and inched provocatively down her thigh, stirring the sequins of her dress. A mouth brushed against her ear.

"Dançar comigo," a voice whispered.

Jeri seized the hand on her thigh and twirled to face its owner. The tranquil eyes of a handsome *paulistano* stared back.

"Dançar comigo!" the man said again with a wide grin.

Jeri released his hand and offered a regretful smile "Não esta noite," she said, shaking her head to the fast beat. She turned before the man could respond and disappeared into the throng of shifting bodies.

Chilly grunted in her earpiece.

Someone's been studying their Portuguese.

Jeri didn't bother to respond. Hours before, it had been decided that the noise of the crowd would be too great for her microphone to work effectively, so in lieu of speaking she would use hand signals to communicate. Trying to convey that she'd learned some Portuguese from a former college roommate just didn't seem worthwhile—especially for the person responsible for her outfit.

Twenty yards.

She paused to get her bearings. Even in four-inch heels she could barely see more than a few feet beyond the crowd.

Keep an eye on your guardian angel.

Jeri looked up. On the north side of the street stood a building with a row of balconies along its upper story. Revelers filled each to capacity, shouting and drinking and leaning precariously over the rusty iron railings. Pressed between two women on the nearest balcony was Sly, a phone cradled in his outstretched hand. Even from a distance, it was obvious his phone's camera lens was pointed at her. *Coming to you live from São Paulo,* Jeri thought irritably, knowing he was broadcasting her every move to the team.

She continued east along the street, painfully aware of the cascade of colored sparkles flashing from the sequins of her skin-tight dress. A short distance on, her earpiece crackled again.

Ten yards.

Jeri paused and let the music once again wash over her. She moved timidly at first, matching the rhythm of those around her. Her eyes flickered up to the balcony where Sly stood. Her colleague nodded and swept the lens of the phone toward someone approaching.

Five yards. You know what to do.

Jeri tossed her strawberry-blonde hair from her face and raised her arms into the air. She closed her eyes and leaned back, giving in to the music. Her steps grew more confident, her movements more seductive. Around her, the crowd opened in response.

Take it up a notch.

Jeri shot an angry look toward the balcony. Without thinking, she seized the hem of her dress and drew it upwards, revealing the smooth white skin of her thighs. As if on cue, the beat of the samba music quickened. Jeri matched it with a rhythmic thrusting of her hips, sweeping her arms back and forth to counter-balance the movement of her lower body. Around her, the crowd quickly gave way to the *mulher bonita*. Jeri moved to the center of the widening circle, her heart pounding. She snapped her legs up and outward in the fast, alternating step of the *Samba Axé*—one of the local styles she'd studied on the Internet. It had seemed so simple rehearsing in her hotel room. But now, performing before the eyes of the crowd, the dance took every ounce of her concentration.

Okay, I think you've got his attention.

Jeri spun and scanned the faces around her. A tall, heavyset man stood just beyond the edge of the circle, his large head looming nearly a foot over those around him. Even without making eye contact Jeri could see that his dark, disheveled hair and patchy beard matched that of the man in the Polaroid photo.

Now listen, I want you to—

Chilly's voice trailed off as the crowd abruptly parted

to reveal a tall, exotically dressed woman. The woman strutted toward Jeri, her mocha-colored body a sculpture of feminine curves and lithe muscle contained by little more than jeweled strips of silver. A tall headdress shuddered with a flourish of silver and vibrant blue feathers with every step, giving the woman the appearance of being even taller than her six-foot frame. Pausing in the center of the widening circle, the woman lowered her head and began to tremble, as if drawing some great unseen energy from the earth. Then slowly, the woman's arms lifted to the sky and her hips began to roll back and forth in a manner Jeri had trouble believing possible. Her movements, which at first seemed random, now synchronized under the spell of the music. Gradually the pace quickened. Moments later, like a serpent preparing to strike, the woman lifted her head and opened her eyes to reveal two piercing, emerald-green irises.

The irises focused on Jeri.

Oh shit.

Jeri stepped back, conceding the center of the circle that had formed around them. Taking her rightful spot, the passista smiled and spun to the crowd, her hips rolling and twisting with almost supernatural control. Then, as if her dominance had not already been established, she launched into the *Samba Axé* with explosive speed, her body and costume melding into a vortex of light and color.

Cheers erupted from the crowd around them. Defeated, Jeri stopped dancing and slipped unnoticed back into the crowd. *So much for getting noticed* she thought, casting an irritable glance at the passista who had just ruined their plans. She was just beginning to look for Sly on the balcony overhead when a large hand fell on her shoulder. Jeri turned and found herself staring at the chest of a tall, broad figure dressed in black slacks and a matching blazer. She looked up into the man's eyes and frowned.

"O que você quer?" she asked tersely.

The man leaned down and placed his thin lips next to her ear. Jeri inwardly squirmed as the man's patchy beard brushed against her neck. "I want many things," he replied in perfect English. "But first, would you allow me the pleasure of buying you a drink?"

～

Watching the live video feed on his phone, Chilly nodded at the sight of Jeri speaking with their recruit. "Contact," he mumbled as the two turned and together made their way through the crowd. He glanced into the darkness of the narrow alleyway at a group of young men passing the parked van and sank further into the shadows of the passenger seat.

Did that really just happen? Tall Tommy's voice echoed in his earpiece. *Did our freshman just get upstaged by a Beyoncé lookalike and still manage to pull in the recruit?*

"Were you worried she couldn't do it?"

No. But if I wasn't worried before, I am now. That bloke's a fucking three-hundred pound monster.

"More like three-forty."

The Australian man sighed. *Maybe she was right about the ambulance idea. He really does look like a heart attack waiting to happen.*

Onscreen, Jeri lead their recruit toward a small bar on the street corner as planned. Chilly smiled at the stark contrast between her lithe figure and the massive bulk following after.

"What ambulance idea?"

Well there's no point in talking about it now, but maybe we should've just picked this guy up in an ambu—

"Hold on," Chilly interrupted, watching their recruit suddenly pause and lean back as if stretching. A moment later the man produced a small bottle from his pocket and dumped an assortment of pills onto his large, paw-like hand.

"Sly, zoom in on that," Chilly commanded

The video feed immediately zoomed in on Javier Salas's thick fingers separating two bluish-colored pills from the rest. He popped them into his mouth.

Chilly's smile vanished. "Tommy, are you still in our friend's hotel room?"

Negative. On my way to you.

"I need you to get back there—now. How quickly can you do it?"

A brief pause followed before the Australian man answered. *Seven minutes.*

Chilly watched Jeri and her recruit enter the bar. "Make it four."

Care to say why?

"Just tell me when you get there. Sly, I need eyes on our freshman."

Give me two minutes the team's guardian angel responded. The video feed went dark.

Chilly frowned and stared out the window. A few blocks away, Jeri and her recruit were ordering drinks as scripted. But if Tall Tommy found what he feared was in Javier Salas's hotel room, everything was in jeopardy. He shook his head in disbelief.

Had he really missed something so obvious?

139

~

Jeri followed Javier Salas's massive bulk through the crowded bar to the counter. Once there, her recruit smiled and hovered bear-like over two men until they graciously relinquished their seats.

"Dois caipirinhas!" he roared above the noise at the bartender. He then turned and studied Jeri with a quizzical expression. "So tell me," he said, speaking once again in English, "what brings such a beautiful American woman to Sao Paulo?"

"What makes you think I'm American?" Jeri retorted in Portuguese.

Her recruit's deep-set eyes glinted with humor. "Only an American would be so foolish as to challenge a passista on her own turf."

"Wait a minute—she challenged *me*!" Jeri exclaimed in English.

Javier pounded his fist against the bar and bellowed with laughter. He gestured at her dress. "Wearing what you're wearing, dancing as you were dancing—any passista would have considered such things a challenge. You're lucky she let you off so easily. The people here take samba dancing as seriously as life itself."

Jeri shrugged. "Perhaps I let *her* off easily."

Her recruit's stare dropped to her dress. "Perhaps so."

The bartender placed two tall drinks in front of them.

"Caipirinha!" Javier exclaimed, raising his glass. "The drink of this wonderful city. And here is to my wonderful new friend, miss—"

"Summer," Jeri replied. "Summer Fields."

"To my new friend, Summer Fields. May her flower be always in bloom." Her recruit laughed at his own joke and tossed back the majority of his drink. "You still haven't told me what brings you to São Paulo, Summer Fields."

"Work." Jeri took a sip of her drink and licked her lips, enjoying the sweet, rum-like taste of the cachaça. "I'm here on assignment."

"Ah, an *assignment*." Javier nodded as if impressed before emptying his glass and motioning to the bartender for another. "And just what kind of assignments do you do?"

"It's a little difficult to describe. You could say I help certain people get to a better place."

Her recruit regarded her with a thin smile. "Such a noble pursuit if I understand your meaning. Would it be appropriate to say that you escort these people to places of great happiness?"

Jeri gasped as if caught by surprise. "You're quite a clever man, aren't you, mister—"

"Salas. But please, call me Javier."

"You're a clever man, Javier. But I take it you're not from around here either."

Her recruit shook his head as the bartender placed another caipirinha on the counter next to him. "Bogota," he muttered, picking up the drink and emptying it in a single gulp. "I'm here on business as well."

"What business is that?"

A dark cloud crossed his face. "My business would be of no interest to you. However, yours is of great interest to me." He leaned closer and placed a hand on Jeri's knee. "I imagine that being escorted by someone such as yourself is quite a privilege, no?"

Jeri glanced down at his hand before smiling. "Quite."

"And just how much would such a privilege cost?"

Jeri appeared to size him up as she took another sip of her drink. *Thank god I don't charge by the pound* she thought morosely. "Four."

"Four *hundred*?"

Jeri laughed.

"Ah, of course," Javier replied with a chuckle. "As they say, the best things in life are free—except companionship." The light in his eyes suddenly transformed into something more sinister. "Very well then, Summer Fields, four thousand sounds fair." His grip tightened vice-like around her knee. "As long as the performance matches the package."

Jeri reached down and gently rubbed his hand until his grip loosened. "I'll make you a promise, Javier of Bogota." She raised her glass and pointed a slender finger at him. "If you don't like the way tonight turns out, you won't owe me a thing."

Her recruit shifted his enormous frame closer and slid his hand further up her thigh. "How can I possibly say no to such a wonderful offer?"

"You can't."

"Well then, it's settled," Javier concluded, the light in his eyes once again friendly. He gestured for the bartender. "Shall we have another?"

Jeri leaned forward and brushed her lips against his cheek. "Make it a double," she said, resting a hand on his thigh. "After all, we have all night, yes?"

Her recruit smiled and nodded, the wide jowls of his face quivering in response. "Yes," he said, his voice a low growl of excitement. "Indeed we do."

~

Tall Tommy strolled back into the sprawling lobby of the Quatro Jardins luxury hotel and took the first available elevator to the ninth floor. Once inside suite 905, he slapped on a pair of latex gloves. "Okay, I'm here," he announced, his eyes sweeping the empty living room. "What am I looking for?"

Go into the bathroom Chilly commanded through his earpiece.

Tall Tommy marched through the master bedroom and paused in the doorway of the bathroom. "Okay, now what?"

Prescription medications. Find everything he's taking.

The Australian man stepped to the vanity and swept his gloved hands around a clutter of used towels, empty liquor bottles, and the chewed remnants of several Cuban cigars. "Plenty of evidence to suggest our friend is enjoying his stay, but no medications."

They're there. Keep looking.

He searched the linen closet and checked for a medicine cabinet before shaking his head. "Nothing."

Try the bedroom.

Walking back into the bedroom, Tall Tommy briefly scanned his surroundings before heading to the nightstand next to the unmade king-sized bed. A collection of empty wine bottles on top rattled as he opened the drawer. "Jackpot."

What's he got?

He pulled out the drawer and dumped its contents onto the bed. "Jesus . . . it'd be easier to say what he *hasn't* got here."

Give me the names.

"Right. Okay, here we go . . . atorvastatin . . . furose-

143

mide . . . nizatidine . . . zafirlukast . . . pioglitazone . . . amoxicillin—fuck, it's a wonder this guy can feel anything."

Keep going.

"Warfarin . . . prednisone . . . cyclobenzaprine . . . ibupro—"

Wait, Chilly interjected. *Say that last one again.*

"Cy-clo-ben-zaprine," his colleague repeated.

A few miles away, Chilly nodded and glanced absently out the window of the van. "Alright, that's all I needed to hear. Clean it up and get back here as soon as possible."

On my way, Tall Tommy replied.

Chilly muted his earpiece and cursed at himself. His hunch had been right. Despite a detailed review of their recruit's extensive medical history, Javier Salas had still managed to slip in a surprise. Nearly every medication in the nightstand matched his known list of ailments and conditions, which included high blood pressure, high cholesterol, acid reflux, pulmonary issues—even type 2 diabetes. But what wasn't in *el hombre voraz's* medical records was the issue made obvious when he'd paused outside the bar—

His back was killing him.

Chilly shook his head. Of course their recruit's back was suffering—the man weighs over three hundred pounds. And the most obvious ailment would be a herniated disc in his spine—which would explain the muscle relaxant cyclobenzaprine. Herniated discs were a common issue for obese individuals like Salas. And yet he'd failed to anticipate it.

Chilly sat quietly for a moment, scolding himself. Prior to now, he'd never missed a diagnosis on a recruit—at least one that might require a change in their method of collection. But none of that now mattered. All they could do was adapt to this new information and finish the collection.

Of course, he already had a contingency plan.

He unmuted his earpiece. "Sly, listen carefully. We're changing the script. Here's what I need you to do."

When he was finished outlining the new plan, Chilly checked the time and glanced at his phone. "Understood?"

The live video feed of Jeri and Javier Salas sitting at the bar moved up and down in response.

"Okay—do it."

The video feed again went dark as Sly put the new plan into motion.

Chilly sighed and clicked his earpiece over to Jeri. "Listen carefully, freshman," he said slowly. "There's been a change of plans."

16.

Jeri stared at her recruit with a thin smile frozen on her face. Next to her, Javier Salas tossed back the last of his drink and pushed the empty glass down the bar.

"Am I boring you?" he asked, raising his hand for the bartender.

"Not at all. Why would you ask?"

"Because you look as if you are not entirely here."

"No, I'm . . . I'm sorry, it's just—" Jeri feigned an uncomfortable laugh and messed with her hair. When she met his stare again, her mouth twisted with embarrassment. "I need to deal with a small . . . issue."

Her recruit gazed back blankly for a moment before erupting in a fit of laughter.

Jeri rose from her seat. "Excuse me," she said icily. As she turned toward the restroom, Javier leaned forward and seized her by the arm.

"You women and your issues," he mumbled, pulling her roughly toward him. "I only hope it's not a monthly one. If so, I should demand a better price."

Jeri's expression softened into an impassive grin. "I agree. If it turns out to be what you think, you should definitely pay more."

Her recruit tossed his head back and laughed again. "I like you, Summer Fields. Very much. You're the first girl of your, shall we say, *kind* that has ever matched my wit." He released his grip and gestured for her to go.

Jeri glanced at the impression marks left by his fingers and leaned toward the greasy nest of hair that covered his ear. "Then you don't know my kind." She turned and marched off. Behind her, Salas's voice bellowed over the din of the bar.

"Volta logo!"

Jeri quickened her pace the moment her recruit wasn't watching. A few steps from the front of the bar, she noticed the sign for the *banheiro* pointing to a narrow, dimly lit hallway. She followed it to an unmarked door and knocked. No one answered. She pushed the door open and groaned at the sight of a filthy toilet pressed against a wall of piss-stained tile.

"Looks inviting, doesn't it?"

Jeri spun on her high heels to find Sly smiling behind her. "What the hell's going on?"

Her colleague motioned her into the bathroom. Once inside, he closed the door and held out his hand. "Give me your tranquilizer stick."

"I don't understand. What's—"

Our new friend's personal drug inventory is even larger than the cartel he works for, Chilly responded in her earpiece. *One of them is a muscle relaxant that doesn't play nicely with the tranquilizer you're carrying. If you hit him with the dose in that stick, he really will be a heart attack waiting to happen.*

Jeri reached two fingers into the cleavage of her breasts and pulled out a black, lipstick-sized cylinder. "Okay, and what am I supposed to use instead?" she asked, handing it to Sly.

Her colleague pocketed the object before handing her another one that looked identical. "Plan B, freshman. See you on the other side."

Before Jeri realized what was happening Sly opened the door and vanished back into the hallway. She studied the object in her hand. "So—plan *B*?"

Oral sedative. Order another round for your friend, twist the cap and drop the contents into his drink. Once he's finished, head for the collection location. By the time you arrive, he'll be ready for a long nap.

Jeri shook her head. "I don't like this. The whole point of the tranquilizer was to knock him out in *seconds*, not *minutes*. If this doesn't work, how am I supposed to stop him from getting what he's already been promised?"

Sly will shadow you to the collection location, and Max will be onsite. Once you're there, just say that you need to use the restroom—and stay in there until he's down. That's it. The rest of the script stays the same.

"Yeah, that's easy for you to say. You're not the one about to take a walk with a three-hundred pound sodomite."

Three-forty.

Jeri rolled the cylinder in her palm. "How much do I give him?"

All of it—and make sure he finishes his drink.

"That's the easy part." Jeri slipped the new cylinder between her breasts and turned toward the mirror. A chill ran up her spine at the sight of the stoic face staring back. "God, I really do look like a whore," she whispered, studying the macabre mask of makeup and colored hair shimmering beneath the stark overhead light.

You mean a four-thousand dollar whore.

"I didn't ask for your opinion." She teased her hair with a few well-placed jabs of her fingers and nodded. "Anything else you want to change tonight?"

Is your attitude an option?

Jeri opened the bathroom door and peered down the hallway. Standing guard at the far end, Sly gave her a brief nod and slipped around the corner. Jeri adjusted her dress and took a deep breath. "Fuck off, Chilly."

Javier Salas could barely believe the evening's fortune.

Two wonderful meals had temporarily satiated his stomach, and the caipirinhas were now slowly melting away his sobriety. But without question, the greatest find of the night had been the American woman who'd materialized before him in the crowd like some fated apparition. How else could he explain such luck? The woman was everything he was searching for—young, beautiful, and as made obvious by her public dancing and general attitude, deliciously fearless. He'd learned from experience that this last trait was particularly essential when selecting a woman to pleasure a man of his sheer physical size. Even the way he'd grabbed her before she departed for the restroom—one of his usual vetting ploys—hadn't aroused any obvious fear in her.

Javier looked up to see his escort strolling back to the bar and felt his appetite stir once again. As she took her seat next to him, he smiled and raised his glass. "So, Miss Summer Fields—have the monthly rains come as predicted?"

His escort shook her head. "I guess my weather forecast was wrong." She grabbed her drink and tossed it back in one gulp. "Should we have one more to celebrate?"

"Yes!" Javier exclaimed, hailing the bartender. With another round ordered, he leaned toward her clumsily. "Perhaps you are correct. Perhaps I don't know your kind at all. But I'm curious—how does a woman of such beauty and wit end up an escort of men?"

His escort regarded him with a cold smile. "You make it sound like I've chosen a less than noble profession."

"Not at all," he replied, impressed once again by her confident manner. "I for one am very thankful for your choice. But you strike me as rather atypical for the profile. And atypical profiles are something I know a great deal about."

"Oh really? Care to explain?"

"I'm not in a position to discuss my profession in any detail. But it would be fair to say that I do something that few other men can do. And I'm paid exceptionally well to do it."

"Well then, we have something in common. And this thing you do so well—does it make you happy?"

The bartender appeared and placed two more caipirinhas on the counter. Javier twisted his mouth in thought. "The money it provides me does," he affirmed after a moment. "And you? Does this escorting business make you happy?"

His escort casually dropped two manicured fingers into the cleavage of her breasts and produced a tube of lipstick. "I like to think I'm helping make the world a better place to live," she replied, pulling off the cap. "One man—or woman—at a time."

Javier's eyes remained on her pale, unblemished bosom. He slid his tongue over his lips and nodded. "I'll drink to that."

He started to grab his drink when his escort's lipstick

slipped from her hand and fell into it with a splash.

"Oh *shit*—" she exclaimed, grimacing with embarrassment as she fished it from the ice and lime. "I'm so goddamn *clumsy* sometimes."

Javier released an irritable grunt and reached for the other glass.

"What—mine? I don't think so." His escort snatched the glass in front of her and drained it empty. When she was finished, she gave him a smug grin. "Drink your own poison, Mr. Salas."

Javier glared at her, anger flushing his round face. Who did this brash whore think she was dealing with? The memory of a previous encounter with an overconfident prostitute came to mind. How quickly her attitude had changed after the first blow had colored the skin of her young face. The second blow had sent crimson streaks of blood running from the corner of her mouth, the very sight of which aroused Javier beyond his ability for self-control. Had it been the fire of terror in her eyes? The way her frail body trembled with the sudden awareness of what he could—and would—do to her? It didn't matter. All that had mattered was his appetite, and his appetite had pleaded for more. He couldn't recall exactly when his fists had stopped. Perhaps it was just before his body had lost its hunger for hers, or perhaps just after. Javier wasn't sure. All he'd been sure of upon leaving the cheap hotel room that echoed with the sound of whimpering cries and labored breath was that he had been satisfied like never before.

And to be satisfied thereafter, he knew his appetite would demand such horrible things again.

Staring now at the woman next to him, Javier imagined a trickle of blood rolling gently down her chin. His arousal

151

flared. *Patience* he told himself, his angry expression easing into a smile. He snatched the drink from the counter and poured it into his cavernous mouth. When he looked at her again, his stare left no doubt as to what he wanted next.

"Would you like to see my lovely view of São Paulo?" his escort asked.

Javier nodded. "It is close?"

His escort rose from her chair with cat-like grace. "Very," she said, running her hands seductively down her dress before taking his hand. "Follow me."

Josefa Rocha looked up at the sound of the front door opening and sighed wearily. *Was this how the entire night would go?* she wondered. She muted the tiny television on her desk and glanced over her shoulder.

Perhaps if she were younger, the sight of an attractive young woman leading a fat, troll-faced man through the hotel's entrance might have aroused her curiosity or prompted a wry smile. But she'd seen far too many things in her sixty-three years to find such things amusing anymore—especially during Carnival. And besides, she was tired. Twice in the last hour she'd been interrupted to assist new guests. The first had been an old Chinese woman who had demanded Josefa haul the woman's luggage up to her room, only to shrug when it came time for the tip. Then, just as the hotel manager returned to her chair to enjoy a classic episode of *A Grande Família*, a grim-faced, massively built man charged through the front door dragging an enormous travel case behind him. Josefa had stared wide-eyed with dread upon seeing the case, which looked large enough to hold an entire year's worth of clothes. Thankfully the man had refused any assistance after checking in, giving her a curt nod with his buzzed head before heading off to the elevator.

Now, just as she was beginning to forget herself in the lives of her favorite sitcom's characters, the pretty American woman who'd checked in the day before staggered into the lobby with a very unexpected-looking companion in tow.

Josefa studied the pair as they made their way toward the elevator and again concluded the woman was a prostitute. Why else had she rented the room but not stayed in it? She was obviously here to prey on the tourists that now filled the streets for Carnival. Nevertheless, the hotel manager was shocked by the woman's first choice for the evening. The only thing that could possibly be attractive about the man stumbling up the stairs behind her was his wallet.

As if reading her thoughts, the man twisted his round, scruffily bearded face around and shot her a murderous look.

Josefa shifted her gaze back to the tiny television screen. She briefly imagined what her tenant was about to do with that *diabo gordo* and shuddered. *To each their own* she concluded, turning up the volume. The sound of a laughing studio audience echoed through the lobby, and the woman and her fat friend were soon forgotten.

Jeri led Javier Salas down the second floor corridor of the dark, musty-smelling hotel and silently counted off the time in her head. The walk from the bar to the hotel had taken just over ten minutes, but her oversized recruit still seemed

153

alarmingly alert and lucid. Reaching the end of the corridor, she paused at the room door and shrugged. "I'll warn you now, it's nothing special," she said, grabbing the key from the overhead doorjamb. "But that's not what you're paying for."

Javier Salas stepped inside and immediately wrinkled his nose at the smell of disinfectant. His dark eyes swept over the sparse, predictable furnishings—a seventies-era dresser, a queen-sized bed flanked by two pastel-colored floor lamps, a large poster of Botticelli's Birth of Venus hanging crookedly over the bed. "Very nice," he mumbled, his words slurring together. He turned and gave her a wry grin. "I'm sure your previous clients were pleased."

Jeri closed the door and took a quick breath, her hand still clutching the knob. "Actually, you're the first."

Her recruit's eyes widened to reveal crimson-stained scleras. "The first in São Paulo?"

"The first in this room." She pointed at a bottle of scotch and two glasses on the dresser. "Why don't you pour us some drinks while I get ready?"

Salas took and a step toward the dresser and stumbled, catching himself against the bed. "Perhaps I've had enough," he laughed breathlessly. He regained his footing and shook his head. "The fucking caipirinhas . . . they don't play fairly."

"Yeah, well, neither do I," Jeri mumbled. From the corner of her eye she saw her recruit reach for her and twisted out of reach. "Whoa—not so fast, tiger," she said flatly, catching the look in his eyes. Before he could try again she slipped inside the bathroom and locked the door.

Everything okay? Chilly's voice echoed in her earpiece.

Jeri turned on the sink faucet and moved to the corner farthest from the door. "Define 'okay,'" she whispered.

Are you in the bathroom?

"Yes."

Good. Stay there. He should be out soon.

"Soon?" Jeri hissed. "You're not exactly inspiring a lot of confidence in me right now. If this guy's on as many drugs as you said, what makes you so sure he's doesn't have a high tolerance for Plan-B?"

I accounted for that possibility in the dosage.

"Well, he didn't act sedated just now when he tried to grab me. Maybe you should stop by and see for—" Jeri froze at the sound of something squeaking behind her. She glanced over her shoulder. "Shit."

What's wrong?

A few feet away, the doorknob slowly twisted back and forth.

Freshman?

"He's trying to come in," Jeri whispered. She walked over to the door and forced a casual laugh. "Is someone in a hurry to get started?"

The doorknob twitched once more and fell still.

Jeri watched it tensely for a moment before returning to her corner. "Just tell me you got the fucking dose right."

Listen to me—Max is just across the hallway. I'm in the alley behind you. It's been fourteen minutes since he was dosed. Worst-case scenario is twenty minutes for full effect, but it will work. Just sit tight until he's down. If he tries anything unexpected, say the word and Max will be in there. Got it?

Jeri nodded, listening to the silence in the next room. Something didn't feel right . . . something about Salas himself. There was no question her recruit was physically imposing, but this wasn't the only thing bothering her at the moment.

What bothered her was something she'd seen in his stare just now when he'd tried to grab her. She'd witnessed it earlier at the bar—a menacing flash of evil, like some creature lurking in the darkness, waiting for the right moment to come out.

Or was she just letting fear get the best of her?

Freshman—got it?

"Yeah, I got it." Jeri leaned her forehead against the lime-green wall tile, thankful for its coldness. "And if he's still standing in twenty minutes?"

A long pause followed before Chilly responded.

Just sit tight.

Jeri shook her head. *Sit tight?* she thought, dropping the lid of the toilet and taking a seat. She turned off the sink faucet and listened intently. A minute later, Chilly's voice broke the silence.

Fifteen minutes.

"Come *on*," Jeri whispered, exasperated. Another agonizing minute of silence passed before she stood and moved to the door. "It's awfully quiet out there," she exclaimed. "You got those drinks ready yet?"

Her recruit didn't respond.

"Hey—are you *awake* out there? Don't think I won't charge you even if you can't manage to—"

A loud crash reverberated from the other side of the door.

"What the hell was that?" Jeri demanded, her voice sharp with concern. "Javier? *Javier* . . . is everything okay?" She pressed her ear to the door, listening for the sound of heavy breathing or any indication that her recruit had finally succumb to the sedative. Once again there was only silence. "Are you going to answer me or not?"

All right. He's probably down.

"Okay," Jeri whispered. "Should I go out there?"

Absolutely not, Chilly commanded. *Max, confirm that he's down with the scope.*

I'm on it, Max answered.

In the corridor outside, Jeri's colleague silently moved to her room door and slipped a small endoscopic camera through the gap at the bottom. A long silence passed before he spoke again. *You seeing this?*

Chilly sighed over the radio. *Yeah.*

"What is it?" Jeri asked, hovering by the bathroom door. "What are you seeing?"

Try the other corner.

Trying now, Max replied.

Another moment of silence followed.

Nope . . . it's the same.

"Will someone please tell me what's going on?"

Something's wedged against the door, Chilly answered. *Max and I can't tell what it is . . . or see past it.*

Jeri shrugged. "It's got to be our friend. He must have collapsed there."

Probably. But I want to be sure. Max, can you get inside?

I can get through the lock, Max affirmed. *But if I start kicking my way in there with him pressed against the door, he's gonna get hurt. Not to mention that I'm a little exposed out here.*

Jeri again pressed her ear to the door. "What's the count?"

Seventeen minutes since dosage.

"And what are the chances he's still conscious?"

Slim to none.

"Right. And if he *has* collapsed against the door, what

are the chances he could be injured or even asphyxiated?"

Chilly sighed. *Not insignificant.*

"Fine—then I'm going out there."

Wait—

Jeri took a deep breath and released the lock. A sense of foreboding rippled through her as she cracked the door open, but she quickly willed it aside. She leaned forward and peered through the opening.

The bedroom was pitch black.

"Javier?"

She looked toward the entry, her eyes struggling to make sense of the darkness. As expected, something large and dark was pressed against the door.

"Javier . . . is that you?"

Jeri opened the bathroom door further to cast more light into the room. As the object at the entry came into focus, her feeling of foreboding suddenly flared into a wave of panic.

Across the room, turned on its side and wedged intentionally against the front door lay the dresser.

Jeri leapt back and slammed the bathroom door closed.

What's happening? Chilly demanded.

Before she could turn the lock, the doorknob stiffened and began to twist beneath Jeri's hand. Terrified, she forgot about the lock and grabbed the knob with both hands, resisting its movement with every ounce of strength she could find. Chilly's voice screamed in her earpiece.

Freshman! What's happening?

"He's still awake!" Jeri exclaimed, feeling the doorknob twist beneath her grip. She anchored her knees against the doorframe in a desperate effort to keep the door closed. "He's wedged the dresser against the front door and now he's trying to—"

An angry growl of triumph punctured the air as the bathroom door was ripped open. The sheer force of the act sent Jeri hurling into the darkness. Before she could regain her senses an unseen hand shoved her roughly to the floor. Jeri spun onto her back and raised her arms in self-defense as her recruit's looming figure appeared over her.

"Javier—wait! I can—"

Javier seized Jeri's wrists and lifted her like a child before wrapping his massive arms around her. The smell of cigarettes and cachaça fell in warm, panting breaths on her neck. "I . . . I don't recall us discussing a change in tonight's arrangement, Miss Fields," he slurred, his wet lips pressed against her. "Do you?"

Jeri gasped as her recruit's tongue began to slowly probe her ear.

"Of course, I know what you're doing," he continued, pressing her against him. "You see, I've been with many, many whores before you. Lovely girls, all of them—at least at the beginning of the night—but none as lovely as you. And so . . . so very smart. Perhaps that should have been my first clue you were up to something. Just when I thought I knew all the devious little tricks of your trade—" His hold tightened, crushing the air from her chest. "The lipstick you dropped in my drink—a sedative, yes?"

Jeri's face flushed with crimson as she fought for breath. "I don't . . . don't know what you're talking—"

Javier squeezed again, choking off her voice.

"So clever you are, waiting for me to pass out so you could take my money. Luckily I have a very high tolerance for such things." He shifted his grip and seized her thigh. "Now—

shall we consummate our earlier agreement? Yes, I believe we shall. Only now, I must insist that your services be rendered for free."

"Wait, *please*—"

Javier started to pull up her dress but then froze at the sound of something large and heavy hitting the entry door. He twisted her around clumsily, nearly falling in the process. "Who is that?" he demanded, his eyes wild and unfocused. Beads of sweat covered his forehead. "Your fucking *pimp*?"

Jeri shook her head. "Nooo," she hissed, frantic for air. She could feel consciousness beginning to fade.

Something smashed against the door again.

Javier released her from his vice hold and wrapped a thick hand around her throat. "Tell him to stop! Tell him to leave now or you will not leave this room alive!" He shook her angrily. "*Do* it!"

Jeri drew in a deep gasp of breath, her mind racing. She had only seconds to get free before her recruit made good on his threat. But even if she did, there was no way she could move the dresser and open the door before he was on her again—and she wouldn't get a second chance to escape.

The pounding on the door quickened. Javier shook her again.

"Tell him—*now!*"

Jeri's eyes flickered around the room. She needed another option. She needed something to throw him off guard. But what? What could she use against him? What could she say to a drunk, semi-sedated egotistical genius whose favorite hobby was abusing prostitutes when he wasn't working for—

She forced herself to smile.

Upon seeing this, Javier's face twisted into an incredulous scowl. "Do you really think I'm *joking*?" he demanded, his fingers tightening around her neck.

"Do you really think I'm a *prostitute*?" Jeri shot back, her smile broadening.

Javier's grip faltered. "What . . . what are you saying?"

"You said it yourself. I'm too smart to be a whore, Javier. Or should I call you *el hombre voraz*?"

A cloud of confusion crossed her recruit's face before mutating into an expression of rage. Jeri caught only a glimpse of his other hand streaking forward before a searing pain erupted across her face. "How the fuck do you know this?" he demanded, raising his hand to slap her again. "Tell me!"

Jeri bit back the pain and forced another smile. "Jose Muñoz told me."

Her recruit's eyes widened with shock. "No," He hissed, stumbling slightly. "El Jefe would *never—*"

"That man outside—do you really think he's here for *me*, Javier? But then, surely you knew this was coming."

Javier slowly released his grip on her throat and shook his head. "What do you mean?" he asked, his rage suddenly replaced with a pleading look of fear. Columns of sweat ran down his face. "Knew *what* was coming?"

Jeri regarded him with disdain and stepped toward the door. "Stop that nonsense!" she demanded, scarcely believing the strength of her own voice. "We'll be out in moment."

The pounding stopped.

She turned and faced her recruit. "A trade, of course." Jeri removed her earpiece and held it out for him to see. "Tonight's encounter wasn't just chance, Javier. We've been watching you for days. We know everything about you—what you do, who you work for . . . the kind of whore you prefer." She slipped her earpiece back into place and smiled. "Tell me—have I played a convincing one?"

Javier's dark eyes slowly focused on her. "What . . . what do mean, a trade?"

"I mean Muñoz and the cartel have decided to trade you for someone else," Jeri replied flatly. "You work for *us* now." She marched over to the overturned dresser and started pushing it away from the door. "Now help me clean up this mess you've made so we can go."

"And who . . . who is . . . us?"

"The Abergils."

"Abergil?" Her recruit mumbled. His round face slackened with disbelief. "The *Israeli* family?"

"Yes!" Jeri snapped impatiently, throwing her weight against the dresser. "Are you going to help me or not?"

Javier hovered unsteadily for a moment before shaking his head. "You're lying," he sneered, stumbling forward. "You lying, deceptive little bitch." A menacing smile formed on his mouth as he raised his hands.

Jeri gave the dresser a final shove before ducking under his grasp and rolling across the floor. "Max—you're clear!"

The room door exploded inward as Max barreled headlong into the room. Jeri looked up to see her colleague's towering physique lean down and collide with Javier Salas. The violent shoulder-to-stomach impact sent their recruit spinning. She watched with morbid fascination as he began to fall—the glint of light on his greasy hair, the rippling skin of his flaccid jowls, the vacant stare of his eyes—until realizing she lay directly in his path.

"Shit . . . *nooo*!"

Jeri scrambled onto her back just as Javier's massive

head and shoulders landed with a dull *thump* on her stomach, pinning her to the floor.

"Max—get him *off* me!"

Her colleague rushed over and seized their unconscious recruit by the shoulders and pulled. As he did, a low growl emanated from the obese man's stomach. Jeri and her colleague exchanged a wary look. Max pulled again and this time Javier's mouth gaped open. An ominous gurgling noise rose from his throat.

"Max, wait . . . he's going to—"

Before Jeri could react, a torrent of vomit spewed from Javier's mouth and splashed onto her chest. The pungent, sickly-sweet smell of spiced meats and stomach bile immediately filled the room.

Max rolled their recruit off of her and frowned apologetically. "Sorry about that." He stood and marched toward the door. "Be right back."

Jeri nodded and closed her eyes. A mixture of relief and exhaustion crashed over her. She fell back against the floor, too tired to care about the vomit now sliding down her skin. Then, without warning, her chest began convulsing. A soft moan escaped her throat, her eyes welled with hot tears. She laid there submissively, letting her body have its way, trying to decide if she was laughing or crying.

Freshman? Chilly's voice reverberated softly.

Jeri opened her eyes to find Max rolling an enormous container into the room. Next to her, Javier Salas lay prostrate, his wide back rising and falling to a slow, steady rhythm. "Our friend's finally asleep," she replied. "Max is putting him to bed now."

Good. And you?

"Covered," she said, the tears now stopping. "In vomit."

I'm sorry to hear that.

"Yeah, I bet you are."

A brief paused followed before Chilly spoke again. *Once he's tucked in, remember to wait six minutes before giving him a cigarette.*

"I know. I remember." Jeri sat up and watched as Max opened the container. Inside, the lifeless body of a large, heavy-set man in clothes that matched their recruit lay bagged and curled in the fetal position.

Two minutes later, Max and Jeri had the corpse unwrapped and arranged on the bed. After planting Javier's watch and wallet on the body and returning the dresser to its original position, they dragged their unconscious recruit into the container, attached a nasal cannula to his face, and adjusted the regulator on a small oxygen tank. Max checked Javier's pulse once again before closing and locking the lid.

"For you," he said, handing Jeri a half-empty pack of cigarettes and matches along with a small bottle of clear liquid. "By the way, good job tonight. I don't know how you came up with that, but it was brilliant." He stood and marched out the door, rolling the oversize case behind him.

Jeri's eyes lingered on the door before turning and walking to the bed. She pulled out a cigarette and slipped it into her mouth. "Chilly?"

Yeah?

"Did you happen to note the time when Salas collapsed on me?"

I did.

She lit the cigarette and inhaled deeply. "And—?"

Twenty-two minutes.

"Twenty-two," Jeri repeated, exhaling a long breath of smoke. She removed the cap from the bottle and poured a thin trail of the clear liquid onto the corpse's hand before continuing up the arm, shoulder and neck to its gaping mouth. "And you said the worst-case scenario would be—"

Twenty.

"That's right." Jeri held up the cigarette, admiring the smoldering glow of its tip. "Okay, I'm going to light up the package now," she announced, slipping it between the corpse's fingers.

No you're not. You're four minutes early.

Jeri stepped back as a small flame appeared on the package's hand. The flame grew quickly, blackening the fingers holding the cigarette and then moving up the wrist. Within seconds the entire arm was ablaze. She tossed the pack of cigarettes and matches onto the bed next to it.

Freshman?

Jeri waited until the face was engulfed in flames before turning and marching into the corridor. "Oops," she replied, closing the door behind her.

What do you mean, oops?

"Looks like I was a few minutes off."

You're kidding, right?

She made her way toward the hotel stairwell. "Oh come on, what's a few minutes?"

Freshman—

"Sorry, can't talk. I need to tell the hotel manager that my john is on fire." Jeri pulled out her earpiece and dropped it into the vomit-stained pocket between her breasts. Behind her, a tendril of dark smoke slipped through the door and curled along the corridor ceiling. "Freshman out."

PART II

Easy?
No, your new life was never intended to be easy.
And yes, at some point in the near future, you will find
yourself questioning the ethics of the agency's actions.
You will find yourself questioning the morality of your
own involvement.

Just remember two things—

Remember the reasons for your recruitment.
Then remember why you have chosen to stay.

Audio Recording #03.173 // 0913
Reference Index: >NewAgentOrientation<
Narrator: Shafer, R. >Shepherd<

17.

Go figure. That was what they'd called it.

It had been her father's idea—one of those silly games he'd invented for long winter days when all of the jigsaw puzzles had been solved and neither of them could stand to shuffle another deck of cards or roll another game of backgammon. The rules of the game were quite simple. Her father would start by asking Jeri a seed question—something subjective or not easily quantified. Questions like *What was the greatest invention ever created?* (she remembered that ice cream had been her immediate answer) or *When will man colonize Mars?* Regardless of the question, or Jeri's answer, her father's next question was always—

And why is that?

This was when the real game began. Jeri now had to defend her first answer with something more concrete. Something like—

Because ice cream is both nutritious and delicious. And because it's both, children eat it and stay healthy. And since healthy children do better in school, they end up smarter than they would've been without ice cream. And as everyone knows, children are our future . . . especially smart children. So really ice cream is helping to make the world a better place.

Next came the third and even tougher question. Her father would stare back at her with the somber face of an interrogator while he decided what aspect of her answer to further question or challenge.

And exactly how nutritious is ice cream?

Everything hinged on the all-important third question. Not only did her answer have to be thorough, its delivery had to be convincing. She always sat up straight and looked her father squarely in the eye.

Extremely nutritious. Ice cream is mostly made of milk, cream and sugar. Milk and cream provide carbohydrates and protein, which are essential to a growing child. They also have vitamins and calcium, which are necessary for both bones and cog— (What was that word again? Oh yeah, cog-nah-tiv) cognitive development. And of course sugar gives children energy.

The corners of her father's mouth would curl up or down depending on his assessment of her third answer. Jeri would then sit back and anxiously bite her lip as he worked up the fourth and final question. If she answered this one correctly—or with enough conviction to appear correct—she won the game. But if she paused too long or wavered in her response, the consequences were—

And who invented ice cream?

Jeri's eyes widened into saucers. *Who invented ice cream? Oh that's easy. Ice cream was invented in the sixteenth century by...by a man named...Thomas...Phil...Philopeus.*

Her father's eyes always revealed the verdict before he spoke. A convincing answer received a simple nod before a new question was posed and the game started over. But when Jeri failed to deliver a convincing answer—as in this case—her father's mouth would twist sideways into a cartoonish smile. He'd then point his thumb at the volumes of Encyclopedia Britannica that lined the living room bookshelf and announce the penalty.

Go figure.

And go figure it out she would, sulking over to the row of glossy numbered spines and quietly pulling out the Propædia to find the answer that had eluded her. *What do you think I should look under?* she would sometimes ask, hoping her father might give her a helpful hint. But his answer was always the same—

What do you *think you should look under?*

(Dramatic sigh.) *Never mind.*

In truth, she'd always enjoyed the hunt for whatever answer had eluded her. Like the game itself, time and boredom seemed to vanish as she sat scouring the volumes of glossy, gold-edged pages for answers. Along the way—and perhaps best of all—other interesting tidbits of information were serendipitously discovered, which Jeri would excitedly relay to her father.

Oh my gosh . . . Dad! Did you know that elephants can smell water up to three miles away? Holy cow! There's a tribe in Papua, New Guinea that cuts off a living tribeswoman's finger when someone dies! No way . . . it says here that the Apollo 11 mission traveled over nine-hundred and fifty-thousand miles to the moon and back. That's crazy!

By the time she was twelve, Jeri's *go figure* responses were detailed and polished. On the rare occasion they weren't based on fact, her improvisational skills and practiced confidence made it nearly impossible to tell the difference. And as the years went by and their silly game continued, her father watched with delight as Jeri's intellectual abilities blossomed. Perhaps he imagined his daughter one day using these skills to trade on Wall Street or conceive a brilliant argument in some high-profile legal case. Maybe he envisioned her as a masterful surgeon, making complex decisions over an open wound as she saved a human life. Whatever his dreams may have been for her career, Jeri now mused, she was quite certain that posing as a prostitute to collect an inebriated, overweight Mafioso with a penchant for rape was not among them.

But tonight, those skills had saved her life.

She raised her glass of whiskey—noting that the shaking in her hands had finally stopped—and silently toasted her father. Curious, she opened her robe and sniffed. The smell of Javier Salas's vomit was gone as well, effectively scrubbed into oblivion by two bars of soap before being smothered under a scented hotel lotion. The penalty was raw, greasy skin that now reeked of vanilla and lavender, but such were the consequences of a thorough vomit eradication.

And besides, there were worse bodily fluids she could have been dealing with.

Jeri was once again examining her limbs for bruises when someone knocked on the hotel room door. She decided not to move or utter a sound until whomever it was had gone. A moment later, the knock repeated. Then a voice broke the silence.

"I know you're in there."

Jeri rolled her eyes. Of course he did. What didn't he know?

"Are you going to open the door?"

She downed the rest of her drink and exhaled a resigned sigh. "What do you want?"

"To make sure you're okay."

"I'm okay."

"To *see* that you're okay."

Jeri rose from the bed with an effort and opened the door. "Shouldn't you be dropping off our new friend?" she asked flatly.

Chilly met her a stare with fleeting look of relief. "Tommy and Max are handling it," he replied. His eyes glanced past her. "Mind if I come in?"

Jeri shrugged and made her way back to the bottle of Jack Daniels on the nightstand. "Drink?"

"Sure. Got any tequila?" He closed the door and turned to find Jeri pouring two whiskeys. "Or a whiskey would be fine."

Jeri handed him his glass. "To being okay," she said, briefly raising her glass before draining it empty. She eyed her colleague expectantly.

Chilly followed her lead and nodded with admiration. "You've got to admire those Kentucky boys."

"Tennessee," Jeri corrected.

"Oh, right . . . Tennessee." He leveled his stare on her. "So—"

"Don't," Jeri interjected, pouring another round. "There's nothing you can say that Mr. Daniels here hasn't already told me." She resumed her position on the bed. "You are free to leave with a clear conscience, Mr. Sam Chilly. Or you can stay and drink with me if you'd like. Just as long as the subject of conversation isn't about me being fine—which I am."

Her colleague pulled out the desk chair and dropped into it wearily. "Alright, what would you like to talk about?"

"I don't know. Something *normal* people talk about?"

Something other than how fucked up my life has become since you shot a tranquilizer dart in my back? Of course, who knows if you and I can even *have* a normal conversation."

"Oh, I think we can. Where should we start?"

Jeri shook her head. "Just start talking and I'll tell you if it interests me."

Chilly nodded and sniffed the air. "Do you smell vanilla?"

"Nope. Next topic."

Her colleague studied her robe. "Is that a hotel robe?"

"Yeah, why?"

"No reason. I just never wear hotel robes. It's the terry cloth—feels like sandpaper on my skin. Plus it's a magnet for pubic hair. I guarantee you that thing's harboring a fugitive from every guest that wore it before you."

"What?" Jeri scanned the front of her robe. To her horror, a curly black hair was tangled in the fabric of her left sleeve. "Fantastic. Thank you for the public service announcement. Next topic."

Chilly rubbed his chin, thinking. "Oh—have you tried the torresmo plate from the room service menu? Too much garlic in my opinion. But the caruru was surprisingly good."

"I've just spent twenty minutes scrubbing vomit off my skin. You really think I want to talk about food?"

"Well, you asked me to pick a topic, didn't you?"

"I did. Now pick another one."

Chilly took another sip of his whiskey and studied the glass. "Jack Daniels. Is that your favorite?"

Jeri glanced at her own glass and frowned thoughtfully. "You could say it's my comfort drink."

Her colleague nodded. "My dad's too. Actually, it was

his *everything* drink. His *comfort* drink, his *dinner* drink, his *had-a-bad-day* drink. Definitely his *had-a-good-day* drink. And if Mr. Daniels wasn't on-hand, Mr. Beam was always waiting on stand-by in the cupboard." He swirled his glass, lost in the memory. "Anyway . . . it's a good one."

"Wow—did we really just go from the room service menu to unresolved daddy issues?"

"Who said it was an issue? My father was a good man. Worked hard, did whatever my mother asked. His worst offense was sitting in his reclining chair every night with a drink and a smoke, griping at the all stupid sons of bitches on the evening news. Other than that he was pretty quiet . . . even more so after he was diagnosed." Chilly drained his glass and looked at Jeri. "So—new topic?"

"No, this one's okay," Jeri replied. "Was it cancer?"

"It was indeed."

"How old were you?"

Chilly fished a pack of Camel Lights from his pocket. "You mind?"

"Seriously? We're talking about cancer and now you want to smoke?"

"Come on, if this agency's taught you anything by now, it's that none of us get to pick what kills us. Besides, a smoke ring is the closest I'll ever get to a halo." He lit a cigarette and took a drag, his expression turning somber. "I was eight when he was diagnosed. And no, it wasn't lung cancer, if that's what you're presuming. It was pancreatic—one of those really nasty cancers that doesn't leave much room for hope. But my father never said a word about it. Never complained, never asked why. In fact, the only time I ever saw him break down was when the chemo took away his taste for whiskey. Funny, huh?

175

Most people worry about losing their hair or getting sick in public. Not him. He could've cared less about that. But being robbed of his evenings with Mr. Daniels?" Chilly paused and shook his head. "He died on my eleventh birthday."

Jeri regarded him silently for a moment. "I'm sorry, Sam. That's . . . awful."

"Yeah, awful. And maybe the best present I ever got." Her colleague eyed her through the coils of cigarette smoke rising past his face. "You'd have to live with someone dying of cancer to understand. Eventually you reach a point when you just want it to be over . . . for everyone's sake."

"What happened to you afterward?"

"Oh, you know, the typical fallout—anger, rebellion, a spectacular display of juvenile delinquency. My mother decided something had to be done before either she went crazy or I went to jail, so we moved to a new town. A few years later she met a nice guy and remarried. He and I didn't get along too well at first, but things eventually settled down. From then on it was typical family dysfunction." He took a drag of his cigarette and poured another whiskey. "Enough about me. What was it like growing up with the great James Stone?"

Jeri shrugged. "What do you want to know?"

"Just start talking and I'll tell you if it interests me."

"He was a great dad . . . the best I could've ever hoped for. He was smart and kind and the most—" She sighed and took a drink. "He was the best."

"And your mom?" Chilly asked.

Jeri narrowed her eyes on him. "I'm sure you've already read all this in my file, but I appreciate you feigning ignorance for the sake of conversation. The truth is, I don't remember my mom. She died of breast cancer when I was three."

"That must've been tough."

"For my father, yes. But not for me. I remember the looks I'd get as a kid whenever someone found out I didn't have a mom. That ridiculous look of pity, that *you-must-have-it-so-hard* stare. But honestly, I rarely gave it a second thought. A mom? Who needed a mom? I had my dad. He was more than enough. And trust me, I had my evidence. Whenever my dad traveled for work I'd have to stay with my aunt—my mom's older sister—and my two bratty cousins. Talk about torture. My aunt was always running around screaming at us to do things or to stop doing things or to come to dinner or go to bed. The only time I'd see her smile was when my uncle got home. She'd look at him and say "your turn" before disappearing into her bedroom to watch TV and forget everyone else existed. Every time I left that house I was convinced I was the luckiest kid in the world for *not* having a mom."

Chilly cocked his head. "You really thought that?"

"Absolutely."

"Sounds a little warped if you ask me."

"Says the guy who thinks his father's death was the best birthday present he's ever gotten."

Chilly took a drag of his cigarette and nodded. "Guess we both have our issues."

"They're not issues," Jeri retorted. "They're just experiences. We were both kids, we both lost parents, and we both found a way to deal with it. It's only an issue if you're still to holding on to the anger—or still trying to figure out who to blame."

Her colleague's dark eyes studied her intently. Jeri adjusted the collar of her robe, sending a fresh assault of vanilla and lavender into the air.

"I appreciate the free therapy," he said finally. "But you might want to consider cutting back on daytime TV. Oh, and by the way, you're wrong."

"About what?"

"About your file. I never read the section about your mother. I was more interested in the section labeled 'potential concerns'—like your bedwetting, for instance."

Jeri gave him a thin smile. "You picked the wrong night for bad jokes."

"Are we still not talking about what I came here to talk about?"

"It depends. What is it you feel so compelled to say?"

Chilly studied his cigarette for a moment. "I missed something tonight. Something that put you in danger. And I'm sorry for that. I did a little research before stopping by. It seems our Plan-B sedative had a delayed effect on our recruit thanks to the blood pressure medication he's taking. It was inhibiting an enzyme in the liver that . . . well, I doubt you want to hear the physiological details, but—"

"But you're saying you missed that one *too*."

"Correct."

"Got it." Jeri finished her drink and poured another. "And this is where I'm supposed to smile and say 'forget about it . . . it's no big deal . . . this stuff happens all the time'—right?"

"Not exactly."

"No? How come? Oh, that's right—because you *never* make mistakes." she said, her tone biting. "Wasn't that what you told me? How we couldn't afford mistakes with so much at stake?"

Chilly's expression hardened. "What's your point?"

"Oh, I'm just doing the math," Jeri shot back. "What's

the statistical probability of someone going from a flawless record to making *two* critical mistakes in a single night—maybe one in a million?"

"So you don't believe me." Her colleague shook his head. "Which means you obviously don't trust me."

"On the contrary," Jeri retorted. "I *do* trust you. That's why I refuse to believe that anything that happened tonight was a mistake. You just needed a few plausible reasons—or "mistakes" as you call them—for changing the script. After all, everything's a test, right? How else were you going to evaluate my ability to deal with the unexpected?"

"Is that really what you think?"

"Do I have a choice?" She gave him a broad sarcastic smile. "Did I pass tonight's test?"

"You mean other than ignoring my order to stay in the bathroom, or lighting the package on fire too early? Sure." Chilly drank his whiskey and took a deep drag of his cigarette. "And what would you say if I told you that tonight's mistakes were real?"

"I'd ask you what's more important—that I trust you, or believe you? Because you can't have both. Not this way. But don't get me wrong . . . I'd love to believe that you might actually be human and make mistakes on occasion. But if you want me to trust you, to risk my life like I did tonight, I have to know that you don't." Jeri leaned over and poured him another whiskey. "So . . . what will it be?"

Her colleague held her stare, noting the sharp light dancing in her eyes like the embers of a fire. He smiled and raised his glass. "To trust."

"To trust," Jeri repeated. "May it last longer than the whiskey."

A brief silence passed as they drained their glasses and exchanged looks. Chilly's stare shifted to the sliver of exposed skin on her chest. "Did he hurt you?"

Jeri looked down, suddenly aware of her own nakedness beneath the thin robe. "No. Just a few bruises."

"Are you sure? Sometimes more serious things don't show up until—"

"I'm sure. Where are they taking him?"

"Salas? He's on his way to Sydney. Apparently the data frameworks he created for online money laundering could also revolutionize critical patient analysis for the healthcare industry . . . like matching global organ donors with recipients in a fraction of the time it currently takes." Chilly paused and gave her a grin that bordered on smug. "Imagine . . . the fat man from Bogota is now going to be a life saver."

"And you really expect him to cooperate?"

"He won't have much of a choice. Either he puts his mind to something useful, or we ship him back to the Muñoz family and feed them a story about Salas working for another drug cartel. Between a mafia-style execution or honest work in the private sector, I think he'll choose the latter."

"Great. And do his new employers know they're also getting a three-hundred pound monster that enjoys recreational drugs and using hookers as punching bags?"

Chilly nodded. "Brilliant minds don't always make for good people, Jeri. I'd love to say this was the first time we've had to deal with this type of thing, but it isn't. But like everything else, there's a protocol. Salas will go through a detox program and some intensive counseling before he's allowed to work. Who knows—he might even come out of this a seminormal person." The tip of his cigarette glowed as he took a drag. "See? Like I said—not *ruined*, just *redirected.*"

Jeri's eyebrows shot up. "Don't tell me you picked Salas and put me through hell tonight just to make that point."

"It doesn't matter what I tell you. You wouldn't believe me anyway." Her colleague snuffed out his cigarette and stood. "I've got to go. Enjoy the whiskey and your aromatherapy. I have to say, the lavender's nice, but I'm not a fan of vanilla."

"That makes two of us." Jeri pointed at a knotted plastic bag by the door. "Speaking of disgusting things, would you mind tossing that out for me?"

"What is it?"

"My dress. Along with dinner and a few drinks."

Chilly walked over and picked up the bag. The dress inside shifted and fell to the bottom with a syrupy thud. "Shame," he mumbled.

"Hardly."

"That was a nine-hundred dollar dress."

"Well, now it's a casualty of war. Hey . . . Sam?"

"Yeah?"

Jeri waited for him to turn and look at her. "How were you recruited?"

The cloud of emotion that crossed her colleague's face was as swift as it was dark. He stood motionless, his stare burning into her. Then, just as quickly as it came, the cloud vanished. His gaze dropped to the floor. "Doesn't matter."

"Why not?"

"Because it's history. Because you can't go back."

"No, but you can at least talk about it."

"I was serious about the daytime TV."

"And I'm being serious now. Why won't you tell me?"

"Because there's nothing to tell. I was recruited just like

you and everyone else. You already *know* what I went through. Dragging out the specific details doesn't . . . " He paused and shook his head. "Trust me, it's much easier to look forward than back."

"Yeah? And what if I don't *want* to look forward? What if I decided I *can't* go forward? Where does that leave me?"

"You don't have a choice. None of us do."

"Bullshit," Jeri scoffed. "Here's a hypothetical question—what if you *had* made a mistake tonight and I had been killed. Would that have changed anything? Would that have changed your resolve for what we're doing?"

"I don't have time for hypotheticals," Chilly replied sharply. I work with facts, with *absolutes*—and I know for a fact that what we're doing is necessary. I also know for a fact that you were brilliant tonight. Christ, for a minute, you had me almost believing we could—" He paused and looked at her, his eyes burning with thought.

"What?"

Her colleague slowly smiled, the light in his eyes fading. "Never mind."

"Come on. Will you please—"

"Two down, one to go, freshman." He said, turning to go. "Don't take your eye off the prize."

"Sam—"

"Good night."

Her colleague vanished through the doorway.

Jeri watched the door close behind him. "Goodnight," she mumbled before rising from the bed and stumbling into the bathroom. She tore off the pubic hair-tainted robe and examined her naked body in the mirror. A patchwork of darkening bruises dotted her arms, chest, and back. The cheek that her recruit had slapped was red but no longer swollen, giving her face an asymmetrical glow. Her shoulders and legs ached. And as she met her own stare in the mirror, it was suddenly obvious that she was now more than a little drunk.

Jeri walked back into the bedroom and grabbed the half-empty bottle of Jack Daniels on the nightstand. "You know what I like about you, Jack?" she asked, topping off her drink. "I can always rely on you to get the job done. And trust me, that's hard to find these days."

She picked up her glass and started to take a drink when she noticed an envelope lying on the desk. Even from a short distance away Jeri could make out the words scribbled on the front—

Keep calm and carry on.

"God*dammit*, Chilly!" she screamed, slapping clumsily at the air. Around her, the room abruptly began to pitch and spin. Jeri leaned down and grabbed the bed, trying her best not to spill her drink. The spinning quickened. "Okay, fine," she conceded, dropping the glass onto the nightstand. She shuffled to the bed and collapsed, her mind giving in to the whiskey and exhaustion before her body reached the sheets.

18.

"Where exactly are we going?"

Adam Cowell glanced out the backseat window of the white Escalade as it slipped south across the Golden Gate Bridge into the city. Up front, the two men in matching Brooks Brothers suits didn't respond. Their silence no longer surprised him. Since his meeting with Security Director Nielsen twenty-four hours earlier, Adam had been under the near constant eye of Nielsen's men—and not once had either of them uttered a sound. Instead, they'd kept the director true to his word—subjecting the research assistant to a barrage of drug tests and psychological evaluations before finally sequestering him in the company's executive retreat house an hour north in Sonoma. Luckily, the overnight accommodations had done wonders for his frayed nerves. The large, Spanish Colonial-style mansion with its stuccoed rotundas and bougainvillea-draped courtyards was as peaceful as it was opulent. By the morning's breakfast, staring out at the rolling landscape of vineyards while picking at an egg white omelet, Adam had even begun to feel something bordering on optimism.

Unfortunately, the feeling vanished when one of the Brooks Brothers received a call and the two men promptly shuffled him back into the vehicle.

Now, as they made their way through mid-morning traffic, Adam once again felt his anxiety begin to spike. He leaned forward and rested a hand on Brooks Brother #2. "Excuse me—could you please tell me where we're going?"

The man glanced down at the pale, freckled hand on his shoulder with a look of repulsion. "Sit back."

"Come on . . . I at least have the right to know where you're taking me."

"Sit back," the man repeated. "Now."

Adam sat back as ordered. "Fine, whatever," he said irritably. "Look, I'm not an idiot. I know you're just trying to rattle me. But you're wasting your time. I haven't done anything wrong. *Any*thing."

The Escalade swerved from the 101 and descended into the Broadway Tunnel. For a brief moment Adam imagined his escorts stopping the vehicle and executing him gangster-style in the darkness, but moments later they emerged from the tunnel and turned right onto Columbus Avenue. "This isn't the way to the corporate campus, you know," he mumbled as they skirted past Chinatown and the Financial District.

Outside, the landscape mutated from opulent high-rises and trendy urban lofts to corrugated garages and dilapidated storefronts. A short distance further, Brooks Brother #1 steered the Escalade into a narrow alley and parked in the shadow of an old warehouse.

Brooks Brother #2 raised his phone to his ear. "We're here. Yeah . . . okay." He stepped from the vehicle and opened Adam's door. "Let's go."

"Where are we going?"

"Get out of the vehicle, Mr. Cowell."

Adam reluctantly stepped from the warm comfort of the back seat. The security agent seized him by the arm and led him toward a nearby service door. Halfway there, the door opened and the muscled figure of Ray Foster appeared.

"I'll take him from here."

Adam felt himself being passed like a fleshy baton as the Velgyn security manager took his arm and pulled him inside. "Jesus—what's up with the man-handling?" he demanded.

"Mr. Nielsen would like to show you something," Foster replied, leading him down a narrow corridor.

"Why aren't we meeting at his office?"

"Because what he wants to show you is here."

"What is it?"

"You'll see soon enough." They followed the corridor to a stairwell and climbed to the third floor. Once there, the security manager directed Adam down another corridor before halting at a closed door. "In there," he said, motioning the research assistant forward.

Adam stepped forward and opened the door. The room beyond was pitch black. "What about the lights?"

"Motion activated."

A ball of fear was gaining mass in Adam's stomach. He glanced at the stony expression on Foster's face and walked into the room. A few steps in, he paused and shook his head. "They're not coming on."

The door closed behind him.

Adam spun in the darkness. "Hey! *Hey!* What the hell?" He stumbled forward, then stopped himself. *It's just mind games* he thought, taking a deep breath. *Stupid little mind games.* He turned and stood for a moment, listening. The room around him was silent. He raised his arms and slowly shuffled forward.

Despite waving his arms, the research assistant didn't notice the table in front of him until striking it with his thigh. He immediately grasped it, his hands sweeping the smooth, cold surface for anything that might reveal where he was or what this was all about. His hand knocked into something warm. He picked up the object up and examined it with his fingers, his mind checking off details as he formed a mental image. *Small, cylindrical, heavy, a power cord on one end, warm—perhaps from recent use?—tapered on the other end to a metal shaft that ends with a thin, disc-shaped—*

His fingers caught the sharp, serrated edge of a blade. Adam furrowed his brow. *A saw* he wondered? He wasn't familiar with power tools. In fact, the only saw he'd ever used was in grad school when he'd had to perform—

He gasped and quickly lowered the saw back onto the table. As he did, his right hand knocked into something else. His fingers nervously explored it, tracing the familiar shape. *A bowl? Yes, a bowl. But what would a bowl be doing here? It would only make sense if this was an—*

Adam took another deep breath and dropped his index finger inside the bowl. A warm liquid covered the bottom. He raised his hand and rubbed his fingers together.

The consistency was right.

A thin whine escaped the research assistant's lips as he frantically felt around for a towel. This time his fingers brushed against something soft. He recoiled his hand in a flash of panic, but his curious fingers came forward and touched it again, stroking the wet stickiness of its smooth surface before pressing into its soft, yielding mass.

Adam stepped back from the table, trying to control

his fear. He wanted to deny the reality of everything he'd just touched, to rationalize it from existence, but the tactile evidence was irrefutable. He listed the items in his head:

a recently used autopsy saw,
a collection bowl filled with warm blood,
a freshly removed human organ.

The darkness around him seemed to deepen, as if taking form and weight. He wasn't just standing in front of an autopsy table. He was standing in front of an autopsy that was still in progress. The obvious question was why. Why here, in this empty warehouse? And why was he being forced to discover it? What did any of this have to do with him or—

Paul Obermeyer.

A cold chill passed through him. Was that it? Was that what—or rather, *who*—was lying in front of him? Not some random corpse, but the charred remains of his former boss and mentor? Adam shuddered at the thought. But still, it made no sense. Why had Nielsen gone to the trouble of putting him in a dark room with Obermeyer's body? Was this some sadistic way of getting him to confess—to force something out of him in a moment of panic?

A cold sweat seized him.

"I didn't do this, you sick *fucks!*" the research assistant exclaimed at the darkness. "I didn't kill Paul!" His heart was now pounding like a fist against his chest, his breath coming in frantic bursts. Disoriented, he leaned forward and reached for the edge of the table, but instead grasped something soft and warm.

To his horror, the object grasped back.

Overwrought with fear, Adam screamed and collapsed to his knees before convulsing into sobs. "I didn't do this . . . I didn't do this . . . oh god . . . I didn't . . ."

"Mr. Cowell?" a voice said softly.

The object grasping his hand offered a gentle squeeze.

"Mr. Cowell, are you alright?"

Adam opened his eyes to find the darkness replaced by the warm glow of incandescent light. He looked at the hand holding his. Beyond it, the gray eyes of Lars Nielsen regarded him with concern.

"I apologize," the Velgyn security director said, glancing up at the ceiling. "I don't know what's wrong with the damn lights in here. Must've gone off while I was in the other room taking a call. No wonder you were terrified—stumbling around in a dark room after Mr. Foster let you in. I rushed in as soon as I heard you shouting, but by then—" He shook his head. "Here, let me help you."

Adam said nothing as Nielsen helped him to his feet, his chest still shuddering with sobs. He glanced around at what appeared to be a large, early-twentieth century storeroom. Old brick walls rose high overhead to a wood beam ceiling. Rusty ceiling fans slapped at the air. On the far wall, in front of a phalanx of ancient-looking filing cabinets, a hastily assembled folding table held a laptop and a large flat screen TV. The research assistant started to look at the table next to him, but instead dropped his gaze to the floor. "Is it him?" he whispered.

The security director raised an eyebrow. "Excuse me?"

"Is it *him*?"

"Is *who* him?"

"Stop fucking with me!" Adam hissed. "I know what you're trying to do. Is that Dr. Obermeyer on the table?"

Nielsen studied the research assistant for a moment before turning to the table. "Dr. *Obermeyer*? Of course not."

"Then who is it?"

It's not anyone, Mr. Cowell. It's lunch."

Adam's attempt at a laugh came out as a thin, incredulous sob. "Oh really?"

Nielsen nodded. "Do you like sushi?"

Adam slowly looked over at the table. A large platter of delicately sliced raw fish glistened under the light. His eyes shifted to the bowl of murky brown liquid sitting next to it. "It can't be," he mumbled, dipping his fingers into the bowl and rubbing them together. The consistency was the same as before.

"Soy sauce," the security director said next to him.

Adam slid a finger along one of the pieces of sushi. *How was this possible? How could he have mistaken a piece of fish for—* He glanced around the tabletop. "Where is it?"

"Where's what?"

"There was a saw here—an autopsy saw." The research assistant held a shaking hand over the spot and nodded with certainty. "You *took* it, didn't you?"

Nielsen raised his hands in a gesture of obliviousness. "Mr. Cowell . . . are you sure you're okay?"

"It was right *here*!" he screamed, slamming his fists against the tabletop. The rows of neatly arranged sushi flipped into the air before falling back onto the platter with a wet, fleshy thud. "I *know* it!"

Both men both looked up as the door opened and Ray Foster stepped into the room, his right hand resting on a holstered sidearm.

"Everything's fine, Mr. Foster," Nielsen said calmly. "Mr. Cowell's just a little disoriented, that's all."

Adam's face twisted into a grimace. "Why are you doing this? I've already told you . . . I didn't have anything to do Paul's death."

Nielsen laid a hand on his shoulder. "I know you have, Adam. But we're not here to discuss that." He motioned to Foster, who promptly marched to the table with the laptop and monitor. "We're here to discuss your date the other night."

"My date?"

The director nodded and grabbed a piece of sushi. "What time did you arrive at the restaurant?" he asked, popping the fish into his mouth.

The research assistant thought for a moment. "Around four."

Nielsen turned to his security manager. "Ray?"

Foster tapped a key on the laptop. A still video image of the path along the Embarcadero leading to the Ferry Building appeared on the monitor next to it. "This was taken at 4:06pm," he announced matter-of-factly. He punched another key and a handful of frozen pedestrians began strolling along the path. The security manager pointed at a figure walking into frame on the left side of the screen. "There."

Adam immediately recognized the pale, pudgy figure in an aquamarine sweater walking toward the Ferry Building's Northwestern entrance. "See, I *told* you!" he exclaimed. He turned to the director. "Do you believe me now?"

"I believe you were at the embarcadero at 4:06 pm, Mr. Cowell. Which, by the way, is a bit early for a date, don't you think?"

"That was her idea. She wanted to meet early because she was supposed to see a friend later that night."

"And you obviously arrived separately."

"Yes."

Nielsen gestured at the screen. "Fine—so point her out to me."

They watched the surveillance footage for several more minutes. "I don't see her," Adam said finally. "She must not have come in this way."

"Okay, we'll try another angle." Foster switched to the recording of the Southwest view.

Moments later, the research assistant pointed at a figure stepping into view from the right. "That's her!"

Nielsen studied the woman casually strolling toward the Ferry Building. From what he could tell the woman was a close match to Cowell's earlier description—approximately five foot-six, with a thin, athletic build and long, dark-brown hair. He turned and nodded. "So that's your accomplice?"

"Accomplice?" Adam gazed at the security director as if he'd gone mad. "What are talking about? This video proves I was on a date!"

"On the contrary—Ray, show us the view from the Northwest camera again. And this time take us forward to around 4:45pm."

"Got it."

"How many times were you in communication with this woman before your date?" Nielsen demanded.

Adam's eyes darted back and forth between Nielsen and the monitor. "I already told Mr. Foster all that yesterday. Like maybe three or four times."

"Give me a precise number."

"Uh . . . four times. Yeah, four times. She contacted me, I responded, she said she'd like to meet, and . . . and I confirmed."

"*She* initiated contact with *you*?"

"That's right."

"And did she also suggest the location of your meeting in addition to the time?"

The research assistant nodded eagerly. "Yes."

"Okay, here we go," Foster interrupted. "We're looking at the northwest corner of the building where Mr. Cowell entered at 4:06 pm. It's now 4:45. On the right side of the screen in the distance is the main entrance. Unfortunately, the camera positioned there was offline at the time. However—" He pointed to the right of the screen. "Look here."

Adam and the Security Director inched closer and watched two figures step from the main entrance and march toward the street. The research assistant's voice hissed softly like air escaping a tire.

"Noooo…"

Nielsen nodded. "Even from a distance you can't miss her—or your aquamarine sweater. And the timing fits. Assuming normal traffic, it takes approximately thirty minutes to drive from the Embarcadero to the Annex lab in Berkeley—putting you back there sometime around 5:15pm. Of course, we already know that at 5:23, you walked back into the lab and spent four minutes collecting something. And that *something* was Paul Obermeyer's encryption key."

Adam shook his head. "No," he muttered, his lips trembling. "It's not possible. I didn't . . . "

The security director placed a hand on his shoulder. "You know Adam, if finding sushi in the darkness was terrifying, imagine what I could do to you if I *really* got creative." He looked at his security manager and the two men exchanged a smile. "But of course, we don't need to worry about that, do we? Because you don't remember any of this." He squeezed

Adam's shoulder reassuringly. "No, all you remember is meeting a beautiful a woman for a blind date, and having too much to drink. Does that sound about right?"

Adam nodded, his eyes welling with tears. "Yes."

Nielsen nodded. "There won't be any more tests, Adam. You've given me everything I need. Mr. Foster is going to walk you out, and our two friends outside will take you back to Sonoma. The only thing you need to worry about for now is getting some rest. Ray?"

The security director absently watched Foster lead the emotionally wrecked research assistant out the door. His first instincts were right—Obermeyer's death and the theft of his encryption key were both masterfully executed by professionals, and Cowell was nothing more than a well-played patsy. Christ, the man had nearly shit himself just fingering some sushi in the dark. Unfortunately, the only value Obermeyer's former assistant offered now was the possibility of remembering something useful. But that was an outside chance, and certainly not worth waiting around for. The director turned and studied the frozen figure of the brunette woman on the monitor. Only one thing was certain—

Their real target was not going to be found so easily.

Moments later Foster returned. "So—what now, boss?"

Nielsen pulled out his cellphone and called up a number. "We keep using our greatest asset," he replied, putting the phone on speaker mode.

"Which is—?"

"Fear."

The phone's ring echoed through the large room. "Federal Bureau of Investigation, Chicago office," a husky female voice answered.

"Pat Vorder's office, please."

A moment later the call was transferred and a man answered with a practiced tone of impatience. "Pat Vorder."

"Pat, it's Lars Nielsen."

"Nielsen? Doesn't ring a bell," the man replied gruffly. "Unless you're talking about that asshole I worked with at Lilly." Both men laughed before Vorder continued. "To what do I owe the pleasure?"

"I wish this was a social call, Pat. But it's not. I'm into something here. Something serious."

"Alright. Whadda ya got?"

"A lab theft two nights back. We're still putting the details together, but it looks like someone got their hands on some very serious materials."

"Define *serious*," Vorder demanded, resuming the tone of an overworked federal investigator. "Are we just talking about some intellectual property, or are we talking about virus samples with bio-terrorism potential?"

"Both." The director eyed Foster. "But I don't want to blow things out of proportion just yet. The reason I'm calling is because I've got a surveillance video that might have captured one of our perpetrators. I need some quick expertise to ID them."

"How quick?"

"You know the drill, Pat. We're measuring everything in hours right now."

"Well, I'd tell you to send it to our forensics guys at the Digital Evidence Lab, but they're working a three-month backlog on cases. You'd need to show some solid proof this was a national security threat to move to the front of the line, but they still couldn't come anywhere close to the turnaround time you're asking for."

Nielsen nodded. The last thing he wanted was a team of mediocre bureau analysts fumbling through their video. "What about private sector consultants? Know anyone you can recommend?"

A long sigh followed as his former colleague thought. "Yeah, I might. We had a criminal case last year that required some video analysis I couldn't get internal resources on. Hired a firm in Boston that did some good work for us. Fast too. But I'll warn you now, they aren't cheap."

"Especially if I want them onsite," the director added.

Vorder emitted an incredulous whistle. "I knew I should've ignored my patriotic sentiments and stayed in pharmaceuticals. Tell me—do those crisp new hundred-dollar bills still chafe when you wipe them on your ass?"

"I'm ready for that contact info, Pat."

"Yep, that sounds like the asshole I knew at Lilly," Vorder scoffed.

The security director jotted down the information and quickly ended the call. He handed the information to Foster. "Get their entire team on the next flight out. Then tell maintenance to get some guys down here and clear this floor. Starting tomorrow this is our new tactical operations center." He turned and pointed at the brunette woman on the monitor. "That's out new target—*Lady X*—and no one goes home until we know who she is. Got it?"

"Got it, boss." Foster pulled out his phone and marched back to the corridor.

Nielsen waited until he was alone before dialing another number. A moment later, someone silently answered on the other end. "It's been a while," he remarked.

"Indeed it has," a low, digitally altered voice replied. "What can I do for you?"

"I may need some help," Nielsen answered, selecting his words carefully. "A young woman has managed to get herself into trouble. The worst kind of trouble. Normally I wouldn't bother. But this one . . . this one definitely has something worth saving." His gaze once again settled on the frozen onscreen image of Cowell's date. "Are you still in the business of saving lost souls?"

"Of course. And I'm always here for a friend."

"Good. That's all I need to know—for now. I'll be in touch."

"Very good," the voice replied. "I'll look forward to your call, and to working with you once again."

Nielsen ended the call. "Lady X," he whispered softly, smiling at the monitor. "You have no idea who's coming for you." He raised his hand to the screen and brushed her cheek with his finger. "But you will soon enough."

19.

"Before we get started, has everyone met Dr. Obermeyer?"

Derrick Birch surveyed the faces around the table as they collectively nodded and looked at Paul. "Great, then let's begin. Chung, you want to kick us off?"

Across the table, a stocky forty-year-old Chinese researcher—nearly departed crewmember #5 according to Birch—stood and began briefing the team on his latest work. Strange terms like *demulsibility* and *kinetic viscosity* colored the conversation, and within minutes Paul Obermeyer found his mind drifting. The briefing continued around the table to a distinguished-looking Middle Eastern researcher named Shahid—nearly departed crewmember #2—before moving on to the energetic, ever-smiling Marcello—*numero uno*! Paul's attention continued to wander until it was crewmember #4's turn.

The attractive, slight-framed Russian researcher named Tatyana Aleksandrov rose and updated the team on improved yield ratios from thermal resonance. When she was done, Dr. Aleksandrov promptly sat and nodded at Birch.

"Very good." Birch turned to Paul. "I know you've only

had a few days to get settled in, Dr. Obermeyer. But would mind giving us a quick update on your progress?"

"Sure." Paul felt all eyes around the table turn to him as he opened his notepad. "I've had a chance to review the incubators and oversee the preliminary samples from the gene sequencers. I should have a first run of plasmids isolated tomorrow, with initial gap sequencing started right after." He paused and smiled at Marcello. "By the way, nice job on setting up the sequencers. I couldn't have done it better myself."

Across the table, Dr. Aleksandrov scoffed. "Marcello didn't set them up," she said, narrowing her green eyes on him. "I did."

"Oh, I'm sorry. I thought it was Marcello."

"And you were mistaken."

Paul held the Russian researcher's stare. "Thank you for setting up the sequencers."

"You're welcome."

Birch studied both of them with a look of amusement before rapping his knuckles on the table. "Alright, thanks everyone for making Paul feel welcomed. Now—let's have a collective reality check." He pressed a button on the computer tablet in front of him. The room lights immediately dimmed.

Paul followed everyone's example and swiveled his chair toward a large screen descending from the ceiling. A blue graph materialized on its surface.

"Here's our current performance dashboard," Birch continued, gesturing at a formation of brightly colored lines rising and falling in various trajectories across the graph. "Alterations to the catalysts seem to have paid off," he said, circling a small uptick in one of the lines with his laser pointer. "Refinement yields are up two-tenths of a percent since the new coatings. Nice work, Chung."

The Chinese researcher nodded.

"Marcello's newest configuration for the cultivators looked promising, but so far the simulations are only showing a one, maybe two percent increase in gross biomass yield. Not exactly the kind of numbers worthy of a full-scale retrograde. Shahid's citrate additives gave us a big boost on the cellular counts in the lab. Unfortunately, numbers from the trial run in one of the cultivators weren't as exciting."

Heads nodded in consent as Birch's laser dot drifted around the graph.

"But here's what I want everyone to focus on." The project leader pressed another button on the tablet and the chart morphed into a table of numbers. He stood and aimed his pointer at the last column. "Our gains in both efficiency and yield have continued to level off in the last four weeks. And even best-case simulations of our current ideas aren't pushing us into viable production numbers." Birch paused and looked around the table. "Short of an eight-point gain in current output, the minister and I will have no choice but to consider Ceres a failure. And we all know what that means."

A few grumbles echoed in response.

"Ceres is ten times larger than any other biofuel facility in the world—and at least four times more efficient," Shahid retorted, shaking his head. "We should be proud of what we've accomplished thus far."

"Absolutely," Birch replied. "We should all pat ourselves on the back for what we've done so far. But it won't change the fact that we still haven't accomplished our goal."

Tatyana gestured at Paul. "Is that not why *he* is here—the *miracle* geneticist?"

Paul looked over to find the Russian researcher gazing at him with something between a smile and a sneer.

"No, that's why we're all here, Dr. Aleksandrov," Birch retorted. "I don't expect Paul to have any more miracles in his pocket than the rest of us." His eyes flashed to Paul. "But yes, I *do* expect brilliant ideas. And the sooner the better."

A union of protests erupted around the table. The project leader curtailed them with a wave of his hand.

"Hey look, I know everyone's tired. I'm tired too. If you need a break, take a break. Hell, take a day off and go wander the compound or play in the sand if you want. There's no question you deserve it. But it won't alter the reality of what we're up against. The only thing that's changed with this mission is the speed at which we're accomplishing it—and we all know time is of the essence. Does anyone disagree?" He nodded at the silence. "Good. Then let's get back to work."

Paul stood and began to follow the others when Birch gestured for him to stay. "How are you doing?" the project leader asked.

"Well, if the purpose of that meeting was to make me feel even more alienated, disliked, and out of my element, it worked."

"Yeah, sorry about that." Birch rubbed at his cleft chin and sighed. "You just have to understand that you're coming here under some particularly challenging circumstances."

"What do you mean?"

"I mean the rest of us have already had a few months to get to know each other and develop a certain camaraderie. Don't get me wrong—putting a bunch of brilliant egomaniacs together is always asking for trouble. We've had a few good battles around here—especially in the beginning. But the five of us have also established a certain amount of mutual trust and respect."

Paul shook his head. "I can't believe I'm asking this, but why didn't you bring me in sooner?"

"Because at the time I didn't know a geneticist was needed. Unfortunately, as I said, we haven't been reaching our goal fast enough. So the decision was made to bring you in. But your presence isn't just arousing the normal suspicions, it's also bruising some very large egos."

Paul took his seat again. "I suppose that explains why Dr. Aleksandrov isn't particularly warm to me."

"Actually, Dr. Aleksandrov's issue with you is another matter entirely. She actually agreed with my decision to bring in a geneticist. The problem was that she had her own candidate in mind."

"What was wrong with her choice?"

"Several things—not the least of which being that he wasn't you. He was also a former colleague of hers, which I didn't like just on principal. Too many *unknown dynamics*, if you know what I mean. But even if I'd agreed it wouldn't have mattered. The guy has a wife and kids. That alone disqualifies a candidate from being brought in by our recruiting firm. Apparently being single is the one ethical requirement they don't deviate from." He laughed and shook his head. "Lucky us, huh?"

Paul gave him a half-grin.

"Don't worry. Tatyana will come around just like the rest of them—especially if you turn out be as brilliant as I expect." Birch's expression turned somber. "But that isn't the only reason I wanted to talk to you."

"Okay . . . what else?"

The Ceres project leader walked over and closed the door. "Do you recall a story in the news from about two years back regarding a private jet that crashed in central Iran?"

Paul shook his head. "Afraid not."

"I'm not surprised. I doubt many people even heard about it. Remote location. Corporate-owned jet. One of those 'mechanical failure' accidents you hear about on occasion. At least that's the story the big three made sure was released."

"The big three?"

Birch nodded. "The world's three largest oil producers—Axcon, Petronus, and GBP."

"So what—you're saying it wasn't mechanical failure?"

"No, I'm saying it wasn't accidental," Birch replied flatly. He sat down next to Paul. "The plane was owned by Hartman Webb—one of the largest surveying firms out there. Companies like Hartman Webb are sanctioned by both governmental and industry regulatory agencies to do two very important things for the oil industry. The first is to identify potential untapped oil reserves and assess their viability based on a simple yield-potential to cost-of-extraction equation. The second is to audit—or, in some cases, re-audit—existing reserves and provide an objective assessment of their remaining yield potential. Now, if this was a perfect world and new oil fields were still popping up like spring daisies, Hartman Webb would be primarily focused on their first job. But that's not the case. In fact, if you were to look over their financial sheets like I have, you'd see that seventy percent of their revenue for the last five years has come from auditing existing fields. Which means—"

"Which means the oil industry is more interested in finding out what's left in the existing pools than what's still out there to find," Paul interjected.

"Exactly," Birch affirmed. "Everyone's suddenly double-checking what they're sitting on. And what does that mean? It means everyone is finally beginning to fear what we already know to be true—the end of oil is coming soon. It also means the big three are in crisis mode. And big companies in crisis mode are like any other big animal trapped in a corner—they'll lash out at anything in order to survive."

"Like sabotaging a plane and literally killing the messenger?" Paul asked with a tone of skepticism. "What would be the point?"

"Business 101. Any company that accepts that their primary commodity—in this case oil—has both a *finite* and *quantifiable* supply remaining also knows that their long-term survival is predicated on one thing—the price of that commodity. The people on that plane had just finished an extensive audit of something called the Dauletabad gas field—one of the largest natural gas fields in the world. They were heading to Dubai to submit their findings to their client when the plane experienced engine failure and fell out of the sky."

"And?"

"Exactly what you'd expect—a big fucking hole in the ground. Six Hartman Webb employees and their pilot all killed. I doubt there was much left of anyone for investigators to identify. And yet,"—Birch's eyebrows arched toward his receding line of brown hair—"the report they were carrying survived."

Paul shook his head. "How is that possible?"

Birch shrugged. "Apparently they lock them in crash-proof cases for just such a precaution. You have to realize that this is highly sensitive information. But regardless of how it survived—or, more likely, how it got there—the report they found was deemed legitimate. And what it said was that the Dauletabad gas field was nearly empty." He quickly stabbed the air with his finger. "I know what you're going to ask—why would the big three go to the trouble of murdering innocent people just to submit a report that *confirmed* what they feared was true—that the world's fossil fuels are running out?"

"Yes—why?"

The project leader gave Paul a devious grin. "Just imagine the repercussions of that information. The moment that report went to their client—a capital market firm owned by a large bank—it sent a shockwave around the financial industry. Suddenly the future of natural gas sounded as dubious as oil. Big investments being made in natural gas infrastructure were immediately thrown into question. Of course, once that report hit the commodities markets, everything went ape-shit. In just two days, natural gas prices rose more than forty percent." Birch's grin widened. "And guess what rose twenty percent right next to it?"

"Oil," Paul mumbled.

"That's right. A price increase of that nature for even a few *weeks* equates to billions in profit for the big three. And don't think they aren't heavily invested in natural gas interests as well. But short-term profits weren't their only objective. No, the true brilliance of their plan was revealed when Axcon, Petronus, and GBP all challenged the validity of Hartman Webb's assessment of Dauletabad—the one supposedly pulled from the wreckage—and submitted lawsuits demanding a re-audit by both another sanctioned auditing firm as well as their own teams of field engineers. Now this was a big deal, because throwing a sanctioned firm's findings into question challenged the whole regulatory structure of the industry. Nevertheless, they won the lawsuit, a re-audit was ordered, and—no surprise—it turned out the original report was indeed wrong. Really wrong. The Dauletabad gas field wasn't nearly empty. In fact, the second firm verified last year that it still has more than eighty percent of its remaining yield potential intact. The big three's own engineers then went in and of course confirmed the same number." Birch shrugged. "That news set off the second panic. Suddenly everyone was questioning the truth about the world's remaining oil reserves. Were they really as bad as these auditing firms were saying? And once everyone began questioning the auditors themselves, it was fairly easy for the big three to get what they were *really* after—a complete overhaul of the auditing and reporting regulations."

"I still don't understand," Paul shrugged. "What does this have to do with me?"

Birch quickly tapped his fingers against the tablet lying in front of him and slid it over to Paul. "This is an email I received from Minister Razam ten days ago."

Paul looked at the brief message on the screen—

Commencement of PAFB audit of Ghawar confirmed. Time is now against us. Acquire whomever necessary.

"Fallout from the Dauletabad report," Birch said somberly. "Both the regulation and international financing communities have taken the side of the big three and demanded new yield assessments of every major oil and natural gas field under their control. The Ghawar oil rights are now partially owned by a non-Saudi investment bank, so it qualifies. The Minister and the handful of Saudi government officials who know what we're up to have been fighting it for months. But at some point you realize that resistance only raises the same suspicions you're trying to avoid. The audit of Ghawar already started last week. But now—just as the big three have wanted all along—the audits are conducted through a collaboration of teams that includes their own geologists and engineers. Which means everyone is going to learn the truth about what's really under our feet here soon. And once they realize there's not enough oil to maintain a refinery of this size and start looking into this operation,"—he paused and drew a finger like a knife blade across his neck—"we're done."

"What do you mean, *done*?" Paul demanded.

The project leader eyed him with a mixture of irritation and pity. "These corporations killed seven people and tossed the world energy market into chaos in order have to exactly this—the opportunity to police the world's oil reserves and see what everyone else is doing. What do you think they'll do when they discover what we're up to here—politely ask us to stop?" He laughed bitterly. "Ceres represents the big three's biggest nightmare—the most commercially viable non-petroleum fuel manufacturer ever created. Trust me, given the chance, they *will* destroy it. And all of us with it. That is, unless we solve our production issues and show the world what we're capable of first."

Paul shook his head. "Jesus Christ . . . are you seriously trying to pin the success of this whole thing on me?"

"Yes."

"And you honestly think a genetic engineer from a pharmaceutical company is going to make the difference?"

Birch nodded. "I told this team that I needed you because you're the best hope we have of making this facility viable in the next six months. The truth is, I hired you because we need Ceres to be viable in the next six weeks, or all this will be for nothing."

"Six *weeks*?"

"Correct. That's roughly when the Ghawar audit will be completed."

Paul sat quietly for a moment, absorbing everything Derrick Birch had said. "You know," he said finally, shaking his head, "if what you're saying is the truth, and the world really does work this way, then maybe we *are* better off dead."

"Don't be ridiculous," Birch scoffed, rising from his seat. "You think I was stupid enough to recruit a quitter for this job? In the last seven years you've been the key researcher behind four different first-in-class drugs for Velgyn Pharmaceuticals. That's *unprecedented*. That's also why you're here. I didn't just pick you because you're brilliant—I picked you because you excel under pressure. So, now that I've applied the pressure—" He walked over and opened the door. "Shall we get to work?"

Paul glared at the project leader for a moment before collecting his notebook. "I hope you know me as well as you seem to think," he said, marching toward the door.

"We'll find out soon enough, won't we?"

"Just remember—I didn't ask for this. And I won't take responsibility for not meeting your expectations if this fails."

"Yes you will."

Paul paused in front of the paunchy, thirty-six year old project leader. "You know what? You're an asshole."

Birched grinned smugly. "Of course . . . which is exactly what this project demands." He spun and marched off. "Have a nice day, Dr. Obermeyer."

Paul watched the project leader retreat down a long

corridor of angular steel beams and reinforced concrete before taking the passageway toward his laboratory. He moved quickly, his mind reeling with this new information. *This can't be happening* he thought as he turned a corner and jogged down a flight of stairs. *Six weeks? Six fucking weeks? It just isn't possible!*

He ducked through a doorway, feeling his face flush with anger. *I won't even have the sequencing done in six weeks, let alone a plan for modeling the alterations.* A short distance further, Paul paused to get his bearings before taking another narrow corridor. The sound of approaching footsteps was lost to his whirling thoughts. *I won't do it. I won't be made to fail like this. Derrick can go fuck hims—* He glanced up just as Dr. Aleksandrov stepped from an adjoining corridor into his path, a stack of boxes precariously cradled in her arms. Their eyes met briefly before Paul barreled into the Russian researcher, launching her sideways through the air. He watched in horror as she crashed against the floor, scattering her payload of boxes. "Oh shit!" Paul exclaimed, rushing forward to help her. "I'm so sorry, Tatyana . . . I wasn't paying attention." The look in his colleague's eyes made him stop.

"Ne trogai menya!"

Paul shook his head. "I'm sorry. I don't—what does that mean?"

"It means *don't touch me!*" Tatyana hissed. She picked herself up, angrily mumbling in Russian as she collected her boxes. "And do *not* call me Tatyana. I am Dr. Aleksandrov."

"Well, I apologize for running into you, Dr. Aleksandrov. Can I help you with—"

"No, you may not," she snapped. "I need nothing from you, Dr. Obermeyer. And I certainly hope you need nothing further from me."

Paul stared after his colleague as she spun and marched down the corridor. He waited until she was a safe distance ahead before following. His earlier thoughts were momentarily forgotten, replaced now by his unspoken response—

Me too.

20.

"Everyone's up and running, boss."

Lars Nielsen nodded at his security manager and glanced around the room. The large storeroom on the second floor of the Velgyn archive warehouse had been transformed into a state-of-the-art operations center. Against an incongruous backdrop of old brick walls were two rows of modern workstations, their surfaces crammed with computers and monitors. A maze of cables ran from station to station before terminating at metal towers stacked with high-powered servers at the end of each row. Buzzing around the room like worker bees in a hive were nearly two-dozen men and women, all clothed in khaki pants and matching polo shirts emblazoned with the same company logo. Nielsen studied the faces around him and leaned toward Foster. "Which one's the ringleader?"

"Follow me." Foster led him toward a group of men huddled around a monitor and paused next to a thin, wiry-framed man with round glasses and a neatly trimmed goatee. "Mr. Evans, do you have a moment?"

"Absolutely, Mr. Foster," the man replied with a tone of just-hired enthusiasm. "What can I do for you?"

Foster gestured at his boss. "This is Mr. Nielsen, our

director of security."

Evans hastily dropped a large Starbucks cup on the desk next to him and offered his hand. "Pleasure to meet you, Mr. Nielsen," he exclaimed, amping the enthusiasm even further. "Nathan Evans, team leader. Do you have any questions I can answer for you?"

Nielsen shook the man's hand and pointed at the screen in front of him. "How do you intend to find her?"

The team leader shifted his gaze back to the monitor. "Well, sir, that's what my team and I were just discussing. We've been reviewing the video assets Mr. Foster gave us. Unfortunately, there's not a whole lot to work with in these files. As you can see,"—he leaned forward and pointed to a magnified image of their target walking toward the Ferry Building—"our subject—*Lady X* as I understand you call her—did a good job of hiding her identity. Between the hair obstructing her face and the large sunglasses, it's pretty much impossible to get anything useful for a facial recognition scan."

"Are you saying you spent all day setting up in here just to tell me this is impossible?"

"No . . . not at all. I'm just saying we can't rely on facial scans for this project." The team leader's mouth curled into a smug grin. "Trust me, Mr. Nielsen. If anyone can figure out who this woman is, it's our team."

"Then I'll ask again—how are you planning to do that?"

"It's called morphetics," a nearby voice answered curtly.

The security director turned to find a young woman with short, spiked red hair and an arsenal of ear piercings typing away at the next workstation. "Excuse me?"

"You asked how we're going to find her," the woman replied, her eyes fixed to one of the several large monitors in front of her. "The answer is morphetic analysis."

"Gentlemen, this is Mary Adler, our biomechanics expert," Evans interjected, shooting his colleague an angry look. "Miss Adler doesn't usually work onsite with our clients, but she's one of the best digital image analysts in the industry."

"What's morphetics?" Nielsen asked.

"Great question," Evans replied. "Put simply, morphetics is an incredible new technology we've developed to—"

The director raised a hand to the team leader. "Miss Adler?"

"Body and behavioral analysis," Adler replied, giving Evans a sidelong *go fuck yourself* glance. "It's built on biomechanics analysis software that was originally developed for the sports industry. Here, I'll show you—"

Nielsen and Foster stepped closer and watched as a still frame of *Lady X* appeared on one of Adler's monitors.

"First, we isolate the subject's body from the video one frame at a time and assign reference points," the biomechanics expert continued. "This takes a while, but it has to be done precisely. Once a frame is done, it looks like this—" She pressed a few keys and the image of *Lady X* was overlaid by an outline of her figure. A myriad of color-coded dots marked her body at selected joints and anatomical features. "From here, we generate a 3D model—"

The director watched as Adler dragged the completed image into a sophisticated-looking application on the second monitor. A few seconds later, a three-dimensional wireframe model appeared on her screen.

"This is what we call the subject's BCI, or *Body Composition Identity*. Every time we add a new frame of reference points from the video, the BCI gets more accurate. And because the video frames we're loading are sequential,"—she tapped a key and the wireframe model began walking forward—"we also get a movement signature. At this point we can re-apply her surface map." Adler tapped another key and the walking wireframe was instantly wrapped in a 'skin' that included Lady X's outfit and long brunette hair. "And there you have it—a completed body print."

Adler spun her chair around and Nielsen noticed that in addition to spiked red hair and piercings, the young biomechanics expert was also a fan of heavy eye shadow and Pussy Riot t-shirts. An intricate tattoo of a rose vine with long thorns curled up her right arm and disappeared under her sleeve. He furrowed his brow. "A body print?"

"A morphologically distinct identity of the person we're after," Adler replied with a tone that suggested her craft had long ago lost its excitement. "You see, looked at separately, a person's BCI and movement signature are not all that unique—maybe one in a thousand. But together they create a body print that's very unique. More like one in a million. A surface map can make them even more so, but surface maps aren't always reliable. If our subject changes anything—hair, glasses, even clothes—the surface map won't match. That's why we don't normally use it in our first round of searches. Anyway,"—she gestured at the rack of computers at the end of the row—"now we'll compile our subject's body print and load it on the servers to start searching against videos that exist in the cloud—or, you know, the Internet—and see what we get. "

The security director nodded. "How long will it take?"

"Hard to say," Evans replied, resuming control of the conversation. "We could get a match in a few hours, or a few weeks. As you can imagine, there's a lot of video content out there on the Internet—especially when you include private security video, which we definitely want to include. For now, we're limiting the search criteria to only include videos uploaded within the last seventy-two hours and within a fifty-mile radius of the immediate area. If we don't see results within two hours, we'll expand the search parameters."

"Fine. Get it going."

"Yes sir." Evans turned and addressed his team of video experts with an air of authority. "Alright everyone, listen up! We're about to commence our search for the subject. Mary's team will continue preparing frames and updating the body print. John's team will refine the search criteria. I want all incoming results reviewed and prioritized immediately and loaded into the system every fifteen minutes for my assessment. Any questions? Good—then let's find our subject before she infects half of the population."

Nielsen leaned toward his security manager as consultants whipped into action around them. "What the hell did you tell these guys, Ray?" he asked quietly.

Foster shrugged. "Remembered what you said our greatest weapon was? Well, I just gave these guys the idea that our Lady X might've stolen something, you know . . . *viral*."

"Like what?"

"Like maybe Ebola."

The security director suppressed a smile. "I said our greatest weapon was *fear*, Ray—not *panic*. Remember, the last thing we need is any of this getting out to the press. All these guys signed non-disclosure agreements, right?"

"Yes sir."

Evans turned and nodded. "Well, gentlemen, now it's just a question of time. Our full team will be here through the night. Tomorrow morning, we'll break into shifts so there's always a team working. Who should I call if we get something?"

"Mr. Foster," Nielsen replied. "But you won't need to call him. Until this is over, he'll be staying here with you." He turned to go. "I'll be back in the morning."

Behind him, the video analysis team leader spoke up again. "Don't worry, sir. We'll find her."

Nielsen paused and stared back at the slumped, concentrating figure of Mary Adler. The young woman gave him a terse nod before focusing on her monitors. "I'm sure you will," he replied, not bothering to look at the project leader. "Just do it quickly."

21.

Hyde Park, London
February 17, 9:14pm
The Regrets of Excess, England

J-

This place is a bust.

Don't get me wrong. I like the eternally gray skies of London as much as any other poor bastard in the throes of a quarter-life depression. But enough already. Kensington hangs on me like the tongue of a tired bloodhound, and I've already lost the scent of everything I came here to find. And decent tequila? Harder to find than a pack of American fags. Yes, I'm talking about cigarettes.

Maybe it's time to take this act underground.

I may speak the language, but the English still mystify me. Does everyone here really speak like this, or am I stumbling between sets of Sherlock and Dr. Who? I swear if one more fair-skinned bar lass peddles me a crumpet, someone's getting a patent-leather kick to the cockney. Has all sense of indecency gone down the tube in this land of tweed-clad candy-asses? What I wouldn't give for a stout beer and a stouter dollymop to nosh up the pain of your absence.

I'm sorry things got so bodged up between us the last time we were together. Don't think I'm not trying, but sometimes when you stoke the fire too early, all you get is a roomful of ashes. All I know is that my heart still burns for you as painfully as it did this morning after that duffer served me gurty pudding in the food hall at Harrods. That's why we have to give this one more shot.

Our kids will be gorgeous, a chuisle mo chroí. I have the artist renderings to prove it.

I'd love nothing more than to continue tickling your inner chi, but I'm off to the circus of Oxford to meet a distant relative. Apparently I have a fourth cousin twice removed on my mother's side that lives in Marlyebone (Photo enclosed). She wants to catch some Sara Dumont film, but I'm hell-bent on seeing that French love flick, Le Trivale. Regardless of who wins, I suspect we'll both be in for a ride.

Ta!
- C

p.s. Of course I won't sleep with my fourth cousin twice removed. Stop watching Downton Abbey.

22.

"If you're here for a wardrobe suggestion, forget it."

Jeri went back to reading her book when a second knock shattered the silence.

"For chrissake…lemme in!" a thickly accented voice demanded.

Jeri rose and marched to the door of her hotel suite. She'd barely opened the door when Dublin's short, pudgy figure pushed past her and marched inside. "It's not like I've got better things to do," he grumbled, fishing a pack of cigarettes from his pocket and dropping onto the couch.

"Sorry Dublin, I thought you were—"

"Enjoyin' a quiet night in are we?"

"I *was*." Jeri took a seat in the chair across from him, wary of getting too close. "Feel free to make yourself at home, but this is a non-smoking room."

The Irishman laughed. "The fook it is. What, is the manager gonna kick me out for smokin'?" He stabbed a cigarette between his scowling lips and ignited the tip.

Jeri leaned forward and snatched it from his mouth. "My rule, not theirs," she said, snuffing it in the ashtray on the coffee table. "So—what's up?"

Dublin stared at the ruined cigarette as if it were a murdered favorite pet. "Change of venue. Chilly wants you on at Bank instead of Oxford Circus . . . just in case."

"In case *what*?"

"In case ya get yer period?" Her colleague pulled out a cell phone and began thumbing the screen. "Fook if I know. He didn't elaborate."

Jeri watched with a mix of amusement and revulsion as Dublin lifted his shirt and absently scratched at a roll of ghost-white skin. "Are you always in a shitty mood, or just when you're around me?" she asked.

"Oh I'm sorry, freshman—do I seem a bit edgy?" The Irishman tossed his phone onto the coffee table. "Maybe you should try *my* job sometime. I'll happily switch places if you like. Ain't like yours, ya know . . . dressin' up all pretty to go poppin' recruits in the arse. I just spent five days scourin' the fookin' boroughs of all London to find tomorrow night's package. And did I? Fook yeah, I did. Pulled off another miracle like the lord Jesus himself. You should try slippin' into the coroner's box in Hammersmith at four in the mornin' to shop for a corpse. We'll see how *your* mood is after."

Jeri considered him for a moment before nodding. "Good—so it's not just me?"

Dublin's eyes flashed with surprise before he slapped his knee and erupted into a fit of hyena-ish laughter. "No, I s'pose not," he hissed between gasps. "Now, for fook's sake—will ya let me have a smoke?"

"Is it a matter of life and death?"

"Of course it is."

"Fine," Jeri conceded. "Smoke away."

"God *bless* ya, freshman." Her colleague lit another

cigarette and took a deep, satisfying drag. "Jesus, I'm beat out," he sighed.

"I don't understand. If you really hate the job so much, why not just quit?"

Dublin studied Jeri through the veil of his smoke. "Habits, love. They don't just vanish with our previous lives, ya know? I might be dead to the rest of the world, but I'm still the same daft bastard I've always been. Why else would I have a kid to support?"

It was Jeri's turn to look surprised. "You have a kid?"

"A boy."

"But, what about the strict rule against any agents or recruits having a family?"

"I suppose it only counts comin' in," the Irishman replied. His lips parted to reveal a nicotine-stained smile. "Ya see, I wasn't exactly an upstanding citizen before Chilly snatched me up. And old habits die hard. Apparently I knocked up this brasser in Galway a few years back. At least that's what the homely bitch says. And it ain't like I can take a DNA test to be sure." His smile faded as he took another drag. "You know the deal. Savin' the world with the likes a' you bastards wasn't any more my choice than yours. But it sure as fook pays good. That little chiseler could go to fookin' Oxford with the money I'm puttin' aside for him."

"And you're telling me that Chilly—mister rule maker himself—knows all about this?"

Dublin nodded. "Sure he does. But of course, he's got his *own* hobbies. Everybody does. I've got my drinking and womanizing, Tommy's got his Playboys, Sly's got his Pokémon Go. And our Chilly-boy? He's got all those broken souls to mend." He caught the confusion in Jeri's expression and continued. "He doesn't know that *I know* about his extra-curricular activities, but I do. You see, Chilly never liked staying in these swanky hotels like the rest of us. Up 'til now, he always picked some shite place in the slums. At first, I just figured he was scoring something for a different kind of habit. I even trailed him a few times to see what he was in to. But truth be told, that boy's got no vices aside from cigarettes and tequila. Turns out he just likes helpin' the dregs of society. Even spied him workin' in an AIDS clinic once, if you can believe that." The Irishman shook his head. "A regular Mother fookin' Teresa, that one."

Jeri narrowed her eyes on him. "What do you mean, up 'til now?"

"I mean he doesn't do it anymore," Dublin replied. "Not since you showed up."

"But . . . *why*?"

Her colleague shrugged. "Who knows. Maybe he's got a new hobby. Or maybe he's just found a new soul to mend that doesn't require a trip to the fookin' slums—like his own, for instance." He ripped the cigarette from his mouth and pointed it at her. "But don't get any fookin' ideas about sayin' anything. That there's our little secret."

"Yeah, of course." Jeri nodded as her colleague slipped a hand into his faded jeans and casually adjusted himself. Despite this, she was certain her sudden feeling of unease had nothing to do with him.

"So—we clear?"

"With what?" she asked, lost in thought.

"The tube, for chrissake. Get on at Bank, not Oxford Circus. Got it?"

"Yep. Got it."

"Ain't feckin' rocket science, freshman." Dublin rose from the couch. "Alright, well . . . I'm off. Can't waste any more precious pub time sittin' here with you now, can I?" He paused and looked her over, his thoughts as obvious as the Bowie album screened across his vintage t-shirt. "Fancy a pint or two with your favorite fixer?"

"What? Oh, thanks for the offer, but I—"

"Don't fraternize with half-witted Irish scumbags?"

"Exactly."

Jeri walked her colleague to the door. There, she paused and looked at him. "Do you know how he was recruited?"

"Who—Chilly? Fook if I know. Why?"

"No reason," Jeri shrugged, suddenly regretting she'd asked. "I was just curious."

Dublin eyed her with suspicion. "Curiosity, huh? I'd be careful, love. If I recall, that shite fookin' killed the cat."

"Maybe. But satisfaction brought him back."

The Irishman's breathy hyena laughter echoed in the entryway. "You know, I like you, freshman. You can sleep with me anytime you'd like."

"Yeah, well, unfortunately you're already spoken for. Speaking of—how did she find you? The mother of your . . . child."

"She didn't," Dublin retorted gruffly. "Like I said, love— habits. For some reason I keep goin' back to tha very things I should be runnin' from." A wry smile pocked the corners of his fleshy cheeks. "Maybe you and I ain't so different." He slapped Jeri on the shoulder and marched into the hallway, a coil of smoke trailing in his wake. A few steps later, he stopped and looked back. "Shouldn't be too hard to figure it out though, ya know?"

"What's that?"

"We both know he was a doctor," the Irishman affirmed, keeping his voice low. "And his accent . . . sounds an awful lot like yanks in—where is it—Chicago? Assumin' he's been doin' this gig for about five or six years now . . . who knows? Might just be enough to go on." He raised a hand in goodbye and strolled toward the elevators. "S'pose you'll be gettin' on the internet now, eh love?"

Jeri waited for her colleague to disappear around the corner before closing the door and snatching her laptop from the counter. Within seconds she was planted on the couch typing a query of "Chicago doctor Sam death" into a search engine.

The first page of results displayed bold headlines containing the word "fugitive". Jeri clicked on one of the links and—to her relief—realized she had stumbled on the story of Sam Sheppard, a Cleveland physician who was famously charged with the murder of his wife in 1954. A quick scan of the page indicated that this particular Sam was the inspiration for the sixty's era TV series *The Fugitive*, which was later followed by a movie of the same name. *Interesting*, Jeri thought, returning to the search results. *And luckily the wrong Sam.*

She broadened her query to "Midwest doctor Sam obituary" and was rewarded with a list of death announcements spanning the last two decades. But nearly fifty Samuel-something obituaries later, she was no closer to a death that appeared to be linked to Chilly.

Undeterred, Jeri cleared the search field on her screen and sat thinking. It had to be out there somewhere. After all, the last thing the agency would do is erase the news of his supposed death. The whole point of faking the deaths of agents—just like their recruits—was to create a credible trail of evidence and information that discouraged any further investigation. The only real question was where to find it.

That, and why Chilly's 'death' even mattered to her in the first place.

Jeri pushed the second question from her mind as an idea struck. She punched "Chicago police report database" into the search engine. A few clicks later, she was inside the Chicago Police Department's public records website and downloading a file of all district police reports from the last ten years. When it was finished, she opened the file and filtered the results by first name. Nearly three thousand reports beginning with "Sam" stared back at her. A quick filtering of unwanted names like "Samantha" and "Samir" reduced the number by half. Jeri then sorted these by date, focusing only on incidents occurring between four and six years ago. Five hundred and thirty reports remained.

Okay Dublin, let's see if you're right.

After studying a list of abbreviated incident codes on the police department's website, Jeri scrolled through the summary of incidents on the screen in front of her. It was soon apparent that the majority of the records were nothing more than traffic infractions and trivial misdemeanors. But halfway through the list, she noticed a curious entry:

Name (F)	Name (L)	Incid Date	Dist.	Code/Desc.
Sam	Lafeen	04/25	18/1834	ATL/MISPER

Jeri clicked back to the department website and looked up the definitions for the listed codes. As expected, neither was in any way ambiguous.

ATL: Attempt To Locate
MISPER: Missing Person

She typed "Chicago Sam Lafeen missing" into the search engine. An instant later, a column of results filled the screen. Jeri scanned several before clicking on a link to a Chicago news station article from nearly five years earlier. Her breath caught in her throat as a younger image of Chilly—face tanned, mouth stretched into a handsome grin—flashed onto her screen. Next to the image, an ominously worded headline jumped out in bold letters. Jeri broke her gaze from the familiar eyes staring back at her and scrolled down to the article.

Lincoln Park man still missing
Published April 28

Nearly three days after a Lincoln Park man went missing, officials say the search continues but hope is quickly fading.

Dr. Sam Lafeen, 30, was last seen walking alone on Lakefront Trail around dusk on the evening of April 25. Police were called to Navy Pier approximately two hours later when a suspicious bag was reported abandoned by the railing just outside of the Shakespeare Theatre. An investigation of the bag by police revealed no dangerous materials, but the bag and its contents were later identified as belonging to Lafeen, a plastic surgeon in his second year of residency at the University of Chicago Medical Center.

Despite an ongoing search effort, no other trace of Lafeen has been found. A search of the waters around Navy Pier by Coast Guard divers yesterday also failed to turn up any evidence.

According to investigators, a handwritten note left in the

missing man's bag may have indicated his intention to commit suicide. A spokesperson for the missing man's family said the day of his disappearance coincided with Lafeen's planned wedding date with his late fiancée, Laura Hammond.

Anyone with information on the whereabouts of Lafeen is asked to contact the police.

Jeri scrolled back to the top of the page and stared again at the photo of her colleague. "Nice to meet you, Sam *Lafeen*," she mumbled, making a sarcastic *tsk* sound with her tongue. She had to admit that the fiancée was a nice touch. But of course, it was also dangerous. Creating a fictitious relationship had undoubtedly required a complex web of lies and false evidence—all of which would've been scrutinized by authorities. So why go to the trouble?

She returned to the search engine and entered "Laura Hammond death." A long list of articles from both local and national news stations flashed onto the screen, all of them echoing the same ominous headline. As she scrolled down the list, a knot of dread formed in Jeri's stomach. Her finger hovered uncertain for a moment before clicking on one of the articles. A picture of Laura Hammond appeared and the knot in her stomach abruptly tightened. When she was done reading, Jeri went back to the results page and methodically read every other related article. When she was finished, she closed the laptop and walked to the window.

Outside, a light rain fell on the streets of London, turning the pavement around Grovsenor Square into a mirror of shimmering black. Jeri watched the passing traffic absently, her mind grappling with the information she'd just uncovered.

A few well-placed articles about Chilly's death could

have been easily dismissed as the work of Chip and the agency. But several articles, linking two tragedies together and authored by both local and national sources? This went far beyond their capabilities.

Which meant some, if not all, of the story was real.

Jeri stood at the window, quietly considering the ramifications. What if it were true? What if Chilly—a man named Sam Lafeen in his former life—truly *did* lose a fiancée named Laura Hammond to a horrible tragedy? Did the rest of the story seem that unbelievable? After all, who *wouldn't* consider suicide if faced with the same tragedy? On the other hand, if it were true, why bring someone in such a state of mind into the agency to begin with?

The more Jeri focused her thoughts on Chilly's story, the less clear the line between reality and fiction seemed to become. Every facet of his "death", if true, led to terrifying conclusions.

But there was something about Laura Hammond herself that worried Jeri even more.

23.

"Need some fuel?"

Paul Obermeyer looked up from a row of monitors to find Derrick Birch standing in the doorway of his laboratory, a large coffee in each hand. He nodded and rubbed his eyes. "What time is it?"

"One in the morning," Birch replied. The Ceres project leader walked over and placed a steaming mug on the counter next to him. "Did you get some dinner?"

"I don't even think I had lunch."

"You need to go get some of Marcello's paella in the kitchen." Birch rubbed at his stomach. "I'm beginning to think he's a better cook than scientist."

"Maybe later." Paul gestured at the two gene sequencers humming quietly next to him. "I want to get these last two plates run and analyzed before tomorrow."

"It already *is* tomorrow."

Paul stood and glared at the project leader. "You're the one that made it clear I'm on a deadline." He marched over to another row of computer monitors flashing long strings of gene sequences.

"You can't hate me for communicating the reality of

what we're up against," Birch countered. "But since we're on the topic . . . any progress to report?"

Paul studied the information onscreen for a moment, then tapped a key. The gene sequences vanished, replaced by a rotating three-dimensional model. He looked at it thoughtfully before gesturing to his colleague. "Come see for yourself."

Birch walked over and narrowed his eyes on the model. "Let me guess—the gene map for botryococcus braunii?"

"Correct." Paul nodded. "Well, at least the functionally relevant parts of it. I was able to accelerate the process by accessing an online genome mapping community called TARO and downloading some sections that were already completed by other researchers. That alone probably saved us a few weeks."

"Excellent. So what now?"

"Now the *real* work begins—figuring out how to coax a perfectly evolved single-celled organism into yielding thirty percent more dry-mass hydrocarbons in half the normal time."

Birch nodded. "Any idea how you're going to do it?"

"Nope."

A smile creased the project leader's face. "Well, you've got about six weeks to figure it out."

"Six weeks," Paul repeated incredulously. "Do you realize it took nature *millions* of years to get our little super-algae this far?"

"Of course I do." Birch raised his arms and glanced around the room. "And now the world's smartest genetic engineer has *millions* of dollars worth of equipment to finish the job." He slapped Paul on the back. "But you do need to eat. How about I grab you some of that paella?"

Paul grimaced as he stared at the monitors, his fingers

punching at the keyboard. "Is it spicy? I don't do spicy."

His colleague laughed. "Of all the things I'd expect you to be shitting your pants over right now, spicy foods isn't one of them."

"Thanks, but I'll just stick with coffee."

Birch shrugged. "Suit yourself." Halfway to the door, he paused and glanced back. "I'll check back with you later this morning. Need anything else?"

"Some help would be nice."

"With—?"

Paul stopped punching keys and sighed. "Look, the only way of achieving anything in six weeks is to run multiple tests concurrently. I'll try methylation, amplification, silencing—everything I can think of—until we get a phenotype that shows promise. But I don't have time to design the experiments *and* set them up. I could use an extra pair of hands to speed up the process."

"Okay," the project leader conceded. "Qualifications?"

"The smarter the better."

Birch scratched at his chin. "I know someone that's got time to spare right now. Even has some experience in your area."

"Fine—they're hired."

"Great. I'll have Dr. Aleksandrov report to you first thing tomorrow morning."

"Sounds goo—" Paul tore his eyes from the screen and glared at Birch. "Wait—*who*?"

"Dr. Aleksandrov. She's completed most of her critical work. Plus she's got a PhD in molecular biology. Might be good to have her here just to kick around ideas."

Paul twisted his mouth skeptically. "I don't need someone to kick around ideas. I need someone to follow my orders. Besides, the only thing Dr. Aleksandrov seems interested in kicking around is my head."

"She's Russian, Paul. What do you expect?"

"What about Marcello?"

"Marcello is redesigning the cultivator intakes. Shahid and Chung are both busy as well. So, you can have Tatyana." Birch raised his hands impatiently. "You want her help or not?"

Paul glanced again at the DNA model rotating on the monitor in front of him and nodded. "Have her stop by tomorrow morning. I should have the incubators set up by then."

"Will do. Goodnight."

Paul continued to gaze at the monitors for untold minutes before remembering his coffee. He stood wearily, exhaustion pulling at his limbs while acid churned in his empty stomach. He picked up the coffee and took a sip only to find it lukewarm and bitter. He took another sip in a desperate hope for improvement before grimacing and tossing it in the trash.

It's decided he thought glumly, glancing around at the sterile emptiness of his lab.

I'm officially in hell.

24.

Sara Benton was terrified.

She refused to look at the object as she ran down the steps of the underground station, her locks of curly brown hair fluttering beneath a white woolen cap. An eclectic mix of Londoners from Borough Market foodies to Hackney hipsters filled the subterranean passageway, but the thirty-one-year-old researcher hardly noticed. She slipped through the Old Street ticket gate with her eyes fixed forward until she reached the northern line platform. Once there, Sara found a bare patch of wall to lean against and took a deep, calming breath.

Had it really happened? she asked herself while a blur of commuters scuttled past. The last hour of her life felt like a surreal dream. Perhaps it had been a dream. Perhaps her mind was just playing a cruel joke.

Of course, there was only one way to be certain.

Sara slipped her left hand from her pocket and glanced down slowly. Even hidden beneath the black leather of her glove, the bulge on her finger was obvious. She touched the sharp, angular edges of its surface with her right hand. A wave of heat blushed her face.

Yes, it had really happened.

The hiss of electro-pneumatic brakes jolted the young researcher back to reality. Sara glanced up at the arriving train rolling to a stop at the platform. With the practiced impertinence of a daily commuter, she stepped forward and pushed her way onto the nearest car, her left hand pressed protectively to her chest. Once on board, she dashed to the nearest open seat and dropped onto the stiff plastic, anxious to be home. *Don't do it* she commanded herself. But of course it was no use. Sara removed her hand from her pocket and looked down.

An avalanche of both terror and elation fell upon her once again.

While the remaining commuters took their seats, Sara looked up to find a tall man with blond hair and GQ-worthy looks standing on the platform. The man's eyes swept the line of subway car windows before settling on hers. To her surprise, Sara felt the corners of her mouth twist upward into a smile as they exchanged looks. The man continued to hold her gaze as the doors closed and the train rolled forward. Moments later, the darkness of the tunnel filled the windows and the man and the station were gone. Sara blinked as if waking and shook her head. *Of all the nights to be flirting, this isn't one of them* she rebuked herself. Her eyes returned to the bulge on her finger. Suddenly the events of the evening became too much to bear alone. She needed to *tell* someone, to hear herself telling someone and know that it was real. But not to a train full of strangers. She needed to tell her best friend—

She needed to tell Mia!

Sara scoffed at the obviousness of this fact and pulled out her phone. It was only after she'd dialed her best friend's number that she noticed the 'No Service' announcement flashing in the upper corner. "Oh bugger off," she exclaimed, raising her phone toward the window in the hope of getting a signal.

"Service's always dodgy around Old Station," a young man seated next to her noted, shaking his head. "Should improve as we get closer to Bank."

Sara thanked him and went back to waving her phone in the air, her finger poised over the call button. "Come on," she mumbled, trying to will a single bar of service into existence. But none came.

She would just have to wait.

∼

Okay, freshman—Tommy just confirmed our friend's on the northern line to Bank, Chilly's voice announced in Jeri's earpiece. *Black coat . . . white cap . . . sitting in the third car. You ready?*

Jeri glanced around the long, brightly lit station. "Waiting at the platform now," she whispered, studying the growing crowd. She turned and retreated further toward the end of the platform. "Though I would like to know why you picked this station over Oxford Circus. This place is packed."

I wanted to make sure you had enough time on the train to find her. And, for your information, Oxford Circus is even busier.

"If you say so. No point in arguing with someone who's always right, is there?"

No, there isn't.

Jeri peered into the ink-black void of the northern underground line and shook her head. "I'm sure I won't have any trouble finding her. Unless—" She reached into the pocket of her overcoat and wrapped her hand around the cold, rubbery grip of the tranquilizer gun. "Unless there's something about this one I don't know about either. Any medical conditions you've forgotten to mention, or perhaps some prescription drugs I should be aware of?"

A long pause followed before her colleague responded. *Two minutes.*

Jeri smiled with an impish sense of satisfaction. "Moving into position." She made her way toward the idling swarm of commuters. "As I'm sure you're already aware, the platform's too crowded for normal comms. I'll let you know when we're heading your way." She swept a hand through her hair—now straight and copper-red— and concealed her earpiece. "Freshman out."

Two minutes later, a whispered hum rose to an echoing crescendo of electric engines and aggravated air as the northern underground line slipped into the station and rolled to a stop. The train's crimson doors hissed open in unison and the platform was instantly transformed into a collision of commuters both boarding and departing. From her vantage point in the crowd, Jeri watched a tall brunette wearing a white cap emerge from the third car and march toward her. She turned and looked away, but there was little chance of being noticed— the woman's attention was fully focused on the cellphone in her hand.

Jeri waited for her recruit to pass before falling in step after. A short distance further, the woman gasped with surprise and slapped the phone to her ear. Curious, Jeri closed the distance between them. She stepped onto the escalator behind her target and listened carefully.

Two steps in front of her, Sara Benton began speaking with breathless excitement.

~

"I thought you were having dinner with Oliver?"

"I did," Sara replied to her best friend's interrogative greeting. "I'm heading home. I would've stayed at his place tonight, but I have an early conference in the morning. So—" She paused and took a deep breath. "We'll just have to finish celebrating tomorrow."

"Celebrating what?"

Sara bit her lip and squealed.

"Celebrating *what*, Sara?" Mia demanded.

Sara lifted her left hand and gazed again at the bulge on her ring finger. "Oh, maybe two carats of flawless round cut diamond in a gorgeously simple setting?"

"Oh my god—he *did* it?" A piercing scream filled the line. "Tell me! I want to know everything!"

"It was crazy!" Sara exclaimed, unable to contain her excitement. She stepped from the escalator and began threading her way through the crowd "We were just finishing dinner at Busabo's when Oliver looks over at me and says 'hey, there's a new nightclub I want to check out.' So the next thing I know, we're walking down Rivington and turn the corner and I swear to god, Mia, there's a string quartet sitting on the sidewalk!"

"Noooo!"

"Yes! And Oliver acts completely surprised and says 'Will you guys play us a song?' and before I know what's even happening they start playing that John Legend song 'All Of Me' and—"

"Oh my god, I love that song!"

"And before I realize what's happening I look over and

238

Oliver's on his knee with this giant ring in his hand and—" Sara paused and caught her breath as her best friend erupted into another fit of screaming. When she spoke again, her voice was low and composed. "He told me I was the love of his life and that nothing would ever change that. Then he slipped the ring on my finger and said 'Will you do me the honor of making me the luckiest man in the world by saying yes?'" A soft peal of nervous laughter erupted unexpectedly from her throat. "So I said yes."

"Oh my god, I'm going to cry," Mia replied, her voice quivering with emotion. "That has to be the most romantic proposal I've ever heard. I can't believe you two aren't spending the night together."

"It's just as well." Sara shrugged as she continued through the arched maze of corridors connecting the northern and central platforms. "Oliver has to be up early as well to assist with a surgery, and I doubt we'd get much sleep tonight if we were together. Oh—and did I tell you? He's taking me to a romantic bed and breakfast in Eastbourne this weekend."

"Oh sod off, you spoiled bitch," her friend scoffed with mock anger. "I knew I should've found him before you did."

"Finders keepers." Sara looked up to find herself standing on the central line platform. "Hey, I'm in the tube right now and reception's a bit dodgy. I want to call Tess and give her the news before the next train. Meet me for a drink tomorrow evening?"

"Yeah, of course. And since you'll soon be the wife of a surgeon, can I assume you're buying?"

"Actually, I think it's traditional for the maiden of honor to buy the first round." Sara hung up as another elated scream pierced the air. She glanced at the crowd growing around her.

A redheaded woman standing nearby caught her eye and smiled. "Sorry for being so loud," Sara said apologetically. She pulled off her glove and held up her hand. "I just got engaged!"

"Oh wow—congratulations!" the woman exclaimed. Her amber eyes briefly studied the ring before searching Sara's expression. "Were you . . . expecting this tonight?"

"Not at all." Sara's gaze fell to the large sparkling stone on her finger. "I think I'm still in shock."

"I'd be in shock too if someone gave me a diamond that large," the woman said with a tone of envy. "He must be a good man."

Sara nodded and watched transfixed as the light played through the diamond. She looked up suddenly. "Oh my god, where's my head? I need to call my sister! I'm sorry . . . excuse me!" She turned and frantically dialed the number. "Tess! Are you sitting down—?"

Behind her, the redheaded woman listened quietly for a moment before pulling out her own phone to make a call.

∾

"Why are you calling me?" Chilly asked.

"Because I need to scream at you without looking like a nut," Jeri replied, marching toward the far end of the platform. "This is just another goddamned *test*, isn't it?"

"What makes you think—"

"Spare me the bullshit," Jeri interrupted, her voice quivering with anger. "I *know* you picked each of these recruits for a reason. Obermeyer to test my resolve . . . Salas to see how I'd react in a crisis. But this one? This one's just—" She turned and found her recruit in the crowd. Even from a distance, the woman's face gave off a glow of happiness as she spoke into her phone. "Call it off, Chilly. Call off the collection."

"And why would I do that?"

"You know why," Jeri said flatly. "She's engaged."

A brief pause followed before her colleague responded. "Engaged?"

"Yes."

"Okay, so . . . what does that matter?"

Jeri briefly pulled the phone from her ear to look at it with dismay. "What does that matter? Are you serious? One of our fundamental rules of collection is that no one with a spouse or children is recruited!"

"That's right. And she has neither."

"Oh come on—you want to destroy two people's lives over a *technicality*?"

"It's not a technicality, it's a rule. And it works. If we called this collection off because of an engagement, what would be next? Calling off a collection because someone got a Valentine's card? Calling off a collection because someone was in love? You have to draw the line somewhere."

"So draw it *here*," Jeri hissed, shaking her head. "Look, this is different. You of all people should understand why this is—"

"What?" Chilly demanded. "What should I understand?"

Jeri looked over at the sound of a low rumble echoing from the tunnel. Moments later, a blur of train cars emerged and rolled to a stop. "Please don't make me do this."

"You know what you need to do, freshman," her colleague replied. "Now show me you can do it."

The sharp click of Chilly ending the call shot through

241

Jeri like a jolt of electricity. She studied the phone in silent shock before slipping it into her pocket. A short distance away, the doors of the central line train slid open and the shuffling dance of commuters played out once again. Jeri looked up and watched the faces around her with cold detachment. Then something caught her attention—a tousle of brunette hair topped by a white cap bobbing toward the train. In an instant her focus returned. She set her jaw and nodded.

Chilly was right. She knew what she needed to do.

Overhead, a calm voice announced the importance of keeping arms and legs clear of closing doors. Jeri pressed her way toward the train, aware that time was now against her. The high-pitched whine of electrical engines stirring to life forced her into a run. The doors of the last car were just beginning to shut when she sprinted forward and jumped. By some miracle she slipped through the closing gap, caught the overhead railing, and landed on both feet. Nearby passengers eyed her with a fleeting look of surprise as the doors sealed shut behind her and the train accelerated forward. Moments later, Chilly spoke into her earpiece.

Still with us?

Jeri turned her mouth toward her shoulder. "I'm here."

Good. You've got fourteen minutes to get your eyes on our friend, freshman. Enjoy the ride.

Jeri took a deep breath and began making her way forward as the central line train raced westward toward the next station. She moved casually through the cars, discreetly studying the faces around her. Four cars forward, she spotted her recruit seated between a grim-faced older woman and a man toting a piece of luggage. The man adjusted his grip on his bag as the train began to slow. Anticipating his departure, Jeri moved closer and slipped into the man's seat as he rose for the next station. A minute later, the train had completed its stop and was again accelerating onward.

Jeri reached up and muted the microphone on her earpiece. She then turned to her recruit and smiled. "So, when's the big day?"

"What? Oh . . . hi." Her recruit smiled, recognizing the woman she'd spoken to on the platform. "We haven't set a date yet," she shrugged. "But I'm thinking next spring. Maybe early June? It's so pretty here in June."

"June is nice," Jeri nodded, glancing around to make sure no one else was listening. Satisfied, she gave her recruit a shrewd smile and motioned her closer. "But can I give you a little advice?"

Sara Benton hesitated for a moment before grinning curiously. "Sure."

As she leaned in, Jeri deftly slipped her fingers under the researcher's long brown hair and seized her neck. "The next time you decide to invent a more effective hydrogen fuel cell," she whispered, pressing her mouth to her recruit's ear, "keep it to yourself."

25.

"Six days, Lars."

The voice of the Velgyn CEO rang with crystal clarity inside the leather-trimmed cab of Nielsen's Jaguar coupe. "Six days since Obermeyer's death, and you still haven't produced a goddamn thing."

Nielsen downshifted and deftly threaded the powerful vehicle through slower moving traffic on the Bay Bridge as he sped back to the Brannan Street warehouse. Ahead, the San Francisco skyline shimmered in the late afternoon sun. "I'm as frustrated by the pace of our investigation as you are, Michael."

"Oh, are you?" Manning retorted. "That's interesting, because I thought *I* was the one that needed this matter to be resolved before the special shareholders meeting." The sound of his fist slamming against his desk reverberated from the car's perfectly balanced speakers. "What is it going to take, Lars—more resources? More men?"

Nielsen clenched his jaw. He'd been expecting this conversation. In fact, he was surprised it hadn't occurred several days sooner. "We're utilizing every resource necessary to pursue the leads in-hand," he answered evenly. "Something should turn up soon."

"That's your most definitive answer—something should turn up soon? And exactly what is your definition of soon?"

A long pause filled the air as Nielsen weighed his response. "Three days. Give me three more days to find something definitive."

"Or?"

"Or I'll hand you my resignation."

A hollow laugh echoed inside in the car. "And what would that solve?" Manning asked. "You walk away and leave me stuck in this crisis with no one to fix it? No, I couldn't allow that, Lars. This situation has the potential to destroy my credibility with the shareholders—if not threaten my position as CEO. And if I'm anything, it's a *trickle-down* kind of leader. I'll give you the next three days to produce something definitive. But don't get any illusions about quitting. We're in this together, in every way possible. Is that understood?"

The security director glanced at himself in the rearview mirror. "Yes."

"Good." Manning ended the call.

Nielsen had only a moment to reflect on the CEO's words before the ring of another incoming call broke the silence. He glanced at the caller ID on the dashboard and answered. "What is it, Ray?"

"Are you in the neighborhood, boss?" his security manager asked.

The Jaguar's engine roared to life as Nielsen downshifted again and shot around another vehicle. "Three minutes away."

"Good. You need to see something."

"Something definitive?"

"Say again?"

Nielsen shook his head. "Nothing. I'll be there shortly."

～

The air inside the archive warehouse held the pungent smell of greasy takeout food and stale coffee. Upon reaching the second floor of their makeshift tactical operations center, Nielsen found Foster and the leader of their hired video analysis team staring at several large monitors on the wall. The team leader dropped his ever-present Starbucks cup on the table and brushed at his shirt as the Velgyn security director approached.

"Mr. Nielsen! It's nice to see you again. I think you'll be happy with what we've uncovered this afternoon."

"What do you have for me, Mr. Egans?"

"Evans," the man corrected, giving an empathetic nod. "Don't worry . . . it's an easy name to forget."

Next to him, Foster gestured at the monitors. "Take a look at this, boss."

Nielsen shifted his gaze to the screen displaying a repeating segment of video taken from a ceiling-mounted surveillance camera. In the video, a procession of people marched through a brightly lit corridor. His security manager held his tongue for a moment before smiling.

"See her?"

The security director was about to shake his head when a woman with straight, copper-red hair and wearing a brown overcoat stepped into view on the left side of the screen and marched along the corridor before vanishing. A moment later the video looped and she appeared once again. Nielsen felt his heart rate rise. Despite the high angle of the camera, there was something distinctly familiar about the woman. "Is that our girl?"

"It's quite possible," Evans replied. "We're continuing our analysis, but so far the morphetic signature looks very promising."

"Define promising."

The team leader glanced over his shoulder. "Mary?"

Behind them, Mary Adler looked up from her own array of monitors and crossed her arms. "The woman in this video matches fifteen out of eighteen morphetic patterns generated by your *Lady X* in the original video," she answered matter-of-factly. "In my book that's a match."

"Let's keep our opinions to ourselves, Mary." Evans looked at Nielsen and shrugged. "As I said, it looks very promising. But we need to do more analysis to be sure."

The security director turned back to the video. "Where was this taken?"

"That's the not-so-good news, boss," Foster responded. "This was taken in one of the international terminals at Heathrow two days ago."

"Heathrow?" Nielsen mumbled. "I thought we were focusing the search here."

"Oh, we have," Evans affirmed. "But we've also been gradually expanding the local search radius since we started three nights ago. Honestly, this was a bit of a fluke. Someone on our team got the idea of scanning a short date-range of security video from the most frequented international airports just to see what we might get." He shrugged and took a sip of his coffee. "And *bam*—we got this."

Nielsen glanced around at the half-dozen analysts staring at their monitors. "And who should I be thanking for this fluke?"

Before her team leader could respond, Mary Adler raised a tattooed arm. "You're welcome," she replied without looking up.

The security director smiled and turned to Foster. "Are you seeing a pattern here, Ray?"

"I am, boss."

Both men turned and glared at Evans, who froze mid-sip with his giant coffee. The bespectacled team leader released a nervous laugh. "Gentleman, there's no doubt Miss Adler's a great analyst, but I assure you this is a team effor—"

"Holy shit!"

All eyes turned to find Adler spring from her chair and run to another colleague's workstation. Her colleague immediately moved aside as she hijacked his keyboard.

"What is it?" Evans asked.

The morphetics expert punched away at the keyboard. Moments later she paused and studied something on the screen. "I knew it," she mumbled, nodding her head. "I fucking knew it."

"What is it, Mary?" Evans repeated, his tone insistent.

Adler turned and looked at Nielsen. "Your briefing was wrong."

Nielsen shook his head. "About what?"

"The second subject." Adler marched back to her workstation and gestured at the monitors on the wall. The surveillance video of *Lady X* taken from the Heathrow terminal disappeared from all but one of the screens. "You know—blue sweater guy."

Nielsen and Foster exchanged a quizzical look as the surveillance video of Adam Cowell walking into the Ferry

Building appeared on the leftmost monitor.

"This is the Ferry building video taken at 4:06pm the night of the incident," Adler said, tapping away at her keyboard. "And this—" She pressed a key and the video of Cowell entering the atrium of the annex lab appeared next to it. "—is the same man again at 5:23pm, right?"

Foster nodded. "That's correct."

"No—that's *not* correct." Adler gave all three men a smug smile upon turning to look at her. "These are two different people."

Evans released a heavy sigh. "Mary, I don't remember authorizing you to—"

Nielsen raised his hand and the team leader fell silent. "Are you sure?"

"See for yourself." Alder pressed another key and the figure of Cowell in both videos were now covered with the familiar color-coded dots of the analysis software. "The body composition identities are somewhat close, but the movement signatures don't match at all."

Everyone in the room watched as the morphetics software repeatedly tried and failed to find matches between the two videos of Adam Cowell.

"But there's more," Adler continued. "I decided to run both body prints against the Heathrow surveillance video and guess what? Four minutes after our *Lady X* walks by—" The video suddenly fast-forwarded and then paused. "—here comes someone that matches sixteen of the eighteen morphetic patterns established by the man who broke into the lab."

As all eyes watched, a pudgy, dark-haired man in jeans and a black sweater strolled across the screen, following in the same direction as *Lady X.*

"Holy shit," Foster mumbled.

The video of the man repeated a few times before Adler paused it. "There's no chance these matches are a random coincidence," she asserted quietly. "The people we're after are in London."

Nielsen quietly studied the man on screen while the impact of Adler's revelation sank in. He turned to Evans. "You have a new role here, Mr. Evans. For the remainder of this project, you and everyone else on your team have one job—to follow Miss Adler's directives."

Evan's mouth dropped open into something resembling a grin. "You're joking, right?"

"Of course, if you or anyone else is unhappy with this new condition, you're more than welcome to go home." Nielsen stepped past the stunned team leader and nodded at Adler. "Alright, Mary—what's next?"

Adler's eyes flashed to Evans with a glint of satisfaction before returning to Nielsen. "Well, the good news is that London has one of the highest numbers of surveillance cameras of any modern city. If we can get access to enough security networks and their file servers, we should be able to search for our two subjects nearly in real-time."

"Good—do it." The security director waved his hand around the room. "This operation is in your hands now. If you need anything, tell Mr. Foster and he'll take care of it. And when you find them, call me immediately."

The morphetics expert nodded. "Got it."

Nielsen pointed at Evans. "Do you have a use for him?"

"I need him to inform the rest of the team. After that—" Adler shrugged. "He can make coffee runs for all I care. That's what he's best at anyway."

Foster turned to Nielsen. "Can I talk to you outside?" The security director nodded and the two men stepped into the hallway. There, Foster gave his boss a troubled sigh. "So does this mean Cowell *really* wasn't involved?"

Nielsen reflected the same troubled stare and slowly nodded. "They must've lured him into the restaurant, drugged him, and then taken his credentials."

"And his fingerprints? How'd they—?"

"I don't know. But we're dealing with some very clever people."

Foster sighed again. "So what are we supposed to do with Cowell—let him go?"

The security director shook his head. "Cowell's the only one who's seen *Lady X* up close. We'll need him to verify her identity once we find her. I'm sure he can suffer at the retreat house a little longer."

"And if we *do* find her? What then? We can't just fly to London and start snatching people off the street."

"No, we can't. But I might know someone who can." Nielsen read the curiosity on his security manager's face and clapped him on the shoulder. "I think it's better if I keep you in the dark on those details, Ray. At least for now." He gestured at the door before Foster could respond. "Get back in there and make sure that Evans idiot isn't getting in anyone's way. And call me when something comes up."

"Whatever you say, boss."

Nielsen lingered in the hallway for a moment, thinking. Whatever it was that *Lady X* and her shadowy accomplices were up to, the theft of Obermeyer's encryption key now seemed to be just a piece in a larger puzzle. Nevertheless, it was the only piece he needed to be concerned with. He reminded himself of this as he pulled out his phone and dialed a number. The call was once again answered with silence on the other end. "Still available?" Nielsen asked, making his way down the stairs.

"At your service," the low, digitally altered voice responded. "How can I help you?"

"Our lost soul called from London," Nielsen replied. "And she has a friend. Do you have anyone there who can assist them?"

"I do," the voice confirmed. "Do you have an address?"

"Forthcoming. But I should mention that these two are being extraordinarily cautious." The security director reached the end of the first floor corridor and paused. "Any mistakes, and I'm afraid they'll be lost forever."

A peal of laughter reverberated from the phone like techno music. "If you recall, I don't make mistakes."

"That's what I thought. I'll call you when I know more." Nielsen ended the call and stepped into the alley outside. A gray smudge of clouds covered the afternoon sky, the bay air cool and wet. An image of *Lady X* marching across the screen was still playing in his mind as he reached his car.

Behind him, the sound of the warehouse door flying open tore the security director from his thoughts.

"You're not going to believe this, boss," Foster said with a hushed tone of excitement. "Adler's already found her. *Lady X* is still in London. And get this—she just got on the goddamn subway."

26.

"What did you just say?" Sara Benton demanded.

Jeri felt her recruit try to pull away and immediately tightened her grip on the woman's neck. "Stop moving, Sara, and listen to me. We don't have much time."

A gasp of surprise escaped her recruit's lips. "How did you know my name?"

"I know everything about you, Sara Benton," Jeri replied. "You're an alternative fuels researcher for Roeh Trivale. You work in their innovation lab on City Street next to Bunhill Gardens. Two months ago, you submitted six patent applications to the British Intellectual Property office regarding a hydrogen fuel cell that you created in conjunction with the development of a new water electrolysis process. You live alone in a third-floor flat in Marylebone across from a pub called The Carpenters Arms. And tonight, your boyfriend—a surgeon named Oliver Webb—asked you to marry him." She eased her grip slightly. "Now—is everything I've just said true?"

Her recruit nodded. "But how do you know—"

"Shut up and listen," Jeri whispered, glancing at the passengers seated around them. No one seemed to have noticed their odd embrace. "Your life as you know it is in danger,

Sara. I don't have time to discuss the details of why, but if you have any desire to see your fiancé again, we need to get you off of this train before it reaches Marble Arch. Do you understand me?"

"I'm not—"

"Yes or no."

"Yes."

"Okay, good. Now listen . . . in a moment I'm going to let go of you. You're welcome to run if you want—and if you do, I wish you the best of luck. But if you trust anything I've just said, you'll remain seated and do exactly as I tell you. Nod if you understand."

Her recruit nodded.

Jeri removed her hand and laughed out loud as if they'd just shared a private joke.

Sara Benton recoiled against her seat and frowned at her assailant, a mix of fear and curiosity swirling in her dark eyes. Unsure of what to do next, she glanced at the passengers around them before leaning toward Jeri cautiously. "What the bloody hell's going on?" she hissed. "Is this a joke? Did Oliver put you up to this?"

Jeri shook her head. "We're stopping at Chancery Lane in less than a minute. Is there anyone you trust that lives near that station?"

"What do you mean my life is in danger?"

"Answer my question."

Her recruit thought for a moment. "No. No, I don't."

"Alright, how about Holborn? "

"No."

"Tottenham?"

"I don't believe . . . wait, yes—Chloe. My old friend

Chloe lives by Soho Square. That's just a stone's throw from Tottenham station."

"Fine, we'll get off there. Now don't say a word until I tell you to."

"Why?"

Jeri held her finger to her mouth and brushed the hair back from her ear. Her recruit's eyes widened in alarm upon seeing the small earpiece she was wearing. She unmuted the microphone. "I've got eyes on our friend," she said quietly, pretending to study her fingernails. Bright light suddenly flooded the windows as the train station rushed into the next station. Around them, passengers rose and began shuffling toward the doors. "Arriving at Chancery now."

Good. Everything okay?

"Everything's fine," Jeri answered, giving her recruit a reassuring nod. "See you soon."

We'll be waiting.

Jeri immediately muted her earpiece. The train stopped and a line of departing passengers slipped past the doors, leaving the car half empty. Next to her, Sara Benton's brow was creased with suspicion.

"What was that all about?" her recruit demanded. "Who are you?"

Jeri studied the attractive, stylishly dressed researcher and weighed her response. There was no question Sara Benton had a right to know what was happening. But without being actually collected, an honest answer simply wasn't an option. Deceiving Chilly and ruining a collection on ethical grounds was bad enough. Revealing the existence of the agency to her would-be recruit would be simply unforgivable. "It doesn't matter who I am," she replied. "*You're* the important one. And speaking of important, I'm curious. This fuel cell you invented—is it a paradigm shifter? Could it really change the world?"

The crease in Benton's brow deepened. "What? I . . . I don't know. I mean, I should hope so." She narrowed her eyes on Jeri. "Is *that* what this is about? Because if it is, I can tell you right now I won't discuss the details of—"

"And once the patents are granted?" Jeri interrupted as the doors closed and the train once again slipped into the darkness of the tunnel. "What then? Do you honestly think you can just produce it? That you'll be . . . *allowed* to?"

Her recruit's mouth twisted into a sneer. "Oh, I see . . . you're with them, aren't you?"

"With who?"

"Of course you are," Benton continued, giving Jeri a contemptuous nod. "You people are just unbelievable. First you tried the polite courtship—the fancy dinners and the big promises. When that didn't work, you tried hacking into our network. Then the legal threats. And now this? Is this the last tactic you employ when you can't get what you want—outright assault?"

Jeri shook her head. "Who are we talking about?"

"You tell me," her recruit scoffed. "Axcon? Petronus? GBP? You've all made your interests clear." She eyed Jeri coldly. "It doesn't matter how much you try to intimidate me. I'm not giving you anything."

Jeri regarded the researcher with bewilderment. Had one—or all—of the big three oil companies really gone to the lengths she was describing to steal her discovery? If so, there was no doubt her would-be recruit had courage—especially if she believed Jeri was some form of corporate-sent assailant. But behind Sara Benton's defiant stare was something else, something much closer to fear—and that was exactly what Jeri needed to exploit.

"You're right, Sara," she admitted. "I'm here because of what you invented. I'm here because of the threat it poses to the big three. And you're right—they will do anything to get what they want. *Anything*. That's why my team and I are here. But I wasn't sent here to scare you." Jeri paused and looked around before leaning closer. "I'm here to collect you."

Her recruit's expression turned quizzical. "*Collect* me? What do you mean?"

"I think you know exactly what I mean." Jeri replied gravely, watching to see if her words had their intended effect. To her relief, her recruit's stony expression began to crack.

"You mean . . . you mean like kidnapped? Is that what you mean?" Benton's eyes darted frantically around at the nearly empty train car. "No, I won't . . . I . . . I have—" she stammered, her voice rising with panic, "I mean, you . . . can't just—"

Jeri grabbed her recruit's hand and squeezed it gently. "Sara, listen to me. I'm not. I'm not going to collect you."

"But you just said—"

"I know what I just said, but I've had a change of heart. That's why I'm sitting here. That's why we're having this conversation in the first place. But you need to calm down, and you need to do everything I tell you to do."

"But why?" Benton demanded, giving her a pleading stare. "Why can't I just *go*?"

Jeri gestured at her earpiece. "Because," she said in a hushed tone, "I'm not the only one sent here to collect you."

Her recruit's gaze shifted from the earpiece to her eyes. "So why should I trust you?"

"Because you're a very smart woman, Sara—which means you know that if there's any truth to what I'm saying, you don't really have a choice." Jeri felt the train begin to slow for the next station. She seized Benton's hand and stood. "Come on . . . we're getting off the train."

"But . . . but this is Holborn. Didn't you say we should get off at Tottenham?"

"I did." Jeri removed her earpiece and dropped it on the floor. She exchanged a brief look with her recruit before lifting her foot and crushing the small device under her heel. She then looked up and smiled.

"Change of plans."

"Take a look." Adler said as Nielsen and Foster rushed back into the operations room inside the Brannan Street warehouse. The morphetics expert pointed at the left monitor on the wall. "That's the northern line platform at Bank Station at 10:03 pm London time—approximately fifteen minutes ago. See the woman standing in the far left corner?"

Nielsen focused his eyes on a redheaded woman in a brown coat standing with her back to the surveillance camera. "Looks just like the she did at the airport," he observed. "So what is she up to?"

Adler tapped a key and the video flashed forward until a train appeared on the platform. As normal play speed resumed, the security director noticed that their target was now standing in the crowd toward the center of the platform. On-screen, the train doors opened and a wave of departing commuters spilled out while boarding passengers began to press forward. Despite the melee of moving bodies, *Lady X* stood firm. "What's she doing?" he asked.

"Waiting." Adler answered.

"For—?"

Next to him, Foster pointed at another figure at the top edge of the screen. "Her."

Nielsen watched as a woman wearing a white cap stepped from the train and moved through the crowd toward their target. As she passed, *Lady X* spun and marched after her. Seconds later, their target followed the unknown woman out of frame toward the exit. "Interesting," he mumbled. "Alright, then what?"

"10:06 pm—Bank Station's central line platform," Adler said, motioning toward the center display. "In the interest of time, I'll play the video at four-times the normal speed." On-screen, the woman in the white cap stepped into view with her phone pressed to her ear. A moment after, *Lady X* walked into frame and stood next to her.

"Okay, so," Foster said, narrating the rapid play-by-play, "white-hat woman ends her call . . . Lady X and her talk for a moment . . . white-hat woman raises her left hand . . . she turns away and makes another call . . . Lady X walks to the far end of the platform and makes a call . . . the train arrives . . . Lady X ends her call . . . white-hat woman walks toward the train—" the security manager paused and glanced at Adler. "Drop it back to normal speed."

Adler punched a key and the video slowed to normal speed.

"Now, check this out, boss—"

From the far corner of the platform, *Lady X* looked on as the woman in the white cap shuffled aboard the waiting train. Seconds passed before she began moving toward the train. The doors began to close and their target broke into a sprint. With brilliant timing, *Lady X* launched herself through the doors of the last car an instant before they sealed shut. A moment later, the train was moving.

Foster turned to Nielsen. "What the hell do you make of that?"

Behind them, Adler spoke up. "Looked to me like she didn't want to get on the train."

The security director stared silently at the display, deep in thought. "Let's see that again."

Adler nodded, then glanced at something flashing onto her screen. "We've got another match!" she exclaimed, punching at her keyboard with blinding speed. "Holborn Station . . . 10:12 pm local time!"

Foster checked his watch. "That was six minutes ago."

All eyes turned to the wall monitors as Adler brought up the video. Once again, the high-angle view from a surveillance camera showed the central line train speeding into a station before coming to a precise stop. "There!" Adler said, pointing out Lady X and the woman in the white cap appearing side-by-side at a pair of open doors. The two quickly threaded their way past the other debarking passengers and marched toward the exit.

"They're together?" Foster asked, shaking his head.

Nielsen studied both women as they moved across the screen. In contrast to Lady X's calm, graceful stride, her companion shuffled forward through an awkward procession of tense, jerky movements. "Not by choice." He turned to Adler. "Is Holborn a connecting station?"

"No," a male colleague sitting next to Adler replied. The

man punched at his keyboard and a detailed map of the London Underground railway appeared on the left wall monitor.

Foster looked at it and shrugged. "I think it's a good bet they've left the station."

The security director nodded and pulled out his phone. "I want the best images you've got of those two emailed to me right now," he commanded Adler before marching out of the room. In the privacy of the corridor he redialed the last number and waited for the familiar click. "My friend left Holborn Station a few minutes ago," he announced calmly. "And she's made a new friend. I'll forward images of them both in a moment."

"Excellent," the digitally altered voice replied. "Shall I pick them up?"

"If you find them, yes." Nielsen looked at his watch. "How quickly can you mobilize your people?"

A low laugh, like steam escaping a pipe, hissed from the phone.

"They're already on their way."

"Why didn't we just stay on until Tottenham?" Sara Benton demanded.

Jeri ignored her recruit's question as they exited the Holborn Underground Station and briefly paused in the brisk night air. She surveyed the central London neighborhood. On the street, a thin stream of traffic rushed past, illuminating the surrounding Victorian façades in fleeting flashes of light. Other than a few strolling pedestrians, the sidewalks were practically deserted. "It's better if we walk," she said, gesturing west.

"Are you ready?"

Benton shot her an uncertain look before nodding.

They walked next to each other in silence, Jeri watching the traffic while her recruit stared anxiously into the voids of darkness between streetlights. A few blocks on, Benton turned and shrugged. "So . . . are you going to tell me your plan or what?" she asked.

Jeri gave her a distracted nod. "Maybe," she mumbled, checking the time on her phone. "But first, I need you to be quiet." Before her recruit could ask why, Jeri again pressed a finger to her lips and dialed Chilly. Her body tensed at the sound of his voice.

"What's up?"

"We have a problem. Our friend just got up and walked to the exit doors."

"Where are you?"

"Arriving at Oxford Circus," Jeri replied. "Two stops from Marble Arch."

"Okay." Her colleague's voice held an edge of irritation. "Why am I not getting any anything from your earpiece?"

"I don't know. It just stopped working." Jeri paused and feigned an exasperated sigh. "Shit. I think . . . yeah . . . it looks like she's planning to get off." A muted click sounded in Jeri's ear as Chilly switched to his radio.

"Sly, are you already in position? Okay, then just stay where you are." A moment later he was back. "Alright, listen to me, freshman. I want you to follow her. But keep your distance and call me as soon as you know where she's going."

"Got it." Jeri ended the call and nodded at Benton. "That should buy us a little more time. But we need to keep moving." She spun and marched several steps before realizing her recruit wasn't following. She turned and shrugged. "Well—are you coming?"

"Maybe," Benton said flippantly. "But first, I want to know where we're going."

Jeri glared at her. "I told you. Your friend's place."

"And what if it's not safe?"

"Then we'll go somewhere else."

"Right. And how do I know this isn't just part of your plan to actually kidnap me? I mean, maybe you're not even talking to anyone." Benton paused and glanced around nervously. "And if you are, how can I be sure they're not telling you exactly where to take me?"

Jeri watched her recruit take a step back and slowly raised her hand. "Sara . . . wait."

"Bloody *hell*," Benton exclaimed, backing away further. "I can't believe I was stupid enough to listen to you. I'd be nearly home by now if I'd just stayed on the train." Her expression hardened with a look of something suddenly decided.

"Don't do it," Jeri warned. "Do you really think—"

Her recruit spun and began running back toward the train station. Jeri cursed under her breath and sprinted after her. Within seconds she was next to Benton and had seized her by the arm. A moving game of tug-of-war ensued until Jeri pushed the taller woman off balance and sent her tumbling into a dark alcove of the building next to them.

"No—my ring!" Benton cried out, hands grasping at the darkness as she fell. Before she could find her balance Jeri shoved her against the building's stone façade. "I'm sorry! I'm sorry! Please don't hurt me! I just . . . I just want to go home!"

Jeri grabbed her recruit by the shoulder and pulled her to her feet. "You know what, Sara? I want to go home too. But

I can't."

"Then why are you doing this?" Benton exclaimed. Her eyes flashed to the gun that was suddenly in her assailant's hand.

"You see this?" Jeri asked, pressing the gun against her recruit's chest. "It's a pneumatic tranquilizer gun. I'm supposed to use this to deliver a fast-acting barbiturate to your lower back that will effectively paralyze you. Now, if you were *really* being collected, this would be followed by another more powerful sedative to keep you resting peacefully during transport." She took a step back. "Terrifying, isn't it?"

"Yes."

"Hold out your hand."

Benton's eyes flashed to hers. "Why?"

"To prove something."

"Please . . . I don't—"

"Do it," Jeri demanded.

Her recruit slowly held out her right hand.

Jeri spun the gun around and slapped it into Benton's open palm. "I get that you don't trust me. But since we don't have time to become best friends, here's a gesture of my sincerity."

Benton studied the odd-looking weapon in her hand. "I wouldn't even know how to use it."

"It's very simple. Just slide that lever forward and pull the trigger. Now—how far is it to your friend's place?"

Benton slipped her fingers around the handle of the gun and cautiously tested the weight of it in her hand. "Maybe fifteen minutes."

"We need to do it in ten." Jeri stepped from the shadow of the alcove and shot an impatient glance at her recruit. "So,

Sara—can we go now?"

Her recruit slid the lever on the barrel forward as instructed and looked up. "Sure," she replied, pointing the gun at Jeri's chest. "After you."

27.

Lars Nielsen marched back into the operations room and addressed his security manager. "What have we got?"

"Mary's got some of her coworkers trying to get us access into the larger surveillance networks in Central London," Foster replied. "That'll give us real-time street views."

In the corner of the room, a short, bearded man with a hand pressed over his phone stood and looked at Adler. "Yo, Mary—Secura says they'll grant us one hour of access to two boroughs in their central city grid. Which two do we want?"

Adler punched a command into her computer. In an instant, a detailed map of London appeared on her monitors. "Camden's the borough where they got off the train. Take that one along with . . . Islington. "

"Got it." Her colleague slapped the phone back to his ear and relayed her request.

"Be careful what you wish for," Adler mumbled, shaking her head.

"What do you mean?" Foster asked.

"Like I said, London has more video surveillance cameras than almost any other city. Those two boroughs alone will have several thousand surveillance cameras—and we're trying to analyze all of them in real-time."

"Good thing you're the best analyst around."

Adler shot the security manager a perturbed look. "Don't patronize me. On the other hand, maybe you should. I work better when I'm pissed off." She turned to her colleague. "Jon—make sure they give us a map of location codes so we know what we're looking at."

Her colleague nodded. "We've got access to Camden and Islington!"

"Good." Adler directed her attention to an Indian man with large eyes and a hawkish nose hovering by a rack of video servers. "Rakesh, run the new search filter only on camera feeds within a half mile radius of Holborn Station for now."

"Got it," her colleague replied. A moment later he gave her a thumbs up. "Search filters are in place. We're now analyzing real-time feeds."

"Okay, let's see what we've got," Adler punched at her keyboard and a collection of video images flashed onto the large wall monitors. "Remember, our system identifies a subject from their movement signature. Even if she's out there, she has to be moving in order for it to accurately—"

"We've got something!" Rakesh exclaimed, pointing to the displays.

Onscreen a dimly lit street appeared. In the bottom right corner, two female figures appeared and marched quickly along the sidewalk.

"White hat on the second one," Foster noted, pointing at the figure a few steps behind the other. "That's got to be them."

Adler looked up from her monitors. "Eighty-four percent match for the woman in the overcoat. That's our *Lady X*.

Rakesh—can you translate the camera's location code?"

Her colleague nodded. "They're on New Oxford heading west. Next intersection is Museum Street."

"Alright, get the feeds from every surrounding camera on-screen so we don't lose them. And record anything with our subjects in it. We might need to analyze it later."

Nielsen pulled out his phone and redialed the last number. "They're on the street," he said quietly. "Heading west on New Oxford approaching Museum." Out of the corner of his eye he saw Foster watching him.

"Very good," the digitally altered voice replied. "My people will be arriving shortly. Black van."

The security director hung up and stepped closer to the monitors. "Strange, isn't it?" he said, studying both women march across the screen.

"What's that, boss?" Foster asked.

"Why aren't they walking next to each?"

His security manager shrugged. "Maybe they're just trying to look like they don't know each other."

"They were walking next to each other out of the train station," Nielsen countered. "So why the sudden change?" He turned to Adler. "Can we zoom in on them?"

"Yeah, just a second."

On the wall monitors, the video feed abruptly zoomed in on *Lady X* and her companion as they continued down the street. Nielsen's gray eyes narrowed on the woman in the white cap. Despite her position behind their target, the woman's movements indicated a nervousness bordering on panic. "Whatever's happening between those two, I don't think it's consensual."

Foster pointed at something on the next monitor. "Your

friends, boss?" he asked in a low voice.

The Velgyn security director glanced over at the patchwork of live feeds from peripheral surveillance cameras on the other monitor. In one of the feeds, a black van could be seen turning onto the street. "I think so," he nodded, watching the vehicle approach their target. "Now we just need everyone to stay calm and—"

On the next screen, Nielsen watched *Lady X* look up and visibly stiffen. Her pace immediately slowed. Foster noticed the sudden change in her behavior as well.

"Boss?"

Nielsen pulled out his phone. "Your team's already been noticed," he hissed at the sound of the click.

"Are you certain?" the voice asked, surprise evident even through its digital filter.

"Get them off the fucking street—*now*."

A brief pause followed. "Understood."

Onscreen, their target was now looking around. "Too late," Nielsen sighed. He watched helplessly as *Lady X* abruptly turned and rushed for a nearby doorway. Caught off guard, her white-capped companion looked up with surprise and hurried after. The security director cursed under his breath.

"What was that, boss?" Foster asked.

"That was us getting outsmarted."

"No—that's not what I meant." The security manager marched toward Adler. "Mary, play that back."

Adler punched at her keyboard and the surveillance video began to rewind. *Lady X* and her companion reemerged onto the sidewalk.

"Okay, play it," Foster commanded. They watched their target again turn and dart for the doorway. "There—*stop*!" The security manager pointed as the video froze and Lady X's companion stood in full view on the screen. "What's that in her right hand?"

Nielsen focused his gaze on the woman and immediately saw what Foster was referring to—the blurry shaft of an object extending from her hand. It was pointed at Lady X.

"Is that a gun?" Adler asked.

The security director silently nodded before returning the phone to his ear. "Tell your team to find a quiet spot and sit tight. This may not be over just yet."

Jeri moved quickly down the narrow corridor and paused in the shadows. A few steps further, the passageway opened into a large central courtyard lined with trash dumpsters. The sickly-sour stench of rotting vegetables and ethnic spices hung heavy in the air.

Behind her, Sara Benton paused and grimaced. "Good god, what is that?"

"I'm guessing a week of leftovers from every restaurant on the block," Jeri replied, looking around.

"Okay . . . and why are we in here?"

Jeri glanced back at the door they'd just come through. "Being cautious."

"What do you mean?" Her recruit followed her gaze and aimed the pistol at the door. "Did you see someone? Is someone coming?"

"I don't know. Maybe they turned, or . . . stopped."

"Who? *Who* must have turned?" Benton demanded, her voice rising to a panicky pitch.

"Put the gun down, Sara. Trust me, if the people after you knew we were in here, it wouldn't make any difference."

Benton spun and aimed the gun at her. "Why did you bring me in here?"

Jeri held her stare. "I saw something that looked suspicious and decided it was a good idea to get off the street. That's what I've been trained to do . . . to think on my feet and make snap decisions. Maybe it was the wrong one—who knows? But it's all I've been doing for the last three months since the life I once knew ended." She paused and shook her head. "And now tonight, in a beautiful twist of irony, I've managed to ruin what was left of my new life in order to save yours. So maybe you could stop pointing my gun at me and show a little fucking gratitude."

"Fine," her recruit replied, holding the gun steady. "You'll get my gratitude *and* your gun back after we get to my friend's flat. So, what now?"

Jeri pointed to the service corridor on the opposite side of the courtyard. "Head that way and go a few blocks north just to be safe. Is that all right with you?"

Benton nodded and waved the barrel of the gun forward. "After you."

The stench of rotting food rose to nauseating intensity as they made their way past the dumpsters to the opposite end of the courtyard. When they reached the door at the end of the northern corridor, Jeri raised her hand and peered cautiously through the reinforced glass at the street beyond.

"See anyone?" Benton asked behind her.

Jeri scanned the quiet residential block. "No, I think it's clear. Are you ready?"

Her recruit tucked the gun back into her jacket pocket

and nodded.

"Let's go." Jeri pressed against the door handle and pushed. The door didn't budge. "Come *on*," she said irritably, shoving her weight against it.

"What's wrong?"

"The door's locked."

Benton stepped forward and raised the gun. "Should I try shooting it?"

Jeri stopped and looked at her. "And what—put it to sleep?"

"Well I don't bloody know . . . I'm just trying to—"

Both women spun at the sound of something crashing against metal behind them.

"What the hell was that?" Benton hissed, aiming the gun at the corridor.

Jeri peered toward the darkness of the courtyard, watching for movement. "Someone must be throwing away trash," she whispered, stepping forward. A strange thought briefly crossed her mind. She turned to Benton. "We have to go back."

Her recruit tore her stare from the corridor. "What?"

"We have to find another way out."

"But—"

"Come on. We're wasting time." Jeri felt her phone vibrate in her pocket and pulled it out to find a new text message from Chilly.

Talk to me. Now.

She tapped out a quick reply and shoved the phone back into her pocket. "We need to go," she commanded, grabbing Benton's arm and dragging her back toward the courtyard.

"But we don't know even who's *here*!"

"Just calm down," Jeri snapped, tightening her grip. "Whoever it is, it's not the people after you." Upon entering the courtyard, she quickly studied the eastern and western corridors before turning to the right. "Let's try west," she said, pulling her recruit after her.

A few steps further, Sara Benton stopped. "Wait," she said, looking toward the dumpsters along the wall. "What's that?"

"What's *what*?"

"Oh my god . . . that's a—"

Jeri spun and clapped a hand over her recruit's mouth to stifle her sudden scream. "Quiet!" she hissed, glaring at her angrily. She studied Benton's terrified expression. "What is it?"

Benton lifted a shaking hand. "Look."

Jeri followed her recruit's gaze to one of the dumpsters. On one side the lid was raised and a carelessly tossed stalk of vegetable hung limply over the side. Something about its pale, limp shape made her look closer. "Oh shit."

"It is, isn't it?"

"Sara—give me the gun."

Next to her, Benton stood motionless, her mouth quivering at the corners.

"Sara, I said give me the—" Jeri heard her recruit's shriek of surprise an instant after the *other* noise—the whispered *psssst* of a high-velocity projectile puncturing clothing and skin. Next to her, Sara Benton dropped the gun and stared down at the silver-colored object lodged in her thigh.

"What is *this*?" Benton exclaimed, seizing the small tranquilizer dart and pulling it free. She held it out to Jeri with a look of both fear and betrayal. "What . . . what did you just do to me?"

"Sara, I didn't . . . I . ." Jeri reached and grabbed the gun. "Where are you?" she demanded, sweeping it at the darkness.

"Heading south on Regent Street," a familiar baritone voice replied. On the far side of the courtyard, a figure moved in the shadows and lit a cigarette. "Wasn't that what you said in your last text?"

Jeri aimed the gun at the glowing tip of the cigarette. "Chilly?"

"Funny, this doesn't look like Regent Street to me." Chilly stepped into the dim light of the courtyard, a hood of smoke twisting over him. He frowned and calmly pointed his cigarette at Benton "You might want to catch her."

Jeri glanced over to find her recruit swaying precariously. She pivoted just in time to catch her. "I've got you," she said quietly, lowering Sara Benton's paralyzed body to the ground.

"It was all . . . all planned . . . wasn't it?" Benton asked between labored gasps, staring up at her with frightened, dilated eyes. "Should've known I couldn't trust . . . trust you."

"I'm so sorry." Jeri gently brushed the researcher's hair from her face. "I swear I was trying to protect you."

"Doesn't matter." Benton's eyes gave her one more fleeting look of defiance before succumbing to the waxy gaze of the sedative. "Both know . . . doesn't change . . . anything."

"Oh, I think you'll find this changes everything," Chilly replied behind them.

Jeri bolted upright. "How did you know?" she hissed, leveling the gun on his chest.

Her colleague studied the gun as he took a drag of his

cigarette. "After your earpiece stopped working—or should I say, after you *destroyed* it—I got worried and started tracking you."

"But—"

"How? Don't worry, I'll tell you later." He gestured at their surroundings. "I have to say, well done, freshman. This is a much better place for the authorities to find the remains of a young woman tragically killed on the night of her engagement. Wouldn't you agree, Sly?"

Jeri looked over to find Sly stepping from behind the dumpster that held the dangling, mutilated hand. "Yeah, I suppose so," he said quietly.

"The noise," Jeri mumbled. "That was you tossing the package in the dumpster."

Sly gave her a somber nod. "Thought that might get your attention." His stare shifted to Chilly. "We were kind of improvising on this one."

"And look how well it turned out," Chilly added.

Jeri kept the gun on him. "I can't believe you'd do this."

"Do what? Let you go off-script again—or plan for it?" He regarded her with a look of disappointment. "You don't even realize what happened here tonight, do you?"

"You mean other than another test?"

"You're right. Tonight was a test. And you failed."

Jeri rolled her eyes. "Maybe in your eyes. But I'd rather fail your fucked-up test than see this woman's life ruined."

Chilly shook his head. "The only reason your recruit is laying there is because you can't seem to find a way to trust me, let alone follow a goddamn script."

"What the hell are you talking about?"

Her colleague stepped forward. "Shoot me."

"What?"

Chilly reached out and grabbed the barrel of the gun. "Shoot me." he commanded, pulling it to his chest.

Jeri felt the gun being torn from her grip and lunged forward. As the barrel rammed into her colleague's chest, she looked into his eyes and squeezed the trigger.

A dull click was followed by silence.

Jeri squeezed the trigger again as a grin slowly grew on Chilly's face. He snatched the gun from her and opened the chamber. "Non-firing round," he said flatly, removing the dart and holding it in front of her. "Also known as a dud."

Jeri stared at it absently. "I don't understand."

"I put this in your gun to make sure it wouldn't work tonight. Your two backup rounds are also duds."

"But . . . why?"

His grin faded. "What's the normal protocol for an agent faced with the inability to carry out a collection due to equipment failure?"

"Abort the collection."

"Exactly."

"But I still don't—" Jeri froze as the reason for her colleague's meaning suddenly became clear. "No," she said softly, shaking her head. "You mean—"

"That's right . . . for once it really *was* a test," Chilly replied. "I knew you were going to have a problem with this collection on moral grounds. But after Obermeyer and Salas, I needed to know if you were capable of actually following my orders. I figured it would go one of two ways—you'd flat out refuse, or you'd see it through and abort the collection as soon as you pulled the trigger. Either way, I wasn't expecting Miss Benton to be harmed. But once again you did something

I didn't expect. You engaged the recruit in your plan—one that I had no intention of collecting in the first place—in order to protect her. So now, thanks to you, we have to bring her in." He dropped his cigarette and snuffed it out with his shoe. "Oh well . . . at least we can all enjoy the irony."

Jeri's face twisted into a grimace. "I didn't shoot her," she snapped, jabbing a finger at his chest. "*You* did."

"I didn't have a choice," Chilly retorted. "The moment you engaged her—not to mention broke communication— you left me and the rest of your team no choice but to bring her in." He stepped over to Benton's body and checked her pulse. "So congratulations, freshman—you're the first agent in the history of the organization to collect someone we didn't even want. Anything you'd like to say?"

Jeri watched silently as he gave their unintended recruit the second sedative. Her eyes shifted to Sara Benton's left hand. Even in the dim light the diamond on Benton's ring finger sparkled like a beacon. She closed her eyes and nodded. "I'm done."

Chilly stood and addressed Sly. "Put her jacket and hat behind the dumpster and toss her shoes into the corridor. Not perfect, but it'll be enough DNA to suffice. Use the cooking oil from the container in the corner when you're ready to burn." He reached into his jacket and removed a small silver dart.

"Did you hear me?" Jeri asked.

"No," he replied, loading the dart into her pistol.

"I said I'm done."

"Done with what—making decisions on your own? Questioning my authority? If that's what you mean, I accept."

Jeri turned and began marching toward the south corridor she'd entered earlier with Benton. Halfway across the courtyard, she froze at the metallic *click* of her pistol being cocked. "That's the second time my gun's been pointed at me tonight," she said without looking back. "But you and I both know that's the only way you're going to keep me here."

The sound of her colleague's approaching footsteps filled the long silence. "You really want out?" Chilly asked in a low, melancholic tone.

Jeri shook her head. "I do."

"Alright," he conceded. "But only on one condition."

"What's that?"

"You follow protocol. You talk to him first."

Jeri turned to find Chilly aiming her own gun at her chest. "You mean—"

"Yes."

She studied his hardened expression and nodded. "Fine, let's go."

Chilly let the gun linger on her chest for a moment before lowering it at her thigh. A thin frown warped his mouth. "After you."

The needle of the tranquilizer dart penetrated the fabric of Jeri's overcoat and jeans before releasing its contents deep within the flesh of her leg. She glanced down at the small silver cylinder, surprised but unafraid. She'd felt this cocktail before—fast acting, with a nice euphoric side effect. Already the warmth was spidering upward toward her chest.

Chilly stepped toward her, the frown still etched on his face. "Sorry, freshman . . . standard protocol for any agent that expresses doubt is collection. But you know I'll catch you if you fall." He reached his hand out and Jeri took it. Her legs were suddenly wooden, her balance gone. She leaned forward and fell gently into his arms. Warmth rushed into her chest as her colleague wrapped his arms around her. She looked up at his tanned face and smiled.

"I know you won't let me fall, Sam *Lafeen*," she said softly, her words beginning to slur. "It's just not in your nature." She watched Chilly's face transform from tenderness to confusion before settling on disbelief. Jeri smiled and closed her eyes. A swirling cloud of happiness enveloped her as her colleague gripped her tightly. She heard his questions, felt the tone of urgency in his voice. And yet, for some reason, the answers were too difficult to form.

But it didn't matter.

Everything was going to be just fine.

28.

"What is the purpose of this?"

Paul Obermeyer registered the icy undertone of the question before glancing up. In the doorway of his laboratory, Tatyana Aleksandrov stood stiffly, her arms folded across her chest. "Good morning to you too, Dr. Aleksandrov," he replied, rising from his chair. "I take it that Derrick didn't explain?"

The Russian researcher marched in and gazed around with a disdainful sneer before leveling her green eyes on Paul. "Mr. Birch only told me you required help. He did not tell me in what areas you lack competence."

"Well, I wouldn't call it a matter of comp—" Paul shook his head and pointed to a row of large, glass-doored instruments. "Are you familiar with microalgae incubators?"

"I am."

"Good. Then you can set up the control samples of all previously used race B stock."

Tatyana raised a stunned eyebrow. "*This* is why I was called here—to be your *assistant*?"

"Yes. I want two sample groups for each generation," Paul continued, "and pay attention to the labels. Generations fifteen through nineteen underwent transposon mutagenesis using bacterial DNA. I want those excluded. Let me know when you're finished." He turned back to his computer, feeling his colleague's lingering stare.

"That is ridiculous. Why would you want those generations excluded?" Tatyana challenged.

Paul exhaled a weary sigh. He had expected Dr. Aleksandrov to question him, to assert her opinion at every opportunity as she had before. He just wasn't expecting it within the first thirty seconds of her arrival. "You have PhD in molecular biology, correct?" he asked, giving her a thin smile.

"I do."

"Then you understand that if I want to concentrate on altering the genes that code for squalene synthase in order to increase cellular oil yield, any samples that have undergone transposon mutagenesis are likely to produce an unstable biofilm matrix—yes?"

A brief look of confusion clouded Tatyana's face before she shook her head. "Not necessarily. Transposon mutagenesis should not affect matrix development unless an enzyme such as isopentenyl phosphate kinase is present."

Paul's smile vanished. "Maybe. But the effects of isopentenyl phosphate kinase as a catalyzing agent have only been studied on prokaryotes—not planktonic microalgae. Your assumption is based on incomplete information."

"And your concerns regarding biofilm matrix development in the mutations are purely speculative," the Russian researcher countered.

Paul held up two fingers to his colleague. "Two samples for each generation. Exclude the mutations. Got it?"

Tatyana glared back stonily. "It's *your* laboratory, Dr. Obermeyer," she said with a curt nod. "I shall assist you as Mr.

Birch requested."

"Good. Thank you." Paul turned back to his computer while his colleague began preparing the flasks for the incubators. He was just beginning to refocus his attention when Dr. Aleksandrov spoke up again.

"But do not expect me to agree with you."

~

Michael Manning swirled the contents of his highball glass and gazed out at the shimmering, star-lit waters of Richardson Bay. "So we *found* her, and then we *lost* her—is that what you're telling me?"

Standing behind him in the CEO's coastal estate library, Lars Nielsen shifted his stance and nodded. "*I* lost her, Michael."

Manning turned slightly, his sharp profile frowning against the dark backdrop of night. "Nonsense. You just told me you had an entire team covering the area." He dwelled on the thought for a moment before shaking his head. "So either all of you are collectively inept, or—what do you call her?"

"Lady X."

"Or this Lady X is simply that good." Manning tossed back the rest of his gin and tonic and marched over to the library's built-in wet bar. "Run me through it again," he asked, pouring another drink. "Starting from the moment everything fell apart."

"There isn't much to run through. As I said, Lady X and a female companion were walking toward an unknown destination when something caught her attention. When she turned to enter the nearest building, we noticed that her companion was holding a gun. After both women entered the building, we monitored the area through video surveillance cameras and waited for our target to make her next move. Unfortunately, her next move was to—"

"Kill her companion, burn the body in a dumpster, and slip unnoticed out a side door during the commotion caused by arriving fire engines," Manning interjected, shaking his head. "And you're certain it wasn't *her* in that dumpster?"

Nielsen nodded. "London authorities have already identified the victim as a local woman named Sara Benton. We checked the surveillance images against her photos and they matched."

"So who was she?"

"An alternative energy researcher for Roeh Trivale. That's all we know right now."

"And what do the London authorities know about Lady X?" Manning demanded.

"They have the surveillance tapes. Nothing more."

"So they know us much about her as we do. And once again Lady X has killed a researcher and turned them into charcoal. Well, you have to hand it to her, our girl's got a great flair for the dramatic." The CEO leveled a dark stare on his security director. "That, or she just enjoys making everyone trying to catch her look like a fucking idiot."

"We've spent hours analyzing the surveillance video around that building," Nielsen said flatly. "However she left, it wasn't on foot."

"Oh, so she just vanished into thin air like Obermeyer's encryption key—is that it?" Manning shook his head again. "What the hell made her run in the first place?"

Nielsen turned to the window and gazed at the undulant silhouette of Sausalito in the distance. "Hard to say," he replied dismissively. The last thing he was going to tell Manning was that his own outsourced interception team may have been responsible. "But whatever aroused her suspicions, I'm quite certain she wasn't worried about us."

"And why's that?"

"Because your assessment of Lady X is correct—she *is* that good. Our target's not in the habit of making mistakes or leaving trails. Quite frankly, it's nothing short of a miracle we've found her at all. But unless her team's still monitoring us, there's no way they could know it's us watching from the shadows."

Manning twisted his mouth with doubt. "No? Then who *is* she so worried about?"

Nielsen shrugged. "It's clear now that ours isn't the only company Lady X and her team have targeted. We're dealing with an international team of corporate terrorists. But they've no doubt got a growing list of enemies."

The CEO released an exasperated grunt. "They can kill every researcher working for our competitors and all the Mickey Mouse impersonators at Disneyland for all I care. But these people fucked with the wrong organization." He pointed his drink at Nielsen. "So how are you planning to find her now? And more importantly—how are you going make sure you don't lose her again?"

"We're paying two London security agencies a significant amount of money in exchange for access to their central surveillance feeds," the security director answered. "As soon as Lady X or her male colleague make another move—and they will—our onsite team will be on them."

"And this onsite team—who are they?"

"Agents from a private security firm. I'm acquainted with the firm's owner."

"Acquainted?"

"Yes."

Manning waved an impatient hand through the air. "And?"

Nielsen turned from the window. "What else would you like to know?"

"A hell of a lot more than you're saying."

Nielsen dropped his gaze to the library's Macassar Ebony floor. "Am I correct in recalling you're a Yale graduate?" he asked, studying the intricate patterns of the rare hardwood.

Manning nodded. "What about it?"

"What's the name of that fraternity of undergraduates there that's known for being so secretive? Skull and—?"

The CEO narrowed his eyes on him. "Skull and Bones."

"That's the one," Nielsen affirmed. "Skull and Bones. One of the oldest and most prestigious societies of any university, from what I've read. Past members—*Bonesmen*, I believe they call themselves—range from former U.S. Presidents and Supreme Court justices to a long list of powerful men. They even have their own private temple on campus called *the tomb* where they conduct all of their secret meetings." He paused and shook his head. "I'm sure it'd be quite interesting to find out what goes on behind those doors. And yet apparently no Skull and Bones member, when asked, will ever say a word about it." The security director looked up at his boss with a prying smile. "Were you a Bonesman, Michael?"

The CEO regarded him silent for a moment before throwing back half of his drink.

"Sorry, I shouldn't have asked," Nielsen continued.

"Even if you were, I'm sure you wouldn't tell me. Your first priority would be to protect your fellow brothers. And we both know that nothing insures protection better than silence—isn't that right?"

"So what are you saying?" Manning scoffed. "Are you and the owner of this private security agent in some kind of secret fucking society?"

The security director shook his head. "Of course not. We simply have some shared past experiences. But for everyone's protection, perhaps we can agree that some questions are best left unanswered. The man in question is someone I trust. I know what he's capable of, and those capabilities are exactly what will be needed when we find Lady X or her colleagues again."

Manning marched over and dropped into one of the large leather couches at the center of the room. "Fine. But I haven't forgotten our earlier agreement. You've got three days to hand me either Paul's encryption key or the woman that took it—or I'll spin this whole goddamn mess into a story of gross negligence on the part of my security team. First, I'll fire everyone on your team just to underscore my resolve. Then I'll set my lawyers to work filing enough suits against my director of security to keep him in legal purgatory for the next ten years of his life. Hell, I'll even talk to those morons on FOX or CNN if our public relations team thinks it'll help. But make no mistake—if you fail to give me what I've asked for, you'll be the one destroyed by this, not me."

"And if I succeed?" Nielsen asked, holding Manning's gaze.

The CEO smiled. "That's what I've always liked about you, Lars. You're not like most people . . . not manipulated by fear." He emptied the rest of his gin and tonic and studied the ice in his glass. "*Executive* Director of Security sounds like a more fitting title for a man who saves the future of this company, don't you think? And I could easily see a three-hundred percent pay raise effective with the title. Not to mention a guaranteed five-year bonus that makes your salary look like a charitable donation by comparison. Does that sound about right to you?"

Nielsen's gray eyes flickered across the room's endless shelves of books as he considered the offer. "I'm sure we can come to an agreement when the time comes, Michael."

"Three days," Manning repeated. "Are we clear?"

"Yes."

"Then I'll ask you again—what else do you need to get these fucking terrorists?"

The security director started to speak when a text message stirred his phone. He glanced at the screen. "A stroke of luck," he replied, a slight grin appearing at the corners of his mouth. He looked at Manning. "I have to go."

The Velgyn CEO said nothing as Nielsen marched from the library. Moments later, the sound of a house staff member bidding the security director a good night echoed from the estate's entryway. Manning stood and paced to the bar. He filled his glass with gin, this time forgoing the tonic. On the counter, pale-faced Geishas gazed back at him from a nineteenth-century Satsuma vase. The delicately painted figures watched the CEO take a drink, their brows drawn downward in expressions of shock and accusation. "The fuck's your problem?" Manning mumbled, returning their gaze. He reached out and shoved the priceless vase onto the floor.

"The first rule of being powerful" he mumbled, careful

to step around the shattered remains as he walked back to the couch. "Everything's a write-off."

~

"I have completed your requests."

Paul looked up from his computer to find Dr. Aleksandrov standing next to him, her head cocked to the side with a look of annoyance. "Just as you have asked," the Russian researcher continued. "Two sample groups for each generation. Testable yields should be available in approximately four hours."

"Great," Paul replied, noting the time. "You do excellent work, doctor."

"Of course I do. Now—" Tatyana's eyebrows rose in a defiant arc. "Do you require *more* assistance, or may I get back to my own affairs?"

Paul suppressed the urge to smile. Despite her gruff manner, his colleague's behavior was quickly proving to be predictable to the point of comic. Regardless of what he said, it was clear she was determined to dislike him. Therefore, he had nothing to lose. "I'm not sure," he replied, deciding to test his boundaries. "I need some time to prepare the exogenous DNA for insertion. Why don't you take a short coffee break while I think up your next task?"

Tatyana's eyebrows dropped. "Absolutely not. I refuse to stand around waiting while you—" She noticed the grin on Paul's face and slowly nodded. "Oh, I see . . . this arrangement is amusing to you. First you demean me with trivial tasks, and then you laugh in the face of my . . . of my . . . "

"Uncooperative attitude?" Paul interjected.

A sudden light flashed from the Russian researcher's green eyes like sparks from a fire. She spun and marched toward the door. "Good day, Dr. Obermeyer—and good luck."

"Wait. Dr. Aleksandrov . . . Dr. Aleksandrov . . . Tatyana!"

His colleague paused in the doorway.

"If you want to go running out of here because I'm treating you the same way you've been treating me, that's fine. All I have to do is pick up the phone and call Derrick, and ten minutes from now you'll be back in here screening useless noncoding DNA sequences just because I asked for it." He sighed and rose from his seat. "Look, I'm here, just like you, against my will. You may have been here longer, but that doesn't mean your life has been any more ruined than mine. Last week I was living in beautiful San Francisco doing research for a top pharmaceutical company. Last week I had a life. Now look at me—sitting in a giant concrete box in the middle of the Saudi Arabian desert with four dead guys and a bitch from Russia."

Tatyana stifled a smile.

"And yet, oddly enough, this just might be the most important thing I've ever done. That *all* of us have ever done. So I'll make you a deal. If you help me, and start acting like we're both equally in this together, I'll start listening to your ideas on genetic engineering." Paul walked over and held out his hand. "Sound fair?"

Tatyana studied his hand. "Do you have any idea how hard it is for a girl in Russia to be accepted into a scientific university? Or to be given even one chance in your chosen field that isn't the work of a secretary? I've spent my entire life proving that I am as smart and as competent as my male peers—and it is exhausting." Her eyes held a lingering look of anger as she met his stare. "I am not here to do menial chores, Dr. Obermeyer."

"Dr. Aleksandrov, if what we're doing can truly change the world, then I don't think there are any menial chores. Wouldn't you agree?"

For the first time since meeting, the Russian woman nodded agreement. "Perhaps not." She took his hand and squeezed it with surprising strength. "Very well . . . I will help you."

"Fantastic." Paul turned and marched back to his desk. "Now—I don't know if you have experience with artificially induced competence, but I need you to prep—" He spun at the sound of his colleague walking out of the lab. "Dr. Aleksandrov?"

"Yes?" she replied from the corridor.

"Where are you going?"

"Did you not ask me to take a coffee break?"

"I . . . yeah, I suppose I did. Hey, would you mind grabbing me a—"

"Excuse me?"

Paul sighed and ran a hand through his hair. "Never mind," he mumbled, making his way to the door. "On second thought, I'll come with you."

∼

"We've got him, boss."

Lars Nielsen nodded at his security manager. "Show me," he commanded, studying the wall of monitors in their operations room. Behind them, Mary Adler sat at her workstation and busily punched at her keyboard.

290

"East London," Foster said as a series of street views appeared onscreen. "On the left is video taken last night at 10:53 pm London time." He raised his hand and traced a dark figure exiting a cab at a quiet intersection and disappearing into a warmly lit façade on the corner. "Even though we can't see his face, Mary's system gives us an eighty-percent match to Lady X's male companion from the airport video."

"What is that—a bar?" the security director asked.

"Yeah, a pub called Ten Bells."

Nielsen looked at his security manager with confusion. "But this was seven hours ago. Are you telling me he's still in there?"

Foster shook his head. "No, we've got video of him leaving at 2:13 am and getting into a cab. Unfortunately, there were just too many gaps in the surveillance coverage and too many cabs on the street to track him."

"So you just dragged me down here to point out another missed target?"

"Of course not," Adler retorted defensively. "We dragged you down here to show you a pattern. Watch the center monitor."

The security director briefly glared at the morphetics experts before turning to the screen. Once again the short, pudgy figure of their second target could be seen exiting a cab and slipping into the corner pub. "Okay . . . so?"

"That was two nights ago, boss," Foster replied. "10:45 pm. Seems this guy not only has a drinking problem, he's got a favorite pub."

Nielsen regarded his security manager with a wide grin and glanced at Adler. "Well done."

The young woman gave him a curt nod. "That's more

like it."

"So what's the play if he shows up again tonight?" Foster asked.

Nielsen considered the question for a moment before gesturing at the door. "Let's take a walk." The two men walked silently out of the building into the cool night air. When they reached Foster's Escalade, Nielsen paused and regarded his second in command somberly. "I want you in London."

"Right away?"

The security director nodded. "If this guy turns up again tomorrow night, I want every appropriate resource waiting for him. Adler and her team can assist you from here, but I want you on the ground. I'll inform my contact that you're coming."

Foster nodded. "Does this mean I finally get a briefing on your guy?"

"I suppose it does." Nielsen surveyed the empty alley around them. "Do you remember Blackwell?"

"You mean the private security firm? Had big government contracts in the Middle East?"

"That's right."

Foster narrowed his eyes on his boss. "Didn't they go out of business after one of their ops teams killed some civilians?

"Firms like Blackwell don't go out of business," Nielsen asserted. "When mistakes happen, they just reorganize and change their names to something less ominous." He paused for a moment, deep in thought. "My contact's name is Marcus," he said finally. "At one point in time he and I were both field agents for Blackwell's Government Services Division, or *GS* as we used to call it. GS specialized in intelligence gathering for the U.S. government—an outsourced version of everything from comm tapping and surveillance to interrogation. There were only eighteen of us in the division initially, all ex-military, all out to prove we were worthy of the job. Of course, this was back when outsourcing was like the western frontier. There were no rules to speak of, no handbooks to tell us our limits. Marcus and I were assigned to interrogation, and both of us quickly developed our own rules of engagement. I was better at the nuance work—the pysch evals and the interviews. Marcus excelled at the messy stuff. He got the *special* cases—the guys who had somehow managed to get through sanctioned interrogation procedures without talking. He developed a list of interrogation methods that fell well outside of our SERE conduct manuals . . . most of which required a special stomach. And he was very good at it. If you needed someone to talk, believe me, there was no better person for the job."

"So why all the secrecy?" Foster asked.

Nielsen regarded his security manager. "The nature of the business. Marcus's results were getting the attention of Blackwell's executives. But his methods were also making a lot of people nervous. Had the government found out what he was up to, it was feared Blackwell would get slapped with some kind of human rights lawsuit—or worse—that GS would be shut down entirely. So the company—which up to that point had fully supported Marcus and his activities—suddenly terminated him and swept all knowledge of his activities under the carpet. But what they didn't realize until Marcus was gone was that their star interrogator had taken a copy of GS's classified operational documents with him." He paused and shook his head. "I'm sure they're still looking for him—and firms like Blackwell definitely hold grudges."

"So how did *you* find him?"

"I didn't," Nielsen answered. "He found me. Right after I took this job in fact. A simple letter in the mail with a name and a phone number."

"And why would he do that?"

"Because I oversee the security of a twenty *billion* dollar pharmaceutical company, and he's a free agent looking for a paycheck."

Foster nodded as his mouth curled into a thoughtful frown. "Do you trust him?"

The security director grinned. "Trust is like money, Ray—you never invest all of it in one opportunity. Marcus will do what we ask. But I want you there to make sure he doesn't do it *too* well. Understood?"

"Understood."

Nielsen glanced at his watch. "Velgyn II has been on standby at Oakland International since this whole thing started. Call me as soon you land."

"You got it, boss." Foster turned and lifted his muscular frame into the SUV. "Anything else?"

"Say hi to my old colleague," Nielsen replied. "Oh, and Ray—don't forget your gun."

Foster patted his jacket just beneath the breast pocket and smiled. "I never do."

As he drove off Nielsen pulled out his phone. "I'm sending someone your way," he said at the telltale click of an answer.

"Oh really?" the digitally altered voice replied. "And why is that?"

"We may have another opportunity tonight . . . probably our last opportunity. I'm not taking any chances."

"Who should I be expecting?"

"If you're as good as you used to be, you already know."

A soft chuckle echoed over the line. "I'll make sure Mr. Foster gets a warm reception."

"Good." The security director replied. "Who on your team will be leading the op?"

"Given it's importance, I'll be handling tonight's pickup personally."

"Excellent," Nielsen replied. "But there won't be a pick-up tonight."

A brief silence followed. "Then what are we doing?

Nielsen glanced down the alley once again and tightened his grip on the phone. "Something else," he said, lowering his voice. "Something unexpected."

29.

"So that's it?"

Jeri looked up at the face of her father poised over his typewriter, his dark eyes studying her reproachfully. She felt herself blush like a child. "What do you mean?" she asked, her voice a breathless whisper.

"I mean are you done?" Her father replied. "Because as far as I see it, there's still some unfinished business."

"With whom?"

"You know who."

Jeri looked down at her body. The warmth had completed its task. She was nothing now, a human still life folded and propped against the wall. "I didn't ask for this."

Her father sighed and sat back in his chair. A deep furrowed scarred his brow. "Did any of us?"

Everything was wrong.

Beneath her, the ground swayed and rolled as if unhinged from the rest of the world. The air burned hot and arid. A constant wind nagged her hair. And that smell—how best to describe it?—the mineral saltiness of sweat mixed with the sweet tang of decay. *This can't be London* her mind pronounced, rising slowly toward the surface of consciousness. *This was somewhere else entirely.*

"Wake up," a gravelly voice commanded.

Jeri opened her eyes and winced at the sharpness of the sunlight. She raised her hand and peered through the narrow slits of her fingers. The silhouette of a man hovered over her. "Chip?"

The silhouette kneeled and a handsome, weathered face materialized. "Just what the doctor ordered," the old man replied, placing a tray of food next to her. "Scrambled eggs with toast, ice-cold orange juice, and three aspirin."

Jeri sat up and gazed at the horizon. Beyond the brilliant white deck of the sailing yacht stretched a sea of languid, blue-green water. "Jesus . . . where the hell are we?"

"Cacela Velha," Chip replied, gesturing behind her. "Beautiful, isn't it?"

Jeri gazed over her shoulder at a white stretch of shoreline a few hundred meters away. Beyond the beach, a hummock furred with scrub brush rose gently toward a small citadel of whitewashed buildings framed by empty sky. "Sure," she conceded, turning back to him. "But that still doesn't tell me where I am."

The old man ran a hand through his shamble of long, salt and pepper hair and nodded westward. "Southern tip of Portugal. Eight miles east is the Spanish border. And over there," he turned and pointed to the southeast, "roughly a hundred and twenty miles southeast, lies the Strait of Gibraltar. Got your bearings now?"

She nodded and looked herself over. Other than her missing overcoat, she was still wearing the same clothes from the night before. A crescent of dried blood on her left thigh sparkled in the light. She touched it and winced at the soreness. "Maybe next time you could just try an Ambien."

"Eat before it gets cold."

Jeri greedily drank back the orange juice and devoured her breakfast while Chip settled into a seat on the yacht's stern pulpit. "Nice boat," she mumbled, tossing back the aspirin. "Yours?"

"Chilly's."

She stiffened. "Is he here?"

Chip shook his head. "Took the dinghy to Manta Rosa to get some supplies. Gives you and me some time to catch up."

"Great." Jeri shoved the food tray aside and crossed her legs beneath her. "What should we talk about?"

The old man's piercing blue eyes inspected her for a moment. "It's good to see you again, Jeri."

Jeri gazed back at the man she used to serve drinks to at the old saloon in Flagstaff. The memory of her former life forced a wan smile. "How's retirement?"

"Quiet," Chip replied, rolling his eyes. "And the real world?"

"Overrated. I thought I might join you."

The old man nodded thoughtfully. "So I've heard." He rose from his seat and dropped into the yacht's cockpit. "Well, I hate to tell you this, but retirement's not what I was hoping for."

Jeri watched as he rummaged through cabinets. "Neither is a career in the clandestine trafficking of human lives."

A moment later Chip held out a pair of sunglasses. "Here, put these on. Goddamn sun'll blind you out here."

Jeri slipped them on and nodded. "Don't change the subject."

"I'm not. In fact, I'm pretty sure I can summarize everything on your mind if you'd like."

"Be my guest."

The old man hoisted himself back onto the deck with surprising dexterity and took a seat next to her. "Dearest Chip—I've decided to quit because I can't tell right from wrong or up from down anymore. I'm seriously questioning the moral prerogative of this agency to do what we do in the interests of the greater good. I also can't help but think there's a better way to do things. And of course, it doesn't help that I'm haunted by the face of every recruit who's life I now believe I've destroyed. Therefore, effective immediately, I've decided to leave the agency and try something else—like maybe starting a charity or saving the whales. Thanks again for ruining my life. Your friend, Jeri." He looked over with a satisfied smile. "How was that?"

Jeri shrugged. "I'm not sure I would've used the word 'dearest,' but the rest was pretty good."

"Thank you."

"And now this is where you reiterate things like *corporate-state oppression* and *macro-morality* in order to convince me to stay, right?"

"Why should I? We both know that none of the things I just said have anything to do with why you really want to quit."

"No? Then why do I want to quit?"

"I don't know," Chip admitted. "Maybe it's something you don't want to tell me. Maybe it's something you don't want to tell yourself. But whatever it is, I'm pretty sure it's a little more complicated than my version."

Jeri scanned the horizon for a moment. "Who's decision was it to bring me into the agency—yours or Chilly's?"

"Why are you asking?"

"Because as far as I can tell, he's done everything possible to see that I fail."

Chip nodded. "Is that so?"

Jeri cocked her head at him. "Do you have any idea what he's put me through just to *test* me?"

"I imagine whatever was necessary."

"I'm serious."

"So am I, Jeri," the old man said firmly. "Listen to me—Sam's done nothing more than train you on the realities of this job. If he's gone out of his way to test you, it's only because he detected a weakness that needed to be tested—that's it. However you feel he's treated you, it's nothing personal."

"No? And what if I told you I knew something about him that suggested how he's treating me is *very* personal?"

"Like what?"

"Like Laura Hammond."

Chip's brow furrowed and suddenly every one of his sixty-plus years was etched plainly on his face. "Who's that?"

Jeri rolled her eyes. "You're a shitty actor." She watched him stand and make his way toward the yacht's bow. "So—is it true?"

The old man pretended to study the rigging lines overhead. After a long moment of silence, he turned and looked at her. "What are you doing?"

"I'm asking you a simple question."

"No you're not. You're trying to pry into things that have no business being opened."

Jeri nodded. "So it *is* true."

Chip's jaw clenched in anger. "Goddammit, Jeri—you don't have the right to—"

"To what, Chip? To know anything about the man who's trying to mentally and physically destroy me? To know if something from his past might be affecting his decisions?" She stood and marched toward him. "Of course I have the right to know! And by the way—fuck you for keeping it from me!"

"Alight, alright," Chip conceded, raising his hands. "And just what do you think I've been keeping from you?"

"Everything! The fact that Chilly was engaged, the fact that his fiancée was murdered, the fact that he tried to take his own life afterward, the fact that—" Jeri paused and checked her anger. When she spoke again, her voice was low and flat. "The fact that his fiancée, Laura Hammond, looked just like me."

The old man stood unmoving, the thin fabric of his polo shirt dancing against his chest. Beneath them, the yacht swayed gently. "What do you want from me, Jeri? A confession? An absolution? Something that makes everything we're doing okay to you?"

"I just want the truth."

"The truth?" Chip scoffed, slamming his hand against the boom. "Here's the truth. We're in a *war*, Jeri. Make no mistake about it. And wars require someone to fight them. I've picked some extraordinarily good people for this fight. Smart, talented people. But not perfect. Perfect doesn't exist. Like everyone else in this world, Chilly has his own tragedies and demons to deal with. Tell me—are you or I any different?"

"So Hammond—?"

"Yes!" The old man ripped the sunglasses from his face and let out an incredulous laugh. "Good Christ, you're tenacious! Yes, she was real! All of it was real—Hammond, their engagement, her death—all of it! Is that what you needed to

Jeri nodded.

Chip glared at her coldly. "Good." He slipped his glasses back on and took a seat on the deck. "Now that *that's* settled," he continued, his voice once again calm, "let's try to have the rest of this conversation without screaming. Voices carry out here."

Jeri walked over and sat down next to him. A long moment of silence passed as they both studied the water. "Thank you," she said finally. "But given what you knew, I still don't understand why you picked him."

Chip sighed. "I don't know. It was—" he paused and shook his head. "You keep presuming that decisions like these are straightforward, or that we always have a choice to begin with. The survival of this agency depends on always being *better*. Better agents. Better tactics. Six years ago, we needed someone that could produce better packages. Somehow we came across the story of Laura Hammond. When I read that her fiancé was a plastic surgeon, I was curious. By the time I'd finished investigating Sam's background, I was certain he was our guy. He was everything we were looking for—brilliant, young, and suddenly without a family. The only concern was whether Hammond's death had made him—"

"Suicidal?" Jeri interjected.

"I was going to say unpredictable." The old man frowned thoughtfully. "Anyway, I spent the next few months studying Sam and learning everything I could about him. I even shadowed him in the evenings. He'd take these long walks to Navy Pier almost every night. I figured he liked the noise, you know—the voices and the laughter? Maybe the sound of kids laughing on the Ferris wheel." He shrugged and shifted his

302

stare to the water. "Then, one night, his posture took on something new. A sudden look of . . . purposefulness. He paced to the end of the pier and stared down at the water, studying the currents. Suddenly I remembered that his wedding date—or what *should* have been his wedding date—to Hammond was just a few days away. That's when I understood his intentions. That's when I knew it was time."

Despite the heat of the sun, a cold chill ran up Jeri's spine. Her thoughts turned back to that night in São Paulo after Javier Salas' collection when he'd stopped in to check on her. The look on his face when she'd asked about his own recruitment had driven her to know the story. Now, with the truth laid bare, everything she believed about Sam Lafeen was twisting upon itself. The cloud of anger she felt toward her colleague was beginning to vanish, a deep sadness filling its place. "What did you do?" she asked, her voice laced with a trace of contempt.

Chip noticed the change of light in her eyes. "I waited," he murmured. "I was already waiting on the pier that night when he arrived."

"And what did you say to him?"

He blinked as if breaking from a trance. "What needed to be said," he shrugged. "That he could let his grief and anger destroy him, or he could use it for a greater purpose. Plus, there were some things about Hammond's death that I knew we could leverage if—well, never mind."

"What things?"

The old man shook his head. "That stays between me and Chilly."

Jeri stood and moved to the side of the yacht. Beneath her, the ship's hull darkened the languid waters in shadow. Her eyes settled on her own distorted shadow, twisting and bending to the will of the currents. "You've used their ghosts against us, haven't you?"

"Excuse me?"

Laura Hammond's . . . James Stone's . . . god knows who else." She turned and shook her head. "And here I thought Chilly was the one I needed to watch out for."

Chip's brow furrowed again. "What are you talking about?"

"Why did you *really* pick me for this agency? For my *brilliance* as you said before? Or was the grieving daughter of the late James Stone just another easy target like Sam?"

"Jeri, don't—"

"Or maybe it was even more sinister than that. Maybe you decided I looked enough like your star agent's dead fiancé to what?—keep him from self-destructing again? Or is the answer 'all of the above'?"

Chip stood slowly, his eyes fixed on her with laser intensity. "I'm going to pretend you didn't ask me that," he replied. "This isn't a goddamn game, Jeri."

"Oh, I disagree. I think that's *exactly* what this is. And you've been exceptionally good at playing all of us—Chilly, me—even my father. I can only imagine what you said to make him hand over his book."

"Same as the rest of you, Jeri—the truth."

Jeri laughed bitterly. "Spare me your self-righteous bullshit, Chip. Anyone unlucky enough to get swept up in your idea of truth is *destroyed* by it."

"No—*saved* by it." Chip countered.

Both of them turned at the sudden drone of an engine echoing over the water. A small boat was speeding toward them from shore.

"You want to talk about your father?" Chip asked, turning back to her. "Fine—let's talk about the man who knew where the world was heading long before the rest of us. The man who gave me the blueprint for this agency through his work. Do you honestly think I just walked in one day and stole it from him?"

"You mean like the life you stole from his daughter? Like the lives you've stolen from everyone you *recruit*?"

The old man's ice-blue eyes narrowed. "Everyone who knew him knew that James Stone was brilliant, Jeri. But do you know what made your father great? Courage. The courage to *give* me his book rather than share it with the rest of the world. The courage to accept what this agency would do— *must* do —for the greater good. And now it's your turn." He stepped closer. "Maybe you haven't realized it yet, but you've completed three collections. Congratulations, freshman . . . it's graduation day. You're one of *us* now."

The rising growl of the approaching boat precluded any further conversation. Jeri quietly exchanged looks with the old man she once considered a friend. Moments later, the engine fell silent and Chilly's tan face appeared at the yacht's transom.

"What'd I miss?" he asked, dropping a bag of groceries onto the deck. His eyes flickered between the two somber faces in front of him as he lit a cigarette. "That much, huh?"

"I was just congratulating our new graduate," Chip answered. "Now she just needs her agency name." He turned to Chilly. "Got any ideas?"

Chilly took a drag of his cigarette and shrugged. "I don't know . . . Agent Ambivalent? Agent Capricious?"

The two men exchanged a quick grin.

"I don't need a new name," Jeri said flatly. "I already have one. It's Jeri Stone . . . and it's not going to change." She smiled at Chip. "Thanks for the talk, old man. One again, you told me exactly what I needed to hear. So—what's the next step in the protocol?"

Chip shook his head. "For—?"

"Leaving the agency."

The old man's smile vanished. "You can't be serious."

"Dead serious."

"You're going to stand there and tell me you honestly don't believe in what we're doing?"

"I don't believe in *anything* anymore. Including you."

Chilly looked at Chip, who simply shrugged and turned away. "Do you realize what this means?"

Jeri nodded. "I do."

"And you're prepared for what I'll have to do to you?"

"Yes." She gazed back at him defiantly. "Are you?"

Her colleague took another drag of his smoke, his dark eyes studying her. "You know what, Jeri," he said finally, shaking his head. "You have no idea what you're—"

"Leave it alone, Sam," Chip commanded behind him, the vitality gone from his voice. "It's done. If she wants to go, we're not going to stop her."

The two men exchanged a tense look.

"Fine," Chilly conceded, turning to Jeri. "So where do you want to do this?"

Jeri regarded him with surprise. "You mean I have a choice?"

"Anywhere but home," Chip answered. "You can't go back."

"So I've been told." She shifted her gaze to the beach in

the distance. "Alright, then I want to go to—"

"Keep it to yourself," Chip said, holding up a hand. "You can tell Chilly once you're on your way. Now, if you don't mind, I'd like to talk to him privately for a few minutes."

"Wait for me on the tender," Chilly commanded tersely, nodding toward the small boat.

Jeri stepped toward Chip. "I guess this is goodbye."

"I guess so." The old man sighed and wrapped his arms around her. "You take care of yourself now, okay?"

Jeri nodded and pulled herself free. The two men lingered in silence on the main deck while she lowered herself into the small boat moored to the stern. She sat and studied the calm, cerulean waters around her for a moment before noticing the yacht's name written across the stern in elegant black lettering. Jeri was still staring at it when Chilly dropped into the tender next to her.

"The *Lorelei*," she said, nodding at the name. "A beautiful water spirit that lures sailors to their deaths."

"Yep," he mumbled, casting off the line.

"Why'd you pick that?"

Chilly took a seat in the stern. "Reminds me of someone," he said, starting the motor. He throttled the motor into a high pitched scream and challenged her with his stare. "Any other questions?"

Jeri shook her head.

"Good." He yanked the steering handle on the motor and the small boat twisted sharply toward shore.

Jeri turned and watched as the *Lorelei*'s sleek profile receded into the distance. On the main deck, Chip's broad-shouldered figure stood stoically. She tried to make out his expression, but the sun and growing distance worked against her. All she could see was a square, stubble-covered jaw set beneath a tangle of salt and pepper hair. Between them, the old man's mouth appeared to be twisted in a grimace.

Or perhaps it was a smile.

30.

"I don't fookin' believe it. Wait, hold on—"

Dublin stepped from the taxi and shoved a five-pound note at the driver. Around him, a sparse collection of street-lights bathed the East London neighborhood in pale yellows. He lit a cigarette and pressed the phone back to his ear. "I'm telling you, it doesn't make any fookin' sense. What? Yeah, I know every freshman struggles. But this . . . *her* . . . I mean, it's just fookin' . . . and you know he ain't exactly been a fookin' saint to her either."

The Irishman paced the street corner, shaking his head. "She give any reason? She said what? . . . what the fook is that s'posed to mean? No . . . no I haven't talked to him yet. Oh yeah? . . . what favor?" He froze in his tracks. "Are you fookin' kidding me? No . . . no fookin' way . . . I collect the packages . . . I don't play the fookin' angel of death too. He can't expect me to . . . what? Remember what? Oh, for fooksake, he still remembers that? Yeah, yeah . . . I know . . . I fookin' know, okay?" He took a drag of his cigarette and shook his head again. "Fine, so where the fook am I going? Where? Where the fook is that? Jaysus *Christ*. Fine . . . fine, tell him I'll be there . . . twelve hours. And tell him we're fookin' square on favors too."

309

Dublin shoved his phone into his pocket and cursed under his breath. He took a deep drag and studied the small crowd collected outside The Ten Bells pub. A nagging thought twisted his mouth into a scowl. "Fook it," he concluded, sucking in one last lungful of smoke. He flicked the half-spent cigarette to the street and marched toward the pub entrance. "I'm gettin' pissed anyway."

Ten meters overhead, the lens of a surveillance camera watched as the Irishman nodded to himself and marched across the street.

Sitting on the cold, shadowed steps of Christ Church cathedral, Ray Foster turned up his collar and pressed a finger to his ear. "Adler?"

"Still running it."

Foster held his stare on the pub's entrance less than twenty meters from where he was now sitting. Around him, the desiccated remains of oak leaves danced in the cold wind. Another minute passed. "C'mon Adler," he said, his tone insistent. "He's probably on his second pint by now."

Five thousand miles away in the Brannon Street operations room, Mary Adler nodded. "Almost there," she replied, her fingers pounding furiously at her keyboard. "Okay—got it. Initial morphetic scan is showing an eighty-seven percent match." She leaned toward her screens and nodded. "Yeah, it's . . . it's him. I'm sure."

"Good. Is the Security Director there?"

"Yes."

"Ask him to call me back in ten seconds." Foster ended

the call and turned the lit screen of his cellphone toward a black van parked just north of the intersection. He waved the phone as instructed. A moment later, a figure stepped from the driver's seat and began making its way toward the pub. The figure passed under a streetlight, revealing a small, wiry-built man with a shock of red hair. His movements, in contrast to his looks, exuded efficiency and confidence. Although they still hadn't met—a plain-dressed woman simply calling herself *the assistant* had greeted Foster at the airport—he was certain of the man's identity. The Velgyn security manager stifled the urge to laugh as the man crossed the street and entered the pub. A moment later, his cellphone buzzed to life.

"Is that Marcus going in?" Nielsen demanded, watching the live surveillance feed on Adler's screen.

"I think so," Foster replied. "Either that or David Caruso just hijacked our operation."

Nielsen grunted. "Appearances can be deceiving."

"Roger that, boss." Foster scanned the pub's curtained windows, hoping for a glimpse inside. "You still sure this guy's as good as you remember?"

"I have to be," the security director replied flatly.

"Why's that?"

"Because if he isn't, we're all out of a job."

∾

"You mind?"

Dublin looked up from his pint to find a short, red-headed man with a scar on his right cheek hovering next to him. The man's finger was pointed at his scarf on the next barstool. "Mind what?"

311

"Mind if I sit there?"

"You being serious?" The Irishman gestured at the half-empty pub. "A million seats and you gotta have that one?"

"My usual spot," the man replied. His hazel eyes shifted patiently to the seat.

Dublin gave the man a hard look before shaking his head. "For fooksake," he grumbled, snatching his scarf and tossing it onto the bar. "There. Take your fookin' seat."

"Thank you." The man sat and ordered a beer. A minute later, he turned and smiled. "See the match?"

"What fookin' match?"

"Manchester at Emirates," the man clarified. "What—not a fan?"

"Of Manchester? Fook no."

"Let me guess—Chelsea?"

Dublin took a sip of his pint and let out a resigned sigh. "Arsenal."

"Ah . . . I should of known," the man nodded. "You've certainly got the look of a *Gooner*."

"S'cuse me?"

"You know—angry, overweight, weak-chinned. Oh, and downtrodden . . . as if life itself had just wiped its ass with you." He tossed back a slug of his beer and shrugged. "Don't know why, but Arsenal always attracts the same sort."

Dublin turned and faced him. "The *fook* you say. And Manchester? The rest of your rag-fook brothers a bunch of ginger-haired little poofs like you?"

The man's hazel eyes regarded him with indifference. "I suppose they are," he said finally, smiling and slapping him on the shoulder. He nodded at Dublin's nearly empty pint. "Buy you another?"

"Only if it comes with the condition you'll shut the fook up."

"I'll take that as a yes." The man ordered another round and fell into silence. Dublin was just beginning to think his wish had been granted when the man turned and pointed at his jacket. "Very nice. Vintage?"

The Irishman gave him a look somewhere between weariness and loathing. "Did I miss somethin'? Does the sign outside say it's fifty fookin' questions night? Of course it's vintage."

The man shrugged as if bored. "Looks almost like the real thing."

"Almost—?" Dublin grabbed his beer and emptied it by half. "I'll have you know that this very jacket once belonged to Lou Reed. In fact, I've got it on good authority that Lou was wearing it the night he and the Velvet fookin' Underground performed their first gig after releasing White Light/White Heat. And you're sittin' there in your gimpy fookin' poof-coat saying it *almost* looks real? This is as real as it fookin' gets."

"May I?"

Before Dublin could respond the man raised his hand and grabbed the jacket's silver-studded collar.

"I don't know," he mumbled, rubbing the black leather roughly between his fingers. "Doesn't look vintage to me."

The Irishman's face went slack. "Get your bloody fookin' fingers off my jacket," he threatened. "Now."

The red-haired man's eyes glimmered with amusement. "I don't even think it's real leather."

"I'm warnin' you, mate."

"Who's Lou Reed, anyway?"

Dublin's balled fist rose from the bar and swung toward

its target. As if anticipating the move, the man shoved Dublin's shoulder back and caught the lop-sided punch in his free hand. Caught off-balance, Dublin started to strike a blow with his other hand, but once again the man anticipated his move, this time pulling the Irishman forward and kicking the stool out from under him. In an instant Dublin was sprawled face down on the ground. He started to rise when the man dropped a foot on his back and pressed him hard to the floor.

"You know, you're right—it *does* look vintage," the man said, rising from his seat. He removed his foot and knelt down next to the Irishman. "My mistake."

Dublin felt a hand pat him gently on the back. He lifted his head and watched the red-haired man rise and straighten his jacket before slipping out the door. Around him, the rest of the bar's patrons gawked silently, unsure of what had just happened. "The fook you lookin' at?" he mumbled, rising to his feet. "What—never seen the consequences of fookin' another man's wife?" He wiped himself off and dropped heavily back onto the barstool.

"You alright there?" the bartender asked.

Dublin waved a dismissive hand and sighed. "Fine," he said, pointing at the tap. "Jus' get me another fookin' beer."

"He's out."

Nielsen leaned closer to Adler's monitor as Marcus stepped out of the Ten Bells Pub and marched back toward the black van. "Alright Ray, go see what he's got for you."

Foster rose from the steps of the cathedral and made his way across the street. His eyes stayed fixed on Marcus as they headed north along the street. Upon reaching the van, Marcus turned and disappeared around the back. Foster slowed and looked into the vehicle's window as he passed. The cab was empty. He followed Marcus around the other side and found the van's side door slightly open. He stepped closer and peered inside.

The muzzle of a gun stared back at him.

"Come in," a voice commanded.

The Velgyn security manager glanced around briefly before stepping inside. He closed the door and turned to the redheaded man leaning against a narrow workbench in the corner. "You must be Marcus."

"And you must be Ray," the man said with a trace of an accent. "It's a shame Lars couldn't join us. But I'm sure he's busy with other matters."

"Mr. Nielsen sends his regards," Foster replied. His eyes shifted to the gun. "Do you mind?"

Marcus glanced at the pistol in his hand as if he'd forgotten it. "Of course." He dropped the gun on the workbench and retrieved a cellphone from his pocket. "I'm not used to having clients involved directly in the work. But I suppose anything's agreeable . . . for the right price."

Foster studied the man as he busied himself with something on his phone. The former Blackwell interrogator looked to be in his mid-forties, with a square, freckled face marred by a scar that ran from the outer corner of his right eye to his chin. A poor suturing of the wound had left it raised and uneven. Although small, he moved with the practiced grace of a boxer or martial artist, and Foster got the distinct sense that from an early age Marcus had required—if not chosen—violence as his preferred means of survival. "So?" he said, sounding less commanding than he'd hoped to. "Did it work?"

Marcus's hazel eyes flashed to Foster with a look of annoyance before returning to the screen. "See for yourself." He tapped the screen once more and tossed over the phone.

The security manager caught it as his own phone buzzed to life. He clicked on his earpiece. "Yes? Hey, boss. Yeah . . . I'm here with him now. Hold on." Foster studied the map displayed on Marcus's phone. A pulsing dot hovered on the southeastern corner of the intersection where the pub was. "Yeah, it looks like he tagged him . . . yes . . . okay, understood." He ended the call and nodded. "Mr. Nielsen's authorized me to obtain anything necessary, including full use of the jet. Whatever we need."

Marcus cocked his head. "We?"

"That's right. I'm part of your team until this is done."

The two men exchanged a silent look.

"I see." Marcus removed his jacket to reveal arms of veiny, tightly corded muscle. "And tell me, Ray—have you done this kind of work before?"

Foster shook his head. "No."

As if on cue, the doors up front opened and two men slipped into the driver and passenger seats. "Let's go," Marcus commanded. He leaned toward the security manager as the van rolled back onto the street. "Well, let's hope you have the stomach for it."

31.

"This doesn't make any sense."

Paul Obermeyer flipped through the pages of analysis results and shook his head. "This can't be right."

"What cannot be right?" Tatyana asked, stifling a yawn. It was well past one in the morning and the sounds of other life inside the Ras Jazan complex had long since fallen silent.

"These readings—" Paul tossed the results on the counter between them. "Hydrocarbon yields in all twenty-three modified samples are even lower than their corresponding control sample. But I don't understand why. The modified algae codon should have only increased lipid production, especially at this light intensity. Even if the codon had failed, it shouldn't have reduced the yield." Tatyana picked up the results as Paul rubbed his beard in thought. "The numbers are too consistent to be genetic," he mumbled absently. "No, this . . . this has to be environmental. Something must have been compromised in the setup. Something in—" His eyes flashed to Tatyana. "Something in the media."

Across from him, the Russian researcher looked up with a deep furrow in her brow. "Excuse me?"

"What media formula did you use for the samples?"

"Exactly what you asked me to use—RFAM-4."

"No, I told you to use RFAM-2," Paul replied curtly. "*Two . . . not four.*" He stepped over to a large instrument and began tapping on its touchscreen monitor. "I would have expected a microbiologist to know that RFAM-4 is optimized for phototrophic bacteria, not microalgae," he said irritably as he called up the formula mix. His finger hovered over the display of compounds. "So let's see what kind of toxic ingredients our samples were subjected to. Three grams of boric acid per liter . . . twenty-four grams of monobasic phosphate . . . calcium chloride . . . Jesus—point eight grams?" Paul turned and looked at his colleague. "No wonder the samples didn't yield higher counts—they were barely staying alive!" He slapped his hand against the device in frustration. "Congratulations, Dr. Aleksandrov—you just *ruined* several days of my work."

Tatyana turned to the last page of analysis results and shrugged. "Not according to this. Did you even read the final summary?"

Paul walked over and snatched the page from her.

"Hydrocarbon readings on samples twenty-four through twenty-nine all show increases in yield," she said flatly. "The increase in sample twenty-six is nearly fifteen percent." A satisfied grin dimpled her cheeks as she crossed her arms.

Paul looked up with a puzzled frown. "Samples twenty-four through twenty-nine? But . . . how did we end up with five extra samples?"

"Do you recall the samples you asked me to exclude?"

"You mean the ones that underwent transposon mutagenesis? Don't tell me you—"

Tatyana nodded. "Yes, I included them anyway. As I said, I did not agree with your conclusions. And I was also curious." She cocked her head triumphantly. "It appears I was right."

"Oh, so you think these results actually mean something—is that it? Here, let me file these results where they belong." Paul crumpled the readout and hurled it toward the wastebasket. "Bacterial mutagenesis—as I've already explained—can generate spontaneous mutations in the cellular matrix that we cannot predict. All you did by including those samples was create a result that can't be traced, documented or even remotely reproduced in the manner or scale this project requires." He shoved the remaining printouts onto the floor. "The next time you decide to ignore my orders and follow your curiosity, remember that *I* am the one that understands genetic engineering around here, not you. In other words, stop wasting everyone's time and leave the thinking to me—got it?"

The Russian researcher's hand shot out with surprising speed and slapped Paul across the face. "I will not be talked to like an insolent child!" she hissed, pointing a finger at his reddening face. "Those results are just as reproducible as the others! Either you are too stupid to see that, or too much of a chauvinistic coward to accept that I could be right!" She spun and headed for the door.

"Wait—where do you think you're going?" Paul demanded, trailing after her. "You can't just walk away, Dr. Aleksandrov. If you're so sure you can reproduce the results, then do it!"

"Go to hell!" Tatyana quickened her pace as Paul fell in step behind her. "I offer you sound scientific ideas, and all you offer in return is insults!"

"*I* offer insults? Wasn't I the one you just called either stupid or a coward?"

"Those were not insults. Those were facts."

"Yeah? Then what should I call an assistant who switches media formulas and intentionally mislabels genetic samples in order to fulfill her own curiosity?"

"A good researcher."

Paul pursued her down a side corridor. "Is that what they call it in Russia? Well, where I come from it's called *sabotage*—and that's exactly the word I'll use when I tell Derrick what you've done."

"My god, you sound like a little child," Tatyana retorted, darting into a stairwell. "I'm quite certain Mr. Birch will understand my intentions. And if he doesn't, fine. What is he going to do—fire me?" A bitter laugh escaped her lips.

At the top of the stairs, Paul grabbed Tatyana's arm and spun her around. "What the hell is your problem?"

"Let go of me," she demanded.

"No, not until you explain—"

Tatyana's hand struck even faster this time, catching Paul squarely across the temple.

"Goddammit, stop hitting me!" he growled, releasing his grip. His colleague turned and marched across one of several suspended walkways radiating outward from the stairwell. "This discussion isn't over, Dr. Aleksandrov!" Paul stepped onto the open metal platform and immediately found himself engulfed in warm, tropical air. Beneath his feet, a network of massive steel pipes hissed ominously as steam rolled off their broad backs. Overhead, brightly colored lines of conduit followed the walkway toward a hulking cylinder of concrete. He looked beyond the swirling veil of steam in front of him to find Tatyana punching at a code panel next to a door that led inside the cylinder. A light on the panel flashed green and the door opened. Paul waited until his colleague stepped inside before rushing in after her. He closed the door behind him and stared into the sudden darkness. "Now—are you going to talk to me like a mature adult, or are you going to slap me again?"

"That depends on you."

Paul turned at the sound of movement to his right. "What are you doing?" he asked. The sharp click of an opened cabinet door was followed by a dull thud of something heavy being placed on a counter. More sounds—muddled together and impossible to distinguish—echoed around him.

"Dr. Aleksandrov?"

"Yes?"

"What are . . . oh, for Christ's sake—would you please turn on a light?"

A moment later, a cascade of overhead light filled the room. Paul winced and focused on a small table in front of him. A half-empty bottle of vodka sat alongside his colleague's discarded lab coat. Next to the table, Tatyana stood staring back at him, a shot glass poised in her hand. "Are you afraid of the dark, Dr. Obermeyer?" she asked.

Paul noted her smug grin. "No, I just wasn't sure—" He glanced past her at the IKEA-style furniture arranged around the large, windowless room. "This must be your apartment," he nodded. "Very nice, at least by Ceres standards. My place has more of a mental asylum look going for it."

"And this place does not?" Tatyana scoffed. "Why else do you think I keep the lights off?" She tossed back the shot and smiled bitterly. "At least in the darkness I can pretend to be somewhere other than here."

"No doubt the vodka helps." Paul gestured at the bottle. "Are you willing to share with a colleague?"

Tatyana refilled the glass and handed it over.

"Nasdarovje," Paul said, raising it. "Isn't that what you say?"

"Close enough."

"Well, here's to close enough." He drank it slowly and smiled. "That certainly beats getting slapped. Thank you."

His colleague took the glass and poured another "Dobro pozhalovat," she replied, tossing it back before pounding the glass on the table. "Now, is there anything else you would like to say before I ask you to go?"

Paul's smile faded. "I'm sorry, Dr. Aleksandrov. I'm sorry you grew up in a world that doesn't treat women fairly. I'm sorry for all the assholes that have forced you to become smug and self-righteous in order to survive. But the truth is, I can't trust you. And if I can't trust you, I can't have you working in my lab. So thank you for your help, but your assistance is no longer needed. Oh, and feel free to tell Derrick whatever you'd like. Tell him I'm an idiot *and* a chauvinistic coward. I'm sure you'll be convincing." His eyes dropped to the soft curve of her breasts beneath the fabric of her shirt. He blinked and looked away. "Anyway, that's it. That's all I came here to say. Thanks again for the vodka."

Tatyana shook her head as he turned to the door. "No," she said, her voice barely more than a whisper.

"No what?"

"I will tell Derrick nothing of the sort. If I have done anything, it is disprove your ridiculous notion that AP mutagenesis is unstable. If anyone should have to defend their actions, it is you."

Paul studied her defiant expression. "You've got to be kidding me." A brief look of surprise crossed Tatyana's face as he marched over and leveled an index finger at her sternum. "If you want to pursue the potential benefits of an inherently unpredictable genetic phenomena, do it in your *own* fucking lab. I'm not here to do theoretical science. I'm here to solve a ridiculously complex problem on a ridiculously short schedule—and the last thing I have time for is defending myself against a microbiologist who doesn't have a fucking *clue* what she's talking about!"

The surprise in Tatyana's eyes abruptly hardened into rage. The flash of her strike came as fast as before, but this time Paul was prepared. He caught his colleague's wrist and shoved her against the wall. "Has anyone ever told you that you're predictable?" he hissed, seizing her other hand. He leaned in and pressed his mouth to her ear. "Now—what are you going to tell Derrick?"

Tatyana turned her head, her short bangs of hair brushing his face. Their eyes met for a brief moment before she leaned forward and pressed her lips to his. Paul felt her tongue force its way into his mouth. The taste of vodka mingled with the soft, flowery fragrance of her skin. His mouth fell into sync with hers and she moaned softly in response. With sudden urgency, her legs began to press against him. Paul shifted his weight to better balance their interlocked bodies when Tatyana's tongue suddenly vanished and she pushed him away. Caught off balance, he opened his eyes to find the Russian woman staring back with a mischievous grin.

"What's so fun—?"

Tatyana's martial arts-style sidekick was perfectly placed. Sweeping his legs from under him, Paul's tall frame twisted in the air like a propeller before crashing sidelong onto the concrete floor. The pain of the impact was just beginning to register when his colleague kicked him onto his back and jumped on top of him.

"Forgive me," she said, straddling his chest. "You were saying something about me being predictable?"

"Never mind," Paul moaned. "I was mistaken."

"Yes, you were. Any good biologist knows that you must study an organism thoroughly before asserting any knowledge of its behavior." Tatyana leaned down. "Have you been studying *me*, Dr. Obermeyer?"

Paul shook his head. "No . . . not really."

"You see? That explains why you know nothing about me. If you did, you would know that I have no intention of taking orders from anyone who does not recognize the value of my knowledge. You would also know that everything I do is done on *my* terms." She paused and smiled. "Of course, I have been studying you."

"Yeah? And—?"

The Russian researcher shook her head. "I admit . . . I do not believe you are an idiot. But of course, what I still don't know is whether or not you are a coward."

Paul's jaw tightened in irritation. "I can assure you I'm not a coward."

"No?" Tatyana shrugged and tightened her legs around him. "Then assure me."

Paul read the thin smile behind her challenge and felt a surge of anger rush through him. He seized his colleague by the neck and pulled her roughly to his mouth.

32.

The Fiat 500 twisted its way north under an orange-tinted canopy of predawn light. On the right, the villas lining the road slipped past in a blur of pastel colors. On the left, an endless colonnade of cypress trees stood in silvery green. Beyond their spindly forms, a vast lake mirrored a constellation of man-made lights flickering on the far shore.

From her position in the passenger seat, Jeri watched the scenery outside impassively, her thoughts materializing and vanishing as swiftly as the objects in the headlights. On the car stereo, an old eighties tune played softly—

> *You and me never were like the rest,*
> *Always runnin' and hidin' to avoid that mess*
> *But troubled followed, right from the start,*
> *And this avoidin' thing's become our art*
> *Want peace and change, love and hope?*
> *Then find your dealer, buy more dope*
> *Cause life ain't fightin' for a cause,*
> *It's checkin' out from all their laws . . .*

Jeri reached out and punched the stereo's power button, happy for the silence. The Fiat rounded another gentle curve and the need for sleep once again pressed against her. She closed her eyes and listened to the drone of the engine.

"Why here?"

Jeri opened her eyes. "What?"

"Why here?" Chilly repeated.

She snapped her head around and glared at her colleague. "Oh, so we're talking again—is that it? After nearly a day of silence, you suddenly feel the need to speak to me? Because if so, I have a question—why this car? Of all the ones you could've rented, why did you pick the smallest car ever invented? And why are we even *driving* in the first place?"

"Cost," Chilly said flatly, steering the tiny vehicle through another turn. "It's not like we have money in the budget to fly a deserting agent to her favorite exit destination. Besides, I thought a nice long drive would give you a chance to think things over . . . maybe change your mind."

"Yeah? Well, the next time you decide to try to change my mind, maybe opt for a bigger car."

Chilly shrugged and pointed a finger ahead. "So—?"

"So *what*?"

"Why did you pick this place?"

Jeri peered out at the dimly lit landscape. "I was here once before," she said after a moment. "With my father. The first big trip we took together. I was maybe thirteen." A smile forced itself onto her face as the memories returned. "I remember having the best time. We rented a boat and spent days just motoring around . . . picnicking on the islands . . . exploring all the beautiful villages along the coast. I don't know . . . I guess I figured that if I have to start all over, this was as good a place as any to do it." A sudden thought swept away her smile.

She turned to Chilly. "You're not taking those memories from me too—right?"

Chilly shook his head. "Only recent memories will be affected."

"Define *recent*."

"The drug targets the prefrontal cortex of the brain where most of your more recent memories are stored. Anything from the last few years could be affected, but the noticeable gap will be the last two or three months. Unfortunately, it's not an exact science. The drug affects everyone differently."

Jeri recalled the name of the drug from their conversation on the Mexican shore two months earlier. "Diaverol," she whispered, staring once again at the rush of passing scenery. "So I won't remember any of this? My training . . . the recruits . . . you?"

Chilly glanced over at her with a pensive grin. "Diaverol doesn't strip away mental records so much as disrupt the associations that provide reference and context. For instance, you might remember an old man sitting at a bar, but you won't know if it was from yesterday or from two years ago. Or you'll remember spending time in a cabin, but you won't recall where it was. You might even remember a strikingly handsome man once driving you somewhere, but for some strange reason you won't be able to recall his name."

"That's odd . . . I don't remember Tall Tommy ever driving me anywhere."

"No, I meant—"

"I know what you meant."

Chilly smiled, and for a moment the tension inside the car's cramped interior seemed to dissipate. "Too bad I don't have anything that can erase your sense of humor."

"Oh, I'd say your personality works just fine for that."

As they rounded another corner, the lights of the next village drifted into view.

"This is it," Jeri murmured, a nervous excitement raising the goose bumps on her skin. Next to her, a high wall of stone abruptly vanished to reveal clusters of ornate houses rising toward the shrouded peak of Monte Baldo. Under the yellow-white glow of the street lights, modern pavement gave way to narrow cobblestone streets. She took a deep breath. "Welcome to Malcesine."

A short distance further, Chilly eased the car to the side of the road and turned off the engine. Jeri looked over to find him staring out the window, his hands still locked around the wheel. "What's wrong?" she asked.

Her colleague looked over with an expression bordering on pain. "Don't do this, Jeri. Don't . . . don't make me *do this* to you."

"What—let me go?" Jeri shrugged. "I don't get it. You didn't have any problem pulling the trigger that brought me in. Why is this any harder? At least this time it's *my* choice."

"You're right. It is your choice. But it's the wrong choice."

"Well, we'll find out soon enough, won't we?" Jeri crossed her arms and sat in silence next to him. "I want to ask you a question," she said finally. "And please give me an honest answer."

"Okay."

"Why was I brought into this agency?"

Chilly shifted his gaze back to the window. "Same as the rest of us," he replied matter-of-factly. "Chip saw something special in you that could be useful to the agency."

328

"And what exactly was that?"

"To be honest, I wasn't really sure at first." He smiled and shook his head. "I was writing those letters to you without even knowing who you really were. But the old man was adamant that you were special." His eyes flashed back to Jeri. "But then, the moment I met you, I knew he was right."

Jeri narrowed her eyes on him. "Chip hasn't retired. He's still behind everything, isn't he—the agents, the targets, the reasons for their selection?"

Chilly's expression turned guarded. "Why do you ask?"

"Come on—hasn't it ever occurred to you that Chip might just be another megalomaniac who's manipulated all of us—even my father—to carry out his own vision for correcting the world order?"

"Maybe. But what if he is? That doesn't necessarily make him wrong. Maybe changing the world *requires* a megalomaniac. Maybe Chip's vision is the best option we've got."

"Or maybe he's just a genius at convincing others to believe him when they're at their most vulnerable," Jeri retorted. "Like a young woman who'd just lost her father, or a suicidal young doctor who was still grieving the loss of his—"

"Don't," Chilly commanded. His hands tightened around the steering wheel. "Look, I don't know what you've chosen to believe in order to make your decision. But don't try to make me a collaborator of your theories . . . especially when you don't know anything about me or *my* reasons for staying in this agency."

Jeri nodded slowly. "I'm sorry. I didn't—"

"Who told you?"

"Who—? No one. After our conversation in São Paulo, I was just curious to know why you didn't want to talk about your recruitment. Dublin happened to mention that you have a Chicago accent, so I did a little searching and the next thing I know I was downloading a database of Chicago police reports. It didn't take long to find the missing person's report for one Dr. Sam Lafeen. Even less time to uncover the reasons why he chose to . . . go."

"Dublin?" Chilly scoffed. "Of all people to be noticing accents."

Jeri looked at him cautiously. "Was her . . . was it really just a random shooting?"

Her colleague pushed the start button and the Fiat's engine whispered to life. "Nothing in this world is random," he said with a tone of finality. He slipped back onto the road and they continued into town in silence. A few turns later, they came upon a rustic, three-story hotel by the water. Chilly stopped the car and reached into his jacket. "Here," he said, handing Jeri an envelope.

Jeri peered inside to find a thick stack of hundred-euro bills. "What's this for?"

Chilly shrugged. "Consider it severance pay. Or maybe *next life* pay is more appropriate since you won't remember where it came from. Either way, it should cover your needs for a while."

Jeri nodded. "I thought you said there wasn't any money in the budget for deserting agents."

"Let's just say if we'd taken the jet, that envelope would be empty."

"So I guess I should be thanking this little Fiat after all." Jeri lingered for a moment, trying to think of something else to say. But nothing would come. "Alright, I'll go check in." She stepped out of the car and turned. "Are you coming?"

Chilly shook his head. "Think I'll go for a drive."

"Didn't we just spend the last nineteen hours doing that? Besides, I thought I wasn't allowed out of your sight. Aren't I still considered a flight risk?"

Her colleague gave her a dismissive shrug. "I trust you," he said, looking at his watch. "I'll be back in a few hours. Just don't eat anything, and only drink water." He looked at her with a distant, clinical expression. "Will you be ready?"

"Yeah. I'll probably take a walk, but . . . yeah." Another awkward moment passed before she closed the door. Chilly started to pull away when Jeri gestured for him to stop. "Not that it matters," she said as he rolled down the window, "but, will it hurt?"

Her colleague gazed through the window at the first traces of dawn edging the sky and sighed. "Of course it will," he replied. "It'll hurt everything we're trying to accomplish."

"No, I meant—"

"I know what you meant, Jeri."

Jeri waited for Chilly to say something else, to look over and smile. But the moment never came. The window slipped back into place and she met her own empty reflection before the car sped forward and vanished around a corner. A sudden urge to run after it shot through her like a jolt of electricity, but it was too late. Sam Lafeen was gone, in every sense of the word.

She turned and walked inside.

33.

Paul awoke with a start.

He couldn't recall when he'd fallen asleep, but the erotic dream that had repeated itself throughout the night still lingered in his mind along with a dull, throbbing headache. He glanced around at the darkness. From his low vantage point, the room seemed oddly familiar. But where exactly was he? The last thing he remembered was—

Something stirred on the mattress next to him. Paul twisted in surprise, wincing at the pain that bolted up his stiff back. His leg connected with an empty bottle and sent it rolling across the floor. The bedsheet fell back to reveal a head of short, brunette hair. Two deep-green eyes blinked back at him.

"Dobro utro," Tatyana mumbled, kicking off the remaining sheet. "That means good morning."

Paul's gaze slowly drifted to her pale, naked body. "Wait, this . . . this actually *happened*?" he stuttered. "I thought I was dreaming."

"I should take that as a compliment." His colleague slapped her hands and several lights around the room abruptly glowed to life. "But I believe most of the credit belongs to the vodka. For a skinny man, you're a very good drinker, Dr.

Obermeyer."

Paul watched with silent wonder as Tatyana rose and assumed a yoga-like pose. Since meeting her, he'd considered the short-tempered Russian attractive. But now, gazing at the lithe, unblemished body standing over him, it was fair to say she was beautiful. He considered reaching up and caressing her leg, but decided against it. "Sorry, but I'm a little confused. I was under the distinct impression that you hated me."

"Nonsense," she scoffed, bending into a new pose. "Your arrogance perhaps, and certainly your narrow-minded approach to research. But I do not hate *you*, Dr. Obermeyer." She looked down and studied his own naked body. "In fact, I find you quite appealing."

Paul nodded. "Likewise." He propped himself onto his elbows and slowly rolled his head back and forth. "Still, I'm surprised. I would've never expected to be a contender against the brilliant Derrick Birch or the dashing Marcello."

"Who said that you are?" his colleague asked dryly.

"Well, that's true. It's stupid of me to assume you haven't—"

"I'm just teasing on you," Tatyana replied, giving him a playful kick before contorting into another position.

"You mean *with* you."

"Yes, I am with you, not them."

"No, I mean . . . never mind." Paul sat up and took a deep breath. The pain in his back was beginning to subside. His bigger concern was the growing queasiness in his gut.

"Derrick is a very nice man," Tatyana continued. "But Derrick is only in love with Derrick. And Marcello is far too good looking to be heterosexual. No, they are only my colleagues . . . like Shahid or Chung. Nothing more."

Paul glanced around for his clothes. "Well, don't worry—I can keep a secret if you can. As long as we both agree this doesn't change anything."

Tatyana dropped her yoga pose and looked at him quizzically. "What do you mean?"

"I mean just because we slept together doesn't mean I've changed my mind. I still don't want you in my lab." Paul noticed his colleague's body abruptly tense and leaned back. "You're not going to slap me again, are you?"

"Is that what you think—that I seduced you as some kind of ploy? So I could assist you in making even more of a fool of yourself?"

"No offense, but if you'd stuck to simply assisting me, we wouldn't be having this discussion."

Tatyana bent down and roughly grabbed his face. "Running samples with AP mutagenesis was my *first* gift to you, Dr. Obermeyer," she said flatly. She stood and gestured at her body. "Consider this my last."

Paul rose to his feet as his Russian colleague spun and marched toward the makeshift apartment's kitchen. "Is *that* what this is about?" He found his pants and hopped after her, putting them on. "You honestly think your little lab experiment holds the answer to increasing yield?"

"Of course I do!" Tatyana grabbed a bottle of water from the refrigerator and slammed the door shut. "And those samples proved I was right!"

"Bullshit! I already told you—regardless of what the samples read, it won't work!"

Tatyana stepped toward Paul with the bottle clutched dagger-like in her hand. "Is it the samples you refuse to trust—or is it me? Are you really going to risk the success of Ceres because your ego refuses to believe a microbiologist may have given you the answer?"

"No." Paul seized the bottle from her hand and pointed it back at her. "On the contrary—I'm trying to protect the success of Ceres from the whim of a self-righteous bitch with a chip on her shoulder so big that she's willing to toss out real science for a fucking hunch!"

His colleague's face twisted into a grimace. "Give me my fucking water!"

"Stay out of my fucking lab!"

"Fine!" Tatyana grabbed the bottle and stormed over to a nearby chair. A long silence followed as she sat and took a drink. "Fine," she repeated flatly, shaking her head. "Do it your way. Do it *only* your way. But I hope you know exactly what it is that you are doing . . . and why."

Paul dropped into the chair next to her before his stomach could attempt a backflip. "Oh, for Christ's sake . . . what difference does it make? The sooner we solve the yield issue, the sooner we're all dead."

"Nonsense."

"Oh—so you really believe they're going to let us walk out of here?

Tatyana shrugged "Is there any purpose in believing otherwise?"

"Come on, think about it—we're already dead to the rest of the world. If there was really as much risk in bringing us here as Derrick and Faheem have convinced us to believe, then why on earth would they just let us go?"

"Because they've said they would."

Paul shook his head. "No offense, but you're the last person I would have expected to trust these guys."

Tatyana offered a bitter laugh. "This has nothing to do with trust."

"Then why would you believe them?"

His colleague's gaze became distant. "Do you remember the person who recruited you?"

"No. Do you?"

Tatyana nodded. "It was late," she replied in a low, weary tone. "I was still working, which was not unusual. Everyone else had gone home to their wives or their families or to . . . something. I was thirsty and had decided to get some tea. So I walked into the cafeteria and turned on the lights and there he was—this man. Dark hair . . . handsome face. I knew he was a foreigner because he was far too handsome to have been from Kaliningrad. We exchanged greetings, he told me he was American, and then he smiled and very politely said 'Dr. Tatyana Aleksandrov, I am here to end your life as you know it.' Of course, I did not believe him. It was only after I saw the gun that I really believed him. By then he was going on and on about why he was there and why I had been chosen. But I wasn't listening. All I could see was the gun. All I could think about was being shot. And all I could feel was terror." She paused and sipped at her water. "I tried to escape, but it was useless. This man, he was . . . he was very clever. It was clear he had done this many times before. So he knew. He knew that I would run. And that's the last thing I remember . . . running for my life."

Paul watched her brush something from her eye.

"Einstein's theory of relativity tells us gravity slows down time, Dr. Obermeyer," she continued. "But terror does the same. Terror can stretch a moment into something far greater and more sinister. In those moments before the life that I knew was about to end, I realized the life that I had always hoped for would never be. The *fermy devushka* who had beaten the odds and become a brilliant researcher was still nothing more than a girl, alone and afraid, whose only true love in life would be her work." Tatyana took another drink and handed the bottle to Paul. "When I woke up and was told where I was and what had happened, I realized the man had lied. My life, as I knew it, had not changed at all. Here I was—still alone and afraid—with nothing but my work."

She stood and faced him.

"There is nothing left to take from me that I have not already given, Paul. But I am tired of being afraid. Tired of being afraid and lonely. So I have decided not to be either in this new life I've been given. It is not that I trust what they say is true—it is that I refuse to accept anything less than what I am owed." She paused and frowned. "Of course, we won't know what they will do until *after* you solve the yield problem. So I will say it again. If you do not wish to listen to my ideas, or to consider solutions other than your own, so be it. You are, as you keep saying, the expert. But again—for everyone's sake, I hope you know what you are doing."

Paul looked up at his colleague's naked form standing shameless before him and nodded. "I will fix the yield problem," he asserted. "But what then? Even if they do let us leave, where are a handful of 'dead' researchers supposed to go?"

"Retirement," Tatyana replied, a thin smile softening her face. "I have always wanted to see Florida. Is Orlando a very nice place?"

"I'm serious. We can't just retire and give up . . . *thinking*. We're scientists—it's in our nature to question, to solve problems. How are we going to do that when we're stuck somewhere between dead and alive?"

Tatyana shrugged. "By doing what every creature must do when faced with an unexpected challenge—evolve into something new."

"Yeah, that sounds great," Paul rose and began collecting the rest of his clothes. "Unfortunately, you and I both know that highly specialized organisms don't like to evolve. One little change and"—he opened a hand to simulate an explosion—"boom . . . disaster."

"Then we must evolve together."

"Sure, that's it," Paul said sarcastically, snatching his shirt from the floor. "The nearly departed crew will form a nice little colony of their own in some hidden corner of the world. I'll hunt, you'll cook, Derrick will tell us all to work faster, the other three will do whatever the fuck it is that they're good at—and six highly specialized individuals will learn to co-exist, each doing their part to survive like any other successful symbiotic—"

He suddenly froze.

Tatyana furrowed her brow at him. "What's wrong?"

Paul looked at her with intense eyes. "That . . . *shit* . . . that just might work."

"What are you talking about?"

"A colony," he mumbled, rushing over and grabbing her shoulders. "A fucking *colony*! Not one, but several . . . working and evolving together. Christ . . . why didn't I think of it before?" Tatyana gasped with surprise as Paul pulled her to him and kissed her. "You're a genius!" he exclaimed, shaking her with excitement. He collected the rest of his clothes and ran to the door.

"Wait—where are you going?" his colleague demanded.

"Meet me in the lab as soon as you're dressed!" Paul opened the door and gave her a fleeting smile before disappearing into a cloud of steamy air.

"So you are allowing me into your lab once again—is that it?" she cried out after him.

"Absolutely!"

Tatyana stood dumbfounded as the sound of Paul's running footsteps echoed across the walkway outside. *A colony? The six of us in a colony?* She considered the idea for a moment before walking over and closing the door. *It would never work*, she concluded, shaking her head.

She didn't even know how to cook.

34.

"Benvenuti a Verona!" The young rental car agent's Ferrari-red lips twisted into a friendly smile at the man stepping up to the counter. "Do you have a reservation, sir?"

"No," Dublin replied. "Last minute trip."

"Of course, sir. Absolutely not a problem." The agent's stare lingered on his bloodshot eyes for a moment before turning to the nearest computer. "And what kind of car were you looking for?"

"Fook if I know. How far's Malcesine from here?"

"Not far at all. You'll take the A22 north to the—"

"Yeah, fine—got it," the Irishman interjected, waving her silent. "Whatever'll get me there tha fastest."

"Yes, of course," the agent replied. Her smile remained while she called up the available options. "May I suggest the Alfa Romeo?" She turned her screen and pointed a manicured nail at a sporty two-door.

Dublin nodded and tossed a credit card and ID on the counter. Out of the corner of his eye, he noticed a tall, broadshouldered man in a black suit step from an arrival gate and check his watch before making his way toward the rental counter.

"Thank you, Mister . . . O'Dooley," the agent continued, studying the Irishman's ID. "And are you traveling for business or pleasure today, Mr. O'Dooley?"

"Neither," Dublin mumbled, watching the man approach. "You expectin' anyone?"

"I'm sorry?" the agent asked.

"Any flights just arrive?"

"Oh, no sir. Nothing scheduled until the flight from Roma at 7:30. But we get a great deal of private charters here." She regarded his leather jacket and disheveled hair curiously. "Did *you* arrive on a private charter?"

"Fookin' eh I did."

"I see. Are you sure I can't interest you in a more luxurious vehicle, Mr. O'Dooley?"

Dublin's lips parted into a mischievous yellow-stained grin. "Only if you come with it."

The agent's eyes promptly widened before falling back to the computer. "Alright . . . here you are," she said, handing him the keys and pointing in the direction of the rental lot. "Enjoy your time in Malcesine, Mr. O'Dooley."

"Right."

The moment the Irishman was gone the young woman's smile transformed into a disgusted grimace. She turned and busied herself filing the paperwork.

"Excuse me?" A voice asked behind her.

"Un momento." The agent spun to find a tall, well-built man in a dark suit leaning against the counter. "Oh, I'm sorry," she said, feeling her face blush. "May I help you?"

"Do you have any vehicles available?" the man asked.

"Yes of course, sir."

The man's gaze flickered to the exit doors leading to the

rental lot. "Small world, but that gentleman you just helped—I think I might know him. Did he mention if he was going to the conference?"

The agent followed his stare toward the exit. "Conference? No, sir, he didn't. Is there a conference in Malcesine?"

The man handed over his ID and shrugged. "I guess he just looked familiar."

"Thank you, Mister . . . Foster. Did you have a particular vehicle in mind, sir?"

Ray Foster nodded. "You know us Americans," he replied, giving her a wide grin. "What's the largest thing you've got?"

∼

Tatyana marched into Paul's laboratory and threw up her arms. "Okay—I am here," she announced. "May I have an explanation as to what this is about, or am I simply here to assist?"

"Both." Paul looked up from a cluster of monitors and quickly pointed toward a large stainless steel cabinet. "In there should be a vial labeled MA-554. Grab it for me."

His Russian colleague hesitated for a moment before reluctantly walking to the cabinet and opening the door. "A storage incubator?" she asked, wincing at the brightly lit interior.

"That's right," Paul mumbled, his attention focused on the screens in front of him. "For cyanobacteria."

Tatyana found the vial marked MA-554 and regarded Paul suspiciously. "Why would you want—"

"Just bring it over here," he insisted.

"Excuse me?"

Paul caught her venomous tone and sighed. "I'll explain in a minute. Now, would you *please* bring that over here?"

Tatyana did as asked. "Your microcystic aeruginosa," she said, handing it over. "Are you planning to drop this into the water supply and poison everyone in the compound?"

"The thought had crossed my mind. But then you gave me a better idea. Here—take a look." Paul grabbed his colleague's hand and pulled her in front of his computer. "It's a rough simulation, but I think it gets the concept across."

Tatyana gazed at the nearest monitor. A collection of small, cellular-looking objects appeared onscreen and began forming themselves into a large, spherically-shaped body. Moments later, a collection of cells even smaller than the first appeared and began to carefully arrange themselves around the outside of the sphere. As soon as they were in place, a thin membrane appeared at the top of the collection and grew outward until it encapsulated the entire spherical body. The Russian researcher shrugged. "What is it?"

"You're the microbiologist," Paul answered, a thin grin on his face. "You tell me."

Tatyana turned and watched the simulation again. "Wait," she gasped, suddenly grasping the meaning of the structure. "You're not suggesting—" She spun and looked at him. "But . . . could it work?"

"Why not?" Paul's grin widened into a smile. "After all, if anyone's made me believe that two very different organisms can learn to work together, it's you."

Tatyana's stunned expression softened into a smile. "I was wrong to call you stupid, Dr. Obermeyer. Especially when you speak such poetry." She leaned forward and kissed him before abruptly marching toward the door.

"Where are you going?"

"Coffee!" the Russian exclaimed, disappearing into the hallway. "We are going to need much coffee!"

35.

She had loved his hands.

Large and soft, strong and gentle. Like her father himself, always there when needed most. How many times had they collected her after a fall, or tossed her laughing into the air? Was there ever a morning walk to the school bus or evening stroll around the neighborhood without his hand wrapped around hers? Well, yes, there was—after those first sparks of adolescent independence appeared and changed everything. But even then she'd secretly missed holding her father's hand, although she would have never admitted as much. Such was the paradox of growing up—learning to evade the unconditional love of a parent only to spend a lifetime searching for it in someone else. But pre-teen girls don't care nearly as much about paradoxes as they do about being cool. And so the handholding—along with the morning walks to the bus stop and the evening walks to nowhere—grew less frequent, until finally one day she realized with both exhilaration and terror what every girl does. That she and her father weren't really so inseparable after all.

But then came the trip.

Her father had announced it the first morning of her

summer break—a two-week tour of Italy. Beginning in historic Rome, continuing to Florence, then onward to Venice before concluding with a three-day rest by Lake Garda in the Italian Alps. The trip of a lifetime! he'd exclaimed, waiting for her reaction. Unfortunately, her thirteen-year-old reaction had been noticeably less enthusiastic. Two weeks without her bicycle, television, or friends? Who does that? she'd asked. Broad-minded people, her father had responded. Her mouth had twisted with doubt. His brow had furrowed into that look that said arguing was futile. It was already settled—they were leaving the next day, and they were going to have fun.

And he was right.

For a young girl who'd never traveled a few states beyond home, Rome was a sensory revelation. None of the travel books she'd lethargically thumbed through on the plane could have prepared her for it—the massive scale of the Coliseum, the impossible complexity of the Sistine Chapel frescoes, the nectary smell of the Campo dei Fiori flower market, the silky texture of gelato on her tongue. Oh—and the tastes! At every turn something new and extraordinary was waiting to be discovered—and with every new discovery came a desire to see and learn more. By their second day in Rome, her only concern about the trip was whether it would be long enough. In the days that followed, as they made their way north through the countryside to the streets of Florence and meandering canals of Venice, the revelations continued: the Ponte Vecchio . . . St. Mark's Basilica . . . the music of the language . . . the art of Michelangelo. Suddenly the renaissance became tangible; science indistinguishable from art. Never before had she experienced a tapestry of culture and history so interwoven and ubiquitous that it could be seen in every façade and tasted in every morsel.

And in the hours spent walking the cobblestone street with her father, talking, pointing, laughing and sharing, her hand had found itself once again wrapped inside his.

Their time in Venice passed in what seemed like moments, and before she knew it they were standing beneath the jagged skyline of the Italian Alps, staring at the cerulean waters of Lake Garda. You pick the place, her father had commanded. Her mouth had twisted with concentration weighing the various options listed in the guide books. Limone sul Garda, with its small town charm and hillside groves of lemon? Salò, with its Roman ruins and long lakeside promenade of restaurants? Or, wait—her eyes widened with excitement as she read further—could it be? A place just a little further north with a castle and a cable car that would take you to the top of Mount Baldo? Her father had simply smiled and gestured for her to climb back into the car. Thirty minutes later, they were standing in the picturesque town of Malcesine gazing awestruck at the pentagonal tower of the Castello Scaligero.

As she stood there next to her father, taking in the view, she knew everything from that moment forward would be different. The world, once limited to the flat pages of web sites and encyclopedias and travel guides, had become real. It was a tangible place of languages and smells and tastes beyond imagination. And best of all, it was right out there, waiting to be discovered. She reached up and took her father's hand, once again comfortable and familiar, and squeezed it until he looked down. I love you, Dad, she'd said, her words nearly lost to the wind. Her father's eyes had gazed down with affection. Welcome to the world, Jer-bear, he'd replied, squeezing back. I love you, too.

A buzzing noise tore her from her memory. She pulled the phone from her pocket and glanced at the message—

It's time.

Jeri gazed one last time at the Castello Scaligero's crenulated walls of white stone—as beautiful now as they'd been when she stood here with her father—before turning and marching back to the hotel.

The third floor suite in the Hotel Lago Di Garda was a throwback to old-world style. Inside her three-room suite, arched niches and lush garden frescoes filled the airy interior, punctuated by windows that stretched from the marble tile floors to a ceiling of quaintly cracked plaster. Jeri left the door open behind her as she passed through the entryway and paused at the nearest window in the living room. Beneath a dome of clouds, the calm waters of Lake Garda stretched before her with the pallid sheen of molten lead.

A moment later, Chilly stood next to her admiring the view. "I can see why you picked this," he said softly.

Jeri nodded without looking at him. "I remember it being bigger."

"The world was a bigger place when we were kids."

"Yeah, bigger . . . and more kind." She turned and regarded him. "So—where do you want to do this?"

Her colleague shuffled his feet. "You'll want to be lying down when I give you the injection. How about the bedroom?"

"Fine."

The sound of someone in the hallway made both of

them turn. A moment later Dublin appeared in the doorway. A large backpack was slung over his shoulder

"The fookin' things I do for you people," the Irishman grumbled as he marched into the suite. He flashed a quick grin at Jeri before locking eyes with Chilly. "What?"

"Got everything I asked for?" Chilly asked curtly.

"You mean everythin' I had only a few hours to scrounge up before flyin' the fook down here? Yeah, I got all that." Dublin tossed the backpack at his colleague and turned to Jeri. "So . . . s'it true? You really want out?"

Jeri caught the glint of sadness in his eyes and nodded.

"Fook me." Dublin leaned closer and gestured at Chilly. "What'd he say to piss you off so much?"

"Nothing, Dub. I just . . . I just decided I couldn't—" Jeri shrugged and nodded. "Seriously, it's better for everybody." She shot a look at Chilly, who was quietly rummaging through the backpack.

"Well, it's a crock of shite if you ask me," Dublin retorted. "I mean, for fook's sake, freshman . . you were s'pose to be the—"

"Drop it," Chilly commanded. "The decision's already been made. The last thing she needs is your opinion on the matter."

Dublin turned and sneered at his colleague. "The fook's your problem? You really just gonna let her go?"

"Yep," Chilly replied. He looked up from the bag. "Okay . . . looks like everything's here. Dublin, why don't you wait for me downstairs?"

"Oh, so I'm being *dismissed* now—s'at it? Sure you don't need anythin' else? Happy to hold Jeri's hand a bit . . . or help you remove whatever's lodged up yer arse."

Chilly stepped closer. "Wait for me downstairs, okay? Or are you having a hard time understanding my accent?"

Jeri watched silently as the two men exchanged looks. A moment later Dublin turned and sighed. "Well, I s'pose this is it, girl. If there's any blessing in all this, it's that you weren't around long enough to fall in love with me. Trust me, it'd been a real fookin' mess if you had."

"Thanks Dublin. I'll miss you."

The portly Irishman stepped forward and embraced her in a bear hug. "No you won't. Not after that fookin' tosser next to us is done with you. But you can try." He released her and nodded. "Take care of yourself now, alright?"

"I will."

Dublin threw one more venomous look at Chilly and vanished into the hallway.

Chilly gestured toward the bedroom. "Shall we?"

Jeri walked into the bedroom and sat down on the edge of the bed. Her colleague closed the door behind them.

"Go ahead and lie down," he commanded, placing the items from the backpack on the nightstand. "Did you eat anything?"

"No. You told me not too."

"I did. But since when have you followed my instructions?"

Jeri smiled. "I suppose I deserve that."

"Yes, you do." He held up a bottle of ibuprofen. "You're going to have a nasty headache when you wake up, and maybe some sensitivity to light. Don't plan on leaving the room for the rest of the day. Oh, and before I forget—" He pulled out a U. S. passport and dropped it on the bed. "Your new identity."

Jeri opened it and studied the name. "This says Jeri

Stone."

"Isn't that what you wanted?"

"Yeah, but . . . won't I wake up thinking that I'm still Jeri Halston from Flagstaff?"

"You won't be sure of anything for a few days while the drug runs its course. But yes, you'll eventually come to that conclusion."

"Which means I'll eventually try to go back there."

Chilly nodded. "And when you do, a man of authority that looks strangely familiar but whose name you won't recall will intercept you at the airport. This same man will pull you aside, flash his badge, and remind you that you were the recent victim of a senseless act of homeland terrorism that not only took a portion of your memory, but also required you to go into a witness protection program. You'll find his explanation very persuasive. And because you won't remember anything about the events he's referring to, you won't resist when he turns you around and escorts you onto a plane back home. Which, by the way, is now in Baltimore." He paused and looked at her somberly. "See how this works?"

Jeri nodded. "And how will you know when I try to go back?"

Chilly turned and picked up a glass vial labeled DIA-VEROL 15mL from the nightstand. He plunged the hypodermic needle of a syringe into the top and carefully measured out the correct dose. "Think back to the day you were brought into the agency," he said, turning the syringe upright and tapping it with his finger. "Remember where you were hit with the tranquilizer dart?"

"Yeah."

"Feel it."

She reached back and gently rubbed the spot on her lower back.

"No, press firmly."

Jeri pushed her fingertips into her flesh. To her surprise, an object roughly the size of a grain of rice shifted beneath her skin. "What the hell is that?" she demanded.

"A GPS microchip," Chilly replied. "Invented for dogs and cats, but it works just fine for our needs too. Has a tiny little battery inside that uses your body heat to recharge. Isn't technology amazing?"

Jeri pulled her hand away. "Yeah . . . fantastic." She sighed and pushed her head against the pillow. "So that's how you found me in London."

Her colleague gave her a thin smile. "Don't feel too special. Everybody gets one—agents as well as recruits." He filled a second syringe from a different vial and handed it to her.

"What's this?"

"I'm going to give you that one first. It's just a strong sedative to make sure that you sleep. It's important to stay in bed as long as you can, okay?"

Jeri studied the needle. A drop of the liquid beaded at the tip like venom from a fang. "What's the point of giving me instructions if I'm not going to remember any of this?"

"Good question." Chilly wrapped her arm with a tourniquet and they both watched in silence as the veins began to rise in the crease of her elbow. His eyes drifted slowly to hers. "Okay—you ready to do this?"

Jeri searched his stare for a moment before shaking her head. "Not yet."

"What's wrong?"

"Nothing. I was just thinking how unique this particular moment is. I mean, here we are, the two of us—alone—and you're about to erase anything we say or do from my memory. It just seems like a perfect opportunity."

Her colleague raised an eyebrow. A thin grin appeared on his face. "For what?"

"For the truth."

His grin vanished. "What's the point? You said it yourself—you're not going to remember any of this."

"True. But then, maybe knowing something for even a moment is better than never knowing at all."

Chilly took the syringe from her hand. "What do you want to know?"

"How did you two meet?"

"You really want to talk about that?"

"Yes."

"Okay . . . fine." He sighed and absently studied the syringe. "First year med school. She was my lab partner in gross anatomy. It sounds disgusting, but there's probably no better way to get to know a person than to cut up a human cadaver with them."

"Did she become a surgeon like you?"

"No. Pediatric oncologist. With a focus on leukemia."

"Pediatric? That sounds . . . difficult."

"Very," Chilly nodded. "It takes a special kind of person to look into the eyes of a sick child and smile when you know what they're in for. Even Laura had a hard time with it. After about a year in practice, she decided to get more involved in research and clinical trials. That's what she was doing at the time of the—" He paused and narrowed his eyes on the syringe. "Anyway . . . she was a good person. Better than I could ever hope to be."

Jeri reached out and touched his arm. "I'm sorry, Sam."

"Yeah. Me too."

"Did they catch the person responsible? I didn't see anything in the articles that—"

"No," he said sharply. His eyes focused beyond Jeri at some distant memory. "They don't let you touch them," he murmured, his voice almost a whisper. "Not when it's a crime scene. I was there within minutes of the call. Everything was so . . . *quiet*. I remember the pattern of the blood on the street, the shape of her body beneath the blanket. I tried so hard to get past them. I just had to see. To know. I remember shouting at the officers . . . punching and screaming at them. Finally two of them pushed me to the ground and said 'You can't, sir. You don't want to. Not like this.' " His jaw tightened. "Any one of the bullet wounds by itself would have been lethal. And she had five. *Five.* That was her reward for being a good person. For getting up to go to work that morning. For walking to her car at the same moment some worthless piece of shit with a gun happened to drive by . . . "

Jeri latched her fingers around his arm and squeezed gently. "It was gang related, wasn't it? Some kind of turf war or drug deal . . . she just happened to be standing in the middle of it."

Chilly's eyes flashed to hers with a look of abject pain. The look abruptly morphed into wonder. "It's remarkable how much you look like her. Same eyes . . . expressions . . . even the way your mouth twists into a frown when you're angry." He poised the needle of the syringe over the blue line of a vein and shook his head. "C'est la vie."

Jeri felt a brief prick as the needle slipped into her arm. "Sam—wait."

"Goodbye, Jeri."

"Goddammit—wait!"

His thumb froze against the plunger of the syringe. "What?"

"That person at the airport—the day I go home?"

"Yeah?"

"Promise me one thing. Promise it'll be you."

Chilly leaned down until his face hovered just over hers. "You won't remember that promise . . . or me."

"Then it won't matter if you make it."

He moved closer. "Close your eyes."

Jeri closed her eyes and leaned forward, finding his mouth with her own. She felt him briefly tense with surprise before opening to accept her. In that moment her senses took on an elevated state of awareness—the warmth of his lips and tongue, the soapy scent of his skin, the sandy texture of his whiskered face. Time stretched into something measurable only by the tempo of the lake water lapping against the shore beyond the window. Gravity loosened its grip and her body began to rise. Everything was spinning toward a singular, inevitable conclusion when a sudden pressure brought Jeri rushing back to reality. She gasped and fell back against the pillow, her stare fixed on Chilly's hand.

The syringe was empty.

She looked at him with disbelief. "But . . . I wasn't ready."

Chilly dropped the empty syringe on the nightstand. "You've got about ninety seconds of consciousness left. Anything else you want to tell me?" He started to pick up the syringe loaded with Diaverol when Jeri reached out and grabbed his wrist.

"Yeah. What if . . . what we both did this?"

"Did what?"

"Got out." Jeri held her grip until he put down the syringe and looked at her. "Think about it—no more scripts and collections and ruined lives. It's not worth it, Sam. You've spent six years doing this—and for what? For the memory of someone you can't get back? I mean, I get it—Chip's done the same thing to me. But this is *not* what my father wanted for me, and you can't tell me it's what Laura would have wanted for you either."

Her colleague shook his head. "You have no idea what she wanted."

"You're right, I don't. But I do know one thing—her life is over, not yours. Christ, Sam, don't you want a normal life?"

"A *normal* life?" he scoffed. "What exactly is that? Being like everyone else? Pretending that none of the things we know about this world are real? What are you suggesting we do? Just say 'fuck it' and have kids, buy a Volvo, and bury our heads in the sand?"

"Yes, I am. And along the way, we could fight the problems of the world on *our* terms. There *are* other ways of fighting this battle, aren't there?"

"Not really."

Jeri glared at him with frustration. Already the room around her was beginning to soften and blur as a result of the sedative. "Chip told me about your recruitment. How he watched you for weeks . . . even following you on your nightly walks. He knew what you were thinking when you stood at the end of that pier studying the water. But he wasn't concerned about your anger, or your pain. When it came to that day, he wasn't worried about you wanting to take your own life—he was counting on it. So you tell me, Sam—do you really want to work for an organization that takes advantage of other's trag-edies for it's own gain? Because I thought that was exactly what we were here to fight against."

Chilly leaned in closer once again. "I hope you sleep well," he said softly. "I hope when all of this is over and you open your eyes, you see a world that's nothing less than per-fect. But you won't. And one day, sooner than later, you're go-ing to wake up and realize this world is not how it should be. You're going to find out all over again that it's full of shadows and deception and evil that's far too clever to be caught by honest means. And eventually, if you take up this fight again, you're going to realize everything we've taught you is true—that the only way to destroy something you hate is to become the very same thing."

Jeri shook her head and turned away.

"You want some more truth? Everything Chip told you about my recruitment is correct—except for one thing," Chilly continued.

"What's that?"

"The old man didn't recruit me. Your father did."

Both of their heads turned at the sound of running footsteps. An instant later the bedroom door shot open and Dublin stumbled breathlessly into the room.

"We gotta go!" he wheezed, his eyes wide with fear. "Somethin'—" the Irishman's words were suddenly clipped off. In one swift motion his mouth clamped shut and body arched violently backwards in rigid attention.

It was then that Jeri noticed the two wires protruding from his side.

Chilly spun and grabbed the syringe of Diaverol from the nightstand as more footsteps echoed from the living room.

His eyes briefly locked onto to Jeri's before he drove the needle into her waiting vein and depressed the plunger. "It's all in his book, Jeri. Do you hear me? It's all in his—"

Jeri watched through a thickening cloud of detachment as he twisted and fell forward, his body writhing and twitching against her. In the doorway, a small, wiry man with red hair lowered the Taser gun in his hand and stepped into the room. A smile creased the long scar on his face while three more men, large and heavily armed, slipped into the room behind him and surrounded the bed. A voice in the back of Jeri's mind commanded her to stay awake, but it was futile. The room began to collapse into a singularity of gray as the redheaded man moved closer. She watched his lips move, but his voice was lost to the sound of her own beating heart. With the last of her will, she reached out and placed a hand on Chilly's still head. Her fingers gently buried themselves within the curls of his dark hair, the warmth of his body enveloping her like a shield.

Then everything faded to black.

PART III

It's inevitable.
All agents will eventually find themselves
in a moment of dire crisis.

It is at this moment,
when everything is weighed and calculated,
that the true measure of the agent is defined.

It is at this moment,
in the darkest depths,
that the agent's new life
truly begins.

Audio Recording #03.173 // 1004
Reference Index: >NewAgentOrientation<
Narrator: Shafer, R. >Shepherd<

36.

"You're neck-deep in it now, Jer-bear."

She looked at the smiling face of her father sitting in his study and felt her face blush with anger. "Seems you are too, Dad."

Her father frowned. "Is that why you're here—to blame me for everything that's happened?"

"No," she whispered, the last of her strength dissolved. "I just . . . I just want answers. I just want the truth."

"The truth? You already have the truth. You've always *had* the truth. The only question now is what you choose to do with it."

The paralyzing agent completed its task and she collapsed against the wall. A fist of panic clenched at her throat. She ignored the darkness narrowing her vision and focused on her words. "Just tell me . . . beyond your book . . . beyond your predictions . . . were you really part of this too?"

Her father rose from his desk and picked up his typewriter. "We're *all* part of this, sweetheart. Most of us just don't know it yet." The muscles in his arms tensed as he lifted the typewriter over his head. "Now—are you ready to face the consequences of your choices?"

She answered with a blink.

"Very good," he said, giving her a satisfied nod. "Here it comes."

Her father tossed the typewriter forward. Its heavy steel body arched through the air toward her head.

Jeri bolted upright and immediately cried out in pain. "Jesus Christ! she exclaimed, grimacing at the brightness. "Turn off the goddamn lights!" She fell back into the bed, acutely aware of the sound of shuffling feet, a light switch being flicked. A low moan escaped her lips. "What the fuck did you do to my head?" she demanded, pressing her palms to her eyes.

"Everything's okay," a calm, feminine voice answered. "Just calm down."

The sound of pills rattling in a bottle rushed into Jeri's ears and stung like a swarm of angry bees. "Stop . . . pleeeease *stop . . .*"

"Here we go," the voice replied. A hand squeezed her shoulder. "You can open your eyes now."

Jeri removed her hands and slowly opened her eyes. The room was now tolerably dark, illuminated only by the glow of moonlight from the window next to her bed. She glanced at the ID band around her wrist before noticing her hospital gown. "Wait . . . what?" She turned to the nurse standing over her. The woman was older, with short, grayish-white hair and a tapestry of soft wrinkles edging her face. "Where am I?" Jeri asked, an edge of panic in her voice.

"Somewhere safe, dear," the nurse replied with a motherly smile. She held out two pills and a cup of water. "Here, take this. It'll help with the headache."

Jeri took the pills and tossed them back without a second thought. The nurse nodded while she drank the water.

"There you go. Good girl."

Jeri handed back the empty cup and looked out the window. "What happened? I don't—" she winced in pain as her attempt to think back stirred another swarm of bees, this one inside her forehead. "I don't remember how I got here."

The nurse frowned sympathetically. "It's okay, sweetheart. Her expression tightening and she shot a quick glance to the side. Jeri looked past her to find a man sitting in the corner of the room, his gray eyes studying her intently. "This gentleman would like to speak with you." The nurse squeezed her arm once again. "I'll be back to check on you shortly."

"Thanks." Jeri watched the nurse leave before shifting her gaze to the man. "Who are you?"

"My name's Lars Nielsen," the man replied. "I'm the director of security for Velgyn Pharmaceuticals." He stood and stepped closer, his pale, Scandinavian looks even more pronounced in the moonlight. His gray eyes remained focused on Jeri. "What's your name?"

Jeri opened her mouth to speak and paused. "I'm—" Her brow furrowed with a mix of confusion and surprise. "I'm," she repeated, running a nervous hand through her hair. The bees in her head stung again, forcing another grimace. "I'm sorry," she said, easing herself back against the pillow. "I'm having trouble thinking right now."

"I understand."

"Can you tell me what's going on?" Jeri asked. The panic in her voice was back.

"No, not entirely," the security director replied. "But I can tell you how you got here." He studied her face for a moment and shrugged. "Perhaps it's better if I come by in the morning after you've rested."

"No, please." Jeri held up a hand as he turned to go. "I'd really like to know."

Nielsen's look of surprise slowly morphed into a thin smile. "Are you sure?"

"Yes."

"All right." Nielsen glanced at a manila envelope he was holding. "Twenty-four hours ago, a team of my men was tracking a man we believe was involved in a crime against this corporation. That man lead us to a hotel room in a small village in Italy . . . and inside that room we found you."

"Me? In *Italy*?" Jeri shook her head incredulously. "No. There's no way—"

"There was another man with you," the security director continued, pulling a page from the envelope and handing it to Jeri. "When my team arrived, they found him injecting you with sedatives along with another drug. This is your lab report."

Jeri briefly regarded the report. A list of indecipherable chemical names stretched down the page. "What does it say?"

"It says you've been dosed with Diaverol," Nielsen replied. "Which is very curious considering what I've been told. You see, Diaverol was designed to fight the symptoms of late-stage Alzheimer's, but didn't make it past clinical trials. It was never available on the market."

"So why was it given to me?"

"I don't know. But I have a theory." The director pulled two photos from the envelope and held them up. "How long have you known them?" he asked, his tone now brusque.

Jeri stared blankly at the photographs of two men ly-

ing face-up on a floor. One of the men appeared to be unconscious. The other stared at the ceiling with dull, empty eyes. "I
don't know them," she replied.

Nielsen clenched his jaw. He held the photos closer.
"Yes, you do."

Jeri regarded him with surprise before looking once
again. She shook her head slowly. "Well, if I do, I don't remember them."

"What's the last thing you *do* remember?"

Jeri tried to think. A rush of images flashed through
her mind like still frames from a moving roll of film, each one
slipping away before it could be studied. A fleeting image of
a window looking out over a lake hung in her mind. When
Jeri tried to focus on it, a hot knife of pain ripped through her
skull. "Fuuuck," she moaned, rubbing her temples. The pain
was equaled only by her frustration. "I can't . . . I can't remember anything."

The security director studied her with detached curiosity. "I see," he said finally, dropping the photos back into
the envelope. "All right, that's enough for now." He closed the
envelope and shoved it under his arm. "We'll talk again after
you've rested."

Jeri felt her face flush with anger as he turned to leave.
"Why would someone do this to me?"

"Because they could." The security director said flatly.

"Wait—will you at least tell me where I am?"

Nielsen paused by the door. "Sonoma, California.
One of the private suites in our executive retreat house. By
the way—would you mind if someone else steps in to see you
tonight? I promise it'll only take a moment." Before Jeri could
respond the security director opened the door and nodded at

someone outside. A moment later, a paunchy young man with a thinning head of reddish-blond hair walked in and smiled at her. "We meet again," the man said with a hint of sarcasm.

"Do I know you?" Jeri asked.

"You mean you don't remember me?"

"I'm sorry, I . . . don't."

"Wow, isn't that ironic?" Adam Cowell's smile twisted into a sneer. "Well, don't worry. I didn't forget you—*Carrie*." The research assistant spat the name out bitterly before nodding at the security director. "That's her."

"Thank you, Mr. Cowell." The security director gestured for him to leave.

Jeri shook her head. "What was that all about?" she asked as Cowell marched from the room. "Carrie? Is that . . . is that really my name?"

"Get some rest." Nielsen opened the door further. In the corridor outside stood a man in a dark suit. The handle of a holstered gun was visible in the gap of his jacket.

Jeri nodded. In the corridor, the eyes of a well-dressed security guard locked onto hers. As the door closed, a menacing grin appeared on his face.

37.

"All right, everyone's here. What have you got?"

Paul nodded at Derrick Birch and drank back the last of the cold coffee in his mug before standing. "Good morning, everyone," he said, nodding to the rest of the nearly departed crew assembled around the conference table. "I know you're all curious to know why I called you in here, but first—does anyone here remember a man named Alexander Fleming?"

Around the table, Birch exchanged curious looks with Marcello, Shahid and Chung as a thin smile appeared on Tatyana's face.

"I guess none of you paid much attention in history class," Paul shrugged. "So allow me to give you a quick refresher course. Alexander Fleming was the Scottish pharmacologist who discovered penicillin back in the nineteen twenties. Since you've forgotten his name, you've probably also forgotten that Fleming won a Nobel Prize for that discovery, and that many credit penicillin as the single greatest medical discovery of all time, saving over two hundred million lives by some estimates." He tapped the screen of the tablet computer on the table and the projector screen lowered behind him. "But what I think makes Fleming's discovery so interesting is how it happened in the first place. You see, Fleming was a brilliant researcher, but apparently not a very tidy one. The day before heading off for a long summer holiday, he strolled out of his laboratory without cleaning his petri dishes or even closing the windows. As the story goes, when Fleming returned weeks later, he started rummaging through his petri dishes and noticed these strange little spots of blue green mold surrounded by a wasteland of dead staphylococcus. And *voilà*—thanks to his messy nature, penicillin was discovered."

Birch glanced at his watch. "We're all very busy, Paul. Is there a point to this story?"

Across the table, Tatyana's green eyes narrowed on the project leader reproachfully. "Yes, Derrick . . . there is."

Birch looked at her with surprise.

"My point," Paul continued, "is that breakthroughs sometimes come not from what we do right, but what we do wrong." He tapped the screen of the tablet again. A large, three-dimensional model of a spherical organism appeared onscreen and began to slowly rotate. "In fact, doing something wrong was what ultimately showed me how to solve the yield problem."

Silence filled the room as the other researchers leaned forward. "Say again?" Birch said.

"I solved the yield problem," Paul repeated. He immediately caught Dr. Aleksandrov's stare. "Sorry . . . I mean *we* solved the yield problem."

The project leader nodded slowly. "Explain."

Paul pointed to the model rotating behind him. "What you're looking at is a single botryococcus braunii cell, which—genetically speaking—is nearly perfect in terms of its morphology, energy conversion and storage. The question I was brought here to answer is as obvious as it is daunting—how do you improve on perfection?"

"Yes!" Marcello said, his dark eyes flickering excitedly between Paul and the screen. "And what's the answer?"

Paul shook his head. "I couldn't come up with one. The truth is, I can't think of single way to engineer a genetic modification to this organism that will increase lipid oil yields to the order required for Ceres to work—at least not in the timeframe I've been given. And if I'd persisted in pursuing this answer, we wouldn't be having this conversation. Luckily for all of us, when I asked for an extra set of hands in my lab, Derrick suggested Dr. Aleksandrov." He tapped the tablet and the onscreen cell model paused. "From the beginning, Dr. Aleksandrov questioned my logic, challenged my expertise, and even sabotaged my research. When I asked her to exclude a group of samples that had been mutated with bacterial DNA, she not only ignored my instructions, she altered the growth media to favor those samples at the expense of mine."

Birch looked at Tatyana. "Is that true?" he snapped.

"Well, technically speaking . . . perhaps," the Russian researcher answered.

"You're telling me you blatantly disregarded Dr. Obermeyer's instructions and destroyed his samples?"

Tatyana narrowed her eyes on the project leader. "Dr. Obermeyer's assumptions were incorrect. I felt it was my responsibility to—"

"Guys," Paul interjected, "it doesn't matter."

Birch shifted his incensed gaze to Paul. "Why? Are you going to tell me she was right?"

"No. Even better—we were both equally wrong."

Birch glanced at the others around the table. "Am I the

only one here who doesn't have a fucking clue what he's talking about?"

Marcello, Shahid and Chung shook their heads.

"Allow me to explain," Paul said, raising his hand. "Despite Dr. Aleksandrov's obvious difficulty in following instructions, her actions forced me to start thinking out of the box. Or, in this case, out of the cell."

Onscreen, the model of the cell shrank and began multiplying into a cluster of identical cells. A thin membrane appeared next, encasing the growing collection within a fragile-looking bubble.

"As you probably know, the botryococcus algae we're using don't live as single free-floating cells, but in multicellular colonies like this, surrounded by a protective biofilm made of lipids. My *original* plan was to seed the cells in these colonies with genetic material from other fast-growth microalgae in order to increase nutrient absorption. Unfortunately, this only resulted a two-percent increase in yield."

On the screen, a bar appeared on the graph and ticked upward slightly.

"What about Dr. Aleksandrov's mutated samples?" Birch asked.

"The samples mutated with bacterial DNA did much better," Paul replied. "Increasing lipid yields as much as fifteen percent."

A second bar graph appeared and rose accordingly.

"So clearly the bacterial DNA is the answer," Birch replied.

Paul shrugged. "On paper, yes. Unfortunately, the mutations are also prone to developing an unstable biofilm—which means the increased yield would be effectively canceled out by the increased rate of die-off in the reactors."

"Or so you believe," Tatyana said under her breath. She and Paul exchanged a quick smile.

Birch shrugged. "I don't understand. Did you solve the yield problem or not?"

"Yes, I did. I mean, we did."

"How?"

"By looking at the problem differently," Paul replied. "You see, all this time we've been trying to make our botryococcus algae more productive by ripping apart its DNA and patching it with the genes of something else, like phototrophic bacteria. In other words, we've been attacking the problem on a *genetic* level. But what if we didn't have to? What if the answer wasn't as much in the genetics of the algae, but in the nature of the algae colony itself? In other words, instead of trying to make a better botryococcus algae through the genetic combination of bacterial DNA, what if we made a colony where the algae and bacteria both lived and worked together, and their inherent individual capabilities were strengthened by the union?" Paul turned to the screen. "Like this, for example—"

All eyes watched as the model of the algae colony began to once again rotate. Small spherical objects suddenly materialized around the colony and started moving toward it.

"We take a phototrophic bacteria—in this case a strain of cyanobacteria that likes the same heat, light and nutrient mix as our botryococcus, and make a few genetic modifications to alter its behavior—which, by the way, is a far easier task than modifying our microalgae . . . "

Onscreen, the small spheres of bacteria quickly passed through the colony's protective membrane and attached themselves to the larger algae cells inside.

"These modifications lead the bacteria to form an ecto-symbiotic relationship. In this case, the algae's waste of polysaccharide carbohydrates becomes an additional food source for the bacteria, and the bacteria's waste gives the algae a much needed infusion of nutrients like vitamin B12 . . . "

Inside the membrane, both bacteria and algae begin dividing and multiplying.

"And there you have it—a new super colony of symbiotic organisms that achieve much higher photosynthetic energy conversion together than either one of them can do on their own." Paul took a breath and turned to his colleagues. "What do you think?"

A long silence filled the conference.

"That's fucking *brilliant*," Birch whispered, awestruck. His gaze slowly shifted from the model to Paul. "And the projected yield?"

Paul smiled at Dr. Aleksandrov. "Tatyana?"

Everyone leaned forward as a third bar appeared on the graph and began to rise steadily.

"Santo cazzo Madre di Cristo!" Marcello exclaimed, reading the number. Next to him, Chung and Shahid both muttered something in their native languages.

"It's true," Paul confirmed. "A *twenty-six* percent increase in efficiency—almost twice the increase we need to make Ceres viable."

"You mean in theory," Birch remarked. "It still needs to be tested in one of the lab cultivators." He watched as Paul and Dr. Aleksandrov exchanged another smile. "What's so funny?"

"We already did," Paul replied. Behind him, the model vanished and was replaced by a table of numbers. "Here are the yield benchmarks after thirty, sixty, and ninety minutes."

The project leader studied the results. "You did it," he said finally, his tone reverential. He stood and seized Paul in a bear hug. "What else can I say? You fucking *did* it!"

"Yes," Paul wheezed. "We did."

Birch released him and turned to the rest of the team. "All right, listen. Normal protocol would be to move to the half-scale reactor. I say to hell with that. Shahid, tell the managers we're immediately undertaking a full-scale trial in reactors one and two. Marcello, oversee the mix. Chung, make sure you're ready on the processing side. I want yields and a complete analysis by tomorrow." The three men nodded and immediately shuffled out of the conference room. The project leader waited until they were gone before turning to Paul and Tatyana. "A super colony," he mused, laughing softly. "Just when I thought I'd fucking heard it all. All right, you two go get some sleep. The rest is up to the engineers and your little orgy of pond scum." Birch marched toward the door. "Great speech by the way, Dr. Obermeyer," he exclaimed as he disappeared into the corridor. "Next time, save the history lesson and get to the fucking point."

Paul's eyes shifted to his Russian colleague. "Congratulations, Dr. Aleksandrov."

"The congratulations belong to you, Dr. Obermeyer, not me," Tatyana replied, stepping toward him. "But I do appreciate your kindness. Forgive me for not being used to it."

"Maybe we can argue about it over a drink. Got any more of that vodka?"

His colleague's stare narrowed on him with suspicion. "Are you hoping for the same results as last time?"

"Depends." Paul leaned down until their mouths were nearly touching. "Are we talking about the slapping, or the other part?"

Tatyana studied his face. "I believe we make a good team, Doctor. However—"

Paul caught the flash of her hand moving toward his face and instinctively recoiled. An inch from his cheek, the hand froze.

"We must continue to work on your courage." Tatyana smiled and brushed a finger gently across his cheek. "I'll expect you ten minutes." She turned and marched toward the door. "And this time, bring your own glass."

38.

The silence was shattered by a slamming door.

Chilly roused himself from a troubled sleep and sat up. Approaching footsteps echoed in the darkness. Beneath him, something hard and cold pressed uncomfortably into his skull. A smell of decay hung in the cool, damp air. He ran his hands over his body, assessing himself for injuries. A sharp pain knifed at his left side upon pressing a hand against his ribcage. The sticky wetness of a laceration covered his forehead. Finding nothing broken or life threatening, he stood and probed blindly at his surroundings. A few feet to either side, his fingers encountered walls made of the same unyielding stone as the floor beneath him.

The approaching footsteps stopped. Chilly froze at the sound of keys rattling and a padlock being turned. Rusty hinges then screamed defiantly as a door opened and the beam of a flashlight stabbed at his eyes. "Jesus," he moaned, shielding his face. "Do you mind?"

"Good morning," a man's voice replied. A hand seized Chilly's arm and pulled him roughly forward. Before he could get his bearings, a blow to his stomach sent him crashing to the floor. "Sleep well?"

Chilly started to rise again when a second blow, this one to his already bruised ribs, dropped him back to his knees. He took a slow breath and nodded. "Great," he gasped. "You?"

"Pretty good. 'Course, the accommodations are much better upstairs." The man stepped forward and switched off the flashlight. His hulking shadow danced beneath a single incandescent light bulb swaying overhead. "Remember us?"

Chilly raised his head and studied the tall, muscled figure standing over him. The man's dark eyes glistened in the dim light while his associate, smaller and with a shock of copper-red hair, circled silently in the shadows. "Vaguely."

"Well, we didn't have time for proper introductions before," the man replied. "My name is Ray Foster. I'm a security manager for Velgyn Pharmaceuticals. The gentleman kicking your ass is Marcus. Just Marcus. And you are—?"

"Confused." Chilly answered. "Where are the others?"

The redheaded man stepped forward and slapped him hard across the face before circling once again. A thin rivulet of blood ran from Chilly's nose and splattered onto the stone floor beneath him. "Thank you, just Marcus," he replied, licking the warm wetness from his lips. He looked up at Ray Foster. "Velgyn? I thought you guys were in the business of helping people."

"That's true. But we make exceptions for murderers. And thieves."

"Do I fall into either of those categories?"

"You fall into both."

Chilly nodded his head. "Okay. Well, if this your idea of a legal incarceration, I'd like my phone call now."

The Velgyn security manager shrugged. "Oops . . . forgot my phone. Though honestly, I doubt it'd work here anyway."

"And just *where* is here?"

"Turkey," Foster answered. "Have you been to Antalya before?"

"The tourist trap of the eastern Mediterranean? Absolutely."

Foster smiled. "A real world traveler, aren't you? Believe it or not, there's a nice beach just a short walk from here. I'm told our company bought this country's largest pharmaceutical manufacturer a few years ago and inherited this relic as part of the deal. I think it was a monastery or something. Who knows. But it's pretty cool. Even came with this convenient dungeon-like cellar. Shame you can't take the tour." His smile faded. "So—where is it?"

"Where's what?" Chilly shrugged.

The blur of Marcus's leg barely registered before searing pain erupted along Chilly's right side. He collapsed against the floor.

The Velgyn security manager stepped forward and pulled him to his knees. "Should we go back to your name?"

"Sure. My name is Michael Bublé. I'm a Canadian born singer and entertainer, and I can assure you that if you do anything to my face or voice, you'll be hearing from my fans."

"You're very funny." Foster gestured at Marcus, who produced a cable tie from his pocket and bound Chilly's wrists together behind his back. "That's good, because you're going to need a sense of humor to get through this next part."

Chilly braced himself as Marcus's next blow landed, this time on his lower back.

Foster once again helped him up. "Want to try that again?"

"Oh, I see—you're the *good* cop. Okay, Ray, you win. My name is Sam."

"Sam what?"

"Just Sam. Like just Marcus."

Foster nodded. "The truth is, *Sam*, I don't really give a shit what your name is. All I want to know is what you've done with it."

Chilly eyed him quizzically. "At the risk of another contusion, would you mind clarifying the *it* you're referring to?"

"I'm referring to the encryption key you and your colleagues killed Paul Obermeyer for. And please—don't waste my time with another bullshit answer. Whatever you and your team were up to, it's over. You're *done*. So let's all just try to play nicely now, okay?"

Chilly's gaze shifted to Marcus's wiry muscled figure still circling in silence. "I want to help you, Ray. I *really* do. But the truth is, I don't have a fucking clue what you're talking about. Maybe it would help if you told me who Paul Oppenheimer is . . . or explained what an enchantment key is. But I doubt it."

The Velgyn security manager eyed him coldly before leaning back and loading up his right arm. His balled fist was hurtling toward Chilly's face when Marcus stepped forward and seized it. Foster glared at the man with a mixture of surprise and anger before wrenching his hand free. Marcus turned to their captive. "Mr. Foster's patience is growing thin."

Chilly regarded him silently for a moment, studying the long scar running down his face. "Are you playing the good cop now?"

Marcus's lips retracted to reveal a row of brilliant white teeth. "Yes," he replied, kneeing Chilly in the groin. He began to circle once again as Chilly doubled over in agony. "You were asking about the others," he continued. "I'm afraid neither of them is doing particularly well. The woman we found you with has lost practically all of her memory. But then, that was your intention, wasn't it?" He made a *tsk* sound and shook his head. "Lovely girl . . . seems so innocent. But of course we all know she isn't. And if she doesn't remember something useful soon, we'll have to find a way to help her. Maybe electroshock therapy. Maybe something more *physically* stimulating. Whatever it takes to get some answers. After all, it's clear that you have no interest in telling us. And we certainly aren't going to get anything from your Irish friend."

"He's not my friend." Chilly said, slowly rising to his feet.

"That's true," Marcus conceded. "Not any more. I'd heard stories of Taser guns accidentally killing people, but this was my first time seeing it firsthand. *Acute stress cardiomyopathy* I believe it's called." He shook his head again. "Maybe if he'd been in a little better shape . . . "

Chilly said nothing as his captor paused and eyed him with a thin smile. He quietly tested the strength of the cable tie binding his wrists.

"Anyway," Marcus continued, "we're even now. You and your people took a life to steal something that wasn't yours . . . and now we've taken a life to get it back. Let's just hope it's the only one we have to take before this matter is resolved." He paused once again in front of Chilly. "So—is there anything you'd like to tell us, Sam? Or should we focus our attention on . . . what was her name again, Mr. Foster?"

"Jeri," Foster replied behind him.

Marcus nodded. "Like I said, lovely woman. I just hope

you got a chance to fully examine her before we interrupted you."

Chilly smiled and leaned closer. "I have to ask," he said finally. "Is that a *real* scar? I mean, I've seen a lot of scars, but yours . . . yours just looks odd to me. It almost looks self-inflicted—like you tried to shave with a pizza cutter. But surely you're not that stupid, are you? I mean, if anyone should know the importance of using the right tool for the job, it should be you, right?"

A brief cloud of anger crossed the mercenary's face before he smiled and took a step back. He turned and gestured at the darkness. "Boys?"

Chilly watched with surprise as two other men, both tall and muscular like Foster, stepped from the shadows.

"Brilliant," Marcus said, gesturing at the floor. The two men seized Chilly and gently lowered him facedown onto the cold stones. "Brilliant is the only word to describe how you and your team carried out the theft of Obermeyer's encryption key. But you're not the only person in this room who knows how to get what they want from someone. So tell me—before we escalate this any further—where is the encryption key now?"

Chilly watched over his shoulder while the two men secured straps around his ankles. Heavy cords were then tied to each strap and threaded through steel rings on opposite sides of the floor. "Would you mind clarifying escalate?" he asked.

Marcus nodded and the two men began pulling the cords.

Chilly's body was immediately dragged backwards, his legs splayed wide apart. The pain in his legs was edging toward the intolerable when Marcus nodded once again and the men stopped.

Ray Foster stepped forward and regarded their captive with a wary frown. "You really want to do this?"

Chilly spat a fresh glob of blood onto the stones next to him and shrugged. "Well, you know what they say. You won't know if you're going to like something until you try it, right?"

Foster exchanged a look with Marcus. The two men wordlessly communicated something as Chilly's handlers tied off the cords securing his legs. Marcus stepped forward. "Thank you, gentlemen. I'll take it from here."

The Velgyn security manager nodded with a look of contempt before he and the two others turned and vanished back into the darkness of the large subterranean room. Moments later, the same door that had awoken Chilly groaned open and closed.

"Just us?" Chilly asked, craning his neck to see what Marcus was doing.

"For the moment."

His captor stepped forward and slipped a thick hood over his head. Chilly felt it being drawn tightly around his neck, sealing him once again in blackness. Behind him, the click of a tool unfolding echoed against the stone walls. He tensed at the sensation of a knife blade penetrating the seat of his pants, its sharp tip grazing his inner thighs as it cut through the fabric. "We're getting to the *escalation* part, aren't we?"

In response to his question, the sliced fabric of his inseam was seized and violently ripped open. Chilly pulled against the straps holding him spread eagle to the floor, but it was futile. A moment later, something cold and syrupy began to drip onto his exposed flesh.

"You wouldn't believe the *infestation* down here," Marcus said behind him. "But it makes perfect sense. Old grain rotting in bags . . . the darkness . . . the damp. All these cozy little places to hide. No wonder they love it so much."

"That's a rather condescending view of the locals, don't you think?"

Marcus laughed softly. "They're everywhere," he continued, his voice low and ominous. "I almost caught one of them. Had it pinned against the wall with my boot. Man, the size of that thing—and those teeth. They don't stir much when the lights are on. But once it's dark—?" He paused and made another *tsk* sound with his tongue. "You can tell they're hungry for something sweet. Something fresh. I'm not sure how long it'll take, but . . . wait . . . speak of the devil—there's one of them now. Poking his head out of the sewer drain." A moment passed and he *tsk*ed again. "Big one."

Chilly sighed. "Is this all you've got—mind tricks and hot syrup? Because if it is, I'll save you some time and tell you there's no—"

A high-pitched screech echoed from somewhere close.

"Well look at that," Marcus whispered. "He brought some friends,"

Chilly blindly turned his head as more shrieks followed. "This encryption key . . . what does it look like?"

"Let's not worry about that now," his captor replied calmly. "You've got other things on your mind. And I admit, I'm awfully curious to find out what happens when I switch this light off."

"I don't think that's really necessary."

"Oh, but I do." Marcus sighed and shuffled his feet. "I'm going have to step out for a few minutes, Sam. But don't worry, you won't be entirely alone."

"Wait, let's talk about this, all right?"

"Back shortly."

Chilly turned his head at the sound of the overhead light clicking off. Almost immediately the nearby chorus of shrieks and squeals rose to a feverish pitch. Something brushed past his shrouded head, paused, and moved off. Then, as if choreographed, a flurry of tentative touches and pokes could be felt along his sides. The pokes grew bolder and more insistent. A small body scurried over his shoulders.

"Marcus? Come on, Marcus . . . I know you're back there—"

Chilly arched his back and tried to sit up, but his legs were splayed at too great of an angle. Twisting to either side only increased the pain of ligaments and muscles being stretched beyond their capacity. Flopping helplessly against the floor, he fought the rising urge to panic as the prodding of small bodies moved steadily up his inseam toward a prize of syrup-covered flesh.

"Goddammit . . . *Marcus*!"

The sensation of something climbing onto his leg spawned another burst of shudders and arm swinging, but the unseen creature held on. Sharp claws pinched at Chilly's skin as more followed, moving upward in short, terrifying bursts of speed. The chorus of shrieks grew higher. A small, shivering torpedo of fur-covered muscle slipped past his fingers. Chilly froze and waited for the next one, his hands at the ready.

And then he felt the first bite.

39.

"Reading, huh? Well, that's a good sign."

Jeri looked up from the wine magazine she was thumbing through and regarded the stout, middle-aged doctor strolling into her room. Behind him, the nurse appeared with a tall orange juice and smiled cheerfully.

"How'd we sleep last night?" the doctor continued.

"Fine," Jeri replied, tossing the magazine aside. "No headaches." She took the large orange juice the nurse offered and drank it back greedily. "Thanks, Margaret."

"Of course, dear." The nurse, who had insisted on being called by her first name, fumbled through her pockets for a penlight and handed it to the doctor.

"Any pain?" he asked, flashing it at Jeri's pupils.

"No."

"Excellent." The doctor switched off the light and smiled. "Yesterday, I asked you to remember five things in a specific order. Will you please recite those to me?"

Jeri nodded. "You name is Dr. Alan Vogel. You have a chocolate lab named Judge. The largest of the great lakes is Lake Superior. Trout are a type of fish. And Nathan's Deli on Fifth Street makes the best corned beef on rye."

Nurse Margaret gave her an approving nod as the doctor jotted some notes. "Very good," he said, looking at her again. "And do we remember anything *new* this morning?"

Jeri's stare flickered around the large, stately bedroom before settling on the view beyond the window. A garden brimming with roses under the shade of queen palms stretched toward a colonnaded portico. In the distance, countless rows of budding grape vines basked in the morning sun on the rolling green hills. "Maybe," she said, shrugging with frustration. "It's hard to say. These images keep popping into my head, but I can't tell if they're real. They seem too vivid to be imagined. But if they *are* real, I don't . . . I don't know what to make of them."

"Give me some examples."

Her gaze remained fixed on the rose garden. "Driving in fog . . . searching for something. Standing on a subway train platform, watching the crowd. Feeling like . . . like I'm supposed to save someone." She paused and swallowed. "A huge man in a black suit, smiling at me in a dark room. Large hands. Strong. He's slapping me, and then…choking me." She shook her head and turned to the doctor. "Do those sound like real memories to you?"

The doctor regarded her somberly. "It's too early in your recovery to know exactly what's real and what's not. As I told you yesterday, your brain's been traumatized and needs—"

"Time to heal," Jeri interjected. "Yeah, got it." She noticed a man standing in the doorway behind the nurse, a manila envelope in his hands. "Good morning, Mr. Nielsen."

"Good morning." The security director's eyes swept briefly over Jeri and the nurse before honing in on Dr. Vogel. "Did I miss anything?"

"Not at all," the doctor replied, stiffening noticeably under Nielsen's pale gaze. "Just checking on our patient's condition."

"How's she doing?"

"Very well." Both men looked at their guest. "No detectible issues with creating new memory since the injection," the doctor continued. "Now we just have to be patient and see what, if any, damage the Diaverol has caused to her memory. We should know more in a few days."

The security director nodded. "Thank you, doctor."

"Of course."

The doctor and nurse both cast a fleeting nod at Jeri before shuffling out of the room. Nielsen closed the door behind them. "Is everyone treating you well?"

"Extremely. I'm starting to feel like a celebrity," Jeri replied. She gestured at the door. "I even have my own private security team waiting outside."

Nielsen nodded. "Do you have any idea why?"

Jeri shot him a surprised look. "I've lost my memory, Mr. Nielsen, not my mind. Given what you told me yesterday, either I'm not as safe as everyone keeps telling me, or you think I'm a lot more dangerous than I really am. Hopefully it's the latter. On another note, I've been doing some reading—" She grabbed the wine magazine on the bed next to her. "It looks like this is definitely going to be the year of the Pinot Noir."

"Would you like some new reading material?"

"Sure. How about Neurological Digest? I'm looking for any article that offers five easy steps to regaining your memory."

"Well, I don't know about that." Nielsen opened the envelope he was holding and pulled out a passport. "But maybe this will help." He tossed it to her.

Jeri caught it and immediately flipped to the identification page inside. "Jeri Stone," she whispered, studying the name. Her eyes shifted to the photograph. "Is this . . . real?"

"It's a valid passport, if that's what you're asking," Nielsen replied. "We found it in the room in Italy, along with some other things."

"Jeri *Stone*," she repeated, listening to the sound of her name. She glanced at her listed address. "Jesus, I live in *Baltimore*?"

"So it says."

"I don't understand. Why didn't you show this to me yesterday?"

"Dr. Vogel made it clear that your mind had already had enough to deal with." The security director's expression tightened. "Are you ready to talk?"

Jeri nodded. "I'm ready for some answers."

Nielsen fished something else from the envelope and walked over to the bed. "Good," he said, gesturing for her to hold out her hand. "Let's start with this."

A small, rectangular-shaped object fell into Jeri's palm. She regarded it curiously. "What is it?"

The security director studied her face intently for a moment. "Press the button on the side."

Jeri pressed the button and watched as an intricately etched shaft of glassy material slid from the protective housing and sparkled in the light. "Okay. And again my question is—"

"It's an encryption key. Used to secure our researcher's computer files from theft. One just like that went missing about ten days ago. It belonged to a researcher named Paul Obermeyer."

"He told you it was stolen?"

"No. But the circumstances surrounding his death do."

Jeri studied the Velgyn security director's face for a sign that he was joking before carefully closing the key. "So *that's* why I'm here," she said, handing it back. "The men you found me with—you think they're responsible."

Nielsen nodded. "Along with a few others."

"Well, you've got them, right? What are they saying?"

"One's dead. The other's still being questioned."

Jeri's eyes widened. "You *killed* one of them?"

"No. Well . . . not intentionally. The high-voltage stun gun used to subdue him ended up sending him into cardiac arrest."

"Too bad," she retorted cynically. "May I speak to the other one?"

"No."

"What do you mean, 'no,'" Jeri retorted, her face flushing with anger. "No offense, but you're missing a piece of computer hardware. I'm missing my whole fucking *life*!"

The security director stared back at her with an expression that bordered on pity. "I know," he said finally. "But he's not here. He's been detained somewhere that allows us to be more, let's just say, *liberal* in our approach to getting answers."

"Okay. And what do you expect me to do in the meantime? Sit around here reading wine magazines, waiting for my memory to return?"

"Unfortunately, yes."

"Yeah, well—to hell with that."

Nielsen took a step back as Jeri slipped off the bed and paced into the bathroom. "What are you doing?"

"First I'm getting dressed, and then I'm leaving," she

replied, closing the door behind her.

"And where do you plan on going?"

"I don't know. Baltimore? At least someone should know me there."

The security director waited silently while she dressed. He shook his head when she stepped back into the room. "I'm afraid I can't let you do that."

"And why's that?"

"See for yourself," Nielsen answered, handing her the large envelope. He turned and sat down on the bed.

Jeri turned the envelope over and watched several photos drop into her hand. "What are these?"

"Still frames taken from surveillance cameras. That first one shows you walking across the embarcadero in downtown San Francisco on the way to your date with Adam Cowell. Remember the young man I introduced you to last night?"

Jeri studied the grainy photo. Despite sunglasses and brunette hair, the woman looked uncannily like her. "The guy that called me Carrie?"

"That's right. He called you Carrie because that was the name you used."

"And why would I have done that?"

The security director regarded her calmly. "Mr. Cowell worked for Paul Obermeyer. Your reason for meeting him that night was to take his keycard so that you and your friends could access Obermeyer's research lab and steal his encryption key."

Jeri's expression slowly mutated from confusion to disbelief. "You think *I'm* involved in all this?"

Nielsen nodded.

"Oh come on . . . be reasonable!" she exclaimed, tossing the envelope and photos onto the bed. "I would never be involved in something like this! Never!"

The security director collected the photos and began shuffling through them. "This is you leaving the restaurant after taking Cowell's keycard. This is you passing a security camera in Heathrow airport six days ago. And this," he said, holding up another, "is you in the Bank Street underground station two days later. See? That's you standing in the corner, staring at the crowd—just like the memory you were describing to the doctor this morning."

Jeri snatched the photo from his hand. "No. It's . . . it's not possible."

Nielsen fished something from his jacket pocket and handed it to her. "This was found in the nightstand of your bed. Care to guess how much?"

Jeri quickly examined the thick stack of Euros and tossed it back. "A lot."

"Fifteen thousand Euros." A long silence filled the room before the security director continued. "I have state-of-the-art analysis confirming your identity in every one of these surveillance videos. I have you in the very same room as the other people we know to be responsible. I have a cash payment. And most importantly, I have Mr. Cowell—an eyewitness confirming you as the person who drugged him and took his lab credentials on the night of Paul Obermeyer's murder. By the way—I had the lab re-run Cowell's blood work yesterday. Can you guess what they found?"

Jeri regarded him with a distant stare. "Diaverol?"
Nielsen nodded.

Jeri turned and marched to the window. She pressed her cheek to the cool glass as a sudden wave of nausea threatened to eject the orange juice in her stomach. "So, what happens now?" she asked, closing her eyes and steeling herself for the answer.

The security director collected the photos and Euros along with Jeri's passport and slipped them back into the envelope. He walked to the door and paused. "Are you hungry?"

Jeri turned and looked to see if he was joking. "Not in the least."

"Then pretend to be and follow me." Nielsen smiled and opened the door. In the hallway, two men in matching gray suits snapped to attention. "Someone very important has invited you to lunch."

40.

Derrick Birch stepped onto the catwalk inside the massive fractional distiller and stared somberly at the collection of researchers, engineers, and managers gathered on the main platform below. Above him, the shimmering network of tubes within Bioreactor Two pulsed quietly like a sleeping, green-blooded serpent. "Okay, everyone," the Ceres project leader exclaimed, raising his hands. "You know why we're here, and you know what this could mean. So, without further ado, let's see what we've got. Samir—?"

A young, bespectacled man slipped out of the crowd and marched up the catwalk. "Ready," he said quietly, holding up a computer tablet.

"Let's start with growth rate and yield," Birch commanded.

The engineer quickly tapped at the tablet screen and showed it to the project leader. Birch studied it poker-faced for a moment before turning to the crowd. "Yesterday, we introduced ten thousand liters of Dr. Obermeyer's hybridized mixture of Botrycoccus with ectosymbiont cyanobacteria to Bioreactors One and Two along with an altered growth media as specified by Dr. Aleksandrov. As of right now, volumetric density within Bioreactor Two indicates a growth rate that is—" He paused and looked again at Samir. "Am I reading this correctly?"

The engineer nodded.

"That is thirty-one percent higher over the same period than any previous version. We're also showing forty percent less die-off at normal pressure and carbon dioxide thresholds."

Below, Paul Obermeyer watched those around him turn and regard each other with wide-eyed shock. A short distance away, the slight, immaculately dressed figure of Minister Razam stood quietly, a slight grin dimpling his handsome face.

"But of course, yield is only *half* of the equation," Birch continued. "We've still got to beat current cellular hydrocarbon densities by at least ten percent."

The collected teams leaned closer in nervous anticipation while Samir called up the latest numbers and handed the tablet to the project leader. Birch read the results and nodded. His gaze fell back to the crowd and locked onto Paul.

"Ladies and gentlemen, prior to this meeting, Minister Razam informed me that two cases of '96 Boërl & Kroff would be chilling in the main kitchen in the event that we pull off a miracle. Well, if you think you're going to get through the rest of this evening—Muslim or not—without having a glass, you're mistaken!"

Below, the crowd erupted in cheers as the project leader turned and raised his arms to the bioreactor overhead. "Ladies and gentleman, it is my sincere pleasure to introduce you to the world's first commercially viable bioreactor. Ceres is truly a living wonder . . . and she's going to change the world!"

The Saudi Minister joined Birch on the catwalk and the two men embraced to the din of more applause. Razam then turned to the crowd.

"On behalf of myself and Mr. Birch, I want to thank each and every one of you for making this incredible achievement possible," the Minister said, his tone earnest and commanding. "Despite all of the many obstacles, despite each of our own personal moments of suffering, we have come together and made this vision a reality. And what a vision it is! Today, after countless trial and effort, we have started the very engine that will drive our global economy into the future. Of course, as with all great achievements that challenge old thinking and demand vast change and acceptance, no one can say when this future will be fully embraced. None of us here is naïve enough to believe it will come easily, or that great forces won't try to destroy everything we've created. But just as surely as the challenges still awaiting us, we all know that Ceres is going to change everything . . . because it *must* change everything. Years from now, when the rest of the world has finally emancipated itself from ideas as unsustainable as the energy upon which it now runs, it will be *this* moment that the historians and storytellers will be talking about. And it is you—the dreamers and the visionaries—who have given it to them. Let us all be proud of what we have accomplished here today."

Another round of cheers echoed through the tall, cathedral-like interior as the Minister embraced Birch again and the two men descended into the crowd. Paul shook hands with Chung and Shahid before finding himself locked in a bear hug with Marcello. "What shall become of our nearly departed crew now?" the Italian researcher lamented, his breath already reeking of alcohol. He rested his head on Paul's shoulder. "We are like brothers, you and me."

"I . . . I couldn't agree more," Paul replied, patting his

colleague on the back. It was then that he noticed Tatyana slipping through the crowd toward him. "Regardless of what happens next, I'm sure we'll stay in touch. Oh look—here's Dr. Aleksandrov."

Marcello released him and cast a sly grin at Tatyana. "He's all yours, Dr. Aleksandrov. Now, if you both will excuse me."

Paul shook his head as the Italian march off toward an arriving tray of champagne flutes. "Do you think he knows we've, you know . . . ."

"Gay men are very perceptive," Tatyana replied flatly. "He probably knew before we did."

Paul noticed the backpack slung over her shoulder. "Where have you been?"

"Making arrangements."

"What kind of arrangements?"

A thin smile creased the Russian researcher's face. "Do you trust me, Dr. Obermeyer?"

Paul was still considering the question when a voice rang out behind him.

"Who needs a drink?"

He turned to find Derrick Birch and Minister Razam standing before them, each holding two champagne flutes. "Oh . . . thank you," Paul replied, reaching for one of the project leader's drinks.

"Fuck you, these are mine," Birch scoffed. "The bar's back there." He grinned at Tatyana. "So, is it safe to say that you two are getting along now?"

"Yes," the Russian researcher replied. "I was just thanking Dr. Obermeyer again for allowing me to assist him in his laboratory."

"It is my understanding that you played a key part in this breakthrough as well, Dr. Aleksandrov," the Minister said, handing her a champagne flute. "Allow me this moment to thank *both* of you."

"All right, I suppose you can have one too," Birch conceded, handing Paul a glass. He raised his own in toast. "Here's to changing the world."

"To changing the world," Paul and Tatyana repeated.

Birch emptied his glass in a single gulp and smacked his lips. "Now—what do you say we all get piss-drunk?"

The minister smiled. "I believe this is an excellent time for me to excuse myself," he replied, bowing slightly. "Please enjoy yourselves tonight. You deserve it."

Paul and the others bid the minister a good evening. When he was gone, Birch turned once again to Tatyana. "Ready for another, Dr. A?"

Tatyana gave him with a brief look of annoyance. "While I'm sure everyone else here is quite eager to destroy their livers, I believe there's still some unfinished work for Dr. Obermeyer and myself in the laboratory." She reached over and grabbed Paul's hand. "Isn't that right?"

Birch's eyes dropped to their joined hands and widened. "Holy shit."

Paul nodded. "That's right, we do. Will you excuse us, Derrick?"

The project leader regarded them with a look of disbelief. "Sure. Of course. Go do your . . . work."

"Thank you. Good night." Tatyana abruptly turned and led Paul toward an exit at the far end of the room. On the other side of the door, Paul paused and pulled her against him.

"What are you doing? Don't you want to celebrate?"

Tatyana reached up and kissed him before offering a mischievous smile. "Of course I do. But not with him. I have another idea in mind. Are you ready for an adventure, Dr. Obermeyer?"

Paul studied her with suspicion. "What kind of adventure?" he asked warily.

His colleague sighed and cocked her head. "Must we have *another* conversation regarding cowardice?"

Paul smiled. "No."

"Good." Tatyana kissed him again, her green eyes sparkling with excitement. "Now follow me."

Inside the Velgyn Pharmaceutical retreat house, the two armed men in matching Brooks Brothers suits escorted Jeri and the security director down a grand stairwell and past large, lavishly decorated rooms before opening the doors to an outdoor courtyard with sweeping views of the surrounding vineyards. "Please," Nielsen said, gesturing to a table set for four beneath a trellis laden with blooming jasmine.

Jeri sat down as requested. "Who else is joining us?" she asked, gazing up at the tapestry of vines and delicate white flowers that hung from the heavy wooden beams. From the corner of her eye she noticed the director's men take flanking positions by the door.

"Michael Manning, our CEO." Nielsen dropped into the seat next to her. "Along with one of his advisors."

Across the courtyard, another set of French doors opened and an attractive brunette appeared with a tray of juices and coffee. "Good morning, Director Nielsen," the young woman said, placing the tray on the table. "Just let me know if you need anything prior to Mr. Manning's arrival."

Jeri's eyes absently followed the woman's slow, sauntering retreat back inside.

"Coffee?" the security director asked.

"Sure," she said flatly.

"I understand that what I've told you isn't easy to accept," Nielsen said, filling her cup. "But none of us know the circumstances that brought you into this. Maybe they're holding someone you love hostage. Maybe they threatened to kill you if you didn't comply. Whatever the reason, there's no point in blaming yourself for what's happened until we know what was leveraged against you."

"Maybe," Jeri sighed, leaning her head back. Beyond the checkerboard pattern of the trellis stretched a pristine California sky. "But it still won't erase the fact I've been involved in something horrible." Her gaze slowly drifted back to the director. "Do you have any idea what it feels like to question everything you believe about yourself?"

Nielsen's gray eyes regarded her somberly. He started to respond when his men opened the doors and a tall, dark-haired man in golf attire strolled casually into the courtyard, a phone pressed to his ear. Behind him, an older gentleman with a round, suntanned face and small, hawkish eyes followed with an attaché case.

"Have you reminded him that he's already signed the contract," the man said firmly into his phone as he took a seat at the table. "Well, if he doesn't like it, tell him we've got word from Bob Downey's people that he'll do the commercial. In fact, I'd prefer him. At least he isn't a goddamn Scientologist." He abruptly dropped his phone on the table and offered a hand to Jeri. "Good morning, I'm Michael Manning. You must be Jeri."

Jeri took the Velgyn CEO's hand and smiled cautiously. "I am. Nice to meet you." Her smile faltered as Manning tightened his grip and leaned closer.

"How are you feeling?" he asked.

"Um . . . better, thanks."

"I'm very happy to hear that." Manning released her hand and gestured at his companion. "This gentleman is Oliver Doling, one of my lawyers. Most people hear the word lawyer and get nervous, but don't worry. Ollie's really just here for the food."

Jeri smiled at the older man, who responded with a terse nod. A moment later their server appeared once again.

"Good morning, Mr. Manning. May I offer you and your guests something for breakfast?"

"Absolutely," the CEO replied. "What's the chef got planned for us this morning?"

"We received a wonderful selection of Maine lobsters this morning and Chef Bottura suggests egg white frittatas garnished with a sea salt infused avocado sauce complemented with Almas caviar."

"Perfect. Let's have that for the whole table."

"Very good, sir."

Manning gestured at the view as the server vanished back inside. "So, Jeri, what do you think of this place?"

"It's beautiful," Jeri replied.

"It is, isn't it? Care to hear the story behind it?"

Jeri noticed a fleeting look of annoyance on the security director's face. "Sure."

"Are you a movie buff?"

"I don't . . . I don't know."

"Right, of course—your memory." Manning shrugged apologetically and poured himself a coffee. "Well, believe it or not, this house was built back in nineteen forty-two by the famous Hollywood director Alfred Hitchcock. According to the story I've been told, Hitchcock was getting ready to make a film called *Shadow of a Doubt*, which he was planning to shoot in one of the studios in Hollywood. Back then, everything was shot in a studio, and Hitchcock had a reputation for spending huge amounts of money on his sets. Kind of like what we spend on drug launch parties, huh Ollie?"

His lawyer grunted irritably.

"Only this particular time there was a problem," Manning continued. "The country was almost a year into fighting the Germans and the Japs, and anything that wasn't going to the war effort was being heavily rationed. So right as Hitchcock was getting started on the film, the U.S. government decided to impose a legal limit on what the studios could spend on each movie set and *boom*—just like that—ruined his plans. But apparently Hitchcock wasn't the kind of man who took kindly to the government or anyone else getting in the way of his movie making. So he said 'To hell with it—I won't use any sets. I'll shoot the entire movie on location.' And you know what? He did. In fact, he shot most of *Shadow of a Doubt* on the streets of a little town called Santa Rosa about an hour north of here. And not only did Hitchcock pull it off, his movie got an Oscar nomination for best story that year." He paused and regarded Nielsen. "I guess sometimes we do our best work when we're forced to rethink everything—don't we, Lars?"

The security director nodded. "Indeed, Michael."

"So what does that have to do with this place?" Jeri

asked.

A thin grin appeared on Manning's face. "As the story goes, even after filming for the movie began, Hitchcock spent months scouting for a place to shoot an important scene that didn't seem to exist in Santa Rosa. He apparently envisioned some grand, Spanish-style house with views of the countryside that was also large enough to film interior shots. But he just couldn't find it. So he went back to the studio, asked for all of the money he was allowed to spend on sets under the new rules, demanded a full advance on his director's fees, and spent the next several months building this house. Of course, not only did it cost him a fortune and delay the movie by nearly a year, it almost cost Hitchcock his relationship with the studio. Can you imagine? The crazy sonofabitch put everything on the line for a *single* goddamn scene." His grin broadened. "But here's the best part. On the night of the movie premiere, some Hollywood reporter who'd gotten wind of the house story walked up to Hitchcock and asked him exactly which scene it was in the film. And Hitchcock, in his usual calm and collection manner, turned to the reporter and said, 'none of them—I decided I didn't need the scene after all!'"

Jeri forced a smile as the Velgyn CEO laughed along with the other two men. "When I first heard that story," he continued, his smile fading, "I wondered—did Hitchcock really care so much about his movie that he was willing to risk everything for it, or was he just showing everyone who was in charge? Which is more important—the work, or the ego? I must have pondered that question for years. Then I became the head of a global, multi-billion dollar company and suddenly the answer was obvious." Manning shook his head and took a drink of his coffee. "Anyway, a few years ago when I found out this place was on the market, I just had to have it. So I asked Ollie here to buy it under the corporation and make it our executive retreat house. Probably not my most rational decision, but I do love to come here." His eyes flashed to Jeri. "It reminds me that beautiful things can persist, even when their very reason for being seems to have vanished."

The intensity of Manning's gaze made Jeri feel as if she'd suddenly been stripped bare.

"When Mr. Nielsen told me you'd been apprehended in Italy, I thought we were finally going to get some answers to this mess." Manning's voice took on a noticeable edge of irritation. "But once again I was wrong. Instead of the bold, mysterious *Lady X* who'd so brilliantly eluded us, we find ourselves left with a quiet young woman who can't even remember her own fucking name. And trust me, Jeri, if anyone wants your memory restored as much as you do, it's me." He paused and narrowed his eyes on her. "And now we're in this predicament together. You and I have had something very valuable stolen from us, and we'd both like to get those things back. Wouldn't you agree?"

Jeri nodded.

"Good. Then let's help each other do that." The Velgyn CEO shrugged and leaned back in his chair. "Of course, my team's already pulled you from the lion's den—not to mention spent a small fortune on your medical needs and recovery. Unfortunately, the only cure for your memory loss seems to be the one thing we *can't* afford—time. So I'll get to the point. I need your help in getting back what you and your friends have taken from me—and I need it now."

"They're *not* my friends," Jeri corrected, eyeing all three men. "What is it you want me to do?"

A thin grin appeared on the Velgyn CEO's face. "Actually, it's very simple—we just want to release you back into the world and see who comes looking for you."

"But that doesn't make any sense. How would they—?"

"Know where you are?" The grin on Manning's face widened. "Lars?"

"You were tagged," the security director replied flatly.

"Tagged?" Jeri shook her head. "What does that mean?"

Nielsen's gaze shifted to her stomach. "There's a GPS microchip in your lower back. Tiny . . . just under the skin. The medical team discovered it when they were examining you. It emits a signal that can be tracked by a computer or a phone— and it's a safe bet the people we're after put it there."

"Are you serious?" Jeri reached back and rubbed at her skin. "Then get it out!"

"Out?" Manning scoffed, shaking his head. "Of course not. Then they couldn't find you."

Jeri looked at him, dumbfounded. "Jesus Christ, I just got away from those people! And now you honestly expect me to go back out there and play the bait for your trap?"

"*We* got you away from those people," Manning corrected, his smile vanishing. "And I would've expected a little more gratitude for doing so."

"Thank you," Jeri said tersely. "But I have to respectfully decline your request."

Doling, the leathery-faced lawyer, leaned forward with a menacing scowl. "I believe you're misinterpreting the nature of our request, Miss Stone," he interjected. "Do you think that your lack of memory somehow absolves you of your involvement in Paul Obermeyer's murder and the theft of his security key? Even if you were coerced into your actions, the evidence

Mr. Nielsen and his team have collected on you is irrefutable. I could easily make you look as guilty in this matter as the people we now seek to find. So let me be very clear—this is *not* a negotiation. This is not us asking for your blessing. This is us telling you exactly what you're going to do. And if you don't comply, your situation is going to become particularly uncomfortable."

"Fine," Jeri retorted. "I'd rather be turned over to the authorities than do what you're asking."

"The authorities?" Doling shook his head. "If we turn you over to anyone, Miss Stone, I guarantee you it won't be the authorities."

Jeri's expression tightened as the meaning of his words sunk in. "Why me?" she demanded. "Why not the *other* guy—the one that did this to me?"

"His value lies in what he can tell us," the lawyer replied. "Besides, he doesn't have a GPS implant like you do."

"Which is good," the Velgyn CEO added. "All the more reason for their remaining team to seek you out. No doubt they're just as desperate for answers as we are. Ah look, here's our food."

Their server reappeared with an armload of plates. Jeri stared absently at the steaming plate of food placed in front of her as the others began to eat. "So . . . say I agree to your request," she said finally. "Say someone does come looking for me and you get them. What happens then?"

"To whom?" Doling asked.

"To me."

"Our interest in you extends only as far as your ability to help us collect what's ours," the lawyer replied without looking up from his plate. "Once the encryption key has been secured, we'll consider your obligations to us fulfilled."

Manning looked over at her with a strange look in his eye. "Of course, who knows? Perhaps when this is over, there's a place for you in *our* organization. You obviously have some very unique skills. Shame to have them go to waste."

Next to him, Nielsen shifted in his chair.

"Where?" Jeri asked, ignoring the strange offer. "Where are you planning to take me?"

"After breakfast, Mr. Nielsen and his men will be escorting you back to San Francisco. We've arranged a suite for you at the Omni—all expenses paid."

Jeri nodded and pushed back her chair. "Fine. Then if don't mind, I'd like go. Now."

"Wow," Manning said, admiring her with a smug grin. "I have to say, I love your spirit. What do you say, Lars—are you and your team ready?"

The security director silently laid his fork on his plate and raised his hand. Behind him, the Brooks Brothers twins stepped forward.

"Excellent," Manning replied. "Ollie and I are going to stay and finish this wonderful breakfast. But don't worry, Jeri—Mr. Nielsen and his men are going to take very good care of you."

Jeri held his stare as she stood to leave. "What was the answer?" she asked.

"Excuse me?"

"Hitchcock. You said you understood him after you became a CEO. So what's more important—the work or the ego?"

Manning gently wiped his mouth with his napkin and leaned back. "Well, since you asked, I'll tell you. The answer is neither—and both. You see, Jeri, when you sit behind an executive desk like I do, you start to see the world a little differently. More clearly you might say. That's when you realize questions like that are irrelevant . . . asked by people who've never tasted power." He paused and let his eyes shamelessly drift over her figure. "The work and the ego? Hell, they're both the same thing."

Next to him, Doling speared a bite of his lobster frittata with his fork and pointed it at her. "Good luck, Miss Stone, and be careful. You're dealing with some very dangerous people here."

Jeri nodded at him. "You're right," she said, feeling Nielsen's men on both sides. Her eyes shifted once again to Manning. "Very dangerous."

41.

"Where are we going?"

Paul followed Tatyana into a service elevator and looked on with surprise as she punched the security code into the operating panel. "Wait—how did you get a security code?"

His colleague smiled. "When I first arrived, I insisted that I be allowed outside after dark to walk. Derrick and the Minister agreed, but required one of the security guards to escort me at all times. That lasted for perhaps two weeks before the guard became bored of the extra duty and just gave me his code."

"So what's out there?"

"Sand."

Paul rolled his eyes. "Of course. And—?"

"Do you like *any* surprises, Dr. Obermeyer?"

The elevator shuddered to a stop. Tatyana grabbed his hand and led him into what appeared to be a large, hangar-like maintenance garage. "This way," she whispered, veering toward an exit door.

Paul glanced over his shoulder. At the opposite end of the garage, a group of men in gray coveralls sat huddled in a tight circle. The noise of voices and laughter echoed through the large space. "What are they doing?"

"Hookah," his colleague replied, tugging his hand impatiently "Come on . . . move your feet." When they reached the door, Tatyana crouched down and quickly punched in the security code. Her smile returned with the soft buzz of the electronic lock releasing.

"Are you sure this is a good idea?" Paul asked.

Tatyana opened the door and they both stared into the darkness. "I am sure." Her tiny frame slipped through the opening and vanished.

Paul shot another anxious look at the maintenance workers. A raucous wave of laughter confirmed that he and Tatyana hadn't been noticed. He stepped toward the door and hesitated. *What the hell are you doing?* a voice in his head demanded. *Get back in the elevator before anyone notices you're missing.*

"Are you coming?" Tatyana exclaimed irritably.

Of course not. Paul Obermeyer is a responsible person.

"Paul?"

Paul cursed under his breath. *Coward!* another voice in his head cried. A bolt of anger surged through him. Without a second thought, he stepped outside and closed the door behind him. The click of the lock sent a strange thrill down his spine.

Fuck it. I'm already dead.

A few steps further, Paul looked up and froze once again. "Holy shit," he mumbled, awestruck by the sheer scale of his stark industrial surroundings. Illuminated by countless high-powered lights, the vast machinery forming the Ras Jazan refinery stretched in every direction beneath the night sky.

"Unbelievable, is it not?" Tatyana said, admiring the

view next to him.

Paul nodded. "Like some kind of alien city. Is this why you brought me out here?"

"No." His colleague pointed toward a large void of darkness just beyond a row of storage tanks. "Do you see that?"

Paul narrowed his eyes on the void and noticed it was shimmering. "What is it?"

"A reservoir," Tatyana answered. "Refining crude oil takes a great deal of water. Almost seven thousand liters per barrel, in fact. So you can imagine how much water this refinery used to require. Of course, now we use it for creating the growth media for the bioreactors."

"Okay."

"One night I walked near the reservoir and I noticed a peculiar smell. It was very strong . . . and very familiar. So I took a small taste. As I suspected, it is salt water."

Paul shrugged. "So?"

"So we must be within a few miles of the source—which could only be the Persian Gulf." Tatyana stepped closer and smiled. "And I wish to see it."

"*See* it?" Paul repeated.

"Correct. With you."

Paul studied her face and realized she was serious. "And how do you propose we do that?"

"There is a truck in a service shed about five hundred meters from here. The keys are in the glove box—I've checked. There is also a map."

"And you honestly think we can just take it for a spin?"

"I already have. Several times around the compound in fact to see what would happen. No one has ever noticed."

"But how would we—"

"An unguarded service gate on the northeast side," Tatyana interjected, anticipating his question. "The security code I was given opens that as well." She grabbed his hand. "I told you, Paul—I have chosen to stop being afraid. What is a life without risk or adventure? We have done what we were brought here to do—we have brought Ceres to life! Are we not entitled to a little fun? To a few *hours* of escape from this steel and concrete prison?"

A long silence passed as Paul considered the question.

Exasperated, Tatyana released his hand and began marching in the direction of the storage shed. "You wish to stay here and get drunk with a bunch of men rather than make love to a beautiful Russian woman on a beach?" she scoffed. "So be it! Dobroy nochi!"

Paul watched his colleague for a moment before breaking into a jog after her. "You win," he said, passing her and picking up the pace. "But I'm driving."

Ray Foster was absently admiring the weathered frescoes on the walls around him when a high-pitched shriek forced him to look up. High overhead, a bat darted around the old monastery's stone vaults and arches with uncanny precision. The Velgyn security manager shifted his weight on the uncomfortable relic of a bench he was lying on and watched the tiny creature's frenetic dance for several minutes before checking his watch. He sat up and regarded the two men seated by the door at the opposite end of the room. "Is this normal?"

The man sitting to the left roused from a half-sleep and raised his eyebrows at him. "Is *what* normal?"

"Come on." Foster pointed at his watch. "A day and a half—and he's still not talking?"

The man shrugged.

"How long does it usually take?"

"It takes what it takes. Everybody's different. Some talk quickly, some don't."

Foster rose and marched toward the door. Both men immediately stood and stepped forward, blocking his path.

"Where are you going?" the second man asked, his stare threatening.

"I want to talk to Marcus. Now."

The guard to his left pressed a finger to his earpiece. "M—you there? Client wants to chat. Yeah . . . okay." He nodded at Foster. "He'll be up in a minute."

Foster spun and paced the perimeter of the abandoned monastery's refectory. His footstep stirred a fresh cloud of dust that rose and sparkled under the temporary construction lights. Two laps around the room, the cellar door swung open and Marcus appeared with a questioning look.

"What seems to be the problem?" Marcus asked.

"Time," Foster replied, stopping in front him. "We're running out of it. Why is this taking so long?"

"This is not a task dictated by time," the redheaded mercenary answered. "Tell me, is your mother alive, Mr. Foster?"

"What did you say?"

"Your mother. Is she alive?"

Foster's eyes narrowed on the wiry man. "Yeah . . . why?"

"Because I'd like to send some men to kill her. May I have her address?"

The security manager stifled a laugh before clenching his jaw. "Fuck you."

"Exactly," Marcus nodded. "Now, imagine if I were serious. What would it take to get that information from you? Do you really know? Do either of us?"

Foster shifted his stare to the door. "I want to see him."

"Why?"

"Because I want to see what you're doing."

"Are you sure about that? I doubt you'd even understand what you're seeing."

Foster leaned closer. "Then you'll just have to explain it to me. Either that, or I call my boss and tell him what's happening here."

Marcus smiled. "Mr. Nielsen knows exactly what's happening here. But I understand. You are, after all, the *client*." He spat the last word out like an expletive and gestured at the door. "Be my guest."

The Velgyn security manager noticed the surprised looks on Marcus's men as he made his way through the doorway. Half way down the narrow stairwell, he stopped and caught his breath. "Jesus . . . what is that smell?"

Behind him, Marcus sniffed the air. "Hard to say," he said, an edge of sarcasm in his voice. "Rotten meat . . . human excrement . . . maybe both? If this is too difficult, you're welcome to go back upstairs."

Foster took a slow breath and continued. Upon opening the lower cellar door, he peered inside and grimaced with disgust. Their captive, naked except for a large pair of goggles and headphones masking his face, hung shivering in the dim light. Tension cords running from wall anchors to his outstretched arms and legs held him upright just inches over the floor. A metal collar wreathed with electrical wires was secured tightly around his neck. Perhaps most disturbing of all, a thick, puss-colored substance was slathered over his arms and chest.

Foster stepped closer. "Can he hear us?" he asked, fighting the urge to gag.

"No." Marcus replied.

"What the fuck's all over him?"

"Durian." Marcus strolled over and nonchalantly swept a sample of the custardy pulp from their captive's arm before holding it toward the security manager. "An Asian tropical fruit. Quite a delicacy, if you can stomach the smell. As I said, its somewhere between rotting meat and human waste, which is probably what our friend thinks he's covered in right now." He shrugged and wiped the foul-smelling pulp back onto Chilly's shoulder.

Foster gestured at Chilly's face. "What are the goggles and headphones for?"

"He's playing a game."

"A game?"

Marcus nodded. "In virtual reality. See how he's moving his head? He's navigating a labyrinth of passageways that has neither an end nor a solution. Of course, he doesn't know that yet. All he knows is that each time he comes to a new passageway, the sounds in his headphones change from death metal rock to evangelical sermons to the screams of a child to something else . . . the next more disturbing than the previous."

"And if he stops?"

Marcus pointed to the collar around Chilly's neck. "Pain. A hundred and twenty volts of motivation if he drops his head. Also deters him from nodding off."

413

Foster watched their captive's head move slowly back and forth and felt a sudden sense of pity. "And you really think all of this will make him talk?"

"This isn't trial and error, Mr. Foster. This is the systematic breakdown of psychological and emotional resistance through exhaustion and sensory conditioning. I'm sure it will work because it always works. It's only a question of time."

"How long?"

Marcus seemed to ponder the question for a moment. Then, without warning, he turned and struck their captive in the ribs. Chilly shuddered under the blow, his body twisting in the air before the tension cords snapped him back into position. The red-haired mercenary studied him with clinical detachment. "Several more hours. His response times are still surprisingly good. We'll know he's closer when he starts talking to himself. Or shits." A smug smile twisted the scar on his cheek. "You'd be surprised what defecating on yourself does to the psyche."

Foster regarded him with a look of disgust. "You actually enjoy this, don't you?"

"I enjoy getting answers, Mr. Foster. The means might be unpleasant, but that doesn't make them—or *me*—any less necessary."

"Well, answers or not, I'm calling Mr. Nielsen in thirty minutes." The security manager shot a final glance at their captive before turning for the door. "Keep me informed."

"Of course. Oh, and Ray—I'm going to make an adjustment to our friend's game program in a moment. Don't be alarmed if you hear a complaint."

Foster nodded at their hired interrogator before making his way past the door. Halfway up the stairs, a terrified scream pierced the silence and reverberated through the narrow stone chamber. The Velgyn security manager paused, the muscles in his jaw tensing as the sound rose and then ended as swiftly as it had come. He turned and looked down at the cellar door, then shook his head and continued up the stairs.

~

Paul's gaze shifted back and forth from the ribbon of unknown road before them to the shrinking view of the Raz Jazan refinery in the Toyota Hilux's rearview mirror. To his surprise, Tatyana had been correct—with the simple entry of her security code, the unguarded service gate had opened. Now, a few kilometers into their unauthorized adventure, his colleague sat next to him in the cab of the truck poring over the map from the glovebox. He looked over at her again. "Tatyana?"

"Yes?"

"Where are we going?"

Tatyana lifted the map toward the overhead cabin light and furrowed her brow. "Perhaps we missed a turn."

"What do you mean, missed a turn? There haven't been any turns." Paul eased his foot off the gas pedal and the throaty hum of the truck's engine softened to a whisper.

"No, no—keep going," his colleague commanded, slapping his arm. "It must be ahead."

"Which direction are we driving?"

"East. Or no—" Tatyana turned the map ninety degrees. "South. Yes, of course. We are driving south."

Paul pulled off the road and hit the brakes.

"What are you doing?"

"You're navigational skills aren't exactly inspiring confidence." Paul grabbed the map and studied it under the light. "Where's the refinery on here?"

Tatyana pointed to a large square labeled in Arabic. "There."

Paul squinted at it, puzzled. "How do you know?"

"What else would be that large in the middle of nowhere?"

"Well, I don't know if we should stake our lives on that argument. But if you're right, there's only one main road in and out, which would be the one we're on now. We've gone just over five kilometers, which puts us right about—" Paul's finger traced the line of the road and paused. "Here. I think the turn you're talking about is another kilometer ahead."

Both of them looked up at a sudden a light on the horizon. Ahead, the twin beams of an approaching vehicle pierced the darkness.

"Well, at least we are not the only ones out here." Tatyana snatched the map back and began studying it once again.

"Yeah, that's what worries me." The Hilux's engine growled once again as Paul steered them back onto the road. His fingers nervously scratched at his beard as the oncoming vehicle drew nearer. "Turn off the overhead light."

"Why?"

"Because drawing attention to the two very non-Arabic-looking people in this truck is a bad idea."

"Ridiculous. No one is going to look at us. And besides, I want to—"

Paul reached over and snapped off the light. A moment later, a white passenger van containing several silhouetted figures sped past. "Could you *please* stop challenging every request I have from now on?" he asked, studying the van's retreating taillights in the rearview mirror.

Tatyana glared at him silently for a moment before retrieving her backpack from the floor. "I believe it is time for a drink," she said, pulling out a large gold-necked bottle and holding it up proudly.

Paul looked over at the '96 Boërl & Kroff in her hand. "Did you steal that from the Minister?"

"Steal is such an unpleasant word, Dr. Obermeyer. I prefer the word *recruit*."

Paul laughed. "How many bottles did you recruit?"

"Two."

"You're right, it's time for a drink." He glanced again at the rearview mirror while his colleague popped the cork and immediately cursed Russian at the stream of froth that splattered onto her lap.

The white van was gone.

"The turn!" Tatyana exclaimed, pointing to a break in the rolling dunes of sand on their left.

Paul steered the truck onto the narrow gravel road while his colleague raised the champagne in triumph. "To not being lost!" she exclaimed, handing him he bottle.

"To not being dead!" Paul retorted, feeling a sudden sense of elation. He took a long drink and clumsily poured some into Tatyana's open mouth, laughing as it spilled over her chin.

His colleague slipped her hand around Paul's neck and pressed her slender frame against him. "Don't look now, Dr. Obermeyer, but I believe you are enjoying yourself," she whispered, her stare shifting to his mouth. "Just as you should be."

Paul fought to keep the truck on the road as his colleague slipped herself onto his lap and began kissing him, her soft lips wet with champagne.

Half a kilometer north on the main road, the brake lights of the white van flashed crimson in the darkness as it slowed and turned around.

42.

Tatyana rolled over and released a deep, contented sigh. "Udovol'stviye," she whispered, a crooked grin dimpling her face. "Christoye udovol'stviye."

Next to her, Paul sat up and admired the moonlit waters of the Arabian Gulf calmly lapping at the sand a few feet beyond their naked bodies. He found the second bottle of champagne hidden beneath his discarded clothes and poured the last remaining drops into his mouth. "Translation?"

"It means pleasure. Pure pleasure." The Russian researcher ran a hand through her hair and gave him a sidelong glance. "Would you agree?"

"I would. Of course, we didn't *really* have to come all the way out here just to—"

Tatyana silenced him with a playful punch to the stomach. "I did. One more night in that compound and I think I would have become crazy." She shivered against the growing chill in the air and put on her clothes. "Tell me about California."

"What would you like to know?"

"Is it as beautiful as I've heard it to be?"

Paul nodded. "Mostly. A short drive south of San Francisco is a place called Big Sur. It's probably one of the most beautiful place I've ever seen. Just pristine coastline and these magnificent mountains rising next to you. There's a restaurant that sits on this high bluff overlooking the Pacific. I was there at sunset once, staring down at the water crashing onto the rocks while a giant condor circled overhead." He paused and shook his head at a sudden wave of homesickness. "It felt like I was sitting on the edge of the world."

"It sounds quite nice," Tatyana replied, studying him in the moonlight. "Perhaps you shall take me there one day."

Paul gave her a pensive grin and threw on his own clothes. "Assuming we're given the chance."

"A chance?" Tatyana grabbed his hands and pulled him to his feet. "Of course we will have our chance! A few days ago you and I solved one of the world's most important energy questions. Tonight we made love on a beautiful, deserted beach. There is no *chance*, Dr. Obermeyer—there is only what we set our minds to do."

"Jesus . . . when did you become such an overbearing optimist?" Paul asked, regarding her suspiciously. His colleague flashed him a broad smile.

"After meeting you, of course." She kissed him again before breaking into a jog back toward the truck. "And besides, who knows what tomorrow may bring?"

Paul stole a final glance at the pristine beach around him before running after her.

～

A heavy coastal fog hung like a shroud over Highway 101 as Nielsen threaded his Jaguar coupe south through morning traffic. Sitting in the soft leather of the passenger seat, Jeri watched the vehicles around them slide briefly into view before fading ghost-like back into the mist. For the first time since their departure from the Sonoma retreat house, she turned and regarded the Velgyn security director. "So whose idea was this?"

Nielsen furrowed his brow, his eyes fixed on the road. "Does it matter?"

"Considering that it's *my* life being put on the line, yes."

"Your life is not going to be put at risk. I promise."

Jeri released a bitter laugh. "You just told me this morning that these are some of the most sophisticated criminals you've ever dealt with."

The security director deftly slipped the sports car into another lane as a slower vehicle appeared in front of them. "That's right, I did," he said, glancing at the rearview mirror. A short distance back, his men's white Escalade obediently followed after. "But now one of them is dead, one's in our custody, and one is working for us. The advantage has shifted to our side. We wouldn't be doing this if I wasn't certain of it."

"So it *was* your idea." Jeri turned back to the window. "What happens when we get there?"

"Two of my men will escort you to the suite," Nielsen replied, a hint of irritation in his tone. "Two more will be posted downstairs. We'll also be analyzing everyone entering the hotel via surveillance cameras."

"And you? Where will you be?"

He glanced over at her. "Close."

"Great. I'll be the bait and you'll be *close*. Sounds like a winning combination." Jeri continued to watch the vehicles drift in and out of view and slowly closed her eyes. A wall of fog appeared in her mind, its opaque tendrils curling and mixing around her. She concentrated on pushing it back and noticed the dark pavement of a road rushing beneath her. Shadowy silhouettes of trees flitted past on the fringes of her vision. She tilted her head as the road turned and rose upward. *Where am I going?* she wondered, a spectator in her own waking dream. The road turned again, her speed now noticeably faster. More trees darted past. Time slowed and her focus began to drift with the fog. Sleep tugged at her consciousness. Then, without warning, a running figure materialized directly in her path. A head turned and looked at her, dark eyes wide with fear. She willed herself to stop, to avoid the body now lunging sideways in a desperate attempt to escape their colliding paths.

But she wasn't stopping fast enough.

"No!" Jeri exclaimed, snapping awake. She reached out and reflexively grasped the dashboard. Next to her, the security director flinched with surprise.

"What's wrong?" he demanded, tightening his grip on the steering wheel.

Jeri took a deep breath to calm herself. "A man," she replied, her voice barely a whisper. "I'm sorry . . . it was just some kind of dream. At least I think it was. He was jogging. He was jogging on a road in the fog and I . . . I think I hit him." She shook her head to purge the lingering face from her mind.

"Paul Obermeyer was wearing jogging clothes the night he was killed," Nielsen said quietly. "And it was foggy." He narrowed his eyes on her. "What did he look like?"

Jeri shrugged as they sped into a tunnel, thankful for the sudden darkness. "Hard to say."

"Try."

"I don't know. Caucasian . . . dark hair . . . thin?"

"What else?"

Jeri sighed and closed her eyes. "A beard, maybe."

"Maybe?"

"Okay, how about *probably*?"

Nielsen nodded. "You just described Paul Obermeyer."

"Yeah, along with a few hundred thousand other men in this city."

The security director felt his jaw tighten as they sped from the tunnel into a landscape of dissipating fog. Ahead, the twin towers of the Golden Gate Bridge rose over the last sage-covered hills of the Marin Headlands. "Welcome back," he said, his tone more sarcastic than intended.

"Thanks," Jeri replied, studying the San Francisco sky-line materializing before her. "I'll try to remember it this time."

∽

Paul broke his gaze from the road and glanced over at Tatyana's figure curled up on the Hilux's passenger seat. "Think anyone's noticed our absence?"

She shook her head sleepily. "Anyone not asleep is quite drunk by now. Especially Derrick."

"True." Paul blinked the drowsiness from his own eyes and smiled. Despite everything that had happened over the last few weeks, he now felt a surprising sense of calm. Perhaps the realization of what they'd accomplished was finally sinking in. Maybe it was the unexpected turn of events with Tatyana. For a moment he even wondered if it had something to do with his falsified death—and the total liberation from his pre-vious life's demands and expectations that came with it. Or maybe it was just the goddamn champagne. Whatever it was, for the first time in recent memory, Paul felt something akin to the freedom of childhood.

And it felt fucking good.

The road turned north to reveal the Ras Jazan refinery shimmering in the distance ahead. Paul focused on it absently as a thought struck him. He eased his foot off the gas pedal and looked at Tatyana. "What if we didn't go back?"

"What do you mean?" she mumbled.

"I mean what if we kept going? Went somewhere else? I bet we're not more than a few hundred miles from Abu Dhabi or Dubai."

Tatyana sat up and regarded him with suspicion. "Has Dr. Obermeyer been replaced by some American cowboy? Because these are not words he would normally say."

"I guess your enthusiasm for adventure is starting to rub off on me."

"And just how far do you expect us to go with no money or identification?"

Paul shrugged. "I don't know. But we have to learn how to live our post-Ceres lives sooner or later, don't we?"

A grin slowly appeared on his colleague's face. "You surprise me, Paul."

"For wanting to keep going?"

"For using the word we." Tatyana leaned over and kissed him on the cheek before sliding her mouth to his ear. "I believe the champagne has affected your judgment," she whispered with a mocking tone of reproach. "Nevertheless, I will follow you wherever you should like to go."

Paul turned and kissed her back. "Good. You can be in charge of the map. But this time, I think—*fuuuck*!"

Paul slammed on the brakes as the truck's headlights

illuminated a large vehicle parked on the road directly in front of them. "What the hell is this?" he exclaimed over the screech of the tires sliding to a stop. Through the haze of brake smoke rising past the headlights, Paul and Tatyana both gazed forward at the white van blocking their path.

"Wait a minute," Paul mumbled, remembering the van they'd past earlier. He turned to Tatyana, the apprehension in her eyes reflecting his own. Before either could speak the truck's doors were flung open and strong arms reached in and seized them. "Hey! *Hey*! What are you doing?" Paul demanded, flailing at his assailant. He looked over to find Tatyana being ripped from her seat. "Get your hands off of her!" An instant later he was pulled from the truck and dropped roughly onto the hard pavement. His assailant kicked him in the side while another pressed the barrel of an automatic rifle into his chest.

"Min ayn anta?" the man exclaimed, staring down with hostile, intent eyes. He jabbed Paul with the rifle. "Min ayn anta?"

"I don't know what the hell you're saying!" Paul retorted, studying his assailants. Both men sported thick beards and wore red and white headscarves. He looked over to find Tatyana sprawled face down on the other side of the truck. Two men were busily groping her chest and legs. "Hey! Get your fucking hands *off* her!"

His armed assailant raised the rifle and drove the stock hard into Paul's stomach. "Min ayn anta? *'Akhbruna*!"

Paul curled into the fetal position, racked with pain. Above him, the two men conversed in short, excited bursts of Arabic. He looked over at Tatyana again and found her staring back at him, a mix of shock and terror in her eyes. "We're going to be fine," he cried out, his voice reduced to a raspy whisper.

The exchange between his assailants escalated into a shouting match before abruptly ending. The man with the rifle glared at Paul while his colleague went to the van and returned with a small black pouch. It was only as the man knelt down before him that Paul realized it was a cloak. "No!" he hissed, snatching the cloak from the man's hand and tossing onto the ground. "Who are you? Why are you doing this?"

A look of surprise briefly widened the man's dark eyes before morphing into anger. "Suker khaljic!" he snapped, slapping Paul across the face. His colleague pressed the barrel of the rifle into Paul's sternum.

"Fuck you," Paul mumbled as the cloak was pulled over his head. The two men lifted him and carried him to the van. "Where you taking us?" he demanded, still reeling from the pain in his stomach. A moment later he was tossed onto a seat in the vehicle. One of his assailants slid onto the seat behind him and seized the cinching rope of Paul's cloak like a leash. Up front, the van's engine roared to life. "Wait—where's my friend? Tatyana!" Paul rose in panic. His assailant immediately pulled on the rope, snapping his head back violently. Before he could regain his balance, the man wrapped an arm around his neck and pulled him back into the seat.

"Alssamt," the man said, his mouth pressed to Paul's ear.

"You're making a mistake! Don't you understand? We're not—" Paul fell silent as the cinching rope tightened around his neck.

"Alssamt," the man repeated, tightening the rope further. With their captive finally silenced, he nodded to his colleague.

The van turned and accelerated into the night.

426

~

The security director drove past the valet line in front of the Omni hotel and parked next to the entrance. Jeri gazed up at the regal stone and brick façade before studying the street. A yellow shaft of sunlight had broken through the thinning fog and settled on the blooming Victorian Box trees that lined the adjacent sidewalk. Something about the light playing through their leaves stirred a distant memory.

"My men will take you inside," Nielsen said, waving off the approaching valet.

"How long do I have to stay here?"

"We'll take it a day at a time. For now, you should just focus on resting and trying to—"

"Right. Got it." Jeri shifted her stare to her hands, which were pressed nervously to her legs. "This is going to sound stupid. I obviously don't have anything to support what I'm about to say, but I . . . I don't feel like someone who's capable of doing what you've told me I've done." She turned and met the security director's stare. "I know I haven't said it yet, but I'm sorry. I'm sorry for what's happened, and I'm sorry for any part I've played in it. I need you know—to *believe*—that the person I am now would do anything in the world to change all of it."

The security director gazed back at her, his expression unreadable. He reached under his seat and produced a thick, hardcover book. "I've been debating whether or not to give this to you," he said, regarding it thoughtfully for a moment before handing it to her. "But apparently it's yours."

Jeri's brow furrowed as she read the title aloud. "*Predictions in the New Business Ecology*—? She looked at Nielsen in confusion. "I don't understand."

"I don't either."

"Where did you get it?"

"From the man you were found with in Italy. It was in his backpack."

Jeri's expression abruptly shifted from curiosity to revulsion. "What makes you think it's mine?"

"Open it."

Jeri opened the front cover. Written neatly at the top of the first page were the words *Property of Jeri Stone.*

"Strange that he has the same last name, huh?" Nielsen added.

"Who?"

"The author . . . James Stone."

Jeri turned the book over and studied the black-and-white photo on the back. The author was young, with large, intelligent eyes and the hint of a smile. Something about his face seemed familiar. "Maybe he's my brother."

The security director shook his head. "I did a little research. James Stone was an investigative reporter from several decades ago. Died long before your time."

"Of course." Jeri shrugged dejectedly. "Well, like everything else, I can't explain it."

Nielsen's stare remained fixed on the book. "There's more."

Jeri followed his gaze to a slight gap in the center pages. She opened it to find a folded piece of stationary tucked inside. "What's this?"

"Read it."

Jeri did as the security director asked. When she was finished, she gazed at him with a look of shock. "Is this a joke?"

Nielsen shrugged. "If it is, I missed the punch line."

Jeri read the neatly penned letter again. "I don't understand. What . . . what is he talking about?"

"I don't know. That's why I'm giving it to you. I thought maybe it would, you know . . . spark something."

Jeri carefully refolded the letter. "I swear to god, I'm about to go *crazy*!" she hissed. To both her and Nielsen's surprise, a peel of laughter escaped her lips. "I mean, seriously—a fucking *apology* letter from the man who erased my life?"

The Velgyn security director said nothing as she crumpled the letter into a ball and let it roll from her hands onto the floor. When Jeri spoke again, her voice was barely a whisper.

"All I want is my memory back. But I'm terrified of what I'll remember when it returns."

"You can't change what you've done," Nielsen said flatly. "But you can remember what that man and the others have done to you." His eyes shifted to her window.

Jeri looked over to find the security director's men standing next to her door.

"Are you ready?" he asked.

Jeri nodded. She turned to open the door when Nielsen grabbed her arm.

"Just in case," he said, handing her his card. "I can be here in a few minutes."

Jeri regarded him with a wan smile. "You have kind eyes, Mr. Nielsen. Most people probably think otherwise, but I can tell."

The security director nodded and one of his men opened her door. Jeri stepped out of the car, the thick book clutched in her hands. After a brief hesitation, she reached down and snatched the crumpled letter from the Jaguar's floor mat. "Then again, maybe I'm a bad judge of character."

Nielsen smiled. "That goes for both of us." He watched his men escort Jeri into the hotel before dialing a number on his cellphone. "Mary—are we up?"

Several blocks south in the Brannan Street warehouse, Mary Adler gazed at the row of monitors in front of her. "We're up," she confirmed. "Linked to four surveillance cameras in the lobby, two in each elevator, one in each ground floor stairwell. No one can get in or out without being recorded and analyzed."

"And the GPS tracker?" Nielsen asked.

Adler turned to a monitor showing a small dot pulsing over a detailed map of the downtown. The dot moved slowly within the footprint of the hotel. "Yep, got it. Not precise, but at least it shows she's in the building."

"Good," the security director nodded. "Keep your eyes open. I'll be there shortly."

43.

J-

You're waking to a world that doesn't make any sense at the moment, but in time it will. In the meantime, all you need to worry about is drinking plenty of water and securing an evening seat at La Pace before the sublimely delicate saffron lavaret filets with venere rice are sold out.

Just remember, the path to anything is an inside job.

What I couldn't say when you knew me, I'll say now that you don't. I know you never asked for this. But you were good. And as the saying goes, whatever doesn't kill you makes you stronger. Our maybe it's what kills you that makes you stronger. Fuck, I don't know. All I know for sure is that our kids would have been gorgeous, mi amor.

Even the illegitimate ones.

XO,
-C

p.s. You have a lot of questions. Put them aside. I need you to <u>concentrate</u> on getting better.

p.p.s. Wherever you go, take this book with you. It was always your favorite.

44.

"Good afternoon, sir. I have two cheeseburgers with fries, an extra order of fries, and a salad?"

Lars Nielsen's security agent nodded mutely and stepped aside to allow the hotel waiter to enter.

"My apologies for the delay, folks," the uniformed young man said as he marched into the large suite and placed the tray of food on the table. "The kitchen's rather crazy right now. Big conference in the Grand Ballroom. Anyway—" He smiled and removed the silver top with a quick sweep of his hand. "Here's your lunch."

Jeri rose from one of the couches and walked to the table while Nielsen's two agents—nearly identical with their dark hair and matching suits—escorted the man out. "Wait," she said, studying the food. "Where's my cobb salad?"

The waiter, an Indian man with large eyes and a thin, angular face, turned and lowered his head in apology. "Sorry, miss, I forgot to tell you. The kitchen was out of cobb salads, so we upgraded your order to an oriental salad with fresh micro greens. Honestly, if you ask me, it's a much better salad." He looked up with a slight grin. "Even comes with a fortune cookie."

Jeri nodded at the plastic-wrapped cookie resting on the edge of the plate. "Fantastic."

"I can bring you something else if you'd prefer."

"No, this is fine."

"Very good then. Enjoy." The waiter bowed and promptly slipped out the door. Jeri watched with mild curiosity as the Brooks Brothers twins surveyed the hallway once more before locking the door.

"You two always eat this well?" she asked sarcastically as they descended on the food.

"Maybe," Brooks Brother #1 mumbled through a mouthful of greasy fries. "Maybe not." He was slightly taller than his colleague, with a square boxer's jaw. Both men gave her a *what-the-fuck-is-it-to-you?* look.

"Right. Well, I think I'll eat in my room." Jeri grabbed her salad and started walking toward the bedroom when Brooks Brother #2 stepped in front of her.

"Hold on," he commanded, licking his fingers. He then shoved them into her salad and slowly poked around.

"What are you doing?" Jeri demanded.

"Checking for contraband." A moment later, he smiled and snatched one of the orange slices from the top. "All clear."

Jeri studied the smirk on his face as he tossed it into his mouth. "Are you here to protect me, or to be a couple of juvenile assholes?"

Brooks Brother #1 shrugged. "Both I suppose. One's the job. The other's just a perk." He grabbed the fortune cookie from her plate and slowly crushed it between his fingers. "If you don't like it, you're welcome to leave. I hear your friends out there would be happy to pick you up."

Jeri looked at his hand. "That's *my* fortune, not yours."

The agent glanced at the pulverized remains of the cookie still sealed within its plastic wrapper and nodded. "You're right—this is definitely your fortune." He dropped it back onto her plate before strolling to the table and grabbing another handful of fries. "Enjoy your salad," he said, exchanging smiles with his colleague.

Jeri marched into the bedroom and shut the door behind her. A heavily sigh escaped her lips. *God, you sure can pick them* she thought, shaking her head.

Go figure.

The words popped into her mind with the unconscious ease of habit. But why? Was this something she used to say—or think—often?

She glanced at the molested salad and dropped it on the nightstand. Her appetite was gone. In its place hung the nagging hunger that now plagued her—the obsession to find and reconstruct the shattered pieces of her past that would tell her who she was.

Regardless of whom she might find.

She lay down on the bed and closed her eyes. For some reason, a passage from the letter written to her by her assailant came to mind—

Now, concentrate on getting better.

Yes! a voice in her head answered. She'd done it on the drive down—concentrated on an image and willed it into focus. Maybe she could do it again. She took a deep breath and tried to clear her thoughts. The muted sounds of the street below washed over her and then, abruptly, something sparkled in her mind. As Jeri focused on it, a shape began to appear.

Sequins and jewels glimmered into view. Then, with sudden clarity—a dress. Minimal and intricate, the tiny dress was laid out on the bed next to her. The image was so real that Jeri opened her eyes and looked, immediately sighing at her own foolishness. *Follow the thought* she told herself, shutting her eyes again. For a few minutes she let her thoughts gently drift with the darkness. The sounds of the city melted away. Then, just as the darkness grew complete, it lifted like a curtain and she was standing in a bright, snow-covered forest.

Follow the thought.

Jeri trudged forward through the deep snow, her eyes scanning for breaks in the surrounding groves of spruce and alpine larch. A track of recent footprints appeared before her and she followed their twisting path down the steep mountainside to a narrow valley clearing. Once there, she paused at the edge of the forest and studied the small collection of weathered wooden cabins that stood next to a frozen stream. Encouraged by the quiet, Jeri made for the nearest cabin and peered voyeuristically into one of the windows.

Contrary to its outside appearance, the cabin's interior was surprisingly white and modern, with bright blue gymnasium mats neatly arranged beneath a long mirrored wall. Along the adjacent walls stood racks of free weights and other exercise equipment. The strangeness of a gym in such a remote place made Jeri turn and reexamine the other cabins. She trudged toward the next one, noting only after she drew nearer that a thin wisp of smoke was rising from its chimney. She stepped onto the small porch and hovered by the door, debating what to do. As if anticipating her arrival, the door opened and a stout, muscular woman with short brown hair appeared in the entrance and nodded.

"'Bout time," the woman exclaimed in a husky voice. "You were supposed to be here an hour ago." She gestured over Jeri's shoulder. "He drop you off at the top?"

Before Jeri understood what was happening she felt herself nod and say yes.

"Figures. God forbid he ever come down here and check on me. Oh well . . . jeet?"

"Excuse me?"

The woman's brown eyes flashed a look of annoyance. "Did you eat?"

"Yes."

"Good." The woman thrust out her hand and took Jeri's. "I'm Whip—your trainer, coach, worst enemy and best friend for the next eight weeks. That's your cabin over there. Step into my cabin without knocking first and I'll break you in two. Talk back to me during training and I'll show you just how cold that stream water really is. The other cabin is the shower and kitchen. I cook, you clean. No exceptions—got it?"

"Got it."

"Then let's get started." The woman stepped outside and closed the door behind her. "Today we'll go easy," she said, marching off toward the gym. "Two hours of basic submission training before lunch, four more after. Oh, and do *not* go wandering around here at night. I have no interest in dragging the frozen, wolf-eaten remains of a newly recruited agent back here again." She turned and glared at Jeri. "Well—you coming?"

Jeri glanced once more at her surroundings. A gust of artic wind stirred her hair. She regarded the strange woman who seemed as cold and unforgiving as the place itself. "Yeah," she nodded, dropping in behind her. "I'm coming."

~

Paul snapped to attention as the van screeched to a stop. Moments later, a door opened and he was dragged onto the street. He twisted his head blindly at the sounds of distant traffic. "Where are we?" he demanded, relenting to the jabs of his two assailants leading him toward an unseen destination. "Where's my friend?"

"La taqlaq," one of the men muttered impatiently.

"Yeah, that's really helpful," Paul retorted. To his surprise, his assailants both chuckled in response.

The ambient sounds of traffic were replaced by the clamor of boots on tile as Paul was pushed inside. There, a new set of hands seized his arm and led him through a maze of left and right turns. During a brief pause for the opening of a door, Paul made out the sound of shuffling feet. Then, without warning, he was shoved forward. Paul tumbled into a wall of bodies and was silently helped back to his feet. The air inside his cloak grew stifling. "For the love of god," he panted, gesturing at his head. "Will you please take this off?"

The hands of his escort seized him again and suddenly the cloak was gone. Paul grimaced at the brightness of the room. The pungent odor of unwashed bodies rushed to his senses, threatening to suffocate him. He rubbed his eyes and looked around.

A roomful of men stared back at him.

Paul turned to his escort, a thick, dour-faced man who wore the same red and white headscarf as his captors. "Where am I?"

The man regarded him with silent disgust before closing the barred door of the holding cell. "Allah yusallmak," he muttered as the heavy steel door slammed shut. He turned and vanished down the corridor.

"Hey . . . wait!" Paul cried out, pressing his face to the bars. "Come back here!" His stare shifted to a large circular crest painted on the corridor wall. In it, a white, sail-shaped symbol and the Saudi Arabian emblem hovered over what appeared to be an open book. A long script in Arabic stretched over the top. But what caught Paul's attention were the word in English written along the bottom—

General Presidency of the Promotion of Virtue and the Prevention of Vices.

"What the fuck is this?" he shouted at the empty hallway. He turned and raised his hands to the other men in the holding cell. "Does anyone here speak English?"

Around him, anxious eyes exchanged looks before Paul noticed a young man pushing his way through the crowd. "Almaʾdirah," the man said, making his way forward. He stepped past Paul and peered cautiously down the corridor. "I speak English," he whispered.

"Fantastic." Paul grabbed him by the shoulders. "Where are we?"

The man, who looked barely older than a teenager, tensed under Paul's grasp. "A station of the mutawa'ah," he said quietly. His eyes widened with a look of reverence. "The enforcers of morality."

"*Morality*?" Paul scoffed. "What are you talking about?"

"Islam," the man replied. His eyes flickered repeatedly toward the corridor. "Sharia law. The mutawa'ah exist to safeguard this law and punish us for our sins against Allah. To-night I was witnessed sinning against Allah and desecrating my spirit through the viewing of pornography. So now I must be punished."

"You're kidding me."

The young man shook his head.

"But we weren't *doing* anything!" Paul exclaimed. "My friend and I were just driving when they took us! These people threw us onto the road and stuck guns in our faces! I don't even know where she is!" He realized he was shaking the man and immediately released his grip. "Look, I'm sorry. But this *must* be a mistake."

"Your companion," the man said. "A woman?"

"Yes."

His expression turned grave. "Then that is your sin. You have been witnessed alone with a woman. Sharia law forbids such things."

"Give me a fucking break. It's the twenty-first century."

The corners of the young man's mouth lifted into a slight grin. "The sins of today are judged no differently than those of yesterday."

Paul rolled his eyes. "Where are we?"

"Hofuf. A city in the Eastern province." The young man's brow furrowed as he regarded the stranger before him. "Where did they find you and your friend?"

Paul shrugged. "It's hard to say. Is Hofuf a large city?"

"Yes."

"Do you think they brought my friend here as well?"

"Yes, I should think so. They'll mean to punish her as well. Of course, the punishment for her sins will likely be greater than your own."

"They must've brought her in the truck," Paul mumbled absently. He turned and again peered into the corridor. "What kind of punishment?"

"Whatever our sins require," the man said flatly. He glanced at the men around them. "For most of us, I should think the whip."

"Goddammit," Paul hissed, seizing the handle of the cell door in frustration. His eyes widened with astonishment as it turned in his hand and the door opened freely.

"What are you doing?" the young man demanded.

Paul glanced over to find a look of terror on the man's face. "It wasn't locked."

"Of *course* it wasn't locked," the man exclaimed, his tone laced with fear. "We are in the house of the mutawa'ah—the enforcers of Allah's will! Who would dare sin in the house of His army?"

"You want to stay here and receive Allah's will? Be my guest." Paul slipped into the corridor and closed the door behind him. "I'm going to find my friend."

The young man stepped forward and shook his head. "It is most unwise for you to do this. They will catch you. They will *kill* you."

"They can't," Paul responded, giving him a wan smile. "I'm already dead."

The young man watched the bold American march off in the opposite direction of his mutawa'ah escort. "Then may Allah protect you," he muttered under his breath, careful not to be heard by the others.

A few feet overhead, the motion-activated surveillance camera automatically turned and focused on the lone figure of

Paul Obermeyer moving down the corridor.

∼

"Why are you always running, Jer-bear?" the baritone voice asked.

She gazed up at the desk in the center of the small study. The face of a young man hovered over a large typewriter. "You're that man on my book."

"That *man* on your book?" He laughed quietly and nodded. "Yes, I suppose I am. And you?"

"Me?" She felt the thoughts in her head stir randomly like leaves in the autumn breeze. "I'm lost."

"Well, you can't be too lost. You found me, didn't you?"

"I didn't know I was looking for you."

"Aren't you looking for your past?"

"Yes."

The man smiled and pointed toward the door. "Well, it's right out there."

She turned and looked down the hallway. A row of encyclopedias lined a shelf on the far wall of the living room, their numbered spines shimmering in the light.

"Still like to play games?" the man asked.

Her eyes remained fixed on the shelf as she considered the question. "I don't remember."

"Yes you do."

Her eyes returned to the man behind the desk. Somewhere deep in her mind, something clicked, like a key turning a lock. The man held her gaze as a thought—a word—that felt oddly familiar formed on her lips. Slowly, almost imperceptibly, a grin appeared on her face.

442

45.

Paul slipped quickly down the narrow corridor inside the mutawa'ah compound, his senses on full alert. A procession of doors to other holding cells lined the walls on both sides. He moved from door to door, peering through the barred window of each as he made his way forward. Every cell was empty. When he reached the adjoining corridor, Paul glanced around the corner and immediately stepped back. A short, corpulent man in the checkered headscarf of the mutawa'ah was escorting a cloaked figure toward him.

Paul didn't have to look again to know who the man was leading. He retreated into the nearest holding cell and waited. A moment later, Tatyana's small figure stepped into view with her escort looming one step behind.

"Waqf!" the man exclaimed, grabbing her by the shoulder. He opened the door to the cell across from Paul and pushed Tatyana inside. A bolt of rage surged through Paul at the sound of his colleague gasping in terror. Without thinking, he opened the door of the cell and lunged forward, ramming the man from behind. Caught off balance, the mutawa'ah man hurtled headlong into the far wall of the cell. The sound of skull colliding with concrete echoed inside the small chamber as the man's body collapsed onto the floor.

Paul turned and grabbed Tatyana. She gasped again in terror and recoiled from his touch. "Hey, hey—it's me!" he hissed, removing her cloak. "I'm here."

"Paul?" The Russian researcher gazed at him through a haze of disbelief. "But . . . how?"

"Are you okay? Did they hurt you?"

Tatyana shook her head and studied the man lying unconscious on the floor. "What have you done?"

"What have *I* done? Hey—look at me. Are you okay?"

His colleague slowly nodded. "I was certain he was going to . . . " She grimaced and shook the thought from her head. "Who are these people?"

"Religious zealots . . . some kind of sanctioned moral authority." Paul shot an anxious glance toward the corridor. "Look, I'll explain later. We need to go—*now*."

"Where are we?"

"A city called Hofuf." Paul looked again at the unconscious man. An idea suddenly struck him. "Here, help me get his clothes off."

Tatyana watched with alarm as he started to prop the man upright. "What? No. Do you really mean to—"

"Yes, now help me."

Tatyana's incapacitated escort moaned irritably at the hands stripping him of his headscarf and white, robe-like dishdasha. "Matha tef'al?" he muttered weakly, gazing at them with unfocused eyes.

"Should we help him?" she asked.

"Sure," Paul replied. "You make him a pillow, and I'll go look for some aspirin." His colleague shot him a lethal look as he slipped the dishdasha on over his own clothes and put on the headscarf. "Okay, let's go."

Paul grabbed Tatyana by the arm and steered her into the corridor. "We'll try going out the same way you—" He noticed the surveillance camera overhead and pulled her back into the cell.

"What is it?" the Russian researcher demanded.

"A camera." He looked at her somberly. "If anyone's watching, they're going to wonder why your head is uncovered."

"And? What do you expect me to do?"

Paul's eyes dropped to the cloak on the floor.

"No." Tatyana replied, following his stare. "I refuse."

Paul picked up the cloak. "Just until we get outside."

His colleague released an exasperated sigh as he slipped it over her head. "For the second time I hope you know what you are doing," she said flatly.

"Me too. Ready?" Paul didn't wait for an answer before steering Tatyana back into the corridor and around the corner. To his relief, an exit door stood at the end of the corridor, the muted light of dawn filtering through its window. He squeezed his colleague reassuringly. "We can do this," he whispered, his eyes focused on their escape route.

Behind them, the groans of their stripped captor grew louder.

"You hear that?" Security agent Scott Harris asked.

His partner, agent Emilio Reyes, raised his eyebrows slightly. "Hear *what*?" he mumbled, his attention still focused on the television.

Harris cocked his head and listened again before toss
ing the television remote onto the coffee table. "Thought I
heard a noise." The Velgyn security agent rose from the couch
and stretched the stiffness from his back and thick, muscled
arms. "Fuck, what time is it?" he grumbled, gazing out the
window of the executive suite at the night-draped skyline of
the city.

"Nine-thirty." Reyes nodded toward the closed door of
the bedroom. "I checked on her thirty minutes ago."

"And—?"

"Still sleeping."

Harris shook his head. "The hell's wrong with her?"

"Nielsen said she'd probably sleep a lot. It's pretty normal if your dealing with shock or, you know . . . depression."

"Yeah? Is that something you have personal experience
with?"

Reyes broke his stare from the television and glared at
his partner. "Yeah, it's called four years of working with you,
asshole."

Harris started to respond but instead paused and
cocked his head again. "Okay . . . did you hear *that*?"

"Nope."

"Christ, Emmy, you need to get your fuckin' ears
checked." Harris marched over to the bedroom door and
palmed the handle.

"Don't wake her up," Reyes warned.

The thirty-six-year-old security agent shot a *fuck off*
look at his colleague and opened the door.

The young woman in their charge was sitting up in
bed. "She's awake," Harris exclaimed over his shoulder without
averting his eyes. He stepped into the room and smiled. "'Bout

446

time."

"What time is it?" the woman asked.

"Late." Harris dropped his stare to the mound of covers over her propped up legs. "Hungry?"

The woman narrowed her eyes on him. "No thanks. I've already seen what you'll do to it."

"Oh, what? Should I play nice with you now? 'Cause as far as I see it, you ain't living too badly for someone that killed one of our people." The Velgyn security agent stepped closer with a contemptuous grin. "How's that memory of yours coming along?" A bolt of satisfaction ran through him at the wounded look on his charge's face.

"Can I ask you a question?" the woman asked.

"What?"

She looked at the door and gestured for him to close it.

Harris glanced back at the living room. His colleague was once again absorbed in some reality TV show. He quietly shut the door.

"Here," the woman said, patting the bedside next to her.

Harris hesitated for a moment before unbuttoning his jacket and making a point of adjusting his sidearm. He walked over and took a seat on the edge of the bed. "Yeah?"

"Look, I'm sorry . . . I think you and I got off on the wrong foot. I know you're here to protect me, and I'm sure that's not easy given everything I've been accused of doing. But you have to understand—" She reached over and placed a hand on his forearm. "I'm not trying to be anyone's enemy. I'm just trying to get through this the best way I know how. Can you understand that?"

Harris studied the hand resting on his arm and shrugged. "Maybe," he replied, irritated at the rush of blood it was causing. "Guess we should figure out a way to get along if we're going to be around each other."

"Exactly. It's not like either one of us *wants* to be here." The woman smiled and squeezed his arm gently. "So why not try to make the best of it?"

A thin, conspiring grin appeared on the security agent's face. "So what was your question?"

"Question?" she whispered, studying his mouth.

"You said you had a question."

"Oh yeah." The woman nodded as if suddenly remembering. "I was just going to ask you if you could explain something."

"What?" Harris asked.

Her eyes shifted to something next to him. "That."

Harris turned and looked. The book that Nielsen had given to her earlier was placed upright on the nightstand. He furrowed his brow. "What, the book? Fuck if I—"

The Velgyn security agent caught a flash of movement out of the corner of his eye. An instant later, the right side of his face exploded in agony as a heavy object collided with his temple and glanced off of his nose. He toppled backward from the bed, dimly noticing the unlikely weapon in the woman's hand as his vision narrowed into darkness.

By the time his concussed head met the floor, agent Scott Harris was unconscious.

Jeri slipped off the bed and quickly checked the Velgyn security agent's breathing before taking his handgun and phone. She moved to the door and opened it quietly.

The second agent was watching TV.

She trained the gun on him and moved forward. Half-way into the suite's large living room, the agent noticed her and rose from his chair.

"What the—" he exclaimed, reaching for his weapon.

"No, no, no," Jeri aimed the weapon at his head. "Don't be stupid. Reyes, right?"

Reyes nodded.

"Toss it over here, Reyes."

The Velgyn security agent tossed his sidearm onto the floor as commanded. "What the fuck are you doing? Where's Harris?"

Jeri motioned him away and picked up the gun. "A word of advice. The next time you decide to detain someone in a hotel room, don't leave an iron in the closet."

"But . . . I don't get it. We're here to *protect* you."

"Is that right? Well in that case, your services are no longer required." Jeri stepped to the side table and grabbed the hotel phone. "Let me ask you a question," she said, hitting the button for room service. "The waiter that brought up lunch—did he look familiar to you?"

Reyes shook his head.

"Well, he did to me."

"Room service." A man's voice answered cheerfully.

"May I speak to the waiter that delivered to my room earlier?" Jeri asked.

"This is he."

"I'm awake, Sly. Chip, are you listening too?"

A brief silence followed before the old man's gravelly voice answered. "I'm here."

"Good. Then get your assess up here. Oh, and Sly?"

"Yeah, Jeri?"

"Can you bring up another salad?"

Paul opened the door and led Tatyana outside. The desert air smelled of dust and diesel fuel. He noticed his colleague starting to remove the cloak on her head and grabbed her hand. "Not yet."

"What do you mean, not yet? I can't see!" she hissed.

"Just wait," Paul said, surveying their surroundings. To their left stretched a narrow alleyway that opened to an intersection about a hundred meters ahead. To the right, a cluster of haphazardly-parked vehicles effectively formed a dead end. Paul studied the vehicles and felt a wave of relief. Parked next to the white van of his captors was their truck. "I see the truck," he said, guiding Tatyana toward it. "Just keep the cloak on until we get inside."

"How far is it?" Tatyana asked.

"Maybe twenty meters."

"And if the keys are not there?"

"We'll worry about that when we get there."

Paul marched his blind colleague quickly down the alley. Upon reaching the truck, they slipped around the other side, safely out of view. Paul grabbed the driver-side door handle and pulled. It was locked.

"Paul?" Tatyana whispered nervously.

"Wait here." Paul marched around to the passenger door only to find it locked as well. He cursed under his breath, unsure of what to do next. A short distance away, the sharp *clack* of an opening door echoed down the alleyway. Paul glanced over his shoulder and froze.

Standing next to the same door they'd exited were two mutawa'ah. Both were staring back at him.

"Paul?" Tatyana whispered again.

"Listen to me." Paul kept his eyes trained on the two men as he addressed his colleague in a low, even voice. "Two of them just stepped outside. I don't think they can see you. Squat down and take off your cloak."

Tatyana dropped from his peripheral vision on the other side of the truck. "What now?"

"Go over to the van and try the door." Paul turned and raised a hand in greeting. The two men exchanged looks before marching toward him. A moment later Tatyana's voice whispered excitedly back at him.

"Unlocked!"

"Find the keys!" Paul hissed, stepping away from the truck.

The two mutawa'ah grew closer. "Man anta?" one of them shouted across the distance.

Paul gestured toward the station door they'd just exited. The men paused and looked over their shoulders. When they turned back, their brows were furrowed with suspicion.

"Man *anta*?"

Paul shrugged. "Man anta?" he scoffed back.

The two men broke into a run.

Paul glanced around for something to use as a weapon when the van's engine suddenly roared to life behind him. He turned and ran, opening the passenger door and lunging inside. "Go! Go! Go!" he shouted, closing the door an instant before their assailants arrived.

Tatyana slammed the transmission into gear and

pressed on the gas pedal. The van's tires seemed to spin for an eternity as the mutawa'ah men shouted and slapped at the door. Then, abruptly, the van leapt forward and the men were gone, lost in a retreating cloud of dust. When they reached the end of the alley, Tatyana swung the large vehicle onto the main road and pressed the gas pedal to the floor.

Paul took a moment to catch his breath before releasing a peal of nervous laughter. "Nice driving."

"Tell me who those men were," Tatyana demanded, her eyes fixed on the nearly deserted road ahead. Her hands, still clutched to the wheel, were trembling.

"A man in my holding cell spoke English," Paul replied. "He called them mutawa'ah . . . said they're entrusted with enforcing Sharia law. Apparently we broke a few of their basic rules of conduct last night. I'm guessing they spotted us on the road and then followed us to the beach."

"You mean they—?" Tatyana sucked in a deep breath in anger. "By what right do they think they can just take us like that?"

"The right of god, apparently." Paul gave her a sarcastic grin. "Not exactly our first time dealing with this problem. Do you think there's a prize for being kidnapped twice in the same month?"

Without warning, Tatyana twisted the steering wheel and swung the speeding van onto a side road. They climbed a steep hill and slipped through the open gate of an industrial complex. A procession of gray, steel-clad storage warehouses shot past the dirty windshield.

Paul started to ask where they were going when his colleague twisted the wheel again. The van twisted and fishtailed into a narrow gap between two buildings, a storm of dust and gravel trailing after them. "What are you doing?" he exclaimed over the din of the engine.

Tatyana regarded him briefly before pressing harder on the accelerator. The vehicle charged forward in response.

A short distance ahead, the sudden void of a steep precipice loomed ominously just beyond the buildings Paul's eyes widened with fear as it grew closer. "Are you trying to kill us?"

"Does it matter?" Tatyana scoffed.

Paul grabbed her arm. "Stop!"

His colleague slapped at his hand.

"Goddammit—*stop!*"

Tatyana shot him a venomous look and slammed on the brake pedal. Caught on the loose gravel, the van slid precariously close to the precipice before shuddering to a stop. The Russian researcher jumped out and cursed angrily at the desert valley below. "B`lyad! *B`lyad!* *B`lyad!* "

After taking a brief moment to collect himself, Paul stepped out of the van. "Tatyana, calm down."

"Tchyo za ga`*lima?*"

Paul marched over and grabbed her. "Be quiet!"

"Nyet!" Tatyana exclaimed, twisting from his grasp. She turned and stormed toward the edge of the cliff. "Why should I be quiet? Why should I be *anything*? Is there not a single place in this world where we can simply live in peace?" She paused and peered over the edge. "At least here we could choose our own end!"

"What the hell are you talking about?" Paul rushed forward and grabbed her again. "What happened to the woman that convinced me to break out of a secure compound just to take a walk on the beach last night?"

Tatyana gave him a cynical smile. "She was shown once again just how powerless she is." She glanced down at his hands now clutching her. "Tell me this is not the life to come for either of us, Paul. Tell me I will not have to live in fear."

Paul pulled her into his chest. "It isn't," he answered, gazing at the view. The dawn light was now painting the horizon in cinnamon orange. In the valley below, the city of Hofuf stood quietly. "And you won't. But we've got to get out of here. We've got to find our way back without attracting any attention—so we'll need to be smart about everything we do." He rubbed her back gently and felt her relax against him. "We'll figure it out together, all right?"

Tatyana pulled herself free and gave him a solemn, solitary nod. "Yes, all right." She followed his gaze toward the city. "So what should we do next?"

Paul walked to the van and rummaged around for anything of use. Beneath the driver's seat he found a thin, flexible stick worn smooth from handling. "What do you think this is for?" he asked, holding it up.

"I know exactly what it is for." Tatyana rolled up her sleeve and showed Paul several long red welts on her forearm. "They used one on me last night."

"Jesus," Paul exclaimed. "All I got was a rifle to the stomach. Speaking of—" He lifted the stolen dishdasha and groaned at the sight of a large bruise painted across his abdomen. "I never thought I'd say this, but I can't wait to get back to Ceres."

"Yes, to our *other* kidnappers," Tatyana replied. "I believe that sentiment is called Stockholm syndrome."

"Do we have a choice?"

"We could drive into town and explain what's happened to the real authorities. It would be easy enough for us to tell them the truth."

"The truth?" Paul laughed. "And how's that going to sound? Yes, that's right . . . our deaths were falsified so that we could be kidnapped to work on a super-secret project here in your nice, quiet desert. Oh, and, by the way—the reason we're in your city now is because we escaped to go screw on the beach and a van full of state-sanctioned religious nuts kidnapped us again! How'd we get here, you ask? Oh that's the simple part—we just stole their van. But feel free to call them if you'd like. I'm sure they'll confirm everything."

He snapped the stick over his knee.

"No one's going to believe our story. No one. And even if they did, all we'd be doing is putting everyone else in danger—Derrick, Marcello, Chung—even Ceres itself. Call it Stockholm syndrome if you'd like, but I'm not willing to risk everything that's been accomplished just because you and I made a stupid mistake last night." Paul hurled the pieces of the stick over the cliff edge and looked at his colleague. "Do you agree?"

Tatyana dropped her head and nodded.

"We have to go down there," he continued, gesturing at the city. "Unless you have a better idea, I say we go in, find a map, and get the hell back to Ceres. With any luck, we'll stay clear of the mutawa'ah."

"I doubt they will be looking for us in the city," Tatyana replied. "More likely they will be waiting somewhere on the road back . . . expecting *us* to come to *them*. That is what I would do."

"Okay. So maybe we ditch the van and find a bus. There has to be some kind of public transportation."

"No. We steal another vehicle," Tatyana retorted defiantly. "We cannot get into any *more* trouble, can we?"

Paul laid his hands on her shoulders. "I'm sorry. I shouldn't have said last night was a stupid mistake." He leaned down and gave her a kiss. "The truth is, until our fanatical friends showed up, I was having a great time."

His colleague eyed him warily for a moment before succumbing to a smile. "Me too," she conceded. "I'm sorry for ever calling you a coward. You are obviously the braver of the two of us."

"Oh, I wouldn't be so sure. I think at one point when you were driving I actually shit my pants. Remind me to wash this robe before I return it." Paul kissed Tatyana again and walked her back to the van. "Okay, are you ready to do this?" he asked, dropping into the driver's seat.

"Yes."

Paul started the van around and drove them out of the deserted compound as the dawn sky continued to lighten. A few miles to the north, the first haunting verses of the *adhan* began to ring out from the slender white minarets rising over the desert landscape. The city's three hundred thousand faithful Muslims washed themselves in silence and aligned their prayer mats toward mecca in preparation for the Salat al-Fajr. Then, in practiced unison, they prostrated their flesh before god.

The morning prayer had begun.

46.

"Welcome back," Sly said cheerfully, marching into the suite. Still in his waiter's uniform, the agency's guardian angel stepped forward and placed Jeri's salad on the table. "Cobb salad, just like you asked for the first time."

Behind him, Chip's eyes flashed to the gun in her hand before shifting to the disarmed Velgyn security agent. "Where's the other one?"

"Bedroom."

The old man nodded. "Sly?"

"Got it."

Jeri narrowed her eyes on Chip while Sly vanished into the bedroom. "What the hell happened?"

"You tell me."

"The last thing I remember was Chilly and I driving to Malcesine." Jeri waved the gun at Agent Reyes. "These guys are from Velgyn Pharmaceuticals. This whole thing is about some encryption key that disappeared when Obermeyer was—" She paused and shook her head. "They showed me photos of them, Chip. Chilly's in their custody somewhere, I don't know where. And Dublin . . . Dublin's . . . ."

"What?"

"They told me Dublin was dead."

The old man winced as if struck by a blow. "Is that true?" he demanded, turning to the Velgyn agent.

Reyes mouth twisted into a sneer. "How the fuck should I know?"

Before Jeri realized what happening, Chip stripped the gun from her hand and rushed over to the man.

"Is that *true*?" he repeated, shoving the barrel into the Velgyn agent's mouth.

"I already asked him," Jeri said impatiently. "He doesn't know anything. He and his partner were here to protect me."

"Protect you?" the old man growled. "What do you mean, *protect* you?"

"Their CEO and security director both know I was involved in what happened with Obermeyer. But since I couldn't remember anything, they decided to use me as bait and see who might come looking for me."

Chip slowly removed the barrel from Reyes's mouth. "Sit down," he commanded, pushing the agent onto the couch. He turned to Jeri. "We already knew it was Velgyn . . . we picked up your tracking signal at the Napa estate. We just couldn't tell what their plan was." His ice-blue eye narrowed. "How in the hell did you get your memory back? You weren't supposed to remember any of this. The agency, Chilly . . . even me."

Jeri read the suspicion in his gaze and shook her head. "No—don't even *think* about going there. I wasn't the one who started this, remember?"

"Then what happened?"

"I don't know! Jesus Christ, Chip—you think I haven't already been asked that same question a hundred times by these guys? I was told their team found me as I was being injected. Chilly must not have given me the full dose before he was stopped. That's all I was told."

Chip's expression slowly softened. "All right," he said, nodding. "I believe you. But we need to know more, and we need to know it quickly."

Sly returned from the bedroom, a bewildered expression on his face. "Damn, Jeri—did you really knock that guy out with the steam iron?"

"It was all I had to work with."

"Well, it definitely did the job. Wait until Whip hears. She's going to be so proud of you."

"All right, *enough*." Chip handed Sly the handgun. "Stay here and babysit these guys. Jeri, come with me."

Jeri followed Chip into the hallway. A few doors down, he slipped his key card into the lock of an adjacent suite and opened the door. "After you," he said, gesturing her in.

Jeri stepped into the room and paused. Around the dining table, Tall Tommy, Max and Art stood scanning blueprints and a large map of the city. An assortment of handguns, keycards and cellphones were scattered on the table in front of them. "What's going on?" she asked.

"Change of plans," Chip replied. "Had you not gotten your memory back and called Sly, we would've still been preparing to enter your room and take you by force."

Art gazed up at her. "Didn't you read the fortune cookie Sly gave you?" he asked.

"The fortune cookie?" Jeri shook her head. "No."

"It was a message to . . . never mind." The agency's forgery expert flipped his ponytail in irritation. "Why do I even bother?"

"Jeri just confirmed that they have Chilly," Chip continued, silencing Art with his stare. "She was also told something else. She was told Dublin is dead."

At the table, Tall Tommy and Max both shook their heads and picked up a weapon.

"So now we have a new mission—collecting the necessary leverage to resolve this mess."

"What do you mean, leverage?" Jeri asked.

"Lars Nielsen," Tall Tommy said curtly. "Velgyn's Director of Security. Forty-three years old, Norwegian descent, creepy gray eyes, drives a nice Jaguar F-Type sports car." He studied her with detached coolness and chambered a round. "But you already knew that."

Jeri glanced at Chip. "You're going to *kidnap* him?"

The old man shrugged. "Do you expect him to give us answers willingly?"

"Of course not. Why would he? In his mind, *we're* the murderers. And now you want to kidnap him? Come on, Chip. Anything we do to him or his people will only strengthen his resolve to destroy us."

Chip regarded her with a determined stare. "They believe we killed one of their people because we need them to believe so. But truly killing one of us? That changes everything. We're working under a different set of rules now. And I'll do whatever's necessary to make sure Chilly comes out of this alive."

Jeri turned to the others. "Look, I understand why you want to do this. But taking Nielsen is only going to put Chilly in more danger."

"We all get that you care about him," Tall Tommy replied flatly. "But *you're* the one that wanted out. And that's the reason we're in this mess."

460

"The hell it is," Jeri shot back. "Don't you get it? These guys were on to us from the start! They had surveillance video of me going all the way back to the night I took Cowell's key card and fingerprints. I don't know how they did it, but I know one thing—it was only a question of time before they caught up to us. So don't even think about putting this on me. You want to blame something? Blame our ridiculous protocols. Blame our god-like arrogance." Her eyes flashed to Chip. "For chrissake—blame *him*."

Chip nodded somberly. "I appreciate that insight, Jeri. I do. And if you were still part of this team, I'd take it under consideration. But you're not—by *your* choice. So forgive me for not wasting my time once again to show you the moral necessity of this job." A look of anguish briefly clouded the old man's face. "Now, if you'll excuse us, we have things to do."

Jeri looked on as the others around the table began to collect their things. "Do you even know where he is?" she demanded.

"His home's in East Bay, " Max replied. "We'll start there."

"How far is that?"

"Thirty minutes."

Jeri shook her head. "He isn't there."

Max stopped what he was doing and glared at her. "Then where is he?"

"Close. He said he'd be close." Jeri turned and marched into the living room, deep in thought. Moments later she turned and nodded. "I know what to do."

All eyes looked at her expectantly. "What?" Chip asked.

"You're going to have to trust me."

The old man cocked his head. "I'm going to need a little

more than that."

"Okay, how about this." Jeri pulled out Agent Harris's handgun and pointed it at Chip's chest. Tall Tommy and Max immediately trained their own weapons on her.

"No!" the old man hissed, waving them off. "What is this, Jeri?"

Jeri gestured for the others to place their guns on the table. "You'll catch up in a minute. But first, where's Obermeyer's encryption key?"

Chip shook his head. "I have no idea."

"Yes you do."

"No, he doesn't," Tall Tommy interjected. "But I do."

Jeri pointed her gun at him. "And—?"

A grin appeared on the Australian man's chiseled face. "Not here."

"Then where?"

When he was finished telling her, Jeri cocked her head in disbelief.

"You've got to be kidding me."

"Nope."

"But . . . why?"

Tall Tommy's grin vanished. "I don't know. Ask Chilly. He was the one that told me to do it."

"You know what? I will." Jeri marched over to the hotel phone and picked up the receiver.

"Who are you calling?" Chip asked.

"Who do you think?" Jeri pulled out Nielsen's card and dialed his cellphone. "Hey, it's me. Yeah, look—I just remembered something. Something important. No, it'd be better to tell you in person. You'll understand when I tell you. Yes . . . but hurry. If I'm right, the people you're after are close." She hung up and smiled at Chip. "He'll be here in five minutes."

"Bringing him to us," Chip said, giving her a grin. "Well done."

"No, not to us—to me." Jeri looked at Art. "Got a sharp knife on you?"

"Yeah."

"Bring it over here." She pointed at her lower back as he stepped closer. "Take it out."

"You mean—?"

"Yes, my tracker."

Art looked at Chip. The old man sighed and nodded. "Do it."

The forger lifted Jeri's shirt and pressed the cold tip of his knife blade against her skin. A moment later he held up the rice-sized device between two bloodied fingers. "We need to dress that wound."

Jeri waved him off. "I'll worry about that later. Just make sure that tracker doesn't leave this room."

"What the hell are you doing?" Chip demanded.

"Collecting leverage—just like you said." Jeri walked over to him and held out her hand. "Give me your phone."

The old man sighed again and handed it over.

"Passcode?"

"Two-three-five-seven."

Jeri punched in the passcode and started swiping through the screens. "Are you going to tell me what it's called, or . . . oh wait—never mind—I found it." She looked up to find his jaw clenched in anger.

"You show Nielsen that, and you risk burning this whole agency to the ground," he warned.

"I doubt it. But if it does burn, maybe something better will rise from the ashes." Jeri marched to the door. "Okay, I've got to go. I know you want to follow me, but I don't think any of us want to see who shows up if I start shooting holes in the ceiling. Besides, we all know you can track me from Chip's phone."

Tall Tommy nodded. "And we will."

"Good. I'll contact you as soon as I have something useful." Jeri looked once more at Chip. "It sucks not being in control of the things happening around you, doesn't it?"

The old man nodded.

"Welcome to *my* world." She turned and slipped out the door.

The others grabbed their guns.

"No," Chip commanded, raising his hand. "Let her go."

Tall Tommy marched to the door and looked outside. The corridor was empty. He turned to the old man. "Are you really going to let this be her show now?"

Chip felt the stare of all three agents on him. He turned and walked to the window. Fourteen stories below, the streets of San Francisco's financial district stood nearly empty. "For now," he replied, watching a sports car turn into view a few blocks away and speed toward the hotel

As the car grew closer, a slight grin creased his face.

47.

Lars Nielsen was just pulling up to the hotel when his cellphone rang. He glanced at the caller name and on the Jaguar's dashboard display and tapped the answer button. "What is it, Mary?"

"I just got a recognition alert on someone in the second stairwell," Adler replied. "It says it's Lady X."

Nielsen glanced toward the hotel entrance. A young uniformed valet was slumped in his chair, fast asleep. "What's her tracker showing?"

"According to her tracker she's still on the upper floor. Hold on . . . I'll check the video myself."

The security director was still gazing at the entrance when someone tapped on the passenger door window. He looked over to find one of his men's pistols pointed at his head.

"It's her," the morphetics expert said excitedly.

The security director took a deep breath and unlocked the door. Jeri slipped into the passenger seat as Adler continued.

"I just looked at the video myself and there's no question. She must've found a way to remove the tracker."

"Among other things," Nielsen replied flatly. "Okay.

'Ihanks, Mary."

Jeri smiled as he ended the call. "It's nice to see you're keeping an eye out for me."

"What did you do to Harris and Reyes?" the security director demanded.

"For the record, your man Harris is quite an asshole. Luckily, we were able to iron out our differences. Don't worry, both of them are humanely hogtied in the bedroom." Jeri gestured forward. "Mind if we take a little drive?"

"Where to?"

"If I remember correctly, the Embarcadero is nice."

Nielsen steered the car back onto the street. "Your memory . . . all back?"

"Almost." Jeri kept the gun on him as they made the short drive east. "I don't remember those last few hours in Malcesine. But I know why I was there."

"Care to enlighten me?"

"Let's just say it was my own choice."

"And Paul Obermeyer—was that your choice as well?"

"Yes. And no."

When they reached the waterfront, Jeri noticed an empty parking spot and gestured for him to pull over. The security director did as commanded and shut off the engine. Across the street, the illuminated clock tower of the Ferry Building glowed like a beacon in the thickening fog.

"Seems we've come full circle," Nielsen said, admiring the view.

Jeri's stare drifted across the thin crowd of couples strolling casually past. A sudden pang of loneliness forced her to look away. "Not quite."

The security director glanced at his watch. "Ten hours

ago, you were terrified of what you'd find out about yourself when your memory returned. So—?"

"So I found what I needed—the truth." Jeri pulled a cell phone from her pocket and held the screen up to him.

"Where did you get that?"

"It's not important. What's important is what you're seeing."

Nielsen held her stare for a moment before shifting his attention to the screen. A small red dot pulsed against a moving map. Next to it was an identification tag that read CER006. He shrugged indifferently. "What is it?"

"Not what—*who*," Jeri retorted. "That little tracker I just carved out of my back? It turns out Paul Obermeyer was given one also."

Nielsen looked closer. The red dot appeared to be moving through a network of city streets, although nothing in the pattern looked familiar. "What—you're telling me he's still alive?"

Jeri nodded.

The security director gently pushed her hand away. "It's a bit late in the game to take me for an idiot, don't you think?"

"If I thought you were an idiot, we wouldn't be having this conversation. On the contrary, I'm betting more than one life—mine included—that you're the most reasonable person involved in this situation."

"And exactly what *is* this situation? Because I can't seem to figure it out."

Jeri dropped the phone back into her pocket. "When it comes to genetic engineering, Paul Obermeyer represents one of the most brilliant minds of his time," she said matter-of-factly. "You and your team have been acting under the belief that he was killed for the purpose of stealing his encryption key and gaining control of his research. But the truth is just the opposite. Obermeyer's death was faked in order to allow us to collect him, and focus his talents on a purpose far more important than the development of a new vanity drug. The loss of his encryption key was just an unfortunate consequence of his collection."

Nielsen regarded her skeptically. "Then where is he?"

"Saudi Arabia."

"Saudi Arabia?" The security director laughed. "Okay. And how do you explain the body that was pulled from the wreckage?"

"The body burned beyond recognition?" Jeri shot back. "The body that—as the autopsy report will show—had its upper and lower jaws crushed from the impact of the steering wheel? The body with no identifiable fingerprints or dental records?"

Nielsen's grin faded.

"What was really found in that wreckage was a cadaver altered enough to persuade you and everyone else to believe it was Obermeyer. That's how it's done—just enough physical and circumstantial evidence to be convincing. But never enough to be absolutely sure."

"And the woman in London—is the same true for her?"

Jeri's eyes widened with surprise. "You were there?" She nodded before he could answer. "The black van . . . that was you."

"Yes," Nielsen affirmed. "Look, if everything you're telling me is true, then why'd you bring me out here? Why are we even having this conversation?"

"Because we both have something the other wants."

"And what do you want?"

Jeri pointed the gun at his phone. "Call your boss. I think he should hear this too."

Nielsen studied the gun in her hand before dialing Manning. A moment later, the Velgyn CEO's voice sounded through the speakers.

"Lars?"

"I'm here with Miss Stone, Michael," the security director answered. "She has something she'd like to discuss with us."

"Miss Stone," Manning said cheerfully over the background noise of a cocktail party. "What can I do for you?"

"It's more about what we can do for each other," Jeri replied. "Would you like to know where Obermeyer's encryption key is?"

"Just a moment." A brief mumbling followed as the CEO excused himself from his social engagement. When he spoke again, the pleasantness in his voice was gone. "What the hell did you just say?" he demanded.

"Miss Stone has recovered her memory," Nielsen said calmly. "She claims to know where our missing encryption key is."

"Tell me."

"I'll be happy to tell you," Jeri replied. "On one condition—that you release the man you're holding."

Surprised laughter resonated from the speakers. "You mean the man that erased your memory?" Manning exclaimed. "*That* man?"

"Yes, that man."

"Okay . . . fine. Tell Mr. Nielsen where the key is, and once it's been recovered, we'll release him."

"No, his release comes first. And I'll want direct contact with him confirming his safety before the key's location is provided."

"Let me get this straight," Manning growled. "After everything we've done for you, this is how you show your gratitude—by ransoming the very fucking thing you stole from us?" He made a clicking sound with his tongue. "You know, Lars, maybe we've been doing this all wrong. Maybe we should just kill Miss Stone's colleague if she doesn't produce the encryption key in one hour."

"I'm not here to negotiate. Any further harm to the man you're holding, and I'll make sure that key is never found. So either we both get what we want, or neither of us do." Jeri gave the Velgyn security director a resolute nod. "It's your choice."

A long silence filled the Jaguar's cabin before Manning spoke again. "Lars, do you have any reason to believe Miss Stone is lying about her knowledge of the key?"

Nielsen's gaze again fell on the gun. "No, Michael, I don't."

"All right then, Jeri—here are *my* terms. We're going to do as you've asked. But Mr. Nielsen isn't going to let you out of his sight until that encryption key is in his hands. And I swear to god, if there's so much as a scratch on that goddamn thing, you're never going to see the light of day again. Those are my terms, and they're not negotiable. Do we have a deal?"

"Yes."

"Good," the CEO said curtly. "Lars, can I speak to you privately?"

Nielsen waited for Jeri's nod of approval before switching the call to his phone. "I'm here."

"Listen to me very carefully," Manning hissed. "Regardless how this turns out, that woman does *not* walk away.

We're dealing with a group of fucking terrorists here, and we will not be caught in a situation like this again. So when this is over, you're going to rip every last shred of useful information out of that bitch's head and give it to me. And then you're going to make her go away. Do you understand?"

"I understand."

"Good. Then release her friend and bring me that fucking key—tonight."

Jeri watched as the Velgyn security director slowly lowered his phone. "Let me guess—he said 'screw the agreement, get the encryption key, and then kill that crazy bitch.' "

Nielsen smiled despite himself. "You could've used me as a bargaining chip," he said, regarding her curiously. "But you didn't."

"I'm trying to fix things, not destroy them further. And like I said, I'm betting you're the most reasonable person among us." She spun the pistol around and placed it on the console between them. "I hope I'm right."

A deep line creased the security director's brow as he picked up the weapon. "Is he really still alive?" he asked, leveling the gun on her.

"Yes."

"Are you willing to bet your life on it?"

"I am."

Another long silence passed as they exchanged looks.

"Then let's find out." Nielsen put away the gun and dialed a number on his phone. "Mary, do you have a body print of Paul Obermeyer? Then make one . . . quickly. Yes, I know he is. I'll be back in five minutes. If anyone else is still there, tell them to leave now. This one stays between you and me, understood?"

471

Jeri gave the security director a puzzled look as he steered the car back onto the street. "Where are we going?"

"To find a dead man."

Moments later they were speeding south along the embarcadero. Hovering ghost-like over the black water, the Bay Bridge vanished into a shroud of deepening fog, its graceful curves reduced to a thousand points of light stretching east into oblivion.

48.

The white van slipped back into the valley at the same moment the sun broke over the eastern sands of the al Khali desert. With the morning prayer complete, Hofuf had suddenly transformed into a bustling, traffic-choked city. Paul watched with growing apprehension as the street around them turned to gridlock. Noting the curious stares of surrounding drivers and passengers, he turned to Tatyana. "I think we need to get off the street."

Tatyana looked up with surprise. "Why? What—?" She glanced around anxiously for a sign of their assailants. On the street, a woman's dark eyes studied the Russian researcher through the narrow opening of her burka. Tatyana brushed a hand through her short crop of brunette hair and nodded. "Yes, we should."

"Hold on." Paul twisted the steering wheel and nudged the van onto the sidewalk before ducking into a nearby alleyway. Twenty meters further, he shut off the engine. "Okay," he said, opening the door. "Let's go."

"Where?"

"I don't know . . . a cafe or somewhere quiet. At least until this traffic subsides."

"But how?" Tatyana gestured at her head. "I will be noticed by everyone on the street. And this is *not* the place for us to be mocking Sharia law again."

Paul nodded begrudgingly. "Okay, then I'll go. I'll find something to cover you with and come back." He started to step out of the van when his colleague grabbed his hand.

"Be careful," Tatyana said, giving him a solemn smile. Her gaze dropped to their interlocked hands. "You are quite literally the only person I have in this world."

Paul leaned forward and kissed her forehead. "That goes for both of us." He stepped out and glanced at the street. "I won't be long. Just stay out of sight and everything will be fine."

Tatyana watched him march down the alley and vanish onto the street. For long minutes afterward she studied the pedestrians that followed after, scanning their appearances for the telltale signs of the mutawa'ah. Finally, racked with exhaustion, she slipped into the back of the van and curled herself tightly in a corner of the floor.

Within moments she was asleep.

"Obermeyer's body print is almost done," Mary Adler announced at the sound of Nielsen entering the room behind her. "Luckily I had plenty of surveillance video from the annex lab to work with. Now maybe you could explain why I'm even doing this in the first—" She spun her chair around and froze. "Holy fucking *shit*! It's . . . it's *you*."

Across the room, Jeri and the Velgyn security director stared back at her. "I'm sorry—do you know me?" Jeri asked.

"You're fucking right I do."

Nielsen raised a hand in introduction. "Jeri, this is Mary. Mary, this is Jeri . . . also known as Lady X."

Adler's heavily shadowed eyes shifted to the security director. "Didn't you tell me she was some kind of, you know—terrorist?"

"I did," Nielsen replied. "And maybe she is. But she's also convinced that Dr. Obermeyer's still alive. Your job is to find me some proof."

Adler studied both of them for a moment. "Alive?" she repeated, crossing her tattooed arms. "Where?"

"Saudi Arabia," Jeri replied. "A private facility near the Persian Gulf."

"Well that's a little vague." The morphetics expert turned back to her computer and started punching at her keyboard. "All right, I'll start with a wide sweep over any open video servers. If we need to go deeper, I'll call Rakesh and see if he can access some private security networks."

Jeri studied her surroundings while Adler got to work. "So what is this—some kind of command center for recovering the encryption key?"

"That's exactly what it is," Nielsen affirmed. "Once I started digging into Adam Cowell's date on the night of Obermeyer's death, it was clear where to start looking." He gestured at the wall of monitors. Playing on each was old surveillance footage of Paul Obermeyer walking through the lobby of the Velgyn annex lab. In one of the sequences, the researcher looked toward the camera and smiled.

"Someone's always watching," Jeri mumbled. She turned to the security director. "So that's how you found me? By analyzing surveillance video?"

Nielsen gestured at Adler. "Blame her. She's the one that found you. And if she finds Obermeyer, she'll also be the one that saves you." He stepped closer. "So help me understand. This group you're involved in, how does it work exactly?"

"I'm not involved anymore, so there's nothing to discuss. Let's just say it exists for the right reasons." Jeri gave him a reproachful look. "Too bad the same can't be said for Velgyn Pharmaceuticals."

The security director shrugged. "What do you mean? Velgyn's a global leader in developing drugs for a whole spectrum of illnesses."

Jeri rolled her eyes. "Give me a break. Do you realize that your company devotes ninety-four percent of its research dollars on non-essential drug development? Half the world could be dying of an infectious disease and Michael Manning would still be spending billions developing a better erection pill. And by the way, the essential drugs you actually *do* produce currently average a three-hundred percent mark-up over market prices. Yeah, you guys are real humanitarians."

"Well, at least we don't kidnap people."

"No, you just kill them."

Nielsen glared at her for a moment before turning to Adler. "How are we coming?"

"Almost ready to start my first search." Adler abruptly paused and looked over her shoulder. "By the way, what happens if I find him?"

"You'll get a nice bonus and another pile of non-disclosure agreements to sign." The security director patted the bulge of Harris's pistol beneath his jacket and pointed at Jeri. "And maybe I won't have to shoot her." A thin smile appeared on his face.

"Whatever," Adler replied, focusing again on her computer. "As long as I get a paycheck when this is over and not a bullet. Okay . . . first search . . . here we go." She tapped a key and sat back.

Jeri looked at Nielsen. "Look, don't get your hopes up. Paul Obermeyer is being kept in an off-the-grid, high security facility. He's not even allowed to go—"

Across the room, something flashed onto Adler's screen. "Holy shit!" The morphetics expert leapt forward. "I've got something!"

Jeri and the security director both turned as an image of a busy street appeared on the monitor wall next to them. Small stands brimming with fruit, cell phones and clothing lined the sidewalk like islands surrounded by a thin current of vendors and mingling pedestrians. In the upper left corner of the image, a man in a traditional Arabic dishdasha and checkered headscarf appeared and began making his way toward the surveillance camera. Hovering halo-like over his head was a small circle indicating a morphetic pattern match.

"Sixty-eight percent match on movement patterns," Adler announced.

"So much for high security," Nielsen scoffed, shaking his head. "But I do like his outfit. Mary, let's keep looking."

Onscreen, the man strolled past several stands before lingering next to a cart piled high with women's garments. As the old, silver-haired clothing vendor turned his attention to two women, the man discreetly pulled an item from the pile.

"Wait—did you see that?" Jeri pointed at the screen as the man tucked the garments to his chest and start marching back the same way he'd come. "He just stole from that street vendor." She turned to Adler. "When was this taken?"

Adler checked the timestamp. "About twelve minutes ago."

Jeri pulled Chip's phone from her pocket and opened the tracking app. "I need a street name," she commanded, zooming in on Paul Obermeyer's current location.

The morphetics expert nodded and punched at her keyboard. A moment later, a string of words in Arabic script appeared over the video on the large monitors. "There."

Jeri studied the name and began searching the area around Paul's location dot. Next to her, Nielsen shook his head.

"We're wasting time," he said flatly.

"Maybe not." Jeri glanced again at the name on the monitors before holding up her phone. "Look—that video was captured three blocks south of Obermeyer's current position. That's him."

The security director shrugged. "So what are you telling me—that you sent Obermeyer to Saudi Arabia so he could dress like a sheik and steal clothes? Is that the greater purpose he was kidnapped for?"

"No, I'm telling you something's wrong. He shouldn't be out on the street like this."

"Look," Nielsen said firmly, "you convinced me to give this ghost hunt a chance. But my faith in your story is running out." His gray eyes remained fixed on Jeri as he addressed Adler. "You've got two minutes to show me something more definitive, Mary."

"And if she doesn't?" Jeri challenged.

Nielsen pulled Harris's gun from his pocket. "Then we go back to the original goal—recovering the encryption key. And for your sake, I hope *that* story is true."

Jeri glared at the security director. "That's him," she repeated. "I'm sure of it. But if you want a second opinion, let's get it." Her gaze shifted to the door behind him. "What do you think, Chip?"

Nielsen smiled. "Do you really expect me to fall for—"

"Who the hell are you?" Adler exclaimed, looking toward the door with alarm.

Nielsen spun to find two men standing a few meters away. One of them, tall and heavily muscled, already had a gun aimed at Nielsen's chest. Next to him, an older man with disheveled, salt and pepper hair stepped forward.

"Sorry we're late," the man replied, his blue eyes shifting from the monitors to the security director.

"Stop right there," Nielsen commanded, training his gun on him. "Who are you?"

The older man smiled. "Oh, come on," he said calmly. "You're the one that put the bait in the water, Mr. Nielsen. Are you really so surprised to see the fish?"

49.

Nielsen studied the older man and his oversized companion for a moment before looking at Jeri. "Is *that* what this is—a ploy to distract me while your team shows up?"

"No." Jeri said, shaking her head. "Obermeyer's alive. Chip—tell him."

"I don't know what she's talking about," Chip replied flatly, eyeing the security director. "But she certainly knew I'd be tracking that phone in her hand." His smile faded. "You know why I'm here."

"Of course," Nielsen retorted. "And you know why I'm here. So where's my encryption key?"

"Can't say," Chip answered. "Where are my friends?"

"Same answer."

The old man nodded thoughtfully. "We're all smart people, Mr. Nielsen. And none of us would be standing here if we didn't have a great deal to lose. So why don't you lower your gun and we'll try to work out some kind of arrangement?"

"Mr. Nielsen and I have already done that, Chip," Jeri interjected. "Max, put your gun away."

Max shot her a contemptuous look and kept the gun on Nielsen. "Miss Stone no longer works for us."

"That's too bad," the security director replied. "She's certainly the smartest among you."

A tense silence filled the room as the three men exchanged looks. Then, at Adler's workstation, a new video flashed onto the screens and started playing.

Nielsen called out over his shoulder. "Mary?"

Hunched behind her desk, the morphetics expert sat motionless, her eyes fixed on the standoff in front of her. "What?" she asked absently.

"What have you got?"

Adler blinked as if awakening from a spell and looked at her screens. "Another one . . . eighty-three percent movement match." She noted the timestamp on the file. "This one's older—about forty-five minutes ago."

"Put it on the wall," the security director commanded.

Jeri turned and watched as the video appeared on the monitors. A man with a black cloak over his head was being escorted down the corridor of a building. His escort, a thick, bearded man in a traditional Arabic robe and headscarf, opened a barred door and shoved him inside. "Oh *shit*," Jeri hissed, shaking her head.

"What is it?" Nielsen demanded, his eyes and gun still trained on Max.

Onscreen, the man's escort briefly stepped into the cell and returned with the man's cloak in his hands. A moment later he slammed the door and walked away. Jeri threw up a hand. "Wait—freeze that frame!"

Adler punched a key and the video stopped.

Jeri pointed to a man's face pressed against the bars of the door. "Can you zoom in on him?"

"Sure." Adler's fingers raced over the keyboard. Seconds later, the face was stretched across the wall of monitors. Jeri sighed and turned to the others. "Look familiar?"

Across from her, Chip looked at the frozen image. His eyes widened with shock.

"Jesus Christ," Nielsen mumbled, staring dumfounded over his shoulder at the face of Paul Obermeyer on the screen. "It's him. You were—"

"Right?" Jeri nodded. "Yes, thank you."

"Mary, play that forward." Nielsen kept his gun trained on Chip while he circled into a better position to watch.

On the monitors, the image of Obermeyer vanished and the surveillance video continued. A short time later, Obermeyer emerged from the cell. The camera followed as he made his way down the corridor.

"Freeze it again," Nielsen commanded. The video paused and he studied the large emblem painted on the wall next to Obermeyer. "That's the crest of the mutawa'ah," he said matter-of-factly.

"The what?" Jeri asked.

"The mutawa'ah. A group of state-sanctioned religious police. More accurately, a group of armed thugs with the authority to punish anyone found violating Sharia law." He shook his head ominously. "Not the kind of people you want to get mixed up with."

Jeri regarded him with surprise. "How would you know?"

"Mr. Nielsen used to work for a private security firm called Blackwell," Chip interjected. "What was the name of the division that handled suspected terrorist interrogations? Government Services?"

The security director shrugged. "Couldn't say."

"I'm guessing some of those radicalized men you were paid to break down at Gitmo got their start in groups like the mutawa'ah," the old man continued. "Nasty work, huh?"

Nielsen grinned. "I can think of worse."

"Are you seeing this?" Adler asked from her desk.

All eyes turned to the monitors as Paul Obermeyer ducked into an open cell. Moments later, a short, cloaked detainee shuffled around the corner with a mutawa'ah escort. The escort shoved his detainee into the cell opposite of Obermeyer's before stepping inside.

To Nielsen's astonishment, the Velgyn researcher suddenly rushed into the cell behind them. "What the hell is he doing? Mary—speed it up."

Adler fast-forwarded the video until the uncloaked detainee reemerged into the corridor.

"Jesus," Jeri gasped. "It's a woman."

The woman's mutawa'ah escort glanced up at the surveillance camera and abruptly pulled her back into the cell.

"Yes," the security director nodded. "And that's Obermeyer."

"What are they doing?" Adler asked.

On screen, Obermeyer reemerged in the mutawa'ah man's dishdasha and headscarf with his female companion once again cloaked. They turned and quickly vanished into the adjoining corridor.

"Taking a very large risk." Nielsen replied. "Mary, can you get an ID on the woman?"

"Don't bother," Chip interjected. "I know who she is."

"Who?" Jeri demanded.

The old man's eyes shifted from the security director. "Tatyana Aleksandrov. An earlier collection for the same project."

"So we've found *two* ghosts?" Nielsen replied. "Well, I don't know what they've done, but if the mutawa'ah find them again, they really will be dead." He waved the end of his pistol at Chip. "And that blood will be on your hands."

"Oh Jesus—enough already." Jeri stepped forward and ripped the weapon from the Velgyn security director's hand. She then marched over to Max and paused inches from the gun aimed at her chest. "They're in trouble, which means we're going to have to figure this out together. Or am I the only one here that gets that?"

"I get it," Adler chimed in from her corner.

Max glanced at Chip and the director before slowly lowering his weapon. "So what do you propose?"

Jeri turned to Nielsen. "Our colleague and the men holding him—where are they?"

Nielsen regarded her with confusion. "I thought we were talking about Obermeyer."

"Just answer my question."

"He's in Turkey."

Jeri's eyes flashed to Adler. "Mary—can you bring up a map of Turkey on these screens, please?"

"Sure thing."

A moment later, a map of Southeast Europe flashed across the wall of monitors. Jeri gestured at the map. "Where in Turkey?"

"Antalya," Nielsen answered.

"Mary, can you—"

"Way ahead of you," Adler said as she tapped at her keyboard. On screen, the map zoomed out and panned south until both Turkey and Saudi Arabia were visible. Two dots materialized next, followed by a red connecting line. The video analysis expert quickly read the number that appeared over the line. "Thirteen hundred and sixty two miles from Antalya to Al Hofuf."

"Thank you." Jeri again looked at Nielsen. "So—do they have access to a jet?"

"What?" The security director caught her meaning and shook his head. "No—forget it. I'm not sending them down there. Too risky."

"For whom? For you, or for those nice guys that killed one man and are now doing god-knows-what to the other?"

"I've got another match!" Adler exclaimed.

On the monitors, the large map was replaced by a high-angle view of Paul Obermeyer pacing down an alleyway in his mutawa'ah outfit. Every few steps he threw a nervous glance over his shoulder.

"What are you doing, Paul?" Nielsen mumbled at the screen as Obermeyer made his way toward a parked van. He sighed in frustration. "It's only a question of time before the mutawa'ah find him."

"Then get your men down there," Jeri demanded. "Look, you're right—we put Obermeyer in this mess. But if you don't help us get him out, we'll *all* share the blame for what happens." She shot a quick look at Chip before continuing. "The man they're holding is named Sam. Tell your men to free him, and then tell him what's going on. Given a choice, he'll agree to help. But I need your word that you'll do everything in your power to protect him from this moment on."

"And what about our agreement?" Nielsen demanded.

"Our agreement still stands. Free Sam, and I'll give you the location of the encryption key."

The security director followed her eyes back to the monitors. Aleksandrov's face appeared through the van's side window as Obermeyer reached the door. Moments later, concealed beneath her stolen burka, the Russian exited the vehicle and the two made their way back toward the main street.

"There's no measure to the catastrophe we'll be dealing with if those two are caught," Jeri said flatly. "This goes deeper than you can even begin to imagine."

Nielsen continued watching until Paul and Tatyana vanished around a corner. "Stay on them, Mary."

"I'm trying."

Nielsen pulled out his phone and dialed his security manager. "Ray—listen to me very carefully. The situation has changed. Paul Obermeyer's alive. That's right. He's with a woman named Aleksandrov in Saudi Arabia, and they need help. Yes, Saudi Arabia . . . and I need you and Marcus's team on the plane immediately to assist them. Tell Marcus that compensation isn't an issue. Adler will have the details and your flight plan by the time you get to the airport." He paused and eyed Jeri. "Also, the man you're holding . . . I want you to release him. His name is Sam. No . . . in fact, I'm being told he may be willing to help."

Chip stepped forward. "Tell him that shepherd's lost the black sheep," he commanded.

The Velgyn security manager briefly regarded the old man with confusion before nodding. "Ray, listen—tell him that shepherd's lost the black sheep. I know, I'm having a hard time believing this too. More details are coming. Call Adler when you get to the plane." He ended the call and noted the time. "All right, you've got less than thirty minutes to pull together everything they need—including a flight plan that won't get them blown out of the sky."

Jeri tossed Chip his phone. "Chip?"

"I'll take care of it." Chip dialed a number and then paused. "Mr. Nielsen?"

"Yes?"

The old man chewed his words for a moment before speaking. "Thank you."

Nielsen nodded and turned to Jeri. "Happy?"

"Hardly. But at least I'm starting to trust my judgment of character again." She gave him a thin smile. "Though I knew you'd do the right thing."

"What made you so sure?"

"Paul Obermeyer. When I told you he was alive, your first questions were about him, not his encryption key. I took that as a good sign." Jeri fished a folded piece of paper from her pocket and handed it to the security director.

"What's this?"

"The location of his encryption key."

Nielsen opened it and read the information. A low, hissing sound escaped his lips. "You're joking."

Jeri shook her head. "It's been there since the night of Obermeyer's recruitment."

The Velgyn security director slowly crumpled the paper between his fingers and let it drop to the floor. "Give Mary the ID code for Obermeyer's tracker so you can monitor their location in real time. And make sure my team gets that fucking flight plan." He gestured at the weapon in her hand. "May I have my agent's gun back . . . again?"

Jeri handed it over. "You're going now?"

"Their flight to Saudi Arabia will take about three hours. I'll be back before they're on the ground." Nielsen checked to make sure the weapon was loaded before walking over to Adler's workstation and laying it next to her hand. "In the meantime, Miss Adler's in charge."

Jeri and the others watched Nielsen march from the room. When they looked over at Adler, the young morphetics expert regarded them with a crooked smile.

"So," she said, waving the gun nonchalantly, "which one of you assholes knows the way to Starbucks?"

50.

Derrick Birch stepped into the conference room and silently poured himself a glass of water before dropping into the nearest chair. Across the table, Minister Razam looked up from the report he was studying and nodded at the Ceres project leader. "Did you enjoy yourself last night, Mr. Birch?"

"Maybe a little too much," Birch replied in a raspy whisper.

A smile creased the minister's handsome, paternal face. "Good. You and your team deserved an evening of celebration. But now the next phase of our work begins." He tapped a finger on the pages spread before him. "Starting immediately, I want systematic documentation and cross-team validation of every step taken to generate these results. We have accomplished what we set out to do. Now we must be certain there isn't a single flaw or error in the manner in which we have achieved it."

"Of course." Birch drained the glass of water and rubbed at his bloodshot eyes. "I'll have everyone on it within the hour."

Razam rose from his seat. "We're almost there, Derrick. But here forward, we can't allow a single moment of rest."

"I understand."

"No . . . you don't." The minister's expression darkened as he began pacing the room. "I received some troubling news this morning. An initial audit of Ghawar has already been submitted to the oil coalition by their engineers."

Birch's hangover suddenly vanished. "What—already? For fuck's sake, that should've taken them *months*, not days. How could they have—?"

"I don't know," the minister replied. "Nor do I know what was detailed in that report. But we should all assume the worst."

The project leader sighed. "Fuck."

"There's more. Last night, our facility manager informed me that several service gates around the perimeter have not been properly guarded as instructed. I've ordered more security personnel on-site, but it's possible that a breach of some kind has already occurred. We shall begin re-screening all support personnel and implementing new security procedures immediately. In the meantime, I need your team—" The minister paused at the buzzing of his cell phone. He glanced curiously at the cryptic name on the screen before answering. "Yes?"

"Minister, we have a serious situation," the caller announced matter-of-factly.

"Who is this?"

"This is your recruiting agency, minister. Do you understand?"

Razam's eyes flashed to Birch. "Yes."

"We're currently tracking two recruits—PO-6 and TA-4—in the area of Al Hofuf. Video surveillance confirms. Both are unsecured and their situation is urgent."

"That's impossible. I just saw them here last night. We were celebrating the—"

"Minister, we don't have time to debate what I'm seeing firsthand," the caller interjected, "so listen to me carefully. We have a team inbound from Antalya, Turkey to assist. I need a flight plan to Hofuf authorized immediately. Can you do that?"

"Yes, of course. Give me the information." The minister produced a pen and paper from his pocket and scratched down the details. "I shall take care of it right away. But please—what do you mean when you say their situation is urgent?"

Across the table, Birch watched Razam's dark, intelligent eyes widen with fear.

"Oh no . . . oh God. Yes . . . yes, they are . . . very dangerous. No, I'm afraid I don't have any jurisdiction or power over such matters. Yes, I'll authorize it immediately. How else may I assist with this?" Razam nodded and abruptly ended the call.

"What was that?" Birch asked.

"A situation," the minister replied, dialing another number. "Let us hope it is not yet a disaster." A torrent of angry Arabic poured from his mouth before he paused and placed a hand over the phone. "Tell Youssef to have two of my vehicles prepared to leave immediately," he commanded Birch. "And check in with your teams. I want to know who saw doctors Obermeyer and Aleksandrov last."

Birch stared at the minister with confusion.

"They're *gone*," Razam exclaimed with uncharacteristic impatience. "And you're coming with me to find them."

≈

Even without the use of his sight, Chilly was certain

Marcus had returned.

There was no point in reacting. Any movement would only re-awaken the pain in his muscles and joints, or further tear the raw, bleeding skin beneath the collars suspending him in the air. Of course, that's probably what his captor was hoping for. More pain. More suffering.

On the screens of the virtual reality goggles covering his eyes, the labyrinth of interconnected chambers and hallways continued to rush past. Despite repeated attempts to remain still, the slightest twitch of his face or turn of his head hurled him ever deeper into the endless, unsolvable maze. Left, right, up, down—the direction didn't matter. It was obvious from the beginning that the goal of the game wasn't to offer some hope of escape, but to nudge him ever closer to madness. Nothing else could explain the death-metal music, or the screams of varying intensity piped into the heavy headphones to keep him awake. Nothing else could explain the electric shock delivered through the collar around his neck when the screams and music weren't enough.

Regardless of his actions, the game played on.

Through some perception beyond his normal senses, Chilly felt the man named Marcus circling slowly around him. Were his mind still sharp, he might have wondered what the strange little redheaded man was doing. Instead, he regarded his captor's presence with the same surrendering acceptance of a broken animal. In the foggy, sleep-deprived depths of Chilly's head, Marcus—like every other facet of his torture—had become an abstraction. A simple, intangible annoyance that refused to fade.

Then, abruptly, Chilly's senses detected something else. It crawled from his neck harness onto his shoulder and paused; a lithe, hairy *thing* twitching with nervous excitement. Tiny whiskers tickled his shoulder. A flickering tongue sampled the rancid shit that covered his body. The creature then turned and jumped to his other shoulder and Chilly took a strange delight in the sudden warmth of excrement running down his back. Beneath the VR goggles, a smile spread across his filth-covered face.

Emboldened by the docile body beneath it, the rat followed its own trail of urine down Chilly's back and clawed to a stop. For a brief moment, the sound of a shouting voice rose above the din of death-metal music in Chilly's headphones. He twisted his head toward the noise. The rat's claws tightened into his skin. Despite the pain, a strange thought flitted through his mind.

Are you arguing with my keeper, ratty-boy?

A hand seized his shoulder. Chilly instinctively shut his eyes as the goggles and headphones were roughly stripped from his head. The muted voice he heard moments before now spoke plainly in his ear.

"Can you hear me?"

Chilly opened his eyes to find Ray Foster standing next to him. He glanced over his shoulder.

The rat clinging to his back was gone.

"Can you hear me?" Foster asked again. "Sam?"

Chilly shook his head as if waking from a nightmare. He slowly met the Velgyn security manager's stare. "Yeah?" he whispered.

"Are you okay?"

"Where's the rat?"

Foster stepped back and waved his hand impatiently. "Get him down."

Chilly looked on as Marcus's two men once again materialized from the shadows and began lowering him to the ground. After hours of suspended movement, the stone floor seemed to pitch and roll beneath him. Alternating waves of pain and relief rushed through his limbs. "What . . . what's next?" he mumbled, stumbling slightly. "A light lunch and some . . . some waterboarding?"

Foster stepped forward and steadied him with a hand. "Here—drink this," he commanded, holding out a bottle. He caught the look of suspicion on Chilly's face and threw back the first sip. "See? Perfectly safe. Just glucose and electrolytes."

Chilly took the bottle and drank back the yellow-tinted liquid. With every swallow he could feel his strength returning. He absently rubbed at his back. "Was it real?"

"What?"

"The rat," a nearby voice answered. Marcus stepped into the light, a smug grin stretching his scarred face. He walked up to Chilly and shrugged. "Who knows? It's so hard to know what's real these days." He turned to the Velgyn security manager. "Would you agree, Mr. Foster?"

Foster's eyes remained on Chilly. "I just spoke with Director Nielsen. It seems the situation has changed. Paul Obermeyer's still alive."

Chilly regarded him silently.

Marcus shrugged. "So what does that mean? Are we done here?"

"Here, yes. But now we've got ourselves a rescue mission. Apparently Obermeyer's with some woman in Saudi Arabia, and they could use our help." The security manager noticed their captive's jaw tighten. He turned to Marcus. "The director's asked for your assistance. Compensation won't be an issue."

The hired mercenary briefly considered the request. "All right," he nodded. "When do we leave?"

"Now." Foster looked at Chilly. "I was told you might be willing to assist us as well. If not, you're free to go."

Chilly cocked his head. "You want my help?"

"That's what I said."

An incredulous smile curled Chilly's mouth. "Wow. You know . . . that is interesting. Don't get me wrong, Ray, you seem like a nice guy. But even if I *could* forgive what you've done to my friends,"—his eyes shifted to Marcus—"do you really think I'd be willing to help after what this little ginger-haired asshole just put me through?"

Anticipating Marcus's enraged strike with his right fist, Chilly pivoted to the left. In one deft motion he slipped his arm around the smaller man's neck and spun him into a chokehold. "This is for Dublin," he said calmly, tightening his grip.

Marcus's men both drew their weapons and leveled them on Chilly.

"Wait!" Foster exclaimed, raising his hands. "Sam, listen—I was given a message."

Chilly smiled at the mix of fear and anger on Marcus's reddening face. "Hold on. This will only take a moment."

"I was asked to tell you that shepherd's lost the black sheep."

Chilly eyes flashed to the Velgyn security manager. "Say that again?"

"Shepherd's lost the black sheep."

Chilly glared at him for a long moment before slowly loosening his grip. Marcus gasped a lungful of air. "You've got my attention, Ray," he said, tightening his grip once again.

"Now, if you don't mind, I'd like my fucking phone."

~

"Stay close," Paul said under his breath as he and Tatyana moved quickly along the fringes of the crowded street. "And keep moving."

Behind him, safely concealed in her stolen burka, Tatyana nodded silently.

Beneath the shade of his headscarf, Paul studied the other pedestrians on the street. To his relief, most wore the same traditional garments as he and his colleague, offering a certain sense of anonymity. Unfortunately—and in direct contrast to Arabic women—eye contact between Arabic men seemed to be a cultural requirement. With each man that passed, Paul felt himself being drawn into a staring contest. Resigned to this fact, he stared back, restraining his instinct to nod in the American gesture for *what's up?*

A few hundred yards further, the carts forming the market began to thin. As the crowd fell behind them, Paul and Tatyana found themselves walking along a wide street bordered by a procession of squat, sand-colored buildings.

"How far should we go?" Tatyana asked once they were safely out of earshot of others

"As far as we have to." Paul glanced across the street at a row of small shops. Over one of the doors hung a sign of an ornately painted coffee cup, with long S-shaped wisps of steam rising from the top. "God, what I wouldn't do for one of those right now," he mumbled, suddenly aware of his own hunger.

Tatyana followed his stare to the sign. "Perhaps they would offer if we asked. We are due for some good luck, yes?"

The morning sun, soft just an hour before, now hung with blood-orange intensity in the cloudless sky, bathing everything in heat and hard shadows. Of the few male pedestrians around them, most were older, with dark faces contrasted by striking white beards. Paul glanced toward the row of shops again. "Maybe. At least they might be able to tell us where the bus station is." He gestured for them to cross the street. "Just remember to let me do the talking."

"Yes, I know," Tatyana shot back.

"They're going to wonder what two foreigners are doing in Arabic clothing," Paul continued. "And without money. We need some kind of backstory . . . like our luggage was stolen. But we can't have them calling the authorities and attracting more attention. I don't know . . . maybe we should—"

Next to him, Tatyana abruptly stopped and sniffed the air.

"What are you doing?" Paul whispered, glancing around anxiously.

"Do you smell that?" his colleague asked, an edge of excitement in her voice. Without waiting for an answer she marched past him toward an open door and stuck her head into the dimly lit interior.

Paul stared dumbfounded as she then disappeared inside. "Tatyana!" he hissed, scanning the street. Realizing she wasn't coming back, he marched after her.

Upon stepping inside, Paul grimaced at the warm, sour smell that filled the small shop. He looked past the racks of hanging garments and sewing machine stations that cluttered the narrow interior to a small table in the back where two men and a woman were sitting. All three pairs of eyes shifted from the strange woman standing before them to the man in the doorway. An awkward moment of silence passed before Tatyana smiled and pointed at a plate of dumplings heaped into a steaming pile on the table. The eyes of the older man at the table widened with surprise as she said something in Russian. Then, slowly, his mouth curled into a thin grin. He gestured at the plate and spoke back to her in clipped Russian. Tatyana nodded and suddenly everyone at the table was smiling and speaking at once. Paul watched the strange scene play out with a detached sense of disbelief. His colleague turned and pointed at him.

"On ne govorit po Rossii," Tatyana said with a shrug. "Angliyskiy."

"Good morning," Paul nodded, a bemused grin on his face. The threesome around the table—Paul now realized they were in fact an older couple and their teenage son—smiled and nodded back. The woman then rose from the table and hurried into a back room to fetch something. Paul stepped forward and took his colleague's hand. "What the hell just happened?" he asked, a clueless grin still stretching his face. "How did you know they were Russian?"

"I know the scent of my homeland," Tatyana replied. She pointed to the plate of dumplings. "They're called syrniki—something of a cottage cheese dumpling. I smelled them the moment we crossed the street."

Paul sniffed the air again. "I think you could smell them from Syria."

"Do not be impolite, Paul," his colleague said flatly. "Besides, that smell may just be the best luck we have been given so far."

The woman returned with two folding stools and her husband and son quickly made room for Paul and Tatyana at the table. As soon they were seated, the husband gestured at the plate of dumplings. Paul took one and nodded in thanks. Across the table, the couple's twenty-something son watched him with a wry grin. Tatyana devoured half of a dumpling in one bite and immediately resumed the conversation in Russian. Within minutes the gestures and smiles around the table evoked the impression that she had been reunited with old friends.

"They are tailors," Tatyana said to Paul over her shoulder. "They were born here, but worked in Tbilisi for many years."

Paul smiled and nodded at the blurbs of translated conversation Tatyana provided while he worked up the nerve to taste the foul-smelling ball of cheese sweating in his hand.

"They returned home during the last Georgian conflict. Our host's name is Mahad, his son is Baasim, and his wife is Ikram. Mahad says that they have been back for almost a decade. Once again it feels like home."

The father of the small family snatched a syrniki from the plate in front of him. "Rasskazhi mne," he said between bites, "chto privelo vas v Saudovskuyu Araviyu?"

The smile on Tatyana's face faltered slightly. Paul studied the faces around the table as she answered, aware that the focus of the conversation had now turned to them. Across from him, the son's dark eyes flickered between Paul and his colleague. When Tatyana was finished, both he and his father nodded their heads in understanding.

"What did you tell them?" Paul asked.

"The truth," Tatyana said, giving him a look. "That we are technicians here for a special project, but we were stopped last night and our possessions and vehicle stolen by several armed men. Knowing that Sharia law does not allow for an unwed man and woman to be out together, we have decided not to speak with the authorities about the situation. We wish only to return to the facility where we work—the Ras Jazan refinery."

Paul nodded, impressed by his colleague's deft handling of the question. Both of them turned to their host, who appeared deep in thought as he grabbed another syrniki. The man glanced at his wife, who in turn rose once again from the table and vanished into another room. Paul leaned toward Tatyana. "You think they'll help us?"

"Perhaps." Tatyana glanced reproachfully at the uneaten syrniki in his hand. "Or perhaps they are waiting to see if you insult them by not eating the food you have been given."

"Ah . . . right." Paul lifted the dumpling in thanks and, with a final glance at its glistening surface, took a bite. As he began to chew, his eyebrows slowly lifted in surprise. Despite the strong smell, the syrniki's texture was smooth and creamy, its flavor mildly sweet. Famished, he stuffed the rest in his mouth and quickly grabbed another.

Across the small table, his host smiled with approval. "Vozmozhno, my mozhem pomoch' vam."

"Spasibo," Tatyana replied.

Paul regarded her quizzically as their hostess reappeared with a platter of cups and a steaming pot of coffee. "Oh thank you, god," he exclaimed, devouring his second dumpling. He leaned toward Tatyana. "What did he just say?"

"My father said we will help you," the son interjected in perfect English. "But first—" He raised a hand and swept it over the table. "We eat."

51.

Jeri studied at the wall of monitors before her, her patience waning. "So you're telling me there isn't a *single* camera in that area?" she demanded over her shoulder.

Behind her, Mary Adler shook her head. "No, I'm telling you there isn't a single camera that's picked up Obermeyer's signature. It's actually not that uncommon. It could be that a camera's broken, or the surveillance server is offline . . . who knows? It just happens. We call it a dead zone."

Jeri nodded. "A dead zone. Fitting name. Is there any way you can—" The ringing of Chip's phone made her pause. The old man stared at it curiously before answering. A brief exchange followed before he turned and looked at her. "Who is it?" Jeri asked.

"Hold on," Chip said to the caller. He walked over and put the phone on speaker mode. "Someone wants to talk to you."

Jeri furrowed her brow. "Yes?"

"I'm fine. And thank you for asking."

A jolt of electricity shot up Jeri's spine. "Sam?"

"Yes," Chilly replied. "Are you okay?"

Jeri's eyes flashed to Chip. "I . . . yeah . . . I'm fine," she said dismissively. "What about you?"

Seven thousand miles away, Chilly relaxed his hold on Marcus's throat to allow the mercenary a breath. "Confused," he said, frowning at the phone Ray Foster was holding in front of him. "I'm here with some people who suddenly want me to be their friend. Perhaps you could explain?"

"Have they released you?"

"They have." Chilly tightened his grip on Marcus's throat once again. "But I'm holding on to some collateral until we're all on the same page."

Jeri caught the unmistakable sound of someone gasping for air. "Okay, then I'll give you the short version. The men holding you are from Velgyn Pharmaceuticals. They want Paul Obermeyer's encryption key back. I was in the process of negotiating your release when we found out Obermeyer and another recruit were in trouble."

"What kind of trouble?"

"Based on what we're seeing, it looks like they were arrested by a Saudi religious group called the Mutawa'ah. They managed to escape from the facility where they were being held and now we're tracking them—well, trying to track them—in the city of Al-Hofuf." Jeri turned and glared at Adler, who shrugged and shook her head.

"Who's the other recruit?" Chilly asked.

"Aleksandrov," Chip answered. "Tatyana Aleksandrov."

A surprised grunt reverberated from the phone. "Never would have put them together."

Jeri sighed. "Look, Sam . . . there are no secrets now. I've given the Velgyn security director the location of the encryption key in exchange for you, but he knows the full story. He agrees that we need to work together if we're going to keep the situation with Obermeyer from turning in to a disaster." Her eyes locked on Chip. "And so does Chip."

A long silence followed before Chilly replied. "Shepherd's lost the black sheep," he said flatly.

"He has indeed," Chip replied.

Jeri gave the old man a puzzled look. "So," she said into the phone, "what do you think?"

"What do *I* think?" Another loud gasp of air was followed by the sound of shuffling feet as Chilly released Marcus and shoved him toward his men. "I think we'd better get our asses to Saudi Arabia."

∽

"Someone's here to see you."

Nielsen caught the icy look Lexi Manning directed at her husband before marching her Pilates-toned figure from the room. Standing at the window, the Velgyn CEO threw back the rest of his drink and turned.

"Lars," Manning said jovially, holding up his empty highball glass. "Get you one?"

Nielsen stepped into the CEO's private library and nodded.

Manning walked over to the bar and poured two gin and tonics. "You'll have to excuse Lexi. She doesn't like answering the door, but the staff had to leave early tonight to prep the boat. We're heading to Catalina for a few weeks after the board meeting. Anyway—" He walked over and handed the security director his drink. "Cheers."

Nielsen nodded curtly. "What are we celebrating?"

A smug grin slowly drew itself across Manning's face.

"Well, you sure as hell didn't drive all the way over here to tell me you don't have it. But I am curious to know if you've done what I asked with our friend."

"Miss Stone is under armed watch, and her colleague is still in the care of my men. I promise you, they'll both get what they deserve." Nielsen took a drink while his gray eyes surveyed the impressive collection of books around them. "Have you read all of them, Michael?"

"Have I—?" Manning laughed and shook his head. "Where's my key?"

"I'll show you in just a moment. But first, I have a question." Nielsen leveled his stare on his boss. "What if I told you I could give you Paul Obermeyer instead of his encryption key?"

"You mean alive and well, or the sixty pounds of charred flesh sitting in a coroner's chamber?"

"You know what I mean."

Manning tossed back a slug of his gin and tonic and shrugged. "Why are you asking?"

"Simple curiosity. You authorized me to do whatever it takes to get Obermeyer's encryption key back. I was just wondering if you would have demanded the same if Obermeyer himself were the one missing instead."

"I see. So this is some kind of hypothetical post-game reflection, is that it?" Manning's mouth curled into something between a smile and a sneer. "Do you know why I'm the CEO of this company, Lars? It isn't just because I can look at any aspect of our business—the financials, the forecasts, the new drug pipeline, the various competitive threats—and immediately see the right path to take. No, what makes me an effective CEO is the fact that I have the *stomach* to lead us down that path. Most people would get mired in the ugly little details of every decision—like firing two-thousand people in the wake of an acquisition, or fighting PETA to keep the animal testing labs open. But not me. And you know why? It's because I don't see money, or people, or cute little fucking bunnies like the rest of you. I only see minions and resources. Minions to be hired, fired and exploited, resources to be consumed—and all solely for the good of the business. Of course, most people would say that that makes me something of an asshole. But I know something they don't. I know that I'm *necessary*. After all, does anyone honestly think a company of this size can be run by someone who lacks the fortitude to always put *its* needs first? Of course not. A morally encumbered CEO would as useless as a doctor who faints at the sight of blood. Do you understand?"

Nielsen nodded. "I do. But you still haven't answered my question."

"Oh, but I have. You see, Paul Obermeyer was a brilliant researcher. But his role was the same as everyone else in this organization—to provide the means to an end. His *research* is the object of value, not his life. If Paul had handed me my new drug and vanished, it wouldn't have mattered if he were dead, missing, or abducted by fucking aliens. I would have already had what I needed. Which means, for all practical purposes, he would have already been dead to me." Manning drained his glass and smiled. "Any more hypothetical questions?"

"No."

"Good. Then give me the goddamn key."

Nielsen took another drink of his gin and tonic and waved a finger at the surrounding walls of books. "Alphabetical by author?"

"Yeah, why?" Manning's brow furrowed in confusion as his security director walked over to the nearest shelves. "What are you doing?"

"Looking for the S's."

"And why the hell would you be doing that?"

Nielsen moved quickly down the rows, tracing an index finger over the neatly ordered spines. "A book was found in the room with Miss Stone. A rather interesting book . . . written by a man with the same last name who died decades ago. Even more interesting than the subject matter is the book's rarity. Seems only a handful were ever published."

"What's it titled?"

Nielsen finger suddenly froze over a wide book nestled in its correct alphabetical spot amongst the others. He gently removed it from the shelf. "See for yourself," he said, showing it to the Velgyn CEO.

Manning stepped forward and read the title. "*Predictions in the New Business Ecology*." He shrugged dismissively. "So?"

"Is it yours?"

"Well, it's here, isn't it?"

"Yes, it is." The security director's stare shifted to the void on the shelf where the book had been. "Along with something else."

Manning followed his gaze. Lying in the back of the void was a small metal cylinder. "What the—?" He grabbed the object and regarded it silently for a moment before pressing a small button located on the side. A shaft of intricately etched crystal slid from the cylinder and shimmered in the light. "Is this what I think it is?" he demanded, handing it to Nielsen.

Nielsen carefully retracted the crystal back into the cylinder before examining the serial number etched along its length. He nodded and handed it back.

"I don't understand," Manning mumbled, staring dumbfounded at Obermeyer's encryption key. "When was it . . . how did they—?"

"Miss Stone told me it was placed here the night of Obermeyer's accident. I'm inclined to believe her."

"But why? Why go to the trouble of killing for something, and then hide it in the house of the very person it belongs to?"

The security director raised an eyebrow. "I thought the encryption key belonged to the *corporation*, Michael. Not you."

Manning's eyes narrowed on him. "I *am* the corporation, Lars. And my executive security director should always keep that in mind."

Nielsen regarded the thick book in his hand. "Quite honestly, I'm not sure I'm worthy of the title. For all of my effort, it was Miss Stone who told me where to find it. And it's safe to say my theory of why it was stolen was wrong as well. Maybe your trust in me is misplaced."

"Don't be ridiculous," the Velgyn CEO scoffed, marching back to the bar. "You're just tired. Go home . . . get some rest. You'll see things more clearly in the morning. Oh, and by the way, I noticed you're still driving that Jaguar. I'll have an Aston Martin dropped off at your house tomorrow. Consider it a small token of gratitude." He dropped Obermeyer's encryption key on the counter and grabbed the gin. "How does red sound?"

"Good night, Michael."

Manning watched his security director make his way

507

to the door. "You still have one more task," he said flatly. "Do I need to worry about your ability to see it through?"

Nielsen paused at the doorway. "By tomorrow morning, Jeri Stone and her colleague will be as dead as Paul Obermeyer."

Manning nodded. "That's all I needed to hear. Oh, and Lars—show yourself out. The last thing I need to deal with right now is Lexi feeling like she's become part of the fucking house staff."

Nielsen made his way toward the front entrance of Manning's Marin County estate. Behind him, the sound of fresh ice cubes falling into a glass echoed from the library. It was only after he was outside that he realized he was still holding the Velgyn CEO's copy of the book.

52.

"Need a drink?"

Chilly opened his eyes to find Ray Foster hovering over him with a bottle of water. He sat up from his chair and yawned. "Sparkling?"

"Still."

He took the bottle regardless and glanced around the cabin of the jet. "How much further?"

"Another hour or so." The Velgyn security manager took a seat across from him and glanced absently out the window. "Gives us a little time to talk."

"Great. I could use someone to talk to right now. As you know, I'm a recent victim of torture." Chilly paused and gestured toward Marcus sitting at the front of the cabin. The mercenary was studying him with a thin smile. "How's his neck by the way?"

Foster shrugged and picked something from his teeth. "I thought maybe we could talk about Paul Obermeyer."

"Why? Were you under the impression I know him personally?"

"What's he doing in Saudi Arabia?"

"Getting into trouble from what you've told me."

Foster nodded. "I get it. You have your secrets, we have ours. But the thing is, whether you want to admit it or not, you're the reason we're doing this right now. So, since we're all in this together now, maybe you'd care to explain what we're up against."

Chilly regarded him with a look of amusement. "Is that what you think—that we're all in this together? Well, Ray, I hate to be the bearer of bad news, but we are most definitely *not* in this together. You can call this little adventure we're on a temporary alignment of interests if you'd like. But when it's over, someone's going to pay for the death of my friend." His stare shifted once again to Marcus. "And we both know who that someone is."

"Did you hear me?"

Paul tore his stare from the ribbon of black pavement stretched before them and looked over at the young man in the driver's seat. "I'm sorry, Baasim—what were you asking?"

The son of the tailoring couple shifted his family's delivery van into a higher gear and leaned closer. "What do you do at the refinery?"

"Oh, um . . ." Paul glanced into the rearview mirror and caught the cautious look in Tatyana's green eyes from her seat between sacks of laundered clothing. In the rear door windows beyond her, the city of Hofuf receded into the vast emptiness of the Khali desert. "We're inspectors for the, you know . . . equipment. Making sure everything is safe. You speak English very well by the way."

"Yes!" Baasim affirmed proudly. "Many people my age

here speak English. It is the language of big business . . . and good movies." His expression turned pensive. "I'm sorry for not telling you when you first arrived. My parents don't like me to speak languages they don't understand."

"It's fine," Paul replied, relieved by the easy subject change. "What's your favorite movie?"

"Anything with superheroes. I love the Marvel Comic movies...Iron Man, X-men, the Avengers." The young man shook his head wistfully. "How cool would it be to have the power to change the world?"

Paul smiled. "Pretty cool."

"I would love to watch a movie in a theatre someday," Baasim continued. "It must be amazing."

"You've never been to a movie theatre?"

"Of course not. They're forbidden here. You would have to go all the way to Bahrain to see a movie."

Paul studied the gleaming dot of an approaching car. Once again he felt his pulse rise as it had with the other vehicles they'd encountered since leaving the city. The dot grew nearer and abruptly divided into two identical black Mercedes. Moments later, both vehicles sped past on their eastward journey toward Hofuf. "Your country has very strict views of what's right and wrong," he said, watching with relief as the vehicles shrank from view in the side view mirror.

"We follow in the path of the Prophet Muhammad," Baasim said with practiced conviction. "The right path is never easy."

Paul nodded. "No shit."

"I'm sorry . . . what did you say?"

"Never mind."

Tatyana's veiled head suddenly appeared between

them. "Do you know how long it will take for us to get there?" she asked in English.

"An hour perhaps. Perhaps a little more." Their young driver cocked his head at a thought. "Will there be a security gate when we arrive?" he asked, his tone anxious. "I only ask because my driving license . . . it . . . it isn't entirely official . . . just yet."

"You can drop us off before we get to the gate," Paul replied. He again caught his colleague's gaze in the mirror and realized they were both sharing the same uneasy thought—

What was going to happen when they got back?

Focused on the immediate threats at hand, neither of them had considered the consequences of returning to their original captors. There was no doubt in Paul's mind that Birch and the rest of the team were now aware of their absence—including Minister Razam. The only question was what they were doing about it. Certainly there would be protocols for such things—searching the grounds, interviewing the security staff, checking the service vehicles. But what troubled Paul wasn't what was being done to find them. He was worried about what the minister would do upon their return. *Disappearing in the night like insolent teenagers* Paul thought sullenly. *What's a fitting punishment?* He mulled the question over in his head as the delivery van sped eastward across the black thread of highway toward the sun.

Thirty miles ahead, a large SUV slowed to a stop and parked sideways to form a makeshift roadblock. The driver and his three passengers quickly checked the magazines inside their Kalashnikov automatic rifles before stepping outside. A hot wind swept at the men's headscarves and long white dishdashas as they focused their eyes westward. Minutes later, as an approaching vehicle drew nearer, one of the men raised the green flag of Saudi Arabia, its Shahada written boldly in white and underscored with a long saber. His colleagues silently raised their weapons.

The mutawa'ah checkpoint was now open.

⌇

"They're leaving the city!" Jeri exclaimed, watching Obermeyer's tracking marker continue to accelerate on the onscreen map. "Based on their speed, they must be in a vehicle. Mary, what's our team's ETA into Hofuf?"

Behind her, Adler punched at her keyboard. "Eight minutes."

Jeri glanced over at Chip. "Support?"

"The minister's almost there," he replied. "Two vehicles."

Jeri refocused her attention on the wall monitors. "Where are you going?" she mumbled, watching the small marker continue along the narrow thread of highway. "Wait," she said, struck with a thought. She again turned to Chip. "Where's Obermeyer *supposed* to be?"

The old man looked at her blankly. "Excuse me?"

"The facility—where is it?"

"It's an oil refinery. I believe it's called Ras Jazan."

Jeri nodded. "Mary, will you please locate Ras Jazan and show it on the map?"

"Yep." Adler once again punched rapid-fire at her keyboard. Moments later, a blue sphere appeared in the lower right corner of the screen and pulsed like a beating heart.

Jeri studied the intertwining lines of service roads leading from the refinery to the lone highway that cut westward through the desert. Her eyes followed the highway's northern and eastern route until she was once again staring at Obermeyer's marker. "Just what I was afraid of—they're going back."

Chip stepped closer to the map on the monitors. "What makes you so sure?"

Jeri gestured at the wide swath of barren desert between the two pulsing dots. "Where else would they be going?"

The old man nodded. "The minister's probably going to drive right by them . . . if he hasn't already."

"Then call him."

"And do what—ask him to pull over every vehicle heading east? We don't even know who Obermeyer and Aleksandrov are with, friendly or otherwise." Chip shook his head. "You were right . . . Chilly and Nielsen's men are the only people equipped to handle this. We just have to let this play out."

All heads turned at the sound of footsteps in the corridor. The Velgyn security director stepped through the doorway and marched directly over to the monitors. "What's our status?" he demanded.

Jeri quickly updated him on the situation.

"Why on earth would they try to go *back*?" Nielsen asked, dumbfounded.

"Why not?" Chip retorted. "It's the closest thing to a home they've got." He excused himself to call the minister with their latest finding.

Nielsen turned to Adler. "Are you okay, Mary?"

"Mostly." The morphetics expert gestured at Max. "Muscle head over there screwed up my Starbucks order. But I decided not to shoot him."

"Good." Nielsen turned and regarded Jeri with a puzzled expression.

"So, was Mr. Manning happy with our arrangement?" she asked.

"Extremely. The key to perhaps the world's most profitable drug discovery is quite literally in his hands again. In two days he'll announce it to the Board of Directors and guarantee himself a year-end bonus equivalent to the GDP of a small country. Plus, he's been assured that you and your friend Sam will be dead by morning."

"And just how were you planning to kill us?"

"I hadn't thought that far ahead yet. But car accidents seem to be a popular choice these days." The security director's grin quickly faded. "I need to know something."

"I can't answer your question."

"You don't know what I was going to ask."

"Of course I do. You want to know why Obermeyer's encryption key was placed in Manning's library. You want to know why it was even taken in the first place. We both know Obermeyer's death would have been written off as a simple accident if we'd just left it at the scene—so why do it?"

Nielsen nodded. "Exactly."

"And I'm telling you I don't have an answer."

"Are you saying you don't *know*, or are you just unwilling to tell me?"

Jeri regarded the security director's pale gray eyes. Beneath their cold surface was a deeper element of honesty and directness. It was this honesty she'd placed her faith—and her life—in when telling him the truth. But now, in the wake of everything, there was nothing left to say. Perhaps more accurately, there was nothing left to gain for either of them to perpetuate the need for complete trust. She gave him a wan smile. "Let's just say, whether I know the answer or not, there must be a good reason for it."

Nielsen started to speak, then paused and slowly nodded. "Right."

A short distance away, Chip ended his call. "The minister is at the airport," he said sharply.

As if on cue, Adler received an incoming call and put it on speaker. Ray Foster's voice reverberated through the control room.

"We're here."

Jeri and the Velgyn security director exchanged nods. "All right," Jeri said, turning to the wall of monitors. "Let's go get them."

∿

"No, you've got it backwards. The Hulk is Bruce Banner. *He's* the physicist . . . not Tony Stark. Tony Stark is the genius engineer."

Paul furrowed his brow. "Are you sure?"

"Yes," Baasim replied, nodding vehemently. "I'm sure."

"And who is Black Widow again?"

The young man looked at Paul as if he'd just committed a mortal sin. "Natasha Romanoff. A Soviet agent who is also a spy, a sniper, and a martial arts expert."

"Does she have any super powers?"

"Do you mean other than being played by Scarlett Johansson?"

Paul laughed. "I see your point. You certainly know your Marvel Comic movies."

"What else is there to do?" Baasim sighed.

"Do you enjoy being a tailor?" Paul asked.

"Do I enjoy being a tailor?" the young man repeated, as if considering the question for the first time. "I like to work with my hands," he said finally with a nod. "Yes, it is good work. Honest work."

Paul started to ask another question when he noticed Baasim's eyes suddenly narrow and turned to follow the young man's gaze. Ahead, a line of stopped vehicles sparkled in the distance. "What's going on?"

"Ya Ibn l Kalb!" Baasim exclaimed, slapping a hand against the steering wheel.

"What is it?" Paul demanded. Next to him, Tatyana's head reappeared from the back. Both of them watched with growing anxiety as they approached the waiting queue.

Their young driver shook his head. "It is a . . . what do you say in English . . . security stop?"

Paul looked at him with alarm. "You mean a checkpoint?"

"Yes, exactly."

"By whom?"

Baasim shrugged. "Military . . . police . . . the mutawa'ah perhaps." His eyes widened with panic. "They're going to ask me for my license! Oh *fuck* me!"

Paul reached over and grabbed his arm. "Baasim, listen to me. Stop the van."

"What?" The young man asked, lost in a sudden haze of fright. "Why should I—?"

"Stop the van!"

Panic stricken, Baasim slammed on the brakes. Two hundred meters ahead, several men in checkered headscarves turned at the sound of the delivery van screeching to a halt. All were shouldering automatic rifles.

Paul tightened his grip on Baasim's arm. "Get out of the van," he commanded. His expression softened at the look of terror on the young man's face. "Look, you don't understand— they're after *us*. We don't want you to get hurt."

Baasim shifted his gaze to Tatyana, who said something to him in Russian. His brown eyes widened and welled with tears.

"When you step out of the van, raise your arms like we're holding a gun on you." Paul continued, watching the men outside. One of them hailed them forward with a wave of his weapon. "Tell them we forced you to bring us here—do you understand?"

The young man gave a slight nod. After a brief hesitation, he opened the door and stepped onto the street.

Behind him, Paul jumped into the driver's seat and rolled down the window. "Raise your arms," he commanded. "Look frightened."

"I am frightened!" Baasim exclaimed, throwing up his arms. "I don't understand!"

"I'm sorry, Baasim. This isn't something we can explain." Paul gestured at the armed men. "Run toward him. You need to make them believe you've been kidnapped. Come on . . . *move!*"

Tatyana slipped into the passenger seat and looked on with her colleague as the young man raced with his arms held high toward the checkpoint. Halfway there, one of the men raised his weapon and shouted something in Arabic. Baasim froze and gestured toward the van. A frantic exchange of questions and answers followed. Then, to Paul and Tatyana's relief, the man gestured for him to pass. Baasim shot a final terrified glance over his shoulder and marched toward the line of waiting vehicles.

"Thank god," Tatyana sighed.

Ahead, the mutawa'ah leader shouted a command. Two of his colleagues abruptly raised their guns at the van and began moving toward them. Paul cursed under his breath. "Remind me to never work here again."

Tatyana turned to him with a fresh look of panic. "What do we do now?"

"Two choices," Paul replied, grabbing the steering wheel. "Forward or back?"

The Russian researcher studied the mutawa'ah men marching toward them and shook her head in defeat. "It would be madness to do either."

Paul nodded. "So why not do both?"

"What do you mean?"

"We passed a chemical plant a few kilometers back. If we can draw these guys back there, we just might have a chance at slipping past them and still making it to Ceres before they catch us. But we have to go now."

Both of them kept their eyes fixed on the men drawing closer. Tatyana slowly nodded her head. "Do it."

Paul dropped the gearshift into reverse and punched the gas. A hundred meters ahead, the approaching men froze and aimed their rifles. "Get your head down!" Paul screamed over the growl of the engine as they accelerated backwards. An instant later, the sharp report of gunfire mixed with the sound of shattering glass and punctured metal. Crouched under the dashboard, Paul blindly spun the steering wheel to the left and hit the brakes. The van swayed violently and rose onto the right wheels for what seemed an eternity before leveling itself. Paul slammed the gearshift into drive and again punched the gas. A fresh barrage of bullets pelted the back of the van as they fled west. Then abruptly, the gunfire ceased. Paul rose into his seat and checked the side view mirror.

Behind them, the two men were racing back to the line of vehicles.

"Jesus Christ—these people are fucking *nuts*!" he exclaimed, shaking his head. He shot a quick glance at his colleague, who was now slumped against the passenger door with her arms folded protectively over her chest. "Are you okay?"

Tatyana didn't respond.

Paul reached over and grabbed her arm. "Hey . . . hey!"

Tatyana let out a loud moan. "Nyet!" she exclaimed, recoiling from his touch. "Nyet!"

Paul pulled his hand away and found it covered in blood. "No no no. Tatyana—talk to me! Where were you shot?"

His colleague slowly lifted her right hand to reveal a wet spot in the fabric covering her shoulder. A pool of dark blood had collected in the depression formed by her collarbone and was cascading in wide rivulets down her arm.

"Fuck! Okay . . . okay. Just sit tight, okay?" Paul kept the gas pedal pressed to the floor and glanced again at the side view mirror. The mutawa'ah checkpoint was rapidly fading into the background. "I'm going to get us out of here and then we'll decide what to do. We're going to find some help, but you have to keep pressure on the wound—do you hear me? Tatyana?"

Next to him, his colleague's head rested lifelessly against the door.

∼

Inside the Brannon Street warehouse, all eyes watched as the pulsing dot of Obermeyer's tracking signal abruptly reversed course on the map.

"Something's up," Nielsen replied, shaking his head. A moment later he was dialing his security manager. "Ray, are you seeing this? They're heading back to you."

"We're seeing it, boss," Foster replied. "We should be intercepting them in a few minutes."

The security director studied the pulsing dot now accelerating westward. "Don't expect them to be alone."

"Understood."

Nielsen turned and stepped out of earshot of Jeri and the others. "Listen to me, Ray. No matter what you encounter, your only directive is to get Obermeyer and yourself out of there safely. Do *not* risk your life or his for anyone else. And don't hesitate to do whatever's necessary to ensure that. Do you understand?"

"Yes sir."

"Give me a status as soon as you can." Nielsen hung up and turned to find Jeri standing behind him. A fleeting look of guilt clouded his expression. "You have to understand—"

"I do," Jeri interjected. "Completely. You see your people as the victims in this madness. Someone else created it, and now they're the ones facing the consequences. You're just trying to protect your own."

Nielsen nodded.

"I feel the same way." Jeri turned and stepped back to the monitors. "That's why I gave Sam the same directive."

．≈．

"Tatyana! *Tatyana*! Come on . . . stay with me!"

Paul glanced again at the growing pool of crimson in the seat next to him. It was obvious she was losing far too much blood. He reached over and pressed his thumb against the entry wound. His colleague gasped with pain. "I'm sorry. I know it hurts. But we've got to stop the bleeding."

Tatyana's eyes briefly opened before once again rolling out of consciousness.

Paul checked the side view mirror. As expected, the glare of a pursuing vehicle was now visible in the distance. He pressed the accelerator to the floor, ignoring the engine howl in protest. "C'mon . . . c'mon," he mumbled, navigating a bend in the road. As the narrow strip of highway straightened before them, Paul noticed two identical cars approaching from the West. He looked closer, wondering if the desert heat or the cracks in windshield from the bullet holes were playing a trick on him.

Ahead, the two black Mercedes formed a side-by-side formation to block his path before slowing to a stop.

"What the—?"

Bewildered, Paul eased his foot off the gas. His confusion only grew when an older, bespectacled man in a suit stepped from the left vehicle and gestured for him to stop. A hundred meters from the vehicles, Paul rolled down the window and stuck his head out to get a clearer look at the stoic figure standing before him.

The minister lowered his hand and smiled.

"Thank god!" Paul exclaimed, sighing with a rush of relief. "I need help!" He jumped from the van and ran to Tatyana's door. "We're going to be okay," he whispered, collecting his colleague's limp body in his arms. The Russian researcher moaned weakly as he pulled her from the van. Behind them, the footsteps of someone rushing to help echoed against the pavement. Paul turned to find a tall, muscularly built man approaching with his arms out. "She's been shot!"

"Give her to me!" the man exclaimed.

"Who are you?" Paul demanded, shocked by the sudden appearance of an American in the middle of nowhere.

"Ray Foster. I'm a security manager for Velgyn Pharmaceuticals."

Paul blinked at him, dumbfounded.

"Are you hurt?" Foster asked. He slipped his arms around Tatyana and lifted her like a weightless child before glaring at Paul. "Dr. Obermeyer—are you hurt?"

"Me? No, I'm . . . I'm okay," Paul stammered. He shook his head as if awakening from a dream. "I don't understand. What are you doing here?"

"I'll explain later." The security manager gestured toward the waiting vehicles and the two men broke into a run. "What happened?"

Paul opened his mouth and a babble of words rushed out. "We were . . . we were just trying to get back and these men . . . these mutawa'ah . . . they were waiting for us, so I tried to get us out of there and they opened fire and—" He glanced over his shoulder as a large SUV cleared the bend in the road and accelerated toward them. "Oh Jesus . . . here they come!"

"Dr. Obermeyer!"

Paul looked forward just in time to avoid colliding into Minister Razam. The older man seized him in a warm embrace.

"We feared the worst," the minister exclaimed. "Come—get inside."

Before Paul realized what was happening a man with a scarred face and fiery red hair shuffled him into the backseat of the nearest Mercedes. "Where's Tatyana?" he demanded.

The minister slipped into the seat next to him. "Dr. Aleksandrov is in the other vehicle."

"She needs a doctor!"

"And she has one." The minister shifted his gaze forward to the approaching SUV. "Now, tell me—have these men seen you up close?"

A hundred meters away, the SUV shuddered to a stop behind the van and the four mutawa'ah from the checkpoint climbed out, all armed with assault rifles. Three of the men raced toward the van while the fourth, short and heavyset, scowled at the two parked Mercedes. Paul recognized the man at once. "He was the one who threw me into the cell," he said flatly.

"I see." The minister lowered the window. "Marcus?"

Outside, the redheaded man turned and looked in.

"I'm afraid we must proceed as discussed," the minister commanded.

Marcus nodded.

Paul got a fleeting look at the smile on the man's scarred face before the tinted window rose back into place. Then Marcus, along with two heavily muscled men Paul hadn't before noticed, began walking toward the van. Concealed in a holster on all three men's lower backs was a large handgun. "What's going on?" he asked, turning to Razam.

"The mutawa'ah have a very antiquated belief in man's path to righteousness," the minister replied softly. "But those who choose to enforce their beliefs with brute force must also accept the same brutal nature of *other* righteous paths. And no path is more righteous than ours, Dr. Obermeyer."

Paul shifted his gaze to the window. The three mutawa'ah had finished searching the van and were now raising their weapons at the approaching men. The fourth, still scowling, raised a hand.

"Tawakafo amkenatekom!"

Marcus and his two colleagues continued to march toward them.

"Tawakafo amkenatekom!" the heavyset mutawa'ah repeated.

This time the three men stopped. Marcus raised his hands in a surrendering gesture and pointed toward the van. To Paul's surprise, he began speaking in Arabic. The four mutawa'ah again turned their heads toward the vehicle. "What's he saying to—"

Catching the mutawa'ah off guard, the two men flanking Marcus drew their hidden weapons and leveled them on the two closest aggressors. In an instant it was over. One by one, the heads of all four mutawa'ah men snapped back like targets at a shooting gallery. Their bodies dropped lifelessly to the pavement.

From the safety of the Mercedes, Paul watched silently, unsure if what he'd just witnessed was real. He slowly turned to the Minister. "Why?" he asked, his voice breathless.

The Minister looked on as Marcus's men grabbed the bodies of the slain mutawa'ah and placed them back inside the SUV they'd arrived in. "There is no room for error in what we're doing here," he replied flatly. "None whatsoever." His dark eyes flashed to Paul with a glint of anger. "Has nothing

I've said or done made that clear to you?"

Paul lowered his head. A sudden, nauseating feeling of guilt overtook the sense of relief he'd enjoyed just moments before. "You don't understand. We did this . . . Dr. Aleksandrov and me. We just . . . we just needed a fucking night away from . . . " His own eyes reflected the minister's anger. "Kidnapping us was one thing. But this . . . this is *murder.*"

"No, Dr. Obermeyer—this is *war,*" Razam corrected. "And like any war, there are casualties and consequences for every action. Dire consequences. *Global* consequences." His expression softened. "The lives of a few are a small price to pay for protecting the greater good. In time, you'll come to understand that."

Paul regarded him coldly. "Maybe. But I never asked for this war. And I certainly never chose to be a part of it." He turned to open the door when the minister seized his hand.

"None of us did, Paul. But that doesn't make it any less real. Or necessary."

Paul walked over and peered inside the open passenger door of the second Mercedes. Tatyana lay sleeping across the back seat, her stolen burka removed and undershirt cut away. A dark-haired man was kneeling over her holding a compress to her shoulder. "How is she?"

"She'll live," the man replied without looking up. "Bullet cleaved through a fair amount of the upper trapezius muscle. There's probably some damage to the scalene muscles, maybe the omohyoid. But no internal organ damage from what I can tell. Did she say anything after she was shot?"

"She said 'nyet' when I touched her."

"Well, regardless of the circumstances, no still means no. Can you take over for a moment?"

Paul held the compress on Tatyana's neck while the man rummaged through a backpack and pulled out a small vial and syringe. He studied the man curiously. "Are you a doctor?"

"Among other things." The man quickly measured a dose with the syringe and plunged the needle into the Russian researcher's arm. "Doctor . . . humanitarian . . . defender of the common man. Recently I even got to try out a new job you might appreciate."

"What's that?"

The man looked up and smiled. "Nightshift security guard at the Lawrence Hall of Science."

Paul studied the man's tanned face and stepped back. "Holy shit. You're—"

"It's nice to see you again too, Dr. Obermeyer," Chilly nodded. "Now, if you don't mind, please put that compress back on Dr. Aleksandrov's shoulder, or I'm going to have to shoot you again."

PART IV

Are you starting to understand?

We are nothing without each other.

And who wants to be nothing?

Audio Recording #03.173 // 1017
Reference Index: >NewAgentOrientation<
Narrator: Shafer, R. >Shepherd<

53.

"Good morning, Michael."

Michael Manning stepped from the elevator of the Velgyn executive building to find his security director waiting in the atrium. "Lars," he said, glancing at his watch. "I'm on my way to the board meeting. Need something?"

Nielsen held up a folder in his hand. "I wanted to give you a final briefing on the investigation. We still have a few details to discuss."

"Fine. You can fill me in on the way to the car." The CEO nodded toward the Mulsanne limousine outside and the two men fell into a quick pace toward the exit. "I didn't hear from you yesterday," Manning continued. "Was everything resolved as we discussed?"

"Nearly." Nielsen produced a document from the folder and handed it over. "Just a few loose ends to tie up."

Manning immediately noticed the City of Berkeley's official seal stamped in red ink on the photocopied pages. "What's this?"

"Obermeyer's death certificate," the security director replied. "The first two pages are the final police report on the accident. Both the investigation team and the Alameda County Coroner conclude that an unsafe rate of speed combined with limited visibility due to fog was the cause of the accident, that the ensuing fire was due to a ruptured gas tank, and that the body found at the scene was indeed Obermeyer's. The certificate was issued and filed with the state yesterday."

"So what am I supposed to do with it?"

"The last page contains an affirmation that we concur with the findings and have no intention of contesting the coroner's conclusions that Obermeyer indeed died of an accident. Apparently it's a standard waiver given to employers or family members in cases where the victim's identity is based on partial or circumstantial evidence."

Manning produced a pen from his jacket pocket and signed the last page without breaking stride. "What else?" he demanded as they marched out of the executive building into the crisp, late-February air.

"A summary of the total cost of the investigation," Nielsen said, holding out another document.

Manning waved it away. "Just give me the total."

A short distance ahead, the driver of the limousine stepped from the car. Nielsen watched the tall, muscled man make his way around the vehicle. "Eight hundred and forty-seven thousand."

The CEO nodded. "Given what that research is worth, I'll consider that a bargain. Anything else?"

"Just one more thing." Nielsen nodded at the limo driver and the large man opened the door. "I'm not sure what to do with the returned asset."

"Returned asset? I'm not following you."

The security director shrugged. "It's probably easier to explain on the way."

"Fine—get in." Manning followed Nielsen into the Bentley's opulently finished interior. He was just noticing the two men sitting across from them when the driver closed the door, engulfing the interior in darkness. "Who are you?" he demanded, punching the door console for some light. The sound of the door lock echoed in response.

"Big day, huh?" the man sitting directly across from him replied.

Manning turned blindly to Nielsen. "Lars, who the hell are these people?"

"Mr. Nielsen already told you," the second man replied. "We're here about the returned asset."

The Velgyn CEO narrowed his eyes on the silhouetted figure. "And exactly what asset would that be?"

"Here, let me show you." The man across from him leaned forward, his face materializing in the dim light of the window. "Good morning, Michael," Paul Obermeyer said calmly. "Did you miss me?"

∼

Manning blinked twice before recoiling as if punched. "Jesus Christ . . . *Paul*?" He shook his head slowly. "I don't understand. You're supposed to be—"

"Dead?" Paul interjected. "Yes, I know." Next to him, his dark-haired companion pressed a button on the door console. The interior of the car filled with soft light.

Manning studied the man warily. "Who are you?"

"I'm the man who killed Dr. Obermeyer," Chilly replied. "But as you can see, I've decided to bring him back to life. At least for this meeting."

Manning turned to his security director as the limousine accelerated forward. "What the fuck's going on here, Lars?"

Nielsen's stare remained fixed on Chilly. "Misdirection," he said calmly. "It's come to my attention that Dr. Obermeyer's death was faked in order for this man and his team to kidnap him—"

"We prefer the term *recruit,*" Chilly interjected.

Next to him, Paul grinned.

"To *recruit* him for another job." Nielsen's stare shifted to the CEO. "You see, I was wrong, Michael. It wasn't Paul's research these people were after. It was his mind."

"Job?" Manning scoffed. His mouth twisted with disbelief. "What job?"

"Nothing that would interest you," Chilly shrugged. "We just needed Paul to help with a small world energy crisis. Which he has. Oh, and while we're on the topic of small miracles, let me just say how happy I am to hear that you found Dr. Obermeyer's encryption key. Strange how things can turn up in the darndest places, isn't it?"

"Listen to me, asshole," Manning retorted. "I don't have time for this right now. So when we get downtown, Mr. Nielsen's going to escort you to the nearest police station while Dr. Obermeyer and I have a conversation with our Board of Directors. And after we're done, he and I will sit down with my lawyers and add up the felony charges we'll be filing against you. Then you'll go away for the rest of your life." He paused and smiled. "Or, if you'd prefer, we can resolve your situation the same way we did with the rest of your team. It's your choice."

Chilly smiled back. "Well, you certainly command

attention when you speak, Mr. Manning. But I'm afraid you have the wrong idea of what's happening. You see, I'm here to explain *your* options, not the other way around."

Behind him, the privacy glass separating the front seat from the limousine's main cabin quietly lowered. A familiar figure sitting next to the driver turned and smiled. "Good morning, Mr. Manning."

"Miss Stone." Manning replied. A long sigh escaped his lips. "I was told you were dead."

"No, I believe you were told I was as dead as Dr. Obermeyer." Jeri raised a pistol over the seat and leveled it on the CEO's chest. "I can only imagine how pleased you must be."

"Indeed." Manning's eyes dropped to the gun. "May I ask what this is about, or are you just planning to shoot me?"

"Of course not. If you were paying attention, you'd know we're not in the killing business."

The Velgyn CEO shot a venomous look at his security director. "Apparently we aren't either. So I'll ask again—what are we doing here?"

"We're here to talk about your special meeting with the Board of Directors, this morning," Paul replied, studying his former employer. "I'm curious . . . what were you planning to tell them?"

"What do you think I'm going to tell them?" Manning leaned forward and seized Paul's knee. "You're a fucking *genius*, Paul. For Christ's sake, I didn't even have to write a speech! All I'll do this morning is stand in front of them and summarize what your own research has confirmed." His eyes glazed over with excitement. "Ladies and gentlemen, after two years of preclinical trials, Velgyn Pharmaceuticals is finally standing at the precipice of producing an entirely new class of drugs that not only slow some of the physiological effects of aging, but the very signs of aging itself. Forget your all-natural creams and your pseudoscience serums. Forget what every medical expert has told you. We have quite literally reached into the depths of science and found the waters of the fountain of youth. And I promise you, once ready, the two-hundred billion dollar anti-aging market will be knocking on our door."

"Behold, a brave new world of vanity drugs for the rich," Jeri replied dryly. "Now, if only you could make a drug that gets rid of all the unwanted poor people out there. No wait—that's what you do every day by pricing life-saving drugs out of their reach."

Manning regarded her coldly. "I hardly have to justify my ethics to someone who kidnaps and steals for god-knows-what purpose. It's time to grow up and accept reality, Miss Stone. Money is the true instrument of change in this world, not moral righteousness."

"Exactly!" Chilly exclaimed. "Which brings us to why we're all here. We wanted to see the look on your face when you got the news."

"News?" Manning's stare shifted back to Paul.

"My research, Michael," Paul said, holding the Velgyn CEO's gaze. "I'm afraid there's a little problem."

～

The smile on Manning's face faltered. "What problem?"

Paul felt the Velgyn CEO's grip tighten on his knee. "A few days ago I made something of a breakthrough in the volumetric growth of a microalgae by inciting a symbiotic relationship between it and a cyanobacteria," he replied, gently prying Manning's hand free. "Now, that may not sound like it has anything to do with the research I did with Velgyn, but the truth is it has everything to do with it."

"I don't understand," Manning scoffed. "What could you have learned in two weeks that you missed in two years of working in your labs here?"

"Call it the uncertainty of life. You see, Michael, in simple terms, I forgot that the world is not a laboratory. Too many things reside outside of our control. And when it comes to gene therapy, that's the problem. All of my research is predicated on one key rule—that unwanted variables in the process of delivering new genetic material to a living cell through viral vectors can be removed or at least largely minimized. In ninety-nine-point-nine percent of cases, that rule holds true. But as I realized last week, there are simply too many times when it may not. And in those instances, the outcomes can be unpredictable . . . or even disastrous."

Next to him, Chilly whistled softly. "I doubt *unpredictable* and *disastrous* are the kind of words the FDA wants to hear when reviewing a new drug for approval."

The Velgyn CEO ignored the comment. "Like what?" he pressed.

Paul shrugged. "A range of things. The very act of using a virus to deliver genetic material to the cells carries the risk of inflammatory response to the packaging proteins. And even if the cells accept the new genetic package, there's no guarantee that it will work correctly. If it doesn't, the worst-case scenario is a mutagenesis that causes abnormal or unregulated cellular division."

"You mean, like—"

"Yes, like cancer."

Manning sat back heavily. "So what are you saying? That these last two years of research are worthless? That everything you've told me is a fucking *lie*?"

"No, the conclusions of my research regarding the gene therapy itself are correct. Unfortunately, the only currently known mechanisms for delivering it to the body are too dangerous to consider viable."

"But . . . but certainly there must be another way—a *safer* way—to deliver the genetic sequence. Right?"

Paul turned to the window. The limousine was now speeding north on Highway 101 toward the city. The sight of green trees and heavy traffic filled him with a sudden joy of being home.

If only I could stay a little longer.

"Right?" Manning repeated.

"Maybe," Paul nodded. "An alternative idea came to me after my breakthrough last week. It would have to be studied and validated of course, but I'm fairly confident it's a much safer alternative to viral vectors."

The Velgyn CEO sighed with visible relief. "Thank Christ. For a moment I thought I was going to be walking into this meeting with only *half* of a miracle drug."

"Oh, but you are." Chilly replied.

"Excuse me?" Manning glared at the smile on his face before looking at Paul. "What's he talking about?"

Paul regarded him coldly. "Mr. Nielsen told me about the conversation you two had the other night. I particularly enjoyed the term you used to describe the rest of us. What was it again?"

"Minions," the security director answered.

Paul nodded. "Well, Michael, I'm sure you can understand why this former *minion* of yours has decided not to share his recent ideas with you. After all, given what I know, I believe I could start my own pharmaceutical company." He leaned forward and patted the Velgyn CEO's knee. "How do you like the term *competitor*?"

Manning's mouth twisted into a sneer. "You can't be serious."

"Of course I am. That's the beauty of being smart, Michael. It frees us minions from the tyranny of megalomaniacal assholes like yourself."

"Well said," Jeri added from the front seat.

The Velgyn CEO studied the faces around him. "So that's what this is—the rise of the disenchanted? And just what do you think this little display of defiance is going to get you? I own your research, Paul. Haven't you read your contract? You're legally required to give me any and all research associated with the development of this drug—regardless of when or where you came up with it."

Across from him, Paul smiled.

"What's so funny?"

"Maybe *you* should read my contract, Michael. If you did, you'd know all such agreements are nullified in the event of my death."

Manning turned to his security director. "Lars, I'd like to reconsider my position of the status of Paul's death."

Nielsen regarded the folder with Paul's death certificate in his hands. "I don't think so, Michael."

The CEO's face tightened with anger. "You're actually siding with this nonsense? With these fucking *terrorists*?"

"No. But what happens now isn't up to you." Nielsen handed the folder to Paul. "It's up to him."

Paul opened the folder and studied the death certificate with his name on it. "You know, last week I was starting to believe I really was dead," he said quietly. "Two days ago I almost was. Strange what it does to you . . . being *nearly* departed." He closed the folder and nodded at Manning. "But I have to say, I'm beginning to see the benefits. Particularly when it comes to this situation. Sorry, Michael, but I think I'll stick with the afterlife."

Across from him, Manning's anger boiled over. He lunged forward and grabbed at the folder. As if anticipating the move, Chilly produced a syringe hidden in his right hand and in one swift motion plunged the needle into the CEO's shoulder. "What the hell was that?" Manning hissed, recoiling back into his seat. His dark eyes held the look of an animal suddenly realizing it was cornered.

"A little something to help you relax before your big speech." Chilly capped the empty syringe and returned it to his pocket. "We both know your position as CEO has been tenuous for some time now, Michael," he continued. "That's why you've been waiting so eagerly for Dr. Obermeyer's research—your own survival depends on it. And in light of what you've just been told, it's understandable that you're upset. I just hope the judge assigned to your case will be sympathetic when you're prosecuted for your crimes."

Manning narrowed his eyes on him. "What the fuck are you talking about?"

"Paul's murder. I mean, isn't it obvious? You've known all along it would be hard enough explaining to the board of directors why more than three hundred million had been spent on an unsanctioned research project, even if it was a success. But a *failure*? That would be disastrous. Of course, Velgyn

Pharmaceuticals would survive, but your position as CEO certainly wouldn't. With the preclinical results looking bleak and your board meeting looming, you needed a back-up plan. So you decided to bury the whole fucking mess—starting with Dr. Obermeyer. You hired a team—us, obviously—to kill him in a way that made his death look like an accident. Then, in a stroke of true brilliance, you had us hide Obermeyer's encryption key in the last place anyone would look—your home." Chilly paused and shrugged. "Unfortunately, Jeri threatened the whole plan when she told Mr. Nielsen where the encryption key had been located the entire time. Faced with this unexpected wrinkle in your plan, you had no choice but to feign surprise, pocket the key, and order your security director to kill us. After all, you couldn't chance any loose ends—right, Michael?"

Manning shook his head at the accusing stares around him "That's the most absurd distortion of the truth you could possibly invent. Not only is Paul alive, his encryption key was delivered to our IT team yesterday. For Christ's sake, a fucking armed escort picked it up!"

"Oh really? Let me guess—was it a couple of big guys in a black SUV?"

"Maybe."

Chilly looked over his shoulder at the limo driver. "Max, did you and Tommy happen to pick up something at Mr. Manning's house yesterday?"

Up front, Max nodded his head. A moment later he fished Obermeyer's encryption key from his shirt pocket and handed it over the seat.

Chilly held up the small cylinder. "I believe a prosecuting attorney would call this 'Exhibit A.' "

Manning shook his head. "Lies. All lies."

"Of course they are. But this was never about the truth. This was about the orientation of the facts. And however you position them, you're fucked." Chilly glanced at his watch. "So, let's talk about your options. As I see it, you have two. The first would be for you to forget this entire conversation happened, walk into that board meeting, and officially announce you're on the precipice of developing a miracle drug. That will of course be a lie, and if you do it, I'll make sure that my theory of Paul Obermeyer's death finds its way into the district attorney's office. As you can imagine, there's really no version of this option that ends well for you, especially considering the testimony that Mr. Nielsen could offer. But I thought I'd throw it out there."

The Velgyn CEO's nod was almost imperceptible. "And option two?"

"Option two would require you to walk into that board meeting and announce the truth—that the tragic loss of Dr. Obermeyer has regrettably left you with only half of the miracle drug you were expecting. But with luck, hard work, and another three hundred million, you might just get there."

Manning laughed bitterly. "You and I both know they'd never go for that."

"No, I imagine they'll laugh you off the stage and announce a new interim CEO by the end of the week. But of course, you'll still end up with a multi-million dollar contract pay-off. Not bad for a man who ordered the death of two people a few nights ago."

"You forgetting a third option," Manning countered. "I tell everyone the truth about all of you."

"You mean tell them that Paul Obermeyer's still alive?"

Jeri replied. "That a secret agency faked his death so that he could help with a global crisis? That they stole his encryption key, but didn't really steal it because it was in your library the whole time? Yeah . . . good luck with that."

The limousine slowed to a stop. All eyes gazed out at the Fairmont Hotel standing regally along an entire city block. "Ah, we're here," Chilly announced, admiring its stone-carved façade. "Looks like a nice place to end one's career." He turned to the Velgyn CEO. "So, have you made your choice?"

Manning regarded Paul intently as Max stepped out and marched around the vehicle. "You're really going to do this? Walk away from years of brilliant research, deny millions of people a life-enhancing drug, threaten the very future of the company—over some petty misunderstanding?"

Paul frowned with disappointment. "The fact that you see what's happening here as nothing more than a *petty misunderstanding* only reinforces my decision." He shook his head dismissively. "Goodbye, Michael."

Manning shifted his gaze to Jeri. "You're a clever woman, Miss Stone. Even more clever than I expected." His eyes flashed to Chilly. "I believe we'll be seeing each other sooner than you think."

Chilly smiled. "Be careful what you wish for."

The Velgyn CEO stepped from the limousine and instinctively adjusted his tie as he studied the hotel entrance. "Oh, and Lars," he said, looking back at his security director. "In case I don't have the chance to say this afterward, you're fired."

Nielsen nodded somberly. "I understand, Michael. As you said, we're in this together." He pulled out his phone and tapped a button on the screen. The sound of Manning's recorded voice reverberated through the car—

"Paul Obermeyer was a brilliant researcher. But his role was the same as everyone else in this organization—to provide the means to an end. His research is the object of value, not his life. If Paul had handed me my new drug and vanished, it wouldn't have mattered if he were dead, missing, or abducted by fucking aliens. I would have already had what I needed. Which means, for all practical purposes, he would have already been dead to me."

Nielsen shut off the recording and tucked the phone into his pocket. "But perhaps we should leave the question of my employment for the next CEO."

Manning regarded the faces inside the limousine one last time before marching toward the hotel.

"Good luck," Chilly exclaimed to the CEO's departing figure. He smiled over his shoulder at Jeri. "All things considered, I think that went pretty well."

"Sure," she replied. "But you don't really expect him to just roll over and accept this, do you?"

"Of course not. But that's already been planned for."

"How so?"

Chilly shrugged. "That's for another time."

Across from him, Nielsen nodded and abruptly stepped out of the car.

"Where are you going?" Jeri asked.

The security director turned and regarded her with a somber grin. "Back to the office. Something tells me I'll be fielding a lot of calls in a few hours. But first, I think I'll take a walk."

"Thank you for your help," Paul said, extending his hand.

Nielsen shook the researcher's hand and stepped over to Jeri's window. "I still have Michael's copy of James Stone's book. If you don't mind, I'd like to keep it. Looks like an interesting read."

Jeri nodded. "I think you'll like it. And who knows . . . it might even change your life."

"Maybe so." Nielsen lingered for a moment, scanning the street. "Good luck, Miss Stone. I hope you find what you're looking for . . . if you haven't already."

"You too, Mr. Nielsen. And thank you. I . . . I owe you. I owe you a great deal."

"No . . . you don't."

Jeri looked on as the security director turned and strolled down the street. Moments later he vanished into the crowd.

"He's a good man," Chilly said quietly from the back seat. "Maybe we should kill him."

Jeri turned and gave him a look.

"Well, not *kill* him. You know what I mean."

Paul glanced at his watch. "If you don't mind, I'd really like to go back and check on Dr. Aleksandrov."

Chilly nodded. "Max, would you mind driving Dr. Obermeyer back over to the hotel?"

"Sure," Max retorted, his eyes studying the half million-dollar vehicle with envy. "But I'm taking this thing for a drive afterward."

"Fine. Just try not to burn it when you're done." Chilly stepped out of the car and looked at Jeri. "You ready?"

Jeri eyed him with confusion. "For—?"

"I noticed a lonely-looking dive bar a few blocks back," he replied, gesturing over his shoulder. "Let's grab a drink."

54.

The walls of the dive bar were a jumbled montage of old sailing gear and faded photos of fishermen standing proudly next to monstrous fish. Jeri took a seat at the counter and absently studied the other patrons scattered around the room as Chilly ordered drinks. A thin smile appeared on her face.

"Remind you of anything?" Chilly asked, noticing her smile.

"Not really. Should it?"

"I don't know. All these places look the same to me."

The bartender stepped over with two shot glasses and a bottle of Jack Daniels. Chilly dropped a hundred-dollar bill on the counter as the first round was poured. "Leave the bottle," he commanded. The young man eyed the bill with surprise before snatching it eagerly and vanishing into a back room.

Jeri picked up the nearest glass and tossed it back in one quick motion. "Is that why you brought me here—to reminisce about the past?"

"No, I brought you here to have a drink. And to thank you."

"Thank me for what?"

Chilly emptied his own glass and immediately refilled

both. "Chip told me what happened in the hotel," he said flatly. "I think it's safe to say that if you hadn't taken control of the situation, I'd probably be occupying a shallow grave in Antalya right now. And I don't want to think about what would have happened to Drs. Obermeyer and Aleksandrov." He shrugged the thought from his mind and raised his glass in salute. "So thank you. You saved us. You saved, well . . . everything."

Jeri held up her glass and stared into the warm, honey-brown liquor. "Not everything. Not him."

Chilly offered a reverential nod. "To Dublin."

"To the crazy Irishman." Jeri tossed back the whiskey and shook her head. "He'd be drinking with us now if it wasn't for my decision to—"

"Bullshit," Chilly interjected. "Dublin was the one who was careless, not you. And regardless, you didn't pull the trigger. As far as the person responsible—" A dark look briefly clouded his expression before he snapped from his thoughts. "None of it was your fault. In fact, all things considered, I'd say you've proven to be exactly what Chip and I expected."

"Which is?"

"The best of all of us."

Jeri eyed him suspiciously. "Is this where you play the apologetic team leader who tells me how much I'm needed and begs me to come back?"

"No," Chilly rebutted, pouring another round. "This is where you play the contritious student who finally admits that what we're doing is right and begs to be a part of the team again."

"I don't think so."

"Then I guess we'll both just have to sit here and drink until one of us concedes."

A thin smile parted Jeri's lips. "That could take all afternoon. And I'm pretty sure it wouldn't end well—for *you*."

Her colleague affectionately patted the bottle of whiskey. "Mr. Daniels and I are prepared for that possibility."

Jeri sighed with impatience. "Alright, fine. You want an apology? I'll give you one. But first, I'd like the truth."

"Regarding—?"

"Those last few minutes in Malcesine."

Chilly's fingers hovered on the bottle. "What about them?"

"Nielsen told me that when his team entered the room, you were already injecting me with Diaverol."

"That's right."

"And how much was in the dose?"

"Fifteen milliliters."

"Fifteen milliliters," Jeri repeated, shaking her head. "Not very much."

"No. But enough to do the job."

"Are you sure about that?"

Chilly smiled. "What do you mean?"

"I mean if you were already injecting me with Diaverol when Nielsen's men entered the room, you had plenty of time to give me the full dose before they stopped you. And if that dose was, as you just said, enough to do the job, I shouldn't have any clue what's happened to me these last three months. Yet here I am, talking and drinking with the very person who injected me, remembering practically everything I shouldn't." Jeri grabbed the shot in front of her and drank it back before giving Chilly a broad smile. "Sounds like a medical miracle if you ask me. And yet you don't even seem that surprised."

A long moment passed as Chilly slowly mirrored her

smile. "Of course I'm not surprised. Since when have you done something expected?"

Jeri's smile vanished. "Why didn't you give me the full dose?"

"Did Nielsen also mention the stun gun that was used to subdue me? Maybe you should try finishing something after getting hit with fifty-thousand volts of electricity."

"Wrong answer."

Chilly laughed and drained his own whiskey. "Then what's the *right* answer? That I just tossed protocol aside and risked the agency and everything we've done on the thin chance you'd remember and come running back?"

"You tell me. Is that the truth?"

The muted sounds of other conversations swirled around them as they exchanged wary looks. "Maybe," Chilly mumbled finally, shaking his head. His gaze dropped to the bottle between them. "Maybe I did have enough time. Maybe I did hesitate. All I know is that Dublin was suddenly at the door, screaming that something was wrong, and a moment later he was on the floor. I had to make a choice. I know I put the needle in your arm. I know I put my finger on the plunger. But after that—?" His eyes flashed to hers. "That's as close to the truth as I can come."

Jeri felt her expression soften as she searched his stare. The shadow of something unspoken was once again lurking there, just beneath the surface. And once again she felt the urge to lunge forward, to reach into the darkness and drag the truth into the light. Or was it just the opposite? Did she really just want to lose herself in the darkness, to forget the light ever existed? The moment stretched into unacknowledged awkwardness while she searched for an answer. Failing to find it,

Jeri turned her eyes toward the bar and nodded. "Then I suppose it'll have to be enough," she conceded flatly, blaming the whiskey for the heat radiating from her skin. She scanned the tidy rows of liquor lining the bar shelves, their labels shimmering in the light. "So . . . where do we go from here?"

Her colleague shrugged. "Well, I suppose I can't be trusted with giving you *another* dose of Diaverol in the hopes of forgetting this whole mess. And god knows you're not capable of following commands. So I guess our only option is to bring you back in and let you build a team that operates the way *you* think it should."

Jeri looked over at him with a blank stare. "What?"

"You heard me."

"But I'm . . . I'm just the—"

"Freshman?" Chilly shook his head. "Not any more. You know what you're doing. Even more, you've proven there are other ways to get what we're after without resorting to violence." He gave her a thin smile. "Think you can handle that?"

Jeri nodded slowly. "My own team? My own tactics?"

"That's right."

Her expression turned skeptical. "Are you sure this isn't just another clever way of getting rid of me?"

"Well, I'll be honest, not getting a lecture on morality every time I have to drop a genius with a tranquilizer dart will be nice," Chilly conceded. He poured another round. "But if you *do* manage to find a better way to restore the world order . . . who knows what could happen?"

A smile crept back onto Jeri's face. "Still, that's a big change."

"Maybe. But a very smart man once wrote 'The single greatest necessity—and threat—to both corporate states and the greater economic ecology is change.'" He raised his glass. "To James Stone."

Jeri raised hers. "To my father."

They drank and shared a moment of silence.

"So—" Jeri slapped her glass on the bar to dismiss the somber air. "Now that I've officially graduated, I guess I need an official agent name."

Chilly cocked his head. "Well, you haven't *technically* graduated, but yes."

"What the hell is that supposed to mean?"

"A second review of your recruit in London led me to conclude that she wasn't the best candidate after all. Luckily she was already drugged, so it was easy enough to deposit Miss Benton back in her flat in Marylebone and lock the door behind us. I'm sure she's written off her memory loss to a night of excessive drinking." He regarded Jeri with a straight face. "She's engaged to be married if I remember correctly, isn't she?"

Jeri studied him for a sign of humor, but found none. "You know, it's moments like this when I'm convinced this whole goddamn ordeal was just a test."

"I told you before . . . everything's a test," Chilly replied. His fingers returned to stroking the bottle of whiskey. "Did you have a name in mind?"

"Well, if I'm going to build my own legitimate team of agents, it seems only appropriate to have a legitimate name."

"Such as?"

"Jeri *Halston* has a nice ring to it."

Her colleague regarded her with surprise. "You can't be serious."

"You said it yourself. My team, my rules."

Chilly read the light in her stare and poured another

round. "It's a brave new world, Jeri Halston."

"It is indeed, Sam Lafeen."

Jeri watched her colleague throw back his whiskey and glance at his watch. She knew with sudden certainty that in the next few minutes he would rise and excuse himself for a cigarette and step outside. She knew with even greater certainty that when she eventually stepped outside to find him, he would be gone. "Another few months then," she said, raising her glass.

Chilly looked over with a fleeting look of confusion before diverting his stare to the floor. "We both have some work to do, don't we?"

Jeri threw back her whiskey and nodded. "In more ways than one."

Behind them, the door opened and a foursome of twenty-something couples entered the bar on a wave of laughter. Jeri watched as they took a table, admiring their effortless, carefree movements, the gentle ease of their smiles. "God, I miss that," she muttered wistfully, realizing afterward that the thought had escaped her mouth.

Chilly shot a look in their direction and rose from his seat. "What—ignorance and empty conversations?"

Jeri nodded. "Yeah."

Her colleague produced a pack of cigarettes from his jacket and looked at the newcomers again. Then, for a fleeting moment, the rigidity of his body softened, as if pressure had been released from some hidden inner valve. "Me too."

She gestured at the pack of cigarettes in his hand. "That time again?"

Chilly gestured at the door. "Be right back."

"Right."

Jeri quietly studied the man who once again had both destroyed and rebuilt her world. In the half-light of the dive bar she committed his face to memory. Her stare dropped to his lips, poised on the brink of a grin, and a sudden certainty that she'd once felt them pressed against her own forced the heat back to her skin. She met his eyes and nodded. "See you around, Sam."

Chilly stabbed a cigarette into his mouth and smiled. "Sooner than you think, Jeri." He marched past the arriving foursome and slipped through the door.

Jeri allowed her gaze to linger on the door for a moment before turning to the bar. She poured her last drink, closed her eyes, and let the warm, honey-sweet liquor roll gently down her throat. In the brief inner silence that followed, her mind searched for a vision of her future, for a fleeting glimpse of the world to come. But only shadows and vague forms would appear.

Go figure.

C. T. WENTE

ABOUT THE AUTHOR

C. T. Wente lives in Sölvesborg, Sweden
with his wife, Linda.

For more information on the author,
please visit www.ctwente.com.

C. T. WENTE

35277131R00307

Made in the USA
Columbia, SC
21 November 2018